A RHYTHMS OF REDEMPTION ROMANCE

To Begin Again

EMILY CONRAD

For Jessica, your friendship is one of my favorite answers to prayer.

PROLOGUE

Voicemail from Michaela Vandehey to Gannon Vaughn, May 16, 1:54 p.m.:

"*G*annon, it's Michaela. I don't know if I should be calling you, but ... I'm sorry about the waterworks. This is harder than I expected. You probably haven't kept tabs on me since *Audition Room*, but I think my label's going to drop me, and I don't know what to do because I've already done everything they asked. I thought you might have some advice. I'm sorry. I shouldn't have called. I hope you're doing well. Do us both a favor and erase this message from your phone and your memory, okay? Sorry. I'm really sorry."

Voicemail from Gannon Vaughn to Michaela Vandehey, May 16, 7:13 p.m.:

"Hey, kid. Sorry I missed your call. Don't put your soul or your peace of mind up for sale, no matter how high they bid. Remember? If you've done everything they've asked, well, frankly, I know. I saw, and I'm glad you reached out. I talked to Adeline and the band. We're contributing a song to a soundtrack, and I've got the freedom to make it a duet. Get away to Lakeshore for the summer. Write new material and reevaluate. While you're here, we'll see if this duet has potential. I had some rental listings emailed to you. Let me know when we can expect you in the studio."

1

---

*P*hilip woke as Clare traced her finger across the bare skin of his back. Serenity and comfort emanated from the contact like warmth from sunshine, but then reality rolled in like a thunderhead.

He'd buried Clare.

The soft touch swept from his spine along his shoulder and out to his deltoid. Instead of continuing into his sight, where he could identify the hand as either belonging to his son or his daughter, the touch turned, scalloping across his shoulder blade.

He let his eyes drift closed again as he waited for the child to finish. The wings he'd had tattooed across his back after Clare's death couldn't raise him to heaven to bring her back to life on earth, but they were a sign of his love for Nila's and Nason's mother. If children had to grow up without a mom, they should at least know how much their dad missed her.

The finger reached his spine and circled there. A red heart marked the center of the wings. It wasn't a fake, useless cartoon heart but a realistic rendition, with chambers and arteries. A vital organ that bled everywhere when it was torn out. Clare's name marked the center, with Nila's and Nason's names swirled in more subtly by the artist.

The soft touch paused on each name, then spread, the whole hand flattening against his back.

A hand too broad to belong to a child.

Philip arched his back away as he twisted between the sheets. His focus fell on his children's nanny, reclined in the space that should've been Clare's. He scrambled to his feet and swiped up the T-shirt he'd tossed over a chair the night before. He'd gone to bed alone. Exactly how he'd expected to wake. "What are you doing?"

"I thought ..." Hillary gathered the sheet to cover skin exposed by her skimpy slip.

Philip pulled the shirt over his head and yanked the lower hem to the waistband of his shorts. "Get out."

"This is the easy solution." Her neck seemed rigid as she rose, taking the sheet with her. The fabric mercifully fell into place, covering her legs. "You want more. I want more. The kids—"

"Out." On second thought ... He checked the clock. Six AM. "The kids cannot see you like that."

"They're sound asleep." She adjusted the sheet. He'd have to burn the thing. "Late night, remember?"

She dared to lob accusations at a time like this?

At Philip's request, Hillary had brought the kids to Awestruck's third secret show of the year. He'd carried a sleeping Nila out to the nanny's car after their last set at midnight, and Nason's happy but droopy eyes had told Philip he would sleep through the drive home. Philip had shut the door and laid his hand on the hood. Sleep made them look so vulnerable, so in need of care he didn't know how to give.

"I wish they had a mom," he'd said.

Hillary had rubbed his arm and opened the driver's door. "You have me."

To take care of the kids. To get them home safely while he and the band wrapped up.

Not to warm his bed.

A physical relationship with the kids' nanny would complicate his household. Since she depended on Philip for her income, it'd also leave him open to sexual harassment accusations and violate his morality agreement with Awestruck. Not to mention his conscience and the memory of Clare.

He pointed to the bedroom door. "You're fired. Get your stuff and get out." Bitterness to match his tone seeped into the back of his throat.

Her neck pulsed with a swallow. "What you did last night—throwing off their schedule like that—isn't good for them. You need me. I'm great with them. And with other things." She lifted an eyebrow as if he'd warm to her offer.

"Out." He roared the command while he retained a sliver of self-control. Better to have to explain a half-naked woman to his children than to fall prey to this scheme.

Hillary scampered from the room, leaving the door open in her retreat.

No young faces appeared in the hallway, no rustling from their nearby rooms.

He sat on the edge of the bed and pushed his fist against his mouth.

If she'd taken the time to let a relationship develop instead of jumping in his bed three weeks into the job, he might've reacted differently. He might've justified one thing and then another.

He knew a thing or two about justification.

But if he took any more risks with the morality agreement, he'd go the way of Awestruck's last bassist, fired for his behavior. Nila and Nason had already lost their mother. They didn't deserve to have everything respectable about their father shatter too.

The kids deserved the world.

Philip could give it to them on a silver platter as long as he stayed with Awestruck. That meant he already had enough demons to hide without acquiring a new one.

MICHAELA VANDEHEY HAD TASTED the dream, and she wasn't ready to let it go.

She placed her fingers on the piano keyboard but lifted her hands without playing a note. The cacophony of her desperation threatened to deafen her to the music that normally hummed through her veins.

Her last experience with such overwhelming nerves had come during her initial performance before the judges on the televised reality competition *Audition Room*. Thankfully, once she'd begun to sing, the music seeped through her anxiety and took her to a higher place. When she was finished, Gannon Vaughn had leaned forward in his seat and compared her voice to not one but two of her idols. He'd coached her to the win, all the while claiming she didn't need him at all.

He'd been wrong.

She'd needed him then, and she needed him now, so much so that she'd cried when she'd heard his kind, "Hey, kid," on her voicemail.

Still, she'd regretted calling Gannon even before she'd finished leaving him the teary message that resulted in his invitation to come to Wisconsin. She'd sounded pathetic. Embarrassed, she would've declined the offer to visit Awestruck's studio if not for her manager, Reese, who'd stressed that Michaela's career depended on her "leveraging every opportunity."

So, she'd come, and now she waited in Gannon's empty studio.

Her phone obliterated the quiet with both sound and vibration, and her tightly strung nerves jolted. Huffing and rolling her eyes, she took out the device to silence it.

She glanced at her father's text as she navigated to the volume controls.

You should call your sister.

"No, thanks." The nearby microphone didn't pick up her mumbling because the security guard or whoever he was that had delivered her from the airport hadn't turned on any of the equipment when he'd left her to await the band.

If only someone would fight for Michaela the way Dad championed Riley.

The murmur of male voices signaled the band's approach.

Panic thrummed. Struggling pop artist Michaela Vandehey singing with one of the top rock bands in the country? An unlikely pairing, even if Gannon had invited her there.

"Make them love you." Her manager's voice, low and gravelly for a woman, didn't match her slender build and feminine blouse. "The headlines would be sensational if they all proposed in the same year."

Michaela had croaked like a frog as she'd suppressed her indignant response. She'd known Gannon and John were engaged, leaving only Philip, their bassist, unattached. But she had her eye on her career, not her love life. She might occasionally flirt her way past a closed door, but leading a man on until he put a ring on her finger for a professional edge was another thing entirely.

Reese had laughed. "Even a summer fling would raise speculations. The publicity could make the difference between a girl fading from the world stage and making herself an institution."

Reese hadn't specified what kind of physical relationship she thought might accompany a summer fling, but in Michaela's experience, that usually involved time in the bedroom. So many had been speaking up and speaking out against the wrongs of men using their power to manipulate—or outright force—women into sexual favors. Surely those activists would call for Reese's head for suggesting Michaela put herself in a situation so likely to go that direction.

The men of Awestruck wouldn't go for it either. Gannon had treated her and the other contestants on *Audition Room* with professionalism, and she could only imagine he surrounded himself with others who would do the same.

A voice sounded in the hall, interrupting her misgivings. "That's nothing. You know who I woke up to find in my bed this morning?"

"Nila?" A second speaker offered the name hesitantly.

Was Nila a girlfriend? A cat?

"No," the first man said. "Hillary."

No one would name a pet Hillary.

They were discussing women. From most others in the industry, sure, she'd expect that. But from Awestruck?

"What'd you do?" Gannon said, his rich voice unmistakable.

If he was invested in the tale, even he wasn't the white knight she'd thought.

After all Michaela had seen, she shouldn't feel this aching disappointment over yet another letdown. She smoothed her fingers over the keys again, reconsidering Reese's advice. Her career had barely begun, and her manager had a point that she couldn't afford to be choosy about her opportunities. She might not go as far as Reese wanted, but a little flirting never hurt.

Anyway, handling womanizers certainly came more naturally to her than accepting the kind of pity that had flowed through Gannon's voicemail.

"Told her to pack her stuff and leave. I'm back on the market." The first speaker entered, and she recognized him from what she'd seen in the media as the bassist, Philip. He had blond hair darkened by brown roots. His close-trimmed beard followed a square jawline. Despite his strong features, something about his eyes looked wounded, as if he'd spent a lot of time narrowing them, trying to figure out where life had gone wrong.

Okay, Reese. She could work with this. She stepped from behind the keyboard.

A couple of years had passed since she'd seen Gannon. He still had the same sharp hazel eyes, toned muscles, and energetic confidence, even if his smile revealed creases that had settled deeper since he'd mentored her on the show.

How old was he now? Thirty? Thirty-two?

Men were allowed to age.

He greeted her with a quick, one-armed hug. "Do you know everyone?" Without waiting for an answer, he indicated the bassist, who stood closest. "Michaela, this is Miller."

She flashed a smile, going along with the formality, though everyone in the room ought to know the names of the others. "Something tells me only the guys call you that."

A spark of amusement lit his eyes. "Philip."

She stepped over to clasp his hand with both of hers. "Nice to meet you, Philip."

"You too." His hand, broad and calloused, slid from hers to pick up an electric bass guitar.

"And John." Gannon nodded toward the drum kit, where the final member of Awestruck settled. She noted the forest tattoo covering his right arm.

Gannon also sported a fair amount of ink on his arms.

Even she had musical notes tattooed on the inside of her wrist.

Only Philip didn't have any visible. Funny that the one who looked the most clean-cut hadn't known what woman he'd wake up to.

"How was the trip?" Gannon asked her.

"Smooth. Your guy was waiting for me, and we didn't hit any traffic." Although, judging by the hours of fields and forests they'd driven through from the airport to Lakeshore in northern Wisconsin, that was a given. "He told me you've been doing a secret concert series. One last night?"

"We've done three. We used the first one mostly to prove John wasn't dead."

John's car wreck, a few months before, had caught her attention—and everyone else's in the industry—but other than a faint scar by his eyebrow, he looked fine now.

"They're also good for trying new songs," Gannon continued. "And connecting with our fans. Our last one will be in late July."

Philip lifted his chin toward his bandmates. "Celebrating these two's independence one last time."

Gannon and John broke into matching grins.

The lead singer reached for his guitar with a glance to Michaela. "Adeline and I are getting married in September, but John and Erin are the most impatient people in the world."

John scoffed and swept up his drumsticks. "A two-month engagement isn't beating any world records."

Philip offered the explanation. "We're doing the last secret show. A week later, John and Erin are getting married. Two weeks after that, we'll be recording the next album. We'll come back, and a little while later, we'll have another wedding."

A busy summer and autumn, but such was life when it had to be lived between tours.

"And you?" She lifted an eyebrow at Philip. "When's your wedding?"

He scoffed. "Not looking for that." His gaze didn't linger on her, signaling he wasn't looking for anything less permanent either.

Hadn't he just said he was back on the market?

Gannon, guitar in hand, looked to her. "Ready to get started?"

"More than." If charming Philip was her only insurance policy to keep her place here, she had her work cut out for her, but what else was new? She'd do what she'd always done—whatever it took to keep her career alive.

2

_P_inching his phone between his shoulder and ear, Philip chased a painkiller with a swig of water. "You only found one candidate?"

Outside the window of Gannon's living room, Lake Superior stretched out of sight, all the way to Canada. Philip's problems were much closer to home.

Nancy, the owner of the nanny placement agency, hesitated. "We've already been through three."

As if the high turnover rate were his fault. The first woman he'd hired on Nancy's recommendation had decided the demands of being a live-in nanny—a rarity in this area—didn't suit her. The second posted pictures of the kids on social media against specific instructions. The third, Hillary ... the less he thought about her stunt that morning, the better.

He clenched his fist. "I need someone who'll work out this time. A bigger agency wouldn't have this much trouble."

"With all due respect, Mr. Miller, the larger agencies are hours away. Their candidates would need to relocate. Formerly, you said you weren't willing to pay for that. If that's changed, I can cast a broader net."

"Fine. Go ahead." But this was her last chance. His kids deserved better care than they'd gotten, and he'd make whatever changes he needed to ensure they received it.

"In the meantime, Audrey can cover some extra days. She's there now, but she needs to leave by five."

Audrey worked part-time, watching the kids every Monday and any Sunday when he couldn't. Her hours allowed him to give the full-time nanny two consecutive days off. The kids complained she was boring, but what six- and eight-year-olds didn't say that?

"I can't make five tonight." For a guest artist, Michaela had a lot of suggestions, and Gannon humored them better than he would've if they'd come from anyone else. "Maybe seven."

"Mr. Miller ..."

"This is the job." For both of them.

The woman sighed. "All right. Audrey has a night class, so I'll cover tonight until seven. But perhaps in the short term, you can adjust your schedule. For the sake of family."

Guilt hardened in his gut. "I'm working for the sake of my family." How did she think he'd pay to move someone here and offer a salary high enough to keep them?

"Right. Of course. I'm sorry." She was thinking of his dead wife, or she wouldn't sound so sincere.

When his career had started, Clare's longing to become a mom had been the one dream he could afford to make reality. He'd worked hard to provide for them, and until her diagnosis, Clare had reveled in taking care of them all. Life had made sense then.

Since, not so much.

He kept coming up short, never the wholesome, nurturing caretaker Clare had been.

Signing with Awestruck had given him the financial means to fill that gap. With his windfall, he planned to hire the best help, establish college funds, and spoil the kids with all the little things along the way.

If only good help weren't so hard to find.

One more failure to add to the list. How hadn't he seen Hillary's true colors sooner, before the kids had gotten attached?

At a rustle behind him, he swiveled his chair from the window. Michaela, all tight jeans, long hair, and shimmering makeup, approached, gaze fixed on a point outside the windows.

Philip's grandfather had once seen a popular actress in person back in the day. "Most beautiful creature I ever saw," he'd said. "Aside from your grandmother, of course."

Michaela had that kind of beauty. Men she passed on the street would wistfully recall the experience fifty years from now. Yet Gannon had called her a "lost kid" when he'd proposed inviting her here for a summer. She'd only been twenty when she'd won *Audition Room* a few years back, but she was struggling to maintain momentum.

Well. She might be lost in some ways, but she wasn't a kid.

He refocused on his call. "I can do interviews Saturday afternoon. However many we have to do."

Another sigh. "I'll set some up."

"And until then ..."

"I'll look after them myself."

He thanked her before disconnecting, then glanced at Michaela.

Her wide eyes, the green of an enchanted forest—too green to be natural—blinked at him, and her glossy lips bowed with understanding. "The trials of being in demand."

"Huh?"

"Interviews all Saturday?"

"Not with the press, if that's what you're thinking. I'm hiring a nanny."

"Oh, right." She slid a hand in her back pocket. "I forgot you've got kids."

He'd never get used to people—strangers—knowing about his children.

"What are their names?" She stepped closer, hand still in her back pocket, hip angled in a way that accented her curves. "They both start with the same letter, right?"

"Nila and Nason." After all, Michaela was a colleague, not a fan or a reporter.

She pulled her long, dark hair to one side, exposing her neck and the thin strap of her tank. "I bet they're great kids. They're lucky to have a loving dad."

They were great, but their only good luck in the father department came from his income.

THE STRETCHING teal of Lake Superior out Gannon's windows could pass for the ocean—just not the view of the Pacific from southern California because pines lined the shore instead of palms.

Michaela hadn't put much stock into the pristine blues of the water pictured in the listing for the condo she'd rented. Since she'd come straight to Gannon's, she hadn't seen the extended-stay property yet, but given it overlooked this same lake, the pictures may have actually undersold the allure.

Maybe this town wouldn't be such a bad place to stay. Assuming the duet went ahead and she wasn't sent packing.

Would Reese give up on her if she failed here?

The worry set off a dull pain in her sternum.

She brushed her hand against Philip's forearm as she settled in the chair next to his. He'd been shifting, about to rise and leave, but at the touch, he froze and focused on her.

Until that moment, his glances in her direction had been fleeting, but she'd captured his attention now.

His irises brought to mind the dark woodwork in one of her childhood friend's homes. The sun lit up the tiny facets of the grain, transforming the deep brown to a rich caramel. Philip's eyes would react to light the same way. She'd stake this gig on it.

A sense of foreboding shot through her.

That home—and Heather, the friend who'd lived there—embodied everything Michaela had never had. She'd walked away from her dream of having a happy family, instead betting everything on singing, when she'd left for *Audition Room*. There would be no take backs, and that made a man whose very glance brought back these memories dangerous.

But she needed the band to champion the duet version of the song for the movie, and her voice alone might not be enough. Befriending Philip was a necessary precaution. More than that, the pain in those brown eyes had ignited her curiosity.

Had he smiled once in the studio? She didn't think so, and coaxing one from him would feel as rewarding as a comped first-class plane ticket upgrade.

"What's a girl to do for dinner around here?"

"What're you in the mood for?" He shifted his arm off the armrest as if to prevent another brush with her. "Your options are family dining, an American grill, and fast food."

"That much variety? How will I choose?"

He chuckled, cracking the first inklings of a smile. "We have a Mexican place and a Chinese place, but if you're hoping for authentic, adjust your expectations now."

"Which one should I pick if I'm hoping for company?"

"Oh." He frowned toward the hall leading to the studio. "Gannon hasn't made plans with you?"

The ends of her hair brushed her forearm as she shook her head.

"I'm sorry. I've gotta get home when we're done here."

She was missing something, some key to unlocking him. "How about someplace family-friendly? Kids have to eat, too, I assume."

"By the time we're done here, they'll be almost ready for bed."

"That's not right." As dysfunctional as her family had been, she'd loved the rare occasions when they gathered around the table like on TV. "You've got to see them. Family dinners are important."

He flinched. "You and the nanny would get along great."

That wasn't exactly flattering, but rather than condescension, Philip's expression seemed to hold regret. Guilt, maybe.

She shifted closer. "I thought you were hiring a nanny. You already have one?"

"All of the above. I had to fire one for inappropriate behavior this morning, so the head of the agency is there now and not happy about the hours."

The story she'd heard him tell that morning fell into place, taking on a completely different meaning. "The one you let go was named Hillary?"

"How'd you know?" He reached for his phone. "She didn't post about it or something—"

Michaela lifted her hands to dismiss the worry. "I heard you telling the story as you walked into the studio. Though I thought it was less of a nanny mishap and more of a one-night stand."

His head drew back as though to distance himself from the suggestion. "That's not how I operate." He laughed softly, still not breaking into a real smile. "And if it were, I wouldn't be telling Gannon and John about it."

"I wondered about that." She pressed her finger against a

seam in the chair, considering how she might ferret out a better understanding of the man beside her. Perhaps she ought to simply count it as a victory that Gannon was still the man she'd known him to be during *Audition Room*.

"Tell you what." She scooted to the edge of her seat and tapped his knee. "I'll stay in Lakeshore as long as necessary to get this song recorded. There's no rush, and family's important. Tell the judgy nanny boss lady you're taking them to dinner. I'll tell Gannon we need to wrap up by five because I made plans."

Questions seemed to bubble behind the quick shifts in his expression, the assessing movements of his eyes. He wanted to know if she was hitting on him, and by the stillness of his body, she guessed the only answer he'd accept was that her interest was platonic.

For now, anyway. How often did it stay that way?

"I could use the company, your kids could use the time with you, and from what I can tell, you could use one less missed dinner to feel bad about."

He gave another joyless laugh and seemed to relax the set of his shoulders. "I guess you've got me there."

She abandoned her seat. "Leave it to me."

3

"Can you get me the unicorn, Dad?"

The machine with the claw and a multitude of stuffed animals waited by the wall. The kids had scoped out the prizes while waiting for the pizzas. Now that they'd eaten their fill, Nila had remembered what Philip had hoped they'd forget.

"Those things are purposely hard to win, sweetie."

"But she's right on top. You can do it."

"Yeah." Michaela elbowed him, laughter in her rainforest eyes as she joined his daughter's campaign. "Come on."

Nason knelt on his seat, boosting himself to his sister's eye level. "I'll get the unicorn for you, Nila."

"That's a good idea." Philip got out his wallet.

"But, Dad—"

He lay a ten on the table and motioned their passing waitress. "Can we get quarters?"

The woman had recognized both him and Michaela earlier. She happily took the money and returned a minute later. Nason guffawed as the coins plinked onto the nicked tabletop.

"But, Dad." Nila's eyes had gone as round and pleading as those on the unicorn she wanted so badly. "Nason will lose."

Her brother shoveled quarters into his pocket like a pirate raiding a treasure chest.

"Let him try. Take turns. If you run out of money, we'll get you a unicorn from the store."

Seeming to recognize her window of opportunity closing with each fistful of quarters Nason squirreled away, Nila grasped a handful of coins. Nason plucked up the remaining three, and the kids beelined for the machine.

Michaela smiled after the children. "Do you think he'll get it?"

"Not a chance."

The waitress brought the bill, and Michaela tried to race him to pay, but he was faster at getting his card out. As the waitress left again, he glanced over at the kids. At the game, Nila allowed Nason the first turn at the controls. She stood at the corner of the machine, pointing and peering in at the unicorn. They were getting along now, but the peace might not last long.

With those two keeping up a constant stream of chatter and questions and needs throughout the meal, he hadn't kept an eye on Michaela or figured out her motive for instigating this. She couldn't like kids this much, could she?

"So." She turned sideways on her chair to face him, pulled her sandaled feet up to rest on a rung, and slung her arm across the back. "This place is quaint."

Philip watched the kids. Easier to keep his mind from straying when he wasn't looking at the low cut of her tank. "You grew up in a big city?"

"Compared to this place." She laid her hand on the table, coming awfully close to touching his arm.

His skin tingled as if she held an electrically charged balloon an inch away.

She apparently didn't believe in personal space, but he'd introduced her to the kids as a coworker. She must have known better than to confuse them—or the rest of the patrons, who were probably more interested than the kids—because she didn't close the gap now.

But Gannon had already given him a sideways glance when she'd announced their dinner plans. Philip had a few guesses why. The lead singer might have felt protective of his protégé. Or his concern might have been for Philip. Michaela didn't strike him as the type in search of a substantial relationship, and Gannon knew Philip had already had his heart broken once.

But he could handle dinner with a beautiful woman without risking his heart. If Gannon's reservations were for Michaela's sake, she was safe with Philip. His conscience was already guilty enough without another complicated relationship.

"I'm originally from Illinois," she said. "About an hour outside of Chicago. You?"

Thoughts of summers spent on his bike or throwing around a football allowed a relaxed breath. His childhood had been ideal, up until the end. "Grew up on a gravel road in the great state of Iowa."

Her shoulders hopped with what looked like glee. "How'd you go from *there* to Awestruck?"

Did she assume his was a rags-to-riches story? He'd never been in rags, but to a glitzy pop star, living on a gravel road probably equated to the same thing.

"The band I was with got discovered at the state fair." He could still smell the fried food and hear the polka music that had played as a label rep approached them after their set. "We moved to California, even went on tour as Awestruck's support band for a while. Those were our glory days, the biggest we ever got. Years later, I ended up available when Awestruck needed a bassist, and here we are." He'd breezed over seas of turmoil. Would she ask about the gap in the story?

Either she already knew and didn't want to risk the troubled waters, or she was completely oblivious. Either way, her enthusiasm didn't falter. "What was it like to get that call?"

He'd downplay it, but he knew a good thing when he had it. He still didn't understand what Gannon and John had seen in him that he'd been their first pick from the very day after they'd fired Matt Visser. "A promotion."

"And the answer to all your prayers, right?"

At the mention of prayer, the pick-me-up of considering his good fortune in getting the job with Awestruck vanished. He hadn't asked God for a single thing since about two months before Clare died, when he'd finally accepted the Lord wouldn't intervene on their behalf.

"Ah." Michaela brushed his arm then folded her hands in her lap. "Not as religious as Gannon, huh?"

"Who is?" Gannon's heart hadn't been broken yet. If God ever ripped Adeline away from him, he'd have some re-evaluating to do. Same for John with his fiancée, Erin.

Michaela's eyes held gentle understanding that seemed free of judgment. Did she have experience with tragedy? Experience that meant they could understand each other?

"How about you?" he asked. "What's your story?"

Her lips lifted with what appeared to be nostalgia. "I caught the bug for performing at a school talent show." She leaned in, her perfume sweet and fresh. "My dad couldn't be bothered to show up. That's why stuff like this ..." She peered over at his kids. "Family time is important."

Nila and Nason were a ticking time bomb, but interacting with Michaela had coaxed him from monitoring the countdown. Her accepting demeanor made conversation easy. He didn't have to be on guard with her the way he did with nannies or his bandmates.

"What was your dad busy with?" he asked.

"My sister. She'd been caught shoplifting that night. Or busted for drinking?" She rolled her eyes with a shrug, but

Philip was well enough acquainted with pain to recognize it in someone else. "Always something with her, but of course, she was his little princess, so why would she ever get in trouble? If I'd pulled half that stuff? Look out. He would've thrown me out and told me to go find my mom."

Sounded rough. "Where was she?"

"Who knows. I'm told she only wanted one kid, so she burned out after a couple of years of having two. Between being the tipping point and resembling Mom, I never stood a chance with Dad and Riley."

"That's awful."

Vulnerability rippled beneath the too-green color of her irises. Then, her expression brightened. "As for my career, you probably know the gist. *Audition Room*, record deal, sales that aren't as great as my label would like."

"Been there. Not with Awestruck, but before." His former band had worked hard, but so many of the factors that affected sales were beyond the artists.

"Then you know being invited here seemed like a miraculous opportunity to me, though I'm not much of a believer either. God loving everyone is a nice idea, but you should hear the complaints I get from church people. If I followed all those religious rules, I'd have no career." She plucked a piece of lint from her pants. "I don't think God's as caught up in right and wrong as people make Him out to be."

"Could be." That would certainly explain how He could take a wife and mother from her family decades before her time.

"Anyway. Getting a shot at this duet is a big deal for me. Maybe like a promotion? Or like trying out for *Audition Room* all over again." She licked her bottom lip, gently bit it, then released it. "If you put in a good word for me and the collaboration, I'd be forever in your debt."

She was flirting, but why? She might've felt the same

connection he had. Or she might only have overestimated his power within the band. He opened his mouth to correct her and put an end to any advances inspired by faulty motives, but an outburst from the claw machine interrupted.

"I told you!" Nila slammed her hand down next to where Nason stood at the controls. "Why didn't you listen?"

Nason's shoulders slumped, and he turned from the game with his mouth screwed to the side.

His son slouched into his seat while Nila stood behind her chair. "Let's go to the store."

"It's getting late, but the next time we're there, we'll get you a unicorn."

Nila plunked onto her chair. "But you said."

"I didn't say we'd go tonight."

"This isn't fair!" Nila's tears and pout were the opening act to a much bigger show, and already the kid drew stares.

Philip rose. "It's definitely time for bed."

Cringing, Michaela stood, and Nason slid to his feet.

Nila folded her arms on the table and dropped her head with a moaning sob. If only Philip could walk out on the theatrics.

He planted one hand on the table and leaned close to her ear. "This is not how you behave when you don't get your way. Keep it up and you won't get a unicorn the next time we're at the store either."

She shuddered and sat back, still pouting but not daring to meet his gaze.

"Let's go." He held out his hand, a risk, because if she refused him, the whole restaurant—and Michaela—would see the truth about him. He wasn't a great dad, and not all was well in his house. But Nila came through. Though her lip continued to quiver, she placed her hand in his.

Outside, he checked that the kids had buckled in before he closed the back door of the SUV. Michaela lingered, one arm crossed over herself as if she were cold. That tank top would've been sufficient for June in California, but it wasn't made for the fifty-something-degree breeze rolling off Lake Superior.

"Sorry about the tantrum." He rubbed his wrist. He didn't like to lose face in front of a coworker, even if Michaela didn't seem daunted.

"They're sweet kids." She glanced down the street. "I happen to be an expert on all things girly. I could swing by the store, pick up a unicorn, and drop it off before you get her in bed. Then, after, you and I could continue our conversation. Get better acquainted." Toying with her lip again, she let her gaze comb over him.

"Better acquainted?"

"Admit it." She rested a light hand on his chest. "You could use a little adult company."

In her heels, she stood about two inches shorter than he did, not much to separate him from bending his head, kissing her, and getting a foretaste of yet another failure.

On tour, turning down temptation had been easy. He could pretend Clare remained a consideration when he wasn't facing day after day at home without her. The shows had been demanding and entertaining. Plus, Gannon and John had always been close by, likely to learn about whatever he did.

Since the tour had ended, though, Philip's life had yawned empty—of both entertainment and accountability. He was lonely and hurting. Life hadn't been kind to him, and maybe Michaela would be.

But he couldn't add that complication to the mix. Not with the kids watching. Not when her real goal might be to cement the collaboration. Not after experience had taught him that he wouldn't find the comfort he longed for in an empty physical relationship. Not when the other solution he'd already enacted was so likely to blow up on him.

Or not. He wouldn't spiral out of control if he kept a firm

hand on the wheel and refused any new detours—including a fling with Michaela.

He stepped back, letting her hand fall away. "Thanks, but that's the last thing I want."

He drove off, leaving Michaela standing in the yellow glow of the single streetlight in the parking lot.

4

She was the last thing he wanted.

Philip was in good company.

If anyone wanted Michaela, she wouldn't be on this desperate mission for attention in the Northwoods of Wisconsin. Though the need to secure the duet had inspired the dinner invitation, her career hadn't motivated the offer she'd made afterward. However, he must not have been as lonely and desperate for distraction as herself. Now, she and her bruised pride had to do the extra work of smoothing things over before Philip told Gannon what she'd done.

If he hadn't already.

How humiliating.

Nearing the peak of its arc, the sun warmed her hair and arms, but the quiet traffic and pedestrians around her on Lakeshore's Main Street left her cold in a way the sun couldn't remedy. She pulled out her phone.

The picture she'd posted of herself and Gannon in the studio yesterday had more likes and comments than anything she'd posted in weeks.

That was something, at least.

She scrolled her feed. Kira K's song still clung to the top of the charts, and the pop artist's vacation photo boasted more reactions than Michaela's picture. She tapped to browse the snapshots she'd captured yesterday, hunting for another to post.

Her sister's name popped up on screen. Because she'd been flipping through pictures, she accidentally swiped to accept the call.

Fantastic.

Admittedly, she should've called Riley after pizza last night. She hadn't because she'd suffered enough rejection from Philip and hadn't wanted to slather on another layer from family. Ready or not this morning, she'd answered, so she lifted the device to her ear and forced a bright tone. "Riley. What's up?"

"Did Dad tell you?"

"He texted that I should call you. Sorry I haven't gotten there yet." She continued down the sidewalk at a slower pace, peering into the realty office. At least she knew she wouldn't find a unicorn there.

"They found a mass."

Michaela's toe caught on a crack, and she drew up short. A mass? As in a tumor? "You have cancer?"

"They ruled out a cyst. They scheduled a biopsy to determine if it's cancer."

They'd lost some grandparents to the disease, but Michaela didn't know any twenty-somethings with the awful diagnosis. "That's awful. When is the biopsy? Is it a big deal?"

"Of course it's a big deal. It might be cancer."

Michaela gulped. "I meant invasive. Is the procedure invasive?"

"They're going to take a chunk out of my body. What do you think?"

Michaela scanned the area, but of course, no one was around to overhear, let alone weigh in on who was to blame for the deteriorating interaction. "I'm really sorry you're going through this. Keep me posted, okay?"

Riley made a noise of protest. "You're not going to ask where the mass is?"

Her other question hadn't been good enough, so no, she hadn't planned to venture another.

"It's on my ovary."

"Okay." At least an ovary wasn't a vital organ, right?

"Look up the statistics on ovarian cancer. Then tell me you don't care."

"I never said I don't care."

"You didn't have to. You're just like Mom, off living your own life without a care for us little people you left behind."

"That's not fair, Riley." Michaela might not be great about returning calls, but she did visit home, and her family did know how to reach her. Meanwhile, they'd had no contact from Mom in years.

"You know what's not fair? Cancer." Riley hung up.

Michaela huffed.

Riley was in a crisis, but did that warrant this treatment? No. Her sister was doing what she'd always done—taking out her frustrations about unchangeable situations like cancer and Mom on Michaela.

Michaela pushed her shoulders back, focusing on a deep breath to calm down and think rationally. The possibility of cancer was scary, but the biopsy results weren't in.

For all any of them knew, Riley didn't have cancer.

In fact, maybe the doctors had told her it was unlikely, so she was spreading word about it now in a bid for attention.

That sounded like something Riley would do.

In the earliest picture of them together, Michaela just a

newborn, Riley had worn a shirt with a tiara, proclaiming herself a princess. From then until Riley entered her wild phase in high school, she appeared somewhere in the background of most snapshots of Michaela, usually striking a hard-to-miss pose.

And Michaela was supposedly the performer of the pair.

Well, Michaela had her own life to tend to.

If Riley was diagnosed with cancer, Michaela would step up, send flowers, mail a card. Whatever people did. And all of it would be more than Mom would ever do.

But most likely, this would turn out to be a false alarm.

So, back to the business of recovering the situation with Philip and, in turn, impressing Awestruck, Reese, and the rest of the world.

She pulled open the door to yet another small shop. She'd already visited a candy store and a touristy T-shirt place, but she hadn't found a stuffed unicorn for Nila. This bookstore occupied what must've once been a family home. Perhaps they'd have a children's reading corner with plush animals for sale.

When she'd declared herself an expert on girliness, she'd underestimated the difficulty of finding a respectable unicorn in small-town Wisconsin. The only department store in Lakeshore, grimy with age, had stocked a ghastly yellow monstrosity she'd left on the dusty shelf. At least her trip through the store's aisles explained the poor fashion sense walking the streets around here.

The difficulty of the feat would make success more impressive. She would find the perfect unicorn for Nila. She knew the pain of growing up without a mom to pick such things out. She wanted to see joy on that little girl's face.

And the only way to Philip seemed to be through his kids.

Had she ever been so soundly rejected in her life?

By Dad and Riley, sure, but not by a man.

If even her looks had begun to lose their allure, no wonder her sales were tanking.

"Can I—?" The saleswoman interrupted herself with a gasp, smoothed her hands over her matronly shirt, and tried again. "Can I help you?"

At being recognized, a flare of triumph shot through Michaela, and her smile came easily for the middle-aged woman. "I'm looking for a stuffed animal. A unicorn."

The woman's face settled into determined lines, and she scanned her store. "I'm afraid I don't stock toys like that here, but I'll tell you what." She hustled behind the sales counter and pulled a pamphlet from underneath. "Your best bet will be The Sea Breeze Gift Shop." The woman tapped the map.

Michaela angled her head, trying to place the bookstore so she could determine a route to the other store.

"Here, you can take it with you." The salesclerk—or owner, she supposed—slid the map over.

Michaela accepted the illustrated paper. All the businesses the mapmaker had marked were within four or five blocks of the lake. Other than to make that one observation, she was useless with a map. She'd have to enter the name of the store in her phone and let GPS navigate her there.

"You must be visiting Gannon."

She lowered the map. "Do you know him?"

"Oh, not personally. My husband plays in the community orchestra with his fiancée. Awestruck moving here really put Lakeshore on the map. I mean, we've always had tourism in summer, but now ..." With a toss of her head, she redirected. "You must know him from *Audition Room*? How sweet to stay in touch. You wonder, watching those shows, if the chemistry is real or all an act."

Chemistry? Her and Gannon? Her smile broadened. "We

had a good time on the show. We're planning a duet. That's why I'm here."

"Oh, wonderful. Well, I'm not the type to call in and vote on a reality show, but if I had known you'd be eliminated, I would've gotten over myself and put in a vote for you. I've always thought the wrong person won that season."

Michaela's smile froze in place like a mask. This wasn't the pick-me-up she'd anticipated. She stepped toward the door. "I won my season, so you must have me confused with someone else."

"Oh ... You're not Jamie Barrow?"

"No, but we competed on the same season, and we're both brunettes. Maybe that's how you got us confused." Michaela waited. At the very least, the lady could realize how insulting she'd been and apologize.

"Oh. Sometimes all those girls look alike with the big, dramatic eyes, and the hair ..." She trailed off and chuckled uncomfortably. "Well, I'm so glad you stopped in. If you need a good book to read on the beach, stop back. And good luck with your unicorn hunt."

Bells rung above Michaela's head as her shoulder pressed against the exit. To think she had expected *Audition Room* to be her big break. Afterward, she was supposed to become a staple in the industry, never again to be relegated to anyone's shadow.

But Riley's shadow had proved much easier to escape than Jamie Barrow's or Kira K's.

Her phone sounded again. Reese.

Let this be good news. She answered her manager's call.

"How's it going up there?"

"Great." The forced enthusiasm took all Michaela's skill as a performer. She continued, praising Gannon's song and how good it was to work with him again.

"How about the rest of the band? Did you connect well with everyone? They were all there, weren't they?"

"They were. I haven't talked much with John, but I got pizza with Philip and his kids last night. We had fun." If she forced any more sunshine into her voice, a solar flare would zap her vocal cords.

"It sounds like you're off to a solid start. Keep me posted."

That was all Reese wanted? She had no news? No plans?

Doom sidled up beside Michaela. She needed to get Reese excited about her again, thinking ahead, campaigning for her career. She licked her lips and borrowed confidence from her imagination. "There is one thing I wanted to discuss for the next album, a way to make it really pop."

"Okay."

"I'd like Evie Decker to produce it."

Silence. *Two. Three. Four. Two, two, three, four.* "She's turned down some of the biggest names."

"We miss all the shots we don't take. I'll start putting together some ideas, and—"

"One step at a time," Reese said. "Let's see how this duet goes. Making a splash with Awestruck could open other doors."

Michaela drew a deep breath. Those who worked with Evie were nearly guaranteed a run at the top of the charts. Same for working with Awestruck. She'd meant to have hope for her career even if she failed with one of the two, but Reese had neatly tied them together.

"You're nervous about Awestruck, but Gannon's always been your biggest fan. Win over one of the others, and you've got yourself a majority. You'll be fine. After Awestruck, Evie will fall into place."

"Okay."

"They're men, honey. Do what you do."

Her stomach sank. Shameless flirting hadn't gotten her as far with Awestruck—Philip, especially—as it had with others in the industry. But she needed this.

Her career needed this.

If she failed, she'd have to find another occupation, and she had no other talents.

She must succeed.

So, she continued down the street to The Sea Breeze Gift Shop.

THE SEA BREEZE Gift Shop had, indeed, stocked a unicorn. One so perfect, Michaela didn't mind hefting it around as she wandered the downtown area, browsing stores and killing time until her afternoon session with the band.

Her stomach gurgled, suggesting she spend some of the remaining hour finding food. She'd seen a little café with a window decal boasting of healthy options—a necessity after pizza last night—but finding it again would be a trick. Downtown Lakeshore wasn't big, but all the streets looked the same to her.

She shifted the two-and-a-half-foot tall unicorn to one hand and reached for her phone in her pocket. As her fingers landed on the smooth surface of the device, a familiar SUV pulled up to the curb half a block away.

Philip got out, a golden opportunity to do damage control one-on-one.

Her arm tightened around the unicorn, and she left the phone in her pocket as she waved a greeting. But he'd already started away from her down the sidewalk. "Philip!"

His step slowed, but he didn't turn.

Didn't he recognize her voice? She started after him, but her own feet grew heavy as a possibility occurred to her. What if he'd seen her before he'd parked and had purposely ignored her?

Shame coiled in her belly, reminding her she'd come on too

strong last night. He'd done them both a favor by rejecting her, but what a fool she'd made of herself.

What would she have done if he'd taken her up on her offer?

She toyed with an earring with her free hand. Didn't matter because he hadn't. To work together, they needed to overcome the awkwardness. Besides, this unicorn was for a noble cause. She didn't need to be embarrassed over doting on an adorable little girl.

She picked up her pace, and simultaneously, Philip turned toward her.

His look of reluctance gave way to a flash of surprise. So he hadn't known it was her calling him after all. Instead of seeming to appreciate the outfit she'd chosen with such care that morning—high-waisted jeans that hugged her hips and a fitted white top with puffy sleeves—he motioned to the stuffed animal. "What's that?"

Relieved he'd steered the interaction that direction instead of to last night, she extended the plush toy toward him. "A unicorn and a Pegasus in one. I'm thinking her name should be Peggy."

The floppy animal hung between them, and though its face was now pointed at Philip, Michaela had seen the thing's big blue eyes. Surely Philip wouldn't be able to resist the poor creature's plea for a new home.

His cheek twitched, and he scanned the surrounding street before fixing a grimace on the animal.

"Oh, come on." Michaela jiggled Peggy so the iridescent wings flapped. "Are you going to take her?"

"For Nila? It's almost as big as she is." He glanced away again, as if looking for an escape. Or maybe he was keeping an eye on the guy walking their way.

The man appeared to be in his early twenties, clean cut

enough that he shouldn't leave Michaela with the desire to cross the street—except that he focused on them with a dark stare.

Michaela inched to the side, giving the man space and hoping Philip would follow. He didn't, so she touched his arm.

That got his attention, but instead of moving aside, he shifted away from her, and the stranger bumped into him.

Michaela sucked in a worried breath, but without a word, the stranger stepped around them and continued away. She watched long enough to ensure he wasn't rounding on her, then turned to Philip, who was stuffing his hand in his pocket, the picture of casual.

"You don't think that was weird?" She shot another look over her shoulder.

"Don't be paranoid."

At Philip's reply, shame lapped at her toes, but was it really paranoia? Hadn't any of his fans ever gone too far or gotten too possessive? Hers had.

The stranger turned off the sidewalk, though from this angle, she couldn't say whether he'd entered a store or an alleyway.

Michaela exhaled relief. "He should watch where he's going."

Philip's gaze dipped to the unicorn, as though Michaela were the one with problems, not the stranger.

This was backwards.

Philip wouldn't know a friendly gesture if it bit him on the nose.

"I saved you a trip to, like, four stores. She would not have been happy with any of the other options." Michaela bumped the unicorn into him then let go, forcing him to catch its fall.

Holding Peggy by the scruff, he surveyed the toy. "I'll see that she gets it." His voice was hard to read.

"She'll love it." She tweaked the unicorn's cheek, picturing the girl's reaction. But then a realization dawned, and her satis-faction fell faster than her record sales. "I should've gotten something for Nason too. I'm sorry. I didn't think of that, but playing favorites isn't cool, is it?"

She of all people should've thought of that. Her expertise didn't extend to toys a little boy might like, but she could've tried.

"It's fine. You didn't have to do this at all. Since you did, I'll make sure Nason gets something to balance it out." He took a step backward and motioned behind him. "I'm getting some lunch, so—"

"Oh, great. I need something too." Food, but more impor-tantly, more time to offer Philip a reasonable excuse for her behavior. An excuse she still hadn't dreamed up.

She lifted her sunglasses and slid them into her hair as she read the nearest awning—Bryant's Subs. The green fabric could use a refresh, and someone ought to clean the grime around the windowsills. "Here? Is the food any good?"

"Gannon and John are at Superior Dogs, a food truck on Main Street, if you want to join them." He motioned back the way she'd come. "Can't beat a Super Superior."

This was no good. He was trying to get rid of her.

She tried a sweet smile. "Then why come here?"

"Can't eat hot dogs every day."

Her gaze slid from him to Bryant's Subs and back again. A hot dog truck was less likely to serve salads. Hopefully the sub place could plate her greens without a side of food poisoning. But why risk her health if Philip spent the whole meal resenting her company?

"You'd rather eat alone?"

He gave a pained smile. "Honestly, I'm not feeling great and might not be the best company, so I'm letting you know your options."

Maybe he did look a little pale. And now that she was

paying attention, his forehead glimmered, damp. It wasn't that hot out. After living in California and Iowa, the guy should be able to handle a Lakeshore heatwave without breaking a sweat. Did he have a fever?

"Are you sure you shouldn't go home?" she asked.

"Eating will help." He retreated toward the restaurant. When he spotted her still tailing him, he pulled the door wide and stood aside, letting her in first.

While she studied the menu, Philip rattled off an order for a roast beef sub. He ran the back of his wrist over his forehead, then paid his bill, collected his food, and carried Peggy to a booth.

When Michaela slid her salad onto the table a couple minutes later, he stood and motioned toward the restroom. "Watch my stuff?"

She ruffled her fingers through the unicorn's bangs. "Didn't want anyone walking off with her?"

"You got me." He covered a yawn.

He really must be feeling off.

"Is it the flu? Or just a wild night?"

"Yeah. Crazy time at the pizza parlor." He turned for the restroom. "My kids know how to party."

Michaela chuckled, though he still hadn't explained his symptoms. His claim that eating would help seemed to contradict both of her theories—that he had a hangover or the flu. But what else could it be?

And since he wasn't taking it seriously and staying home to avoid spreading germs, the hangover seemed most likely. It saddened her to think of him sitting alone at home, drinking. She liked the guy she'd started to get to know at the pizza restaurant. Liked his questions, liked his sympathy.

Her determination to make him smile quadrupled, but he still wasn't on his way back, so she busied herself staging the scene for a social media post.

When Philip returned, he stopped beside the booth and cocked his head in an unasked question. She'd placed her salad in front of Peggy, rested a fork against one of the unicorn's hooves, and put her water against the other front hoof.

"What? She's hungry." Laughing, Michaela motioned him to take his seat. "It'll be a fun picture."

"Me having lunch with a unicorn."

She grinned. "Not just any unicorn. Peggy."

He studied her for a beat, then a hard-earned smile edged onto his haggard face. He dropped into the booth and unwrapped his sandwich as if she weren't hovering with her camera app at the ready. As he took his first bite, she snapped the shot, then tapped to review her work.

Hilarious.

"Want to see?"

"Not really." The amusement lingering in his expression softened the refusal.

"You guys should consider putting a unicorn on the cover of your next album."

Philip didn't reply as she flipped through filters. After she finished the post, she pulled her salad back to her side of the table. Across from her, the unicorn, with its fresh white fur and doe-like eyes, looked the picture of youth and joy next to Philip.

In the unattended minute since their last exchange, the haunted look had returned to his eyes. "What was that last night? If you're just trying to get close to me any way you can so I'll do you a solid with the guys, it's not going to work."

Wow, the man could be direct when he wanted to be.

She drizzled oil and vinegar over her salad. "Maybe I just thought we had enough in common that it'd be worth getting to know each other better with a little more conversation."

That was the truth, but not the whole truth. She was attracted to him, had hoped he might be interested in her, and had been willing to see where that would lead. Maybe it would've done her some good with the collaboration, but that hadn't been her primary motivation. She'd simply wanted to be less lonely for an evening. Was that so bad?

Philip gave her a long look, as though he doubted her, then lifted his sub. "I don't bring women home, even for conversation, because of the kids."

She should've thought of that. They might get confused or get their hopes up if they saw their dad with a girlfriend.

Michaela had spent years wishing for a loving mother who'd take her shopping, do her makeup, and give her advice like other girls had. She would've settled for an older sister who took her under her wing instead of one who constantly shooed her away. "Do they miss having a mom?"

"They miss *their* mom."

Right. Kids who'd had a good one were probably more particular than Michaela would've been. And a man who'd loved his wife and the mother of his children might know something about loss, but that didn't mean he'd seek comfort with Michaela.

Shame prickled her cheeks. She'd never have made the offer if she'd known the rejection, awkwardness, and confusion that would follow.

The sooner they returned to business as usual, the better.

"So ... we're good?" she asked.

"We were never *not* good."

Liar, liar.

But as he continued to eat, he didn't seem sick anymore, so he may have been telling the truth about his mysterious illness. She stabbed her plastic fork into her greens and glanced again at the unlikely pair across from her, the man and the unicorn.

She'd made a mistake, but he'd let her join him and take that picture, showing a willingness to tolerate her that meant he probably wasn't trying to talk Gannon out of working with her. That would have to be good enough.

Meanwhile, since she'd tagged both him and the band's account, the shot would get lots of views. Maybe enough to edge out Kira K's vacation. Whether she broke through Philip's defenses or not, landed the duet or not, she'd benefit from the world knowing she kept such famous company.

5

"*D*o the kids have any fears or quirks your nanny should know?"

For the other candidates Philip had interviewed that day, he wouldn't have put much thought into his answer because he didn't intend to hire them. But Ruthann Presley came with stellar references, ten years of experience, and a sense of humor the kids would love.

Unfortunately, she'd already received offers from other families. Families she wouldn't have to move six hours north for.

At this point, he was the one in the hot seat, not her. "They're both ... nervous about the dark, I guess. Sleep with nightlights, but nothing unusual." He rubbed his hands together, wracking his brain. Questions about his kids should be easy. "Nila also has nightmares sometimes."

"What are the dreams about?"

He reached across himself, scratched his shoulder blade, then crossed his arms. "Being left alone. The dreams started during last year's tour. She's afraid people she cares about won't come back."

The difficult admission didn't seem to surprise Ruthann. "She lost her mother, and trauma tends to introduce some fears. We can work on that. Or ..." She froze a moment then lifted open hands. "I mean, whoever you hire could partner with you on the issue."

Partner. A nice idea. He also appreciated that she'd laid blame on Clare's death and not his absences.

"I'm hoping she'll feel better if she and Nason can stay in one place, no matter where my job takes me. They won't have to change schools and friends. At home, I need someone who'll be a constant for them. When I'm here, the nanny will stay in the apartment. When I'm gone, she'll move into a room in the main part of the house."

"Nancy mentioned that." She acknowledged the head of the placement agency, who sat next to Philip, then refocused on him. "How does the band's schedule work?"

"We tour heavily every other year. Home this year, gone most of next. I'll come home when I can, but during school breaks, the nanny will bring the kids for visits wherever I am."

The discussion continued for another half an hour until Audrey, the part-timer, brought the kids home from the zoo.

Nila clutched the stuffed unicorn from Michaela under one arm and the tulle of her knee-length skirt in her other hand as she eyed the newcomer. "I like your skirt."

"Thank you. I wear one every day." Ruthann smoothed her hands over the orange fabric of her ankle-length skirt. "Yours is cute too."

Nila muted her answering smile by biting her lips together.

"Do you know how to make cupcakes?" Nason asked.

Ruthann's mouth broke into a grin.

Nila released her lips to ask, "Unicorn cupcakes?"

Audrey confirmed they had the ingredients—for normal cupcakes, anyway—and Philip hung in the background as Ruthann and the kids tackled the task.

The woman had a way with the kids. She appeared to be about his age. The age Clare would be. If she wore long skirts every day, Philip would bet she was religious. Not a surprise, as she'd listed a church daycare on her resume. Convictions ought to mean Ruthann wouldn't surprise him the way Hillary had. She'd probably also obey his ban on posting pictures of the kids online.

Besides, having a Christian influence in the kids' lives wouldn't be bad. Clare had made him promise to keep taking the kids to church. She'd probably thought continuing to show up in the Lord's house would cure his ebbing faith. Not the case, though, and he'd been attending services less and less.

Guilt over breaking his promise weighed heavily. He'd have to get the kids there tomorrow. Hopefully, if they adopted Christianity as their own, God wouldn't disappoint them the way He'd disappointed Philip.

How had Clare been at peace with Him, even as she'd died?

His phone sounded with a text, preventing him from having to stare down the deep, dark hole of that question.

Michaela had messaged. *How does Nila like Peggy?*

He'd been enjoying Michaela's company. She seemed to regret the tactic she'd tried at the pizza place, and once she'd laid off the flirting, her kindness and sense of humor had come through.

The unicorn sat at the table, waiting as Nila helped pour batter into the muffin pan. The remote-control truck he'd picked up for Nason had captured his son's interest for all of five minutes while Nila had yet to let Michaela's gift out of her sight. *BFFs, but she renamed her Helga.*

As he resumed observing the kids, his thoughts circled back to church and God. The cloud of guilt and disappointment loomed again, but then his phone dinged, a break in the sky.

Helga? Michaela had written. *She's a pegacorn, not a Scandinavian wench!*

44

He snorted, drawing a glare from Nancy. He would've replied despite the silent rebuke, but Ruthann slid the pan into the oven, wrapping up their project. Audrey took back over with the kids, and he and Nancy showed the new candidate to the apartment that came with the job.

He unlocked the separate entrance at the back of the house, flipped on the light, and stood to the side so the women could precede him inside and up to the second-floor apartment. His phone had dinged again, but he forced himself to focus. Whoever he hired would be an important part of the family, and he couldn't afford to choose poorly again.

"Mr. Miller? A word?" Nancy leaned her head to signal him to hang back. When Ruthann had rounded a corner, Nancy pulled a contract from the portfolio she carried. "If you want to hire her, you'd better make the offer today."

He took the contract. "Okay."

Nancy exhaled, relief lifting her features. The sooner they filled the position, the sooner Nancy wouldn't have to sub. She bustled into the living room, following Ruthann, while Philip checked his messages.

Michaela again. *What are you up to?*

Nanny interviews, remember?

Oh right. How's that going?

Good. I think I found one. He sent the reply, then met up with Ruthann in the living room. She'd finished her walk-through. He liked her, but as he looked at the contract, doubts surfaced. He'd thought the previous nannies would work out too.

"How soon would you be available?" Nancy leveled a stern look at him. Apparently, she thought him too slow with an offer.

Ruthann seemed unfazed. "My current family is moving. They're okay if I stay on to help until the end but also said they'd understand if something came up sooner."

45

"Perhaps a week, then?" Nancy's eagerness sent Philip into a panic.

He stared at the contract, but the writing blurred. Was Ruthann the right choice? If only he could get Clare's input. Or, really, any opinion besides Nancy's. She wanted to fill the role to free up her schedule. Gannon and John didn't know about kids. Michaela didn't, either, but she'd picked a unicorn Nila loved.

Michaela probably wouldn't like Ruthann's long skirts, no frills hair, or her open, makeup-free face.

But he needed a nanny, not a beauty queen, and even considering Michaela's preferences regarding a childcare decision left him uneasy. Decisions about nannies should fall to parents, and enjoying Michaela's company was a far cry from being that serious about her.

If only Clare were here to weigh in.

"If I accepted a position here, I could move within a week." She focused on Philip. "Is this a job offer?"

Clare was the key to this. If Clare had to choose someone other than herself to raise her kids, what would she do?

He pulled in a deep breath, focusing on the woman, all she'd said, how she'd connected with his children.

Clare would choose Ruthann.

"It is." He extended the contract. "I think you'd be great with the kids."

"Wonderful." Ruthann seemed to skim the first couple of lines before offering a smile. "I'll read this over and pray about the position, then get back to you by Tuesday."

"And you could start the following Tuesday?" Nancy asked.

Philip cut between her and Ruthann before the older woman scared away the best candidate they had. "If you need a couple of extra days to think about accepting—or two or three weeks before moving—we'll make do."

"Thanks, but Tuesday should be fine. I've been looking for a couple of weeks, so I have a clear view of my options. It's decision time."

Philip saw both women out and locked the apartment as they drove off. With a sigh, he checked to see Michaela's latest text. Maybe she could lighten him up again.

Want to do something later?

And there it was. She still wanted into his life, but why? She certainly wasn't looking to settle down. Did she want friendship, help convincing Awestruck to pursue the duet, or a casual hookup?

Clare had forgiven him for all his other failings, but sleeping around would've betrayed her trust irreparably. Sure, she'd died, and that wasn't supposed to be a consideration anymore. In the wake of her death, he'd sought comfort in places both Clare and God would've hated—to no avail. The string of women had left him disgusted with himself and more bereaved than ever. He'd sworn off casual sex.

That or help with Awestruck seemed Michaela's most likely motivations.

He typed his reply to her. *Sorry, can't.*

He'd treat the emptiness another way. He watched his screen for a long moment after sending the message, regretting the abrupt decline. She might be bored and lonely—he knew how that felt. He wouldn't fall into bed with her, but her company would make suffering through a service more entertaining.

He sent a follow-up message.

But you're welcome to come to church with us in the morning.

MICHAELA PARKED her rental car at the back of the lot and watched vehicles pull in, on outfit patrol. The women in their twenties seemed to favor jeans, while some of the old ladies wore bright dresses cut in styles that would've been all the rage twenty-five years before. A few of the little girls wore party dresses. A crowd wearing this much of a mishmash of styles had no room to judge Michaela in her silky peach-and-gold shirt dress.

Philip pulled in and parked his SUV two rows away. As he got out, she crossed the lot.

He wore dark jeans with brown leather shoes and a green polo that loved him. His shoulders, especially.

She lifted her sunglasses to the top of her head and squinted in the yellow morning sun. "I am having the hardest time figuring you out, Philip Miller."

More than sunlight seemed to glimmer in his eyes as he opened Nason's door without taking his gaze off Michaela. "Why're you trying to figure me out?"

If she wasn't mistaken, he was glad she'd come.

"You prefer to be an enigma?"

A smile lifted the corner of his mouth, but instead of answering, he offered his hand to his son. "You remember my friend Michaela?"

Nason took his hand, staring up at her as if they hadn't shared pizza a couple of days before.

As Nason half-frowned at her, Philip focused behind her. "Nila, come say thank you for Helga."

She turned. The girl must've exited the other side of the van and come around. She wore a simple blue dress with buttons down the front and rubbed the toe of her sandal into the asphalt while fingering the locket on her necklace. Michaela didn't usually turn to mush over kids, but with curly hair and wide eyes, Nila was uncommonly cute. Or perhaps the draw was something else. The fact that the girl was both motherless and acting shy, signaling she might need the kind of help and protection Michaela hadn't received.

Riley hadn't received motherly care either. She'd texted an

apology yesterday for comparing Michaela to their absent mom, saying something about how the threat of cancer, especially since it might prevent her from having any more children, had caused her to think more about Mom. She'd taken it out on Michaela, and she was sorry.

Michaela suspected that Riley's true regret wasn't so much the sentiment, but rather the fact that she'd spoken it aloud. The apology was an attempt to return them to the status quo, where resentment could simmer unacknowledged, never to be resolved.

They'd been at this so long that Michaela didn't know how to improve the situation. So, she'd simply replied that she understood, and then she'd messaged Philip.

Now she was here with him and his adorable children, and if she could be a bright spot in a little, motherless girl's life, she would be. Maybe it would spare Nila just a little pain down the line.

"Look, we match!" Michaela motioned to her own dress. "Mine has buttons too. Yours is lovely. Did you pick it out yourself?"

The question drew out a sweet smile but not an answer. But, as they headed toward the building, Nila fit her hand in hers, shooting joy through her.

Nason bumped along between Michaela and Philip, still gripping his dad's hand.

To keep Nila, who seemed most likely to understand, from overhearing, Michaela dropped her voice as she said what she'd been thinking since she received his invitation. "I thought you weren't religious."

"Their mom thought church was a good idea." As he spoke, Philip scooped up a lagging Nason.

She pried her focus from his flexed bicep. The one he used to carry the son he'd had with someone else. Someone who apparently retained a role in his life. No wonder Michaela couldn't make progress with him.

How foolish, her hope of filling a gap for Nila. First, she knew nothing about kids—except that she probably wasn't the best role model. Second, the girl had her own mother.

She lowered her voice even more. "I didn't realize you two were still close."

Philip gave her an indecipherable look as they approached the doors.

People in the lobby greeted them, ending the conversation.

In the main room, Philip motioned Michaela into the row of seats first. "I have to take the kids out for their class partway through."

She released Nila's hand. She didn't have a place in the girl's life, anyway. Of course, she'd be left here alone.

Michaela Vandehey and *alone* were synonymous.

Philip must've read the look on her face because he chuckled as he settled beside her. "I'll come back."

She took a deep breath, trying to calm her overreactions. Church, the few times she'd attended, did seem to bring out her emotional side. But she'd been a hormonal teen back then. What was her excuse now?

A man approached the microphone in front, and everyone quieted.

Funny. She wanted the opposite reaction when she stepped on stage.

The man started singing, accompanied by a white-haired lady on the piano and a teen on guitar. The people around Michaela lifted their voices more loudly than Philip. He sang backup vocals for Awestruck, but she could only hear him on one of the songs.

Perhaps he didn't know the music any better than Michaela did.

Finally, the last song's lyrics appeared on the projection screen.

She'd heard "Amazing Grace" enough on TV and in movies to join in. Philip, too, seemed to pick up volume.

Even as she sang, no pose or expression felt appropriate. She wasn't used to standing so still, putting so little personality and emotion into a song. Given the lack of stage presence up front, this was like a concert with no focal point. Yet a few members of the audience lifted their hands as if desperate for some superstar to stretch out and touch them.

True believers.

Her childhood friend, Heather, the one with the old woodwork in her house, had been one of those. After hanging out with her too long at youth group and Bible camp, even Michaela tried to believe. Said the prayer and everything. But as much as she'd reached out to God, He hadn't stretched her way.

She'd been left doing everything for herself, as always.

When she reached for her fans, they reached back. They got far more excited to see her, in fact, than the most passionate people here got about God. Church people could learn a thing or two about worship from pop concerts.

After the singing, Philip escorted the kids out.

Up front, the pastor took the mic. "Let's pray." He bowed his head, and the people around her followed suit.

Michaela lowered her eyes to wait out the prayer, but minutes dragged by, and the guy droned on. Would he mention every person in attendance by name? Maybe God preferred specific prayers?

"For those suffering with cancer, Lord, we ask that you act as their Great Physician and heal them."

Michaela's focus jumped to the pastor. Last night, because of Riley's mention of how ovarian cancer might affect her ability to have more kids, she'd done what Riley had suggested and looked up statistics.

The numbers were scary.

Not only might Riley not be able to have more kids, her life was at risk if the mass turned out to be cancer. For all Michaela's difficulty getting along with Riley, she didn't wish her harm. If God could prevent Riley's mass from being cancer, Michaela ought to try to get Him on their side.

She closed her eyes and tipped her face down, listening, as the pastor prayed in more detail for the church's cancer-stricken. Then he paused, either to tackle the next set of problems or to end the prayer.

"And for Riley," Michaela mumbled. "Don't let her be sick."

Maybe she couldn't match the religious wordiness of the guy up front, but she'd covered the bases, hadn't she? For good measure, she kept her eyes closed until the pastor finally wrapped up the prayer.

When she opened them again, Philip was seated beside her. She hadn't heard him return. Had he heard her? Probably not, since he looked as bored as she'd felt during most of the singing.

He noticed her looking, and his lips tipped up at the corners in a quick acknowledgment before he fixed his focus forward again.

Business as usual. He hadn't heard.

Good. The whole thing was superstitious. After all, people enumerating their concerns to God was probably as useful as Reese sitting Michaela down to explain how badly her sales were tanking.

She already knew, and so did God.

Maybe He was just as helpless and desperate as Michaela was.

6

*M*ichaela parked in Gannon's drive for her Monday session with Awestruck, humming her favorite lines from the song for the soundtrack.

The crowd loudly chanting your name, can't see you like I do or love you the same.

If you'll be mine, mine alone, I'll see you through, I'll bring you home.

Gannon put his heart into performances, and she pictured how the song would play out on stage, him promising her the world if she'd put him first.

Yes, please.

But the lyrics weren't trying to convince her—or her persona in the song, anyway—to give up relationships with other men. The line urged her to *come back from the dark edge of fame.*

That could do with some revision.

The lyric fit the movie's storyline but didn't have broad appeal to spread beyond the soundtrack. The sea of faces that came to their shows and sang along as their music blared from stereos—those people probably hadn't even had their fifteen minutes of fame, let alone stumbled across any dark edges of it.

But a song about wanting their loves to choose them? Longing for faithfulness, longing to capture their crush's full attention? *That,* they'd relate to, and she'd captured the feeling in a new lyric. Convincing Gannon to accept the change would pose a challenge, but when had she ever shied away from one of those?

She gathered her purse and water bottle and headed for the walkway.

The man himself swung open the door, but his greeting seemed distracted.

She bit back her suggestion as she followed him in. It could wait until the time was right. "How was your weekend?"

"Good." He didn't turn as he walked ahead of her toward the studio. "But I hear Kim Piel's weekend wasn't."

"Who's Kim Piel?"

"She owns the bookstore in downtown Lakeshore. Her husband knows Adeline from the community orchestra and plans to help teach music lessons at the non-profit we're starting." Gannon drew his phone from his back pocket and tapped on the screen. "The orchestra had a rehearsal last night."

Oh. Right. The woman who'd mistaken her for Jamie Barrow. "What's going on with her?"

"She's upset."

He slowed to pass her the phone, which displayed a post Michaela had done while shopping downtown Friday. She'd captioned it with the story about finding a unicorn for a new little friend, with begrudging thanks to a local who didn't know which brunette from *Audition Room* Season Eight was which.

You can call me many things, she'd written, *but don't mistake me for a loser.*

She'd considered before posting that Jamie might take offense. But the shopkeeper?

"I didn't name her."

"But she knows, and you didn't rein your fans in when they ridiculed her." He pointed her attention back to the phone.

Michaela glanced at the comments, though she'd read them as they came in. "These really aren't that bad. People say worse about me all the time, and no one reins them in."

They'd reached the studio, but Gannon stopped outside the closed door. The set of his shoulders belied his easy expression. He wasn't on her side. "You chose a public career. Kim Piel didn't, and she's part of a community that's been good to us. Adeline and I are starting that non-profit to teach kids music here because we want to give back to them, not open them up to public ridicule."

"All I posted was the truth."

Annoyance flitted across his forehead and around his mouth. "It wasn't necessary. You complained because you were offended, and you knew your fans would take your side. Delete the post and apologize."

"Apologize?" At a sound behind her, she turned. John advanced down the hall, so she lowered her voice. "For mentioning the truth? For what fans said?"

She wasn't a twenty-year-old nobody auditioning for a reality show anymore, but Gannon's even confidence reminded her she didn't call the shots here. And okay, maybe she could see how Kim Piel minded, but really? A big confrontation over a silly post?

Gannon opened the studio door for her and John. Philip stood behind the control room window, the door gaping open. He and John expertly avoided eye contact with her.

They'd known, she realized. Known Gannon had planned to talk to her about this.

Her defense might as well be public. "Mentioning the mistake might've been petty, but what she said hurt my feelings moments after I found out my sister might have cancer. It wasn't a great day. Maybe I deserve a break too."

She couldn't summon tears on cue, but she didn't need to.

Gannon's head tipped with surprise and sympathy.

John, who'd taken a seat on one of the couches, gave her the slightest of sad smiles before he focused on the door to the control room.

Through the glass, Philip's eyes were trained on her with what appeared to be concerned shock.

Her play for sympathy had worked a little too well. She squirmed, wishing for a take back.

"I'm sorry to hear that," Gannon said.

She nodded once. "Look ..." She swallowed, distracted by the man on the opposite side of the glass. Why did Philip stare as though she'd announced an imminent death? "It's not confirmed yet. They're going to do a biopsy. And you're right. I shouldn't have mentioned what happened in the store in a post."

Gannon rubbed his hand over his mouth. The muscles in his jaw flexed, but he didn't speak.

"I'll apologize to her and delete the post like you asked." She coated her voice in honey. "I'll make it up to her."

"Good." Gannon's gaze darted toward the control room. "What kind of cancer?"

She tracked his line of sight as Philip entered the room, for a moment unsure if Gannon's question had been pointed at him or her. "She has a mass on her ovary. Chances are it's not cancer. She's young and healthy. I'm sure in a couple of months, we'll have forgotten all about this little scare."

"You never know." Philip picked up a bass and slung the strap around his back.

Gannon winced, still—*still*—watching Philip.

"When's the biopsy?" This from John.

Her face heated. She and her sister hadn't made it that far in the conversation. "Soon."

"You going to go be with her?" Philip asked.

"Like I said, it's probably nothing, and I really, really want this chance with you guys, if you're ..." She had no idea how she had walked in with ideas and ended up groveling. "As long as you're not giving up on me, I really want to collaborate with you."

"If you need to visit your sister, we're your biggest supporters." Gannon rested his hands on his guitar. "If this collaboration happens, it happens. If it doesn't, your sister is more important than any music."

She tried to ward off his serious tone with a dry chuckle. "You haven't met my sister."

"If things aren't good between you, that's all the more reason to go." Philip's voice cut with judgment. "Get right with her before it's too late."

Get right with her? How, when her sister misconstrued even the most innocent questions Michaela had asked?

She retreated behind the keyboard. "Let's take this down a few notches. The news rattled me, maybe more than I realized. But we don't know she has cancer. I shouldn't have let the situation cloud my judgment. I also shouldn't have brought it up. If it's all right, I'd like to focus on work."

Philip, who'd somehow become a major concern for Gannon and John, judging by the way they watched him, already had his bass ready to go. That gave the other two little choice but to follow suit.

WORK TENDED to distract Philip from other concerns, but not today. After a few hours of forcing himself to focus, Philip held up his phone as his excuse to step from the studio. In the hall, he checked that no one had followed him out, downed a painkiller, and pulled up Nancy's text.

Ruthann accepted the position. She'll move this weekend and start a week from tomorrow.

He texted his thanks as he wandered onward. In the kitchen, he got himself a glass of water. He could've replied and gotten a drink without leaving the studio. But the drug hadn't had a chance to help yet, and he didn't want to be with the others.

Didn't want to be anywhere.

He braced his hands on the counter. He ought to be glad about Ruthann.

"I wasn't expecting that."

Philip turned to see John entering the kitchen.

Hours had passed, but Gannon and John had been keeping a close eye on him since Michaela had mentioned her sister. He should've known someone would tail him out. At least John was less likely to pry.

"I can handle a mention of cancer without falling apart. It's been years."

John nodded but kept studying him.

Good thing the drummer couldn't see through all of Philip's lies so easily.

"You guys didn't tell her, did you?"

John shook his head with an exaggerated frown that meant that they had seen no reason to.

"Good. If her sister's going to go through something similar, let's not scare her with Clare's story." Though how Michaela didn't know on her own ... He'd been shocked when she'd asked if he was still close with the kids' mom yesterday, but he'd rather dodge her questions than her pity.

"Every situation with cancer has to be different, right?" John kept his stance open, concern and not recrimination in his tone.

Philip drank about half his glass of water. The differences didn't worry him. The similarities did. "Going for a biopsy feels about the same, no matter what." He'd felt nauseated the entire time they'd waited for Clare's results. He spent hours plodding mindlessly through his daily tasks, all the while pleading to God to give them good results. "At that point, everything's unknown. It's traumatic, even before you get bad news."

"*If* you get bad news."

"Right." He wiped his mouth with his wrist, but then drank more to have something to do. When Clare got the call confirming her diagnosis, he'd held her for hours while she cried and talked. He'd suppressed his own reaction in order to be strong for her. Once she recovered enough to move on with her day, he'd driven to a park and sobbed. "Cancer is horrible. That's all."

All he would say, anyway.

He finished the water and set the glass in the sink. When he turned, he found himself still the center of John's attention.

"You two spent some time together."

"Me and Michaela? A little, but it's not like that. Anyway, she's not the sick one."

"Okay." John's tight smile hinted that he knew Philip wasn't telling him everything. He stepped back to let Philip lead their return to the studio.

The pill he'd taken had eased into his system. To numb his pain, he'd need more, but the dose would get him through the rest of the day—as long as he wasn't thinking about cancer and its victims. The ones the disease had stolen. And those in its sights.

TOWARD THE END of the day, normalcy seemed to have returned to the studio, and Michaela would never get a better chance.

"How about we change, 'Come back from the dark edge of fame' to 'Come back and rekindle our flame'?" Accompanying herself on the keyboard, she sang the revision.

Gannon's expression soured. "What's wrong with the original?"

"It's not relatable. Besides, if we sing this, people will think *we're* on the dark edge of fame. It's a public image issue." That should help her cause. Gannon cared about his image more than most because he spoke so publicly about his faith.

He crossed his arms. "You had no problem singing about a series of alcohol-inspired one-night stands."

"You're right, I didn't have a problem with it—until it was too late. I'm here *because* of that song. The response was ..." She'd done "No Love Lost" believing what she'd been told.

It was just a song. It would sell. She owed everyone who'd helped her get as far as she had the profits they'd gain off a hit like that.

And the lyrics alone might have been all right.

But, she'd also gone along with their provocative vision for the music video.

Reese had called the approach artistic and empowering. "You'll send the message to women everywhere that they don't have to be ashamed of their bodies."

She'd chosen to believe her so deeply that the vulgar response had shocked her. As did the outrage from the parents of her younger fans. The music video showed no more than many others out there. Still, the reaction made her regret the choice. Big time.

A few months later, Reese reported her label was disappointed with her sales. After she'd gone so far to ensure success, the fiasco felt like the ultimate betrayal. She'd sold herself out and gotten failure in return.

With no pride left, she'd called Gannon, looking for help,

though she'd known he wouldn't be happy about the video. "You don't want to know what the response was."

"I can imagine."

He may as well have said, "I told you so." And he *had* warned her during *Audition Room* to stay true to her values, to refuse anything that made her uncomfortable. But she couldn't go back. Only forward.

She replayed the line, singing her version of the lyrics again.

Gannon pulled out his most dashing smile. "I'm letting you tell me to come back from the dark edge of shame a verse later. Whatever they think of you, they'll think the same of me. And our video will be a lot less controversial."

He'd seen the one for "No Love Lost," then. Or perhaps he'd only heard of it and had purposely avoided watching it.

She wanted to melt into the floor.

"Trust me, kid."

Trust had gotten her into this mess. She looked to the others for help.

John had been at the drums most of the afternoon, but now he sat on the couch, advising instead of playing. "It'd change the whole meaning." And from his tone, change would be a bad thing.

She turned farther, but Philip's bass leaned on its stand. She pivoted, but she didn't see him in the control room either. "Where's Philip? He'll agree with me."

Gannon crossed his arms, smirking. "Not sure he would, but his nanny has to leave by five tonight. You didn't see him go?"

"It's only four." When he'd stepped out, she'd assumed he'd return.

"You two don't need the rhythm section yet, anyway." John swung his feet onto the armrest of the couch, crossed his ankles, and scrolled on his phone.

Gannon toyed with the melody. Based on where he'd picked up, he was working on the final verse, which they had yet to write, and not the section she'd proposed changing.

"What was up with him today?"

"With Miller?" Gannon looked to John. Very unlike him to play clueless and defer to someone else.

The drummer didn't take his focus off his phone. "He didn't explain."

Gannon tried a line for the last verse. Michaela made a face, and he came back with another variation.

Was he really dismissing her suggestion so quickly? Sure, she'd made a mistake with that music video, but she still knew how to relate to fans. "So that's a no on my lyric suggestion?"

"With the right final verse, it'll all fall into place."

She'd never convince him otherwise, and he'd made something of himself without betraying his morals. Record companies were fighting each other with ludicrous bids to sign his band. As always, she needed his help to succeed, not the other way around.

Though John and Gannon didn't seem to be in a hurry to call off the collaboration over her post, they also didn't seem too concerned about whether the song came together.

She still needed Philip. Still needed to win him over.

More than that, she *wanted* to.

He didn't let many past his defenses, and she never could resist a challenge to number among a select few. She'd made some progress with him already, swapping stories and beliefs at the pizza restaurant, sharing lunch, sitting through church. Through it all, she'd seen his loyalty. He looked out for Nila's and Nason's best interests, even when it cost him, like when he refused relationships to not confuse his kids. Though he wasn't religious, he attended church because the kids' mom asked him to. And what of that haunting concern on his face earlier? Could it be he was becoming loyal to Michaela too?

She'd heard a couple of warm laughs from him and had witnessed a few smiles starting to lighten his normally weighted features. How might she go about earning a full, unreserved grin?

She'd have to find out more about him—and Gannon and John didn't seem willing to share details.

No problem. That was what the Internet was for.

7

$\mathcal{T}$hat evening, Michaela turned onto a tree-lined private drive on the outskirts of Mariner, a town even smaller than Lakeshore. Philip's house guarded the top of a rise she wouldn't think of as a hill if it weren't such a flat area. A couple of lights shone inside.

He'd claimed he didn't invite women over because of the kids, so she'd searched the Internet to find out when children under ten usually went to bed. Now that it was past eight thirty, they shouldn't see her, and she would have Philip to herself.

She parked in the looped drive, then sent a text.

Hey, I'm out front. Can we talk?

She darkened the screen and tapped her fingernails on it, waiting.

A minute later, a knock on her window startled her. Given the distance between him and the car, he'd stood as far away as possible to rap on the glass. His hair stuck up in a couple of places, and if he hadn't appeared so quickly, she would've guessed he'd been sleeping.

She hopped out and tucked her phone away. The sun nestled low and golden near the horizon. Despite the remaining light, the air had cooled. She couldn't wait to get back to someplace with more normal, warmer June temperatures, but she could get used to whatever sweet floral scent lingered in Philip's yard. Low bushes dotted among the landscaping hung heavy with large blooms, the only obvious flowers.

He crossed his arms, stance wide and eyes narrow.

She hoisted a smile. "You're probably wondering how I found your place."

His mouth pinched.

She plowed ahead. Coming uninvited to tell him what she'd learned—also uninvited—might be as ill-conceived as trying to crash an invitation-only A-list party in LA. But after what she'd read about him, everything from the way he'd turned her down after pizza to the look he'd given her at church to his complicated beliefs about God made more sense. He'd been hurt. A compassionate ear could do him wonders and transform their relationship. "Turns out, I have at least one fan left in the world, and she works at Mariner General Home. She told me."

"Okay."

"What kind of flowers are these?" She crossed to touch one of the pale pink blooms along the front walk.

"Not sure."

"They smell amazing." The petals fanned into an area the size of her hand. "And they're gorgeous."

Philip stayed a few feet away. "They were here when we moved in."

"I'll have to ask around. Maybe my new friend at Mariner General Home knows."

Posture stiff, Philip eyed the road. Surely Michaela didn't have to specify that she wouldn't actually bring a stranger here.

She straightened and motioned to the door. "Are you going to invite me in?"

His hesitation stretched a couple of beats too long, but she held still, waited out him and his wounded eyes. If only she'd realized sooner what he'd experienced, her priorities would've been different from the start.

If she could be the listening ear and supportive friend Philip needed, perhaps he'd step up to meet her needs, the ones that were so much more vital than a collaboration. Acceptance, understanding, support.

Love.

He was capable of great love.

She saw that now more than ever, and if he let her, she'd show him she could be loving too.

"Sure, okay." He seemed to take care with the latch, opening the door quietly.

Her heel clicked loudly with her first step off the rug in the foyer, so she slipped out of her shoes. Philip studied the sandals as if he were adding up the consequences of letting her make herself at home there.

"I know about your wife." The sentence came out muted.

He ran his hand under his eye and continued farther into the house.

She followed him across the tile and onto the living room carpet, a warm beige. Ample windows overlooked sloping farm fields all the way to the golden sun. From here, he could watch it set every night, but he'd taken a seat on the couch, eyes trained on the coffee table.

"Are you okay?" she asked.

His brow wrinkled as his gaze met hers. "Yeah. You? Why'd you come here?"

"Because I'd rather hear about Clare from you than from the Internet." She watched for cues that she'd stepped onto thin ice and found none. All this time, his wife had been the key. She'd felt so foolish for bringing up Riley, but if she'd kept her mouth shut, she wouldn't be here. "How'd she die?"

"Breast cancer, but it was years ago."

"When I mentioned my sister, you seemed troubled."

"Okay." He watched his hand as he made a fist, opened his hand, and did it again, over and over.

Her whole body ached to cover that fist with her palm. Or hug him. "Philip."

"Yeah?"

"I've only known you a little while, but it hurts to see you so sad."

"Don't take it personally."

His strong front only made this more tragic.

"I wish I could help." She almost reached toward him, but she stopped herself. "Maybe talking ..."

"There's a gene mutation." He spoke quickly, as if he'd been waiting to speak with as much longing as she waited to touch him. "If you have it, you're more at risk for some cancers, like breast and ovarian. It's inherited."

"Oh." Michaela tried to think through his side of things, the implications. Her mind spun uselessly, wheels stuck on the fact that she hadn't expected him to start talking so easily. "Are you telling me about Clare, or are you warning me that, because my sister might have ... Maybe I ...?"

"Clare had the gene. We found out too late to take extra precautions."

"You think my sister should be tested. And me."

He lifted his hand as if to quell undue concern. "I don't know your family history. Chances are, genetics aren't the cause. It's just, when you mentioned where the mass was ..."

"I'll ask about it."

Portions of sky outside the windows had morphed into pink and purple as the sun eased closer to the tree line. Did the kids ever see such a late sunset? Nila would love those colors.

Nila. Sweet, unicorn-loving Nila.

Oh no.

Nila had half her mother's genes.

Philip leaned forward, elbows on his knees, hands clasped behind his neck.

Fear clawed at her throat, nearly silencing her, but ignorance wouldn't change a thing. She needed to know. "Tell me about this gene."

He tipped his face, obscuring her view with his forearms. "I didn't mean to scare you. I shouldn't have mentioned it."

"It's okay. I'm not scared." Such lies. She was concerned for her family. She was downright scared for Nila.

"Even if your sister did have it, not everyone in a family gets the same genes. And bad genes aren't a guarantee someone will get cancer. And cancer treatments advance every year. Maybe something they do now would've saved Clare." He spoke as if he'd preached this to himself often, but something dropped from his face. A tear? "Like I said, with more screenings, they would've caught Clare's earlier, which also would've helped."

Michaela eased closer and slid her hand around the inside of his elbow. The smooth, warm skin there stretched over muscle, but the load he carried had to be heavy, even for him. "Philip."

He covered his eyes.

"Philip, does Nila have the gene?"

A deep ache for a girl she barely knew suspended the moment. Too long.

No wonder he wasn't religious.

She rested her head on his shoulder. Her prayer about her sister yesterday had been pointless if God would let an adorable child like Nila inherit something so horrible.

"We don't know." Philip ran his hand heavily over his face and leaned back into the couch, forcing her to sit up, though she didn't release his arm. "Nason could have the gene, too, but the risk of cancer is higher for women. Still ... Clare thought they should decide for themselves when they're older if they want to be tested. At the time, I agreed, but ... Nila takes after her mom more and more, and I can't imagine finding out one day she's—"

"Are you talking about me?" Nila, dressed in princess pajamas, rounded the couch.

Michaela withdrew her hand from Philip, her arms tense with a desire to gather the girl in a massive hug.

In a jerky movement, Philip sat up and scrubbed his hands over his face again.

His daughter arrived at his side, rested a hand on his knee, and peered into his face. "Dad? Are you sad?"

"No, baby girl." He'd somehow swept away the grief that had been obvious moments ago. "What are you doing up?"

"I heard someone come." She gave Michaela a winning grin, a mix of gaps, baby teeth, and adult teeth. "Hi."

"Hi, sweetheart." She tried to force bravado as well as Philip had, but emotion roughened her voice.

The girl refocused on her father. "Do I get new jeans? Because if I get to decide like you said, I want pink ones."

If Philip felt as pained at her innocent misunderstanding as Michaela did, he covered perfectly. "Pink jeans? Don't you already have pink jeans?" His tone turned teasing, and he reached to tickle Nila. "And pink dresses? And a pink tutu?"

With a giggle, she hopped out of range. "Maybe. But I don't wear the tutu anymore." Tickling Nila seemed to take too much of Philip's effort, and he lowered his hands. Nila took the reprieve as a chance to explain to Michaela. "It's too small, and I don't have dance class anymore."

Before Michaela could reply, Philip rose and motioned Nila toward the stairs. "Come on. Let's get you back to bed."

The girl squirmed past him and pitched herself across the cushions, grinning. "We should have a sleepover on the couch."

"You've got to go to bed." If Philip had reached for Michaela the way he reached for his daughter, Michaela would've had a hard time resisting.

Nila nestled herself into the back corner of the couch. "But I like it here." She craned her neck to Michaela. "Do *you* like it here?"

Her cheeks burned as she nodded. She liked being here very much.

Far too much.

Instead of trying to coax obedience from his daughter, Philip scooped her up, one arm beneath her knees, the other around her back. Once he'd straightened with her in his arms, the girl put her hand on his cheek. "I love you."

Philip flinched first, then narrowed his eyes with playful suspicion. "I love you, too, but that doesn't mean you get to stay up."

Over her protests, he carried her to the stairs, set her on her own two feet, then followed her up.

Michaela stared after them. She knew all about the kind of attraction that drew her eyes to his shoulders and arms. She knew about the buzz of a new romance, the high of a first kiss.

But the tenderness in Philip's relationship with his daughter opened an ache she'd never experienced before. An ache for something lasting. An ache for not just a boyfriend but for this. For family. The family she'd dreamed of but never had.

She'd been a kid when her mom had left. Dad and Riley considered Michaela the last straw that had precipitated that departure. And apparently, now Riley considered Michaela like Mom. Despite how Michaela had suffered for Mom's choice, the woman hadn't gotten in touch, even when Michaela won *Audition Room*. Family, for Michaela, had been a place of pain, so she'd looked for acceptance and security elsewhere. On stage, from the masses.

That had proved a painful pursuit too.

Philip's family had experienced more than its share of pain, and they faced the possibility of suffering a great deal more.

But relationally, this home glowed with security and acceptance. Love.

All the things she'd hoped for from fame.

Fame, at least the secure, lasting kind, continued to prove elusive, but perhaps if that never worked out, she'd found a way to meet those longings through family instead.

And his name was Philip.

BY SOME MIRACLE, Michaela hadn't seemed to notice Philip's state when she'd arrived.

When the last tour had ended, he'd come home clean. Sobriety hadn't been easy on the road, mostly because scoring would've been. But traveling with Awestruck revolved around his strengths—music, the band, crazy travel schedules, adoring fans. Carried by those highs, he'd abstained.

At home, life revolved around his weaknesses—relating to the kids and providing the care they needed. Nila, especially, had taken his extended absence and their subsequent move hard. On top of her recurring nightmares, she'd spent weeks crying and moping, and the revolving door of nannies hadn't helped.

Thanks to Awestruck, he had all the money he could spend, but he couldn't buy what the kids needed, and he didn't have it in himself. They needed Clare, and he couldn't bring her back. He was failing.

Eventually, he'd turned to numbing the aching disappointment the way he'd done in the past.

Despite the morality agreement required to join Awestruck.

By signing the contract, he'd agreed to a list of behaviors: not using his role in the band to take advantage of women, keeping any use of legal substances like alcohol from impacting his performance, and avoiding illegal activities. Violating those promises could cost him his place in the band.

So, he'd treated women with respect. He didn't drink. Not often, anyway, and never when it would impact Awestruck. The pills he took were legal if one had a prescription.

He didn't, but no one had noticed when Philip started using them.

Of course, back then, he'd been taking fewer.

Over the last few months, his fear of discovery had grown with his habit.

Maybe fear had exaggerated how noticeable his problem was. Maybe it wasn't that big of a deal at all. Michaela hadn't noticed anything about his behavior or appearance when she'd arrived, and his so-called problem enabled him to cope. What choice did he have?

He left Nila in the care of her nightlight, then detoured to his bathroom. He wanted to get back to Michaela. Her beauty drew him, but so did her talent for making even a mundane meal at Bryant's Subs interesting. She made it easy to talk about Clare, and her concern for his daughter made him feel less alone than he had since he'd lost his wife.

At the sink, he rinsed his face.

The mirror reflected the same image as always. He'd trimmed his beard that morning and shaved the scruff off his cheeks and neck—a daily routine to maintain the appearance his kids knew. The beard also distracted from his tired eyes, cheeks that had thinned out. If Gannon or John had noticed the twenty pounds he'd put on during the tour or lost since, they hadn't said anything.

Michaela hadn't been around long enough to witness that change, and nothing about him now would give away what he'd been up to before she came. His body had grown accustomed to the painkillers. He rarely took enough to get high anymore. Simply keeping withdrawal symptoms at bay caused enough trouble.

Because he'd gone through his stash too quickly, he'd been in withdrawal that day at Bryant's Subs. Thankfully, Kory had replenished his supply, and so when the mention of ovarian cancer had shaken him earlier, he'd made it through the day and then had come home and done what he'd had to do to relieve the suffering.

The high had faded before Michaela had stepped foot in the living room. He would've taken more, if not for her presence. Even now, the bottle in his medicine cabinet tempted him.

But what if there was some peace and comfort to be found with Michaela? The pills would be there after she left. He tossed the towel on the vanity and returned to the living room.

A lock of Michaela's hair fell over her shoulder, and she toyed with the ends. "Asleep?"

He nodded. She hadn't moved from in the middle of the couch. When he hesitated to return to the place beside her, she scooted back and patted the spot he'd vacated.

He eased into the seat.

She propped her arm on the back of the couch and rested her head. "I do believe you're a good guy, Philip Miller."

"Not really."

"No?" She tucked her feet under herself so her knee nearly touched his thigh. "I think you're too hard on yourself. I mean, we all have our faults. Do things we regret."

"In your case?"

"When I first started getting to know you, it was to get on your good side, so I could have an in with Awestruck. But during that first dinner, I thought we connected, so I thought ... Well, I came on too strong." Her eyebrows hopped as if hitting a speed bump of shame. "I've had a rough couple of years." She swallowed hard, and her normally alluring lips pursed. "I'm not proud of who I've become, especially in some moments."

He understood that struggle. He had no business sending her on a guilt trip, given his own choices. "I can't judge you, but no matter what kind of connection we have, I can't do you favors with the guys."

"I understand. And, honestly, I'm grateful." She leaned her head on her arm again, relaxed. "This whole thing ends happily for me. I tried to secure a collaboration, but instead I ended up getting to know a man I actually like. One who turned out to be pretty honorable."

The truth about him boiled like acid in his gut. "You're making me out to be something I'm not."

"Lighten up." She nudged his shoulder. "Your kids adore you."

Michaela had only seen them on relatively good days, but he didn't argue. It felt good to have someone believe in him—and for that someone to be Michaela ... He'd suspected her of seeking a relationship for all the wrong reasons, but he'd been straight with her, and she'd reaffirmed her interest. Maybe he'd misjudged her. Everyone needed genuine connection, even beautiful pop stars. As a single-father rock star, he would know.

"When is your sister's biopsy?"

"Friday." She sighed, gazing at him. "She and I aren't close. I don't get along with her or my dad. If this turns out to be cancer, I'll go when I can. But there's no way I can stay all the way through until the results a week later."

"If the Awestruck collaboration is the only thing on your plate, you can."

"No. If I stayed the whole time, the test results wouldn't matter. We'd kill each other before cancer had a chance." She gave a wry smile. "She's supposed to go home the day of the biopsy, so I'll go Friday morning, come back Sunday. Be a good sister and daughter, and hopefully, it'll turn out to be nothing so I can be grateful she's all right—and for the one good thing I got out of the scare."

"Which is?"

"I don't know why I didn't research you right off the bat, but because of your reaction earlier, I did. And then I came over here, and you actually talked to me. I finally feel like I know you."

Her expression was all too trusting.

He rose, paced to the darkened windows, and turned to lean against the frame. He'd warned her she thought too highly of him, but his conscience prodded him to do more. To tell her about the pills.

Michaela shifted to the edge of the couch, watching. "You don't regret telling me about Clare and Nila."

"No. I just ..." They'd had a moment. There might be more to her than he'd thought. She wasn't really in a place to judge him. But that didn't mean she wouldn't. "It's been a long day."

"Okay." She stood.

When he opened the door for her, the exterior lights illuminated the flowers she'd complimented. He asked her to wait and collected shears, a baggie, and a damp paper towel from the kitchen. On returning, he passed the shears to her. "Pick yourself some, if you like them so much."

"Really? Thanks." She gathered a bouquet of about six of the flowers. The scent of this moment, like crisp rose petals and expensive perfume, would stick with him for ages. Her hair fell over her shoulder, echoing her graceful movements, and the bouquet looked fit for a wedding. If only he could offer her more.

A kiss for the road.

A promise of a relationship.

The truth.

Her eyes glimmered as she held the flowers out, hands high on the stems.

He wrapped the damp towel around their cut ends, then finished with the baggie and a rubber band. A process he'd learned from Clare.

She tucked the flowers into the crook of her elbow and lifted the other arm for a hug.

The soft press of her body against his, someone who seemed to care, someone he liked being around, made the truth kick for release. He could tell her about the pills, how he'd been buying them illegally, how he'd been on them every time she'd seen him.

But then what?

Their conversation tonight had changed nothing. As soon as Michaela left, he'd find the fastest path to oblivion. The fastest path away from the warehouse of images of what Clare had gone through. The surgeries, the hair loss, the chemo, the way both the disease and the treatment had ravaged her.

Those same threats hung over his daughter, and he couldn't save her. He hardly knew how to parent the kids in normal situations, let alone in life-or-death ones.

Painkillers offered a respite from his failures and the doom hanging over them all.

Yes, if he made a misstep, his habit could cost him his job. Depending on how things went down, pills could cost him his freedom or his kids or his health. All of the above. But only if he made a mistake, and he was careful.

He couldn't take the risk of telling Michaela.

He ended the hug, opened her car door for her, and sent her off.

8

*I*n her embarrassment over the post, could Kim Piel have removed her store from Lakeshore?

Unlikely, but Michaela would have sworn the shop was on this corner. She let the car coast past one small business after another. Humming, she leaned closer to the steering wheel for a better view of the awnings and signs. None featured books.

She gave in and switched from her poor sense of direction to GPS, which directed her to a spot a block off Main Street and two blocks ... east? ... of where she'd thought the shop had been.

Huh.

She parked, pushed open her car door, and planted her heeled sandal on the asphalt. The new tune she'd been humming followed her down the sidewalk until the ringtone she'd assigned to Reese interrupted.

She stopped in front of the bookstore's window display to answer, again hoping for good news, again finding her manager only wanted an update.

But nothing would get Michaela down today. Not apologizing to Kim Piel, not Reese's lack of motivation.

"The collaboration is coming along." Her foot tapped to the new melody. "I've even got an idea for a song of my own. It's catchy. Evie will want in."

"A new song?" Reese hadn't sounded this interested in her in ages.

The tune grew louder in Michaela's mind, and she nodded to the music. "Let me work on it a bit longer, and I'll send you a recording to share with Evie's team, see if there's a possibility—"

"I have to know the inspiration."

Michaela tucked her chin as memories of the night before set off hopeful tingling in her chest. The first strains of the new song had come as she'd left Philip's, giddy with the scent of flowers and the relationship breakthrough.

He'd opened up. He trusted her. Liked her.

"Philip and I are becoming friends. He lost his wife to cancer, and my family's anxious about Riley's biopsy, so ... This comes at a good time. We can be there for each other."

"You have feelings for him, or you wouldn't be writing a song about him."

"Maybe a little." Or a lot. He needed someone to brighten his life, help him move past the pain, and face the future. She needed love and acceptance. They worked, just like the song their evening together had inspired worked.

"It'd be great for your career."

Michaela grinned at the vote of confidence in her song. "It really will be. Wait until you hear it."

"Not the song, honey." Reese's low voice carried a dry tone like no one else's could.

"Oh." Like fireworks aimed at each other, conflicting emotions popped, one on top of the last. First, hope because Reese thought she had a chance with Philip. Second, worry, because she didn't want anyone, even Reese, thinking her interest in him was career motivated. "Nothing happened. And this isn't about a headline."

"Of course not. But my job is the business side of things, and from that perspective, he's a great choice. He's famous already, the press will love the timing, and I've heard about their contract negotiations. Even rock stars would have trouble blowing all that money on drugs and women."

"The guys in Awestruck are not into any of that."

"Forget I said anything if you're uncomfortable with being half of a power couple."

A power couple? The phrase implied Michaela brought something to the table too. The publicity could benefit them both.

Reese ended the call, and Michaela pulled open the door to the bookstore. She took a breath of paper-scented air, tempted to start humming again. That would contradict the remorse an apology required, so instead, she exhaled slowly and tried to relax her smiling facial muscles.

No one manned the counter nor stood in the visible part of the children's book area. She turned to the taller shelves that dominated the rest of the sales floor.

Floorboards creaking beneath her feet, Kim stepped from the aisle marked "poetry" and "literature." On spotting her, the woman wiped her palms on her wide hips.

"Hi." Michaela allowed a small smile like the one she'd use to coax Nila out of shyness. "Kim, right?"

"Yes. Michaela." She lowered her chin, as if weighed down by the serious effort it took to avoid another mistake.

She cringed. "About that. I'm sorry I brought up the misunderstanding in a post. I shouldn't have. I deleted the whole thing, comments and all."

"I told Julian not to say anything." Kim bustled past and fussed with paperwork at the checkout. Embarrassed in a way that reminded Michaela of how she'd felt over the wrong foot she'd started on with Philip.

The memory of their exchange in the parking lot of the pizza restaurant brought with it an extra gust of regret.

"I'm glad he did." Michaela approached the sales counter. "You didn't sign up for a public career, and I shouldn't have yanked you into mine. It wasn't kind. I'm sorry."

On the word "kind," Kim raised her gaze, assessing.

Michaela strained to remember what Gannon had said when he'd called her out on the post. "It's good to give back to communities."

A wrinkle of surprise appeared on Kim's forehead.

How exactly had Gannon worded what he'd said about communities? She'd already apologized twice, but she felt bad for Kim. Also, she needed the duet not only for her career, but for the reason it provided to be around Philip and his adorable kids.

The thought of the kids inspired an idea.

"I'd like to give back to the community and make it up to you." She swept a hand toward the shorter bookcases surrounding the colorful children's area. "What if I read to some kids here? As like a ..."

"A children's story time?"

She'd been thinking of a photo op for the store, but a story time did sound nicer. "Yes. Having celebrities here ought to bring in customers, and ... there are kids around, right?"

"Lakeshore has quite a few young families. The children love story hours."

Another idea sparked. If Philip, Nason, and Nila joined her, an hour or two would fly. "I'll talk to the guys. Maybe they'll join us. Gannon was just saying how much he appreciates Lakeshore."

At Gannon's name, Kim's shoulders seemed to lower. She

must trust him a lot more than she did Michaela. "Okay. That could be nice."

"We'll post about the event. I bet we can bring in quite a crowd."

"Oh, don't." Kim's hand fluttered with her objection. "We'd be overrun with people wanting to see the stars, not buy books. How about I invite some local families, and they can spread the news by word of mouth? We'll keep it small."

Word of mouth could get out of control, too, but let the woman have her way. Then she couldn't complain about Michaela.

"Great." She opened her calendar app. "I'm going away this weekend, but I could do the weekend after." She paused, eyes fixed on her sister's name, since her upcoming trip was to travel home for the biopsy. By the weekend she'd offered Kim, she ought to know whether Riley had cancer. If the diagnosis was confirmed, Awestruck would encourage her to visit home again. But she wasn't close with Riley. If she and the band scheduled an event that Saturday, they couldn't send her home. "I'll check and see if the guys are free then too."

"The last weekend in June?"

"Exactly." Michaela tapped and added the event. "I'll call you after I talk to the guys."

"Okay. Do that." Kim's smile didn't show the carefree relief Michaela had hoped for, but it did mark some progress, and she'd consider that a victory.

Michaela stepped back onto the street. Within two strides, the new melody caught back up with her.

If Philip's fifteen-year-old self had seen what went into writing music for an album, he might've more seriously considered "pursuing a stable career," as his biology teacher had advised. Most days, creating in the studio beat out other work, but when ideas were sparse and someone got hooked on a vision that wasn't catching, he could see the allure of making a living by teaching kids to dissect frogs.

Gannon, the one with the vision this time—most times, actually—paced with his cell phone in hand, the call on speaker but the microphone tilted toward himself. "There's something here. The sound doesn't—"

"It's not just my opinion, or I wouldn't bother." Though Tim's tone had remained neutral until now, annoyance edged in. "Dodge said it first."

So Awestruck's manager, Tim, had their longtime producer, Dodge, on his side. Philip, too, would agree it was time to give up on the song, if he cared to rock the boat by speaking his mind. Thankfully, at some point, if "Tenacious" remained unremarkable, John would eventually talk Gannon out of the song.

For now, the drummer stayed neutral—silently observing—and Philip followed suit.

Gannon splayed his hand. "Dodge has ruled out songs prematurely before."

"Then develop it more. In the meantime, why haven't I heard anything from your work with Michaela?"

"Because we've only been at it a few days. The song's not written yet."

"Neither is 'Tenacious.' You sent that."

To cover his laugh at Tim's dig, Philip clenched his hand in front of his mouth. Anger flared across Gannon's face, and he motioned to John as if to ask, *Can you believe this guy?*

"Easy." John's single-word of caution earned a couple of beats of silence.

Then, Tim started up again. "Look. To command the amount you deserve, we've got to have the makings of your best album yet. Even if 'Tenacious' comes together, you need more standout material. I've got an idea you're not going to like, but I'd put money on it being the runaway hit of the album, and you know I don't gamble."

"You want to buy a song." Gannon's words smoked with anger. If Tim heated his temper much more, something would combust. But Philip had come on board when Awestruck was already in the process of recording the previous album. He hadn't seen the part before that, when they'd written the songs. Maybe Tim goaded Gannon every time.

"Think of it as another collaboration." Tim had broken out his sweet-talking manager voice. "And this one's basically in-house. He doesn't even want to get paid."

All their songs were in-house. Gannon sometimes worked from an idea Philip or John suggested, but the bulk of the song-writing fell to their lead singer and guitarist.

"Who wrote it?" Gannon asked.

"Matt."

John sat forward, focus locked on the phone as if he knew who they were talking about.

Philip didn't.

The lead singer asked the question, a suspicious edge in his voice. "Matt who?"

"Visser."

Now *that* name rang a bell. Matt Visser had been Awestruck's last bass guitarist. After Matt had gotten fired for reckless partying that had endangered a minor, Gannon and John had hired Philip to take his place.

Matt was the whole reason for the morality agreement they'd had Philip sign before he could join the band.

The agreement Philip was violating by taking painkillers he'd obtained illegally.

Air rushed from his lungs. Philip had never been on equal footing with Gannon and John. He hadn't been with them from the start and didn't share their brother-like bond. Before his dismissal, Matt had racked up years of history with these two. If they considered him a brother, and he returned a changed man ...

"Not interested." Gannon's declaration cut across Philip's spiraling thoughts. "There's a reason he's not in the band anymore."

And that reason was mostly drugs. Philip turned his face. A mess of cords snaked between amps and the drum kit.

"He's not asking to get back in. He wrote a song. He's offering it to Awestruck. Says it's his way of making amends or something. Whatever, it's classic—everything you stand for from start to finish. He even fit in a Bible verse."

"Which one?" John asked.

"I don't know. Bea's the one who said it's a verse. Reaping whirlwinds? It has to be one of the most Awestruck songs I've ever heard."

Philip's line of sight rose to catch John's chin lift as the drummer eyed Gannon. One vote for buying the song.

Going through with this didn't mean they would push Philip out. He didn't party the way Matt used to. Philip kept his problem much quieter. Much tamer. Doctors prescribed painkillers all the time.

Philip had first taken them after a major surgery in high school. He'd quit a few times over the years, but the tranquility they offered called like a siren when disappointments battered him. Like when he reached the pinnacle of career success only to find that his kids needed more than he had to give.

Were pills really so wrong? At least he hadn't abandoned his children.

If he had a real problem, Gannon and John would have noticed in the last few months.

Since they hadn't, they wouldn't catch on now.

Unless Philip had raised Michaela's suspicions last night.

He'd spilled a lot more than he should've. He'd cried, for heaven's sake.

How would he face her when she showed up for her daily session?

"What do you think, Miller?" Gannon asked.

He'd missed a chunk of the discussion, but judging by his bandmates' expressions, nothing had changed. Gannon didn't want Matt's contribution, but John was interested.

To avoid suspicion, Philip couldn't show his fear, and the most fearless choice would be to invite the danger closer. "If the song is that good, we should give it a chance."

"We'll get back to you." Gannon ended the call, and for a few moments, they all remained quiet.

"Matt deserves a shot at redemption." John didn't direct the statement at anyone, but the words pierced Philip. How far would John go to make room for Matt? What did redemption look like?

"He doesn't have to get his redemption with us," Gannon returned. "He's cleaned up and relapsed before. I don't want to get back on that train."

"You won't even listen to the song?" John's disbelief was evident in his voice.

Gannon eyed the wall clock, chest rising with a deep breath. "I don't see the point."

"You're holding a grudge."

"I'm choosing whose reputation I want associated with Awestruck."

John's narrowed eyes suggested he had more arguments, but instead of raising them, he announced they needed a break and left without waiting for a consensus. Gannon watched him go, jaw pulsing, then stalked to the control room to turn off the equipment.

Philip stole out to his car, drove to one of the lakeside parks, and took the prescription bottle from his center console. He ought to chuck this into the lake. Give up the habit before pills cost him his pride, his job, his clear conscience.

But with Matt threatening his job, his past with Clare an aching wound, and the embarrassment of showing Michaela his weakness, he needed the pain to stop.

He deserved these pills as much as anyone in physical agony, and if it took a few more to get through the day, so be it.

MICHAELA TRIED fresh lyrics for her new song as she walked the hall to the studio. After the first day, she'd been given the entrance code so she could let herself in for her sessions with the band. She was a little early today. If she happened to find the room empty, she'd test the tune on the keyboard, maybe record what she had so far.

But instead of unused equipment, she found Philip in the studio.

Even better.

She set her purse aside and got a bottled water as he worked on a bass line for a song she didn't recognize. She settled on the couch across from the stool where he perched. "Where are the other two?"

"Not back yet."

She slid her feet from her sandals and curled her legs on the cushion. "So it's just me and you."

He blinked and looked away, an indication that last night hadn't set *him* to singing. She'd interpreted the hug and flowers to mean his feelings matched hers. Had she misread him? Her new song faded to a whisper.

The studio door swung open, and John scanned the room. "Not back?"

"No sign of him." Philip barely glanced the drummer's way,

so at least she wasn't the only one who couldn't command his attention.

"Sign of who?" she asked. "Gannon?"

John nodded once, much more interested in Philip than her. "I had Tim send Matt's song to me."

Philip rested his arm on top of the guitar, suddenly focused. "And?"

"It's made for us."

Since neither man offered an explanation, Michaela struggled to piece together the meaning.

Philip rubbed his forehead with the back of his hand. "Okay. So what now? Because all he wants to do is fix 'Tenacious.' If he even considers it broken."

John gave a wry smile. "He does, or he'd be back."

Had the band disagreed on something this morning?

John continued to pay her no mind. "Do you have a problem with it?"

What was "it" now? Matt's song? Whatever that was?

Philip sighed heavily. "If you think it's made for us, it's fine."

"You're sure?"

"I'm on board with whatever's going to set us up best for the new contract. If we have to go through Matt, so be it."

"Awestruck has never been about the next contract." Gannon brushed past John and let himself into the control room.

At the matter-of-fact statement, Philip looked more annoyed than chastised.

John's expression seemed to indicate that Gannon's objection could be safely ignored.

Michaela felt anything but safe. Philip and Gannon disagreed with each other about something, and she couldn't play both sides. An argument could spread, threatening her collaboration with them—let alone a relationship with Philip.

She cleared her throat. They'd agreed on something just

yesterday: her post about the bookstore owner. Maybe telling them about her morning would give them a little common ground. "I apologized to Kim Piel."

Gannon gave a tight-lipped nod as he emerged from the control room. He must've turned on the recording equipment, meaning this conversation would be added to what must be a massive library of Awestruck's sessions. Since she wasn't at a mic, hopefully her voice would remain indistinguishable.

Not that history would care about a conversation where she ate humble pie.

"I'm doing a story time for the local kiddos." Hopefully her enthusiasm would show Philip how much she enjoyed kids. His, anyway. "It can't happen this weekend because of Riley, but we agreed on the one after. You guys have to join us."

"Can't." John lobbed the answer from behind her, like an unexpected dodgeball in gym class.

She floundered.

"John and I will be gone." Gannon picked up one of his guitars, posture tense.

She eyed them. "Where to?"

Band divorce court?

"John's bachelor weekend. Plans are all set." Gannon wasn't angry at her, but his no-nonsense tone kept her on guard like dark music in a murder mystery.

She tried to force a few lighter notes into the score. "Where are you going?"

"It's a secret." Gannon paused in fiddling with his guitar to motion to John. "He doesn't even know."

"Okay." She pivoted toward Philip. Kim had lit up at the mention of Gannon. Michaela couldn't show up solo. Besides, Nila and Nason had inspired this. "Are you going on the trip too?"

"The kids need me home." He studied her as if looking for a

way out of the reading, but finally he nodded. "They'd probably go for a story time. We can come."

She gave him a grateful nod.

Set with his guitar, Gannon led them into the soundtrack collaboration. The band focused with bristling intensity, as if the song was the last thing keeping them together.

9

Something important would happen here tonight.

Hard to believe the setting, this deep into farm fields and woods, where Michaela's phone didn't even get reception, could be so pivotal. After a tense few days in the studio, she still hadn't drawn out the full story. The campfire at John's house on Thursday night seemed like the drummer's way of trying to make peace before they broke for the long weekend. She couldn't risk missing it in case he succeeded.

Or failed spectacularly.

She followed Gannon's SUV down the driveway and parked beside it in the open area by the garage.

A woman exited his passenger's seat. This had to be his fiancée, Adeline. She was pretty in a girl-next-door sort of way. But then, Adeline hadn't tried very hard. She wore about two minutes' worth of makeup and had dressed in shorts and a T-shirt bearing the logo of a local ice cream shop.

Yet this was the woman Gannon had left LA for, bringing Awestruck with him. They were all here, Michaela included, because Adeline called Lakeshore home.

Envy tightened around Michaela's limbs. No man had ever

uprooted everything to follow her. Her own father had never even flown out to California to visit for a weekend.

Since Adeline had been the one to tattle to Gannon about Kim Piel, they weren't destined to be friends, but for the sake of the collaboration, she could pretend.

She mustered enthusiasm as she met up with them. "The famous Adeline."

Adeline's lips lifted sweetly. "The famous Michaela. Only in your case, the famous part's actually true."

"You've walked a few red carpets." If Michaela kept this saccharine look on her face much longer, she'd attract all the mosquitos in a ten-mile radius. She let the expression fade as she and Adeline followed Gannon along the side of the house.

"It's not the same, and that's okay with me." Contentment smoothed both her voice and her expression. "I prefer my quieter life."

"A quiet life? You're engaged to the wrong guy."

"I can do quiet." Gannon slowed to put his arm around Adeline. On the narrow path, the move forced Michaela to walk behind them. Especially since Gannon carried a large canvas tote that appeared to contain a blanket and bug spray.

Michaela hadn't packed provisions, nor had she considered how she could end up the odd one out if Philip wasn't there yet but John, Gannon, and their fiancées were. His SUV hadn't been in the drive, but the electric blue sports car off to one side could've been his alternate ride.

The song she'd written the night he'd given her flowers had grown stagnant. Awestruck hadn't lingered together since, so she'd had no opportunity to connect with him again. Never before had one of her relationships come to life, inspired music, then died before she could even finish writing the piece.

He would come around. As long as Awestruck didn't self-destruct in the meantime.

She followed Gannon and Adeline down a boardwalk along

the side of John's home to a treehouse-like deck. Steps led down to a trail that snaked into the woods. Pine needles slid onto her sandals, and a stick poked the arch of her foot. "No one warned me to wear hiking boots for this."

"It's not far." Gannon eyed her footwear. "You'll be all right. Just look out for snakes."

She froze. "Snakes?" Awestruck could dissolve without her. Witnessing whatever happened tonight wasn't worth encountering slimy, legless reptiles.

Adeline swatted Gannon's stomach. "Be nice."

In the fading light, he spared Michaela a smile. "No dangerous snakes, but John did see a bear once."

Adeline gave him a warning look, but neither of them took back the statement.

Bears? Also, he'd specified "dangerous" snakes, which meant others slithered about.

Great. Here she'd thought the worst things she'd face out there were Awestruck tension and mosquitos. She watched the ground to keep from impaling her foot on stray sticks—no need to let anything else threaten her when bears and snakes roamed the woods.

A quarter of a mile later, the scent of smoke welcomed them to a grassy clearing. Two people—neither of them Philip— stood silhouetted by a car-sized bonfire. A pair of dogs ran over, and Adeline knelt to say hello to the pit bulls.

Gannon continued toward the fire. Over the music that played, he called complaints to John about starting without him.

He could do quiet, sure.

When Michaela reached the gathering by the fire, Gannon introduced John's fiancée, Erin. Blue tips highlighted the woman's pixie cut, so she—not Philip—likely owned the sports car.

Michaela swatted a mosquito. This would be a long night.

She borrowed bug spray because she preferred smelling like summer camp over having a bunch of red welts to contend with. Erin claimed the lawn chair beside the one Michaela chose and chatted easily. The woman worked as a mechanic, apparently as content as Adeline with a life lived off stage, despite her famous fiancé.

With hardly a pause, Erin switched from talking about the auto repair shop to asking Adeline how work was going.

"We hired a director for Key of Hope." Adeline turned to offer Michaela an explanation. "I'm starting a non-profit called In the Key of Hope Music Lessons for kids from low-income families. Music has made such a difference in our lives." She shot a sappy look to Gannon, then refocused on her companions. "Have either of you met Lina, Awestruck's social media manager?"

Michaela and Erin both shook their heads.

"She wanted a change of scenery, so she's going to relocate here and split her time between Awestruck and Key of Hope. Meanwhile, we asked for Tim's advice choosing a property, and ever since, he can't stop meddling. He's negotiated down the price on pretty much every service we pay for."

Sounded like a beneficial kind of meddling to Michaela. Tim was one of the best in the business, and his negotiation skills no doubt carried over. If only she had someone like him in her corner instead of Reese.

"Speaking of Tim, meddling, and Awestruck ..." Erin leaned toward Michaela and lowered her voice. "Have you heard the song?"

Confused, Michaela rubbed her collarbone. "Which one?"

"The one Matt wrote." Adeline matched Erin's quiet tone, interest shining in her eyes as if she didn't mind the change of subject in the least.

Fifteen feet away and engrossed in their own conversation, the guys had no chance of overhearing. Especially when the popping fire and music were factored in. Michaela studied her companions with new appreciation. Erin and Adeline might prefer to avoid the spotlight, but they kept a pulse on Awestruck.

"What's the story with him?" Michaela had spent a couple of hours digging online to find answers. According to her searches, the only Matt tied to Awestruck was their last bassist, so she assumed he had to be the guy in question. "I met him when they performed on *Audition Room*, but details on why he left were hazy."

"He partied." If Adeline minded the detour from their question, she hid her annoyance, her answer confirming that Michaela had identified the correct Matt. "They tried to help him and then to tolerate him, but he got worse and worse. Finally, Gannon fired him. They wrote a morality agreement into the contract to make the expectations and repercussions more straightforward before hiring Philip."

"After that, one of Matt's friends overdosed." Erin didn't keep her voice as quiet. "Matt went to rehab. He's supposed to be a new man."

Gannon and John hefted a pallet onto the fire. They stepped back to watch the flames engulf it, unconcerned about anyone else.

"You don't believe it?" Michaela asked.

"I don't know him." Erin shrugged. "John says it's possible."

"Gannon says it's too soon to say."

Erin leaned back in her chair, all pretense of a confidential conversation gone. "It's been almost a year since he cleaned up."

"I was there the night he was fired." Adeline's soft-spoken manner continued, but rather than a tactic to maintain secrecy, Michaela realized the volume was a matter of habit. "Earlier that same day, he claimed he wanted to quit cold turkey. The whole thing was a play to save his spot in Awestruck. He thought they'd brought me in to replace him."

"You?" The question burst out. Michaela couldn't picture this mild-mannered woman on stage at all, let alone with Awestruck.

Adeline's only reprimand was another smile. "I was Awestruck's first bassist, when we were all in high school. I stick to upright bass these days."

"Don't be so modest." Erin leaned heavily on her armrest, coming close to Michaela. "She played on the last album too."

"Philip did most of *Letting Go*. I played on 'Phoenix.' Other bassists stood in on other songs before they hired Philip."

Another Internet search was in order. This one would help pass the time waiting for her flight to visit her sister tomorrow.

Adeline, the apparent expert on Matt's time with the band, continued. "Matt contributed to songwriting back in the day, but he was down to the bare minimum by the time he got fired."

"Tim says 'Whirlwinds' is the most Awestruck song he's ever heard," Erin offered.

Adeline cut Erin a glance. "Whatever the secret is to getting John to talk, you must've found it."

Erin grinned. "He feels strongly about giving the song a chance."

"Gannon thinks Matt might want to oust Philip."

Whoa. No wonder this week had been tough in the studio. Especially for Philip.

"I heard the song." Erin brushed a mosquito from Michaela's arm. "John tried telling me how they could flesh it out, but I know nothing about music. That's why we were wondering what you thought."

"You haven't heard it?" Michaela looked to Adeline.

The fellow musician gave a tiny shake of her head and shot a glance at her fiancé. "Gannon doesn't want to work with Matt again, so he hasn't listened to it himself, let alone played it for me."

Funny for Michaela to think of her mentor harboring a grudge.

She liked these women. "And it'd be crossing enemy lines to ask John for a copy," Michaela guessed.

Adeline chuckled. "I haven't gotten that desperate yet. They've worked together for a long time. They'll figure it out. But I am curious."

"I haven't heard the song either." Michaela hoped they'd appreciate a glimpse inside the studio enough that they wouldn't be annoyed with her for pumping them for information. "They've been moody all week. When Gannon and John said they couldn't do the story time next weekend, I thought they refused because, at the rate they're going, they knew they'd scare the children, not entertain them."

"They wouldn't let a little disagreement interfere with that." Erin tilted her head toward the men. "Still friends, see?"

The two bandmates did look chummy, but Philip's absence concerned her. With his job in jeopardy, why hadn't he come to the campfire?

"Is Michaela going to the party?"

Philip shifted his shoulder blades against Nila's headboard. If he'd known how much time he'd spend sitting here, waiting for her to fall back to sleep after nightmares, he would've gotten her one covered with padding and fabric. But who would want to believe their kid would suffer bad dreams this often?

He brushed his fingers across Nila's forehead and slipped a soft curl behind her ear. "Michaela's probably already at the party, but I'm not sure. Now, why wouldn't I be sure?"

She giggled. "Because you're here with me."

Audrey, the part-time nanny, claimed he shouldn't be. She suspected his daughter made up nightmares to get more time with him. This one had occurred immediately after Nila went to bed, as Philip was leaving for the bonfire. She'd come to him crying but not flushed or shaking like other nights.

But maybe a little girl who so feared being left alone—who *had* been left, first by her mother, and then by him on tour—maybe that little girl deserved to call the shots every once in a while, whether she'd suffered a nightmare or not.

"Will you sing to me?"

"Do you promise to be asleep by the time I finish?"

She nodded and jammed her eyes shut.

He closed his eyes, too, and tipped his head back against the wall. He and "Amazing Grace" had been through a lot together. Clare had shown her love for the song by using it as a lullaby with both kids.

They'd sung the hymn at her funeral.

Afterward, Nason wouldn't fall asleep without hearing the familiar melody. The first few times, what had calmed his son had set his own tears to streaming, but he'd eventually grown numb to the grief. Nason outgrew lullabies. Older, Nila had witnessed all those nights Philip had sung the song for her brother. She'd asked for it regularly ever since.

How odd he'd felt, singing "Amazing Grace" with Michaela at church. She had the pipes to do it the kind of justice neither he nor Clare ever could, but she hadn't put her heart into the hymn.

So much the better.

As he wrapped up the second verse, his phone indicated a message. Nila shifted, probably a quiet way of telling him he hadn't fulfilled his end of their deal yet.

He continued into the third verse as he took his cell from his pocket and read the message.

Nila shifted again, and he realized he'd faded out after "His word my hope secures."

"He will my shield and portion be as long as life endures." In the breath between verses, he read the message.

The seemingly innocuous words from his dealer carried a deeper meaning and, once again, changed his plans for the evening.

A few short lines later, Nila had fallen asleep—or pretended she had, as promised. He clicked off the bedside lamp and headed out.

10

The sky went dark, and nine o'clock came and went. Michaela grew increasingly aware of how early she needed to leave for her flight to Illinois in the morning. The others passed s'more supplies, but she lifted the borrowed blanket and laid it over the arm of her chair.

The Awestruck drama she'd expected hadn't happened. Aside from the conversation with Adeline and Erin, no one had mentioned the song or Matt. Thanks to whatever kept Philip away, their relationship would stay paused until after she got back. She ought to care more about Riley and her biopsy anyway.

"I'm sorry to bow out early, but I've got a flight tomorrow."

Gannon lifted the marshmallows he roasted for himself and Adeline away from the flames. "Tell your sister we're praying for her."

Hopefully that would do some good. She supposed it wouldn't do any harm.

"I will." She waved and stepped away from the fire.

The long grass of the meadow buffeted her toes, and she wrapped her arms around herself to ward off the cool air. At the edge of the clearing, the woods made a dark maze of rustling leaves, croaking frogs, and reaching branches. The display on her phone still showed no signal, and hunting for one all evening must've done a number on her battery. Thanks to that, now even her flashlight wouldn't last long.

She'd better not get lost.

Or run into a bear.

She set off down the trail and walked for longer than she'd expected. Worried, she turned a slow circle. She recognized that stump, didn't she? Doubt nudged her, but she kept on. A pale shape shifted in front of her, obscured by a bend in the path and trees. *Moonlight on a branch. Not a bear.*

A stick cracked.

"Hello?" Fear immobilized her joints. "Who's there?"

No one answered, but two footfalls later, Philip appeared, his white T-shirt glowing in the light from her phone. He held up his arm to protect his eyes. "Hey. What's the deal?"

"You scared me!" She'd meant to sound angry, but relief and excitement trilled in her voice. "Why didn't you say something?"

"Seriously." He kept his arm raised and motioned with his other hand for her to lower the phone.

Nah. She enjoyed having him at her mercy. Besides, his biceps looked amazing at that angle in this light. "I thought you were a bear. You owe it to me to see me safely to my car."

"I just came from there. No bears." Was he slurring?

She lowered the light and stepped closer. "Where have you been? The party started hours ago."

"Nila had a nightmare." He averted his face, but the pines around them couldn't overpower the scent of alcohol.

Talk about having him at her mercy.

"Philip Miller, you've been drinking."

"Michaela Vandewald, so what?"

"Vandehey." She put her hands on her hips, and the phone

light pointed behind her, leaving her in shadows with Philip. "So nothing. But I bet Gannon will have a thing or two to say about it."

"He doesn't care if I have a drink now and then." Philip's white T-shirt reflected the faint moonlight, and his beard outlined the contour of his jaw while his brow left his eyes dark.

She could discern little else, and she longed to reach out and touch him, fill in with her hands what she couldn't see of the textures of T-shirt, hair, skin. His stance warned her off advancing, though. One wrong move, and he'd go face the others or retreat to his car.

"This is more than one drink. Did you drive here like this?"

"I'm fine to drive." With a dismissive laugh, he took a step past her.

She lowered her hands, and the light shined across his back and the easy fit of his well-worn jeans. "You could've hurt someone, and I bet a DUI would violate Awestruck's morality agreement."

"What do you know about the morality agreement?" Suspicion lowered his voice as he turned back, but when he spoke again, his tone took on a flirtatious note. "Researching me?"

Well, yeah, but the code of conduct hadn't come up until the women mentioned it tonight.

"If you go out there, they'll have a lot of questions for you. They fired a guy for partying, right?"

"This is different."

Maybe, but she knew how much he had on the line. If she saved him from throwing everything away, she'd earn a spot in his life. The melody of her new song whispered through her mind. "Are you sure they'll agree? I've never seen Gannon drunk, even at after-parties where most everyone else got hammered."

"They're expecting me."

Not in this state, they weren't. "Text that you can't make it and let me help you."

"I don't need your help. Relax. It's fine."

His continued insistence worried her. If she failed to prevent this disaster, she might not get to keep seeing him. And what effect would his sudden unemployment have on his kids' lives? "You do need help, because you're either going out there and losing face with your band, you're letting me drive you home, or I'm calling the police about a drunk driver. You're lucky you didn't get in a wreck on the way here."

He shifted and lifted an arm for balance. Had his foot struck a fallen branch, or was he having trouble on level ground? "Luck had nothing to do with it. I'm fine." Balance regained, he spread his arms, as if that proved something.

"Your drinking doesn't offend me. If I were you, I'd want to drown my sorrows, too, and you seem to have done a pretty effective job of it. But Gannon's going to care, and if something happens on your drive home, you'll care too."

He ran his hand over his hair and turned his face toward the clearing, not visible from this point in the path. Dropping his arms, he took a step in her direction.

She laid her hand on the inside of his elbow and led him from what would've been a disaster with Gannon toward a solution she hadn't entirely worked out yet.

She could give him a ride home, but what about his car? Leaving the vehicle here would raise questions.

He covered her hand, still in the crook of his elbow. "You just want time with me."

She groaned but didn't pull away because he was correct. He'd tortured her by avoiding her for days, and she wasn't about to miss this opportunity to be with him. That didn't mean she'd go easy on him, though. "Don't tell me you're an arrogant drunk."

"I'm not drunk."

"You are."

"Pot*a*to, pot*ah*to."

She rolled her eyes. She'd known some men to get aggressive and belligerent when they'd been drinking, but the way Philip laid his hand over hers seemed sweet. Still, he *was* drunk, and she wanted him, not booze, to choose her.

She untangled their hands and put some distance between them.

In the driveway, she found that somehow, his SUV was parked in the space beside her own car.

If she called for a tow, the driver could spill the story publicly. Or simply dally so long that someone from the fire would discover them before they escaped.

They'd have to hide Philip's SUV nearby, walk back, and take Michaela's car. Sober tomorrow, Philip could retrieve the vehicle.

Then he'd call her, thank her a million times, and pledge his undying gratitude.

She held out her hand. "Keys."

"I can drive."

"Fighting me on this is pointless."

"I'm bigger than you." He squared his stance to her. He was bigger and in far better physical shape, that was for sure.

She clenched her stomach against a flare of attraction. He wasn't hitting on her. Or if he was, his advances wouldn't count until he'd sobered up.

"You might be bigger, but I'm not afraid to call the cops on you if you drive." Besides, with him so messed up, she could probably knock him off balance with one finger.

He huffed, retreated a step, and pulled the keys from his pocket.

She swiped them. "Besides, I don't believe for a minute you'd do anything to hurt me." She motioned for him to get in the passenger seat.

"About that." He started around the nose of the vehicle. "Sorry."

She stopped, thumb on the unlock button. "What?"

"I've been mean to you this week." He continued to the passenger's side, out of sight.

"Mean to me? What are we, in fifth grade?" She pressed the button and popped open the driver's door.

Philip got in and bent to take a plastic shopping bag from the floor. As he placed it in the second row of seats, paper crinkled, liquid sloshed, and something rattled. She could imagine only one reason for a paper bag to be in a plastic one.

"That's not open, is it?"

"Not at the moment."

"Give it to me."

"No."

Unbelievable. His children behaved better. "Philip."

"Michaela."

Gripping the keys so tightly the ridges dug into her fingers, she got out. He owed her. He owed her so much. When she opened the back door for the bag, Philip had his hand inside it. His fist rattled as he drew it out. The fact that he'd left the alcohol for her to stow away didn't comfort her.

Philip used pills? Loyal, understanding, wounded Philip.

She couldn't regret safeguarding his job, but she was out of her depth if he was on more than alcohol.

Mind spinning, she put the bottle in the far back, out of reach, and got behind the wheel. Philip sat in his seat as if nothing had happened, but his pocket bulged with what had to be a pill bottle.

Real subtle.

As she drove down John's drive, she debated asking. At the street, she turned right.

"My house is the other way. There's nothing this direction."

"Good." She peered down the tunnel created by the headlights and the trees, only a narrow strip overhead open to the sky. "That means John has no reason to come this way."

She navigated slowly, peering into the woods. Finding an acceptable hiding place took about a mile—far longer than she'd hoped. A tiny dirt road with no address marker led into the forest. She drove past a bend that would block the view from the main road and parked near concrete barriers that prevented passage. Hopefully there wasn't an active worksite on the other side.

"Out."

"Why?"

He might revolt if she shared her plan to leave his SUV hidden here.

"Because I'm getting out, and you were mean to me, so joining me is the least you can do." She slid from her seat. As soon as he'd followed suit and closed his door, she locked the vehicle. "Walk with me."

He took his time but finally passed behind the vehicle to join her. She started toward the road, but he tripped, either over an exposed root or his own feet, and landed with a grunt.

To think this was the same guy she'd watched carry his children so easily. The respectable father. The skilled musician.

Michaela circled back and extended a hand. "You all right?"

"Yup." He pushed up, got one foot planted, then paused on one knee as if to strategize before rising. He wobbled on the way up but stayed vertical.

They crunched down the dirt-and-gravel lane to the paved street, then started the long, dark trek toward John's house and Michaela's car. On level asphalt with someone beside her and her eyes adjusting, she didn't bother with her phone light. She did wish again for hiking boots as blisters turned her toe and heel tender.

This whole effort could be for naught if someone saw her car still in the driveway. Where would they assume she'd gone?

Hopefully Gannon wouldn't remember her poor sense of direction and launch a full-fledged rescue effort.

"If you'd wanted a moonlit stroll, you could've just asked."

She used both hands to push her hair behind her shoulders. Seeing those pills had steeled her willpower against him. What were they, and how often did he use? "You've been avoiding me all week."

"Oh." He sounded genuinely disappointed with himself. "I'm sorry."

"How do I know you mean that when you're drunk and high?"

He lifted his hand and rubbed his mouth hard enough that she could hear the bristle of his beard over the crickets, between frog croaks.

He hadn't denied being high.

She looked up to the sky visible past the forest canopy. Stars amassed overhead in ways she hadn't seen since attending Bible camp with Heather.

"I think you're a nice person," he said. "I like you. But I'm not a guy you want to get involved with."

He liked her? Not enough, given his penchant for ignoring her. But by helping him tonight, she might win his affection. "Tell me what you're into, and let me decide for myself."

"I'm not into anything."

"Liar."

"Bingo." He kept step with her, face toward the road before them.

They walked in silence a quarter mile. Under other circumstances, this would be romantic.

She chided herself. She kept thinking that—*under other circumstances*—but she couldn't change the situation she'd been dealt.

Something stirred the leaves. An animal?

She had no defense. This fumbling version of Philip

couldn't protect her beyond mustering enough bravado to get himself eaten first. Still, she stepped closer to him, and when he enclosed her hand in his own, she didn't fight the warm reassurance. For a few yards, the touch kept her mind off their surroundings.

Then, a bird flapped across the road, bringing memories of a vampire story she'd read at far too young an age.

She needed a better distraction. She closed the fingers of her free hand around Philip's forearm. "Why tonight? Did something happen that made you—"

"You know why I haven't talked to you all week?"

"Why?"

"Because I said too much last time." Breath laced with the scent of the alcohol carried the statement.

She dug mints out of her purse. They might not do the trick, but she could try. "Here."

He took a few and popped them into his mouth. He crunched them, then cleared his throat. "That's no fun."

Was he disappointed she hadn't fed him his next high? As if he weren't already messed up enough.

"We talked about Nila. Why would that be a problem?"

"I don't tell anyone about Nila. I don't even think about Nila —her genes—when I can help it." He swiped at his neck, probably after a bug. "How far are we going?"

They had walked a little over halfway, but the less he thought about what they were doing, the less he'd fight her.

"So why did you talk to me?" she asked.

"Because you show up at inconvenient times."

"Which means what?"

"I talked to you when I shouldn't have." He might as well be communicating through only predictive text on his phone.

So frustrating.

Still, he wasn't choosing silence, and he hadn't chosen it Monday night. Which meant there were some similarities.

Her last hope that tonight was an exception to the norm sank. "You were on something then too."

"I'm always on something. But don't worry. My supply's been cut off."

Relief swept across her as suddenly as the bird had appeared over the road a few minutes earlier. "How?"

"Don't know. He can't get it anymore. Guess he's bad at his job."

Such casual references to a drug dealer—that had to be who he meant, right?—took getting used to, considering she'd thought Philip was clean until less than an hour before. Still, he'd shared good news. No supply meant Philip's demand— and his ability to pay—wouldn't score him more. "This is it, then? Once you use up what you have, you're done? Just like that?"

"Just like that."

"You can do that? Quit?"

"Yes." His voice carried confidence.

If only he hadn't also called himself a liar.

She peered up at him, but she'd never learn from studying his face how big of a problem he had. How tragic. She was attracted to him, and not just physically. She admired his love for his kids. She appreciated how, even tonight, he remained safe. Handsome too. And famous. And rich. And so sad.

If only …

She tipped her head against his shoulder. Both his arm and worry settled around her. Poor Nila and Nason. His habits, whether they involved abusing drugs or mostly just sadness, had to affect them in a myriad of ways. In no shape to drive, he also hadn't been in the right mind to make childcare decisions.

"Where are the kids tonight?"

"In bed."

"Who's watching them?"

"The nanny."

For the kids' sake, she had to press. "I thought she didn't start until next week. Is it the boss lady again?" He'd mentioned someone in charge of the nannies watching the kids Michaela's first day in Wisconsin. If he'd have to face someone with some authority when he got home, would his state cause him trouble there too?

"Not her. This is the other nanny."

"How many do you have?"

"As many as it takes. Look." He dropped his arm from around her and shot a look back. "How far are we walking?"

"Almost there." She picked up the pace, and a few minutes later, they came to the cars, all quiet and dark in the drive.

Tension left her neck as she steered herself and Philip away from more drama with the band. She made her way down unfamiliar country roads, guessing at the directions until her GPS found its bearings and routed her toward Philip's.

Since the substances he took seemed to make him more talkative, she ought to press for information about what he'd been taking. But when she glanced over to start asking questions, she saw that he'd fallen to sleep.

She left him that way until she pulled into his driveway. Shaking his shoulder woke him, but he remained groggy and struggled to identify which of his keys would open the locked front door.

By the time they entered, a college-aged woman in a neon orange sweatshirt approached, head cocked at a leery angle. So at least he'd had a nanny on duty, as he'd claimed.

Philip caught his foot on the edge of the open door and bumped Michaela.

She braced him before he fell.

"Oh." The nanny frowned and punched a code into the pad that controlled the security system. She scrutinized first Philip, then Michaela. "Is he all right?"

"Yup." Her defensiveness welled. The guy had enough problems without extra judgment. "Just sick. He'll be fine." She put an arm around Philip's waist and walked him through the living room.

The staircase ascended to a dark hall. If he'd struggled with the door, mounting the steps would pose a significant challenge. Was his room even up there?

He moved ahead.

Bright orange in her peripheral vision warned her the nanny continued to look on.

A few thumps yanked her focus to Philip. He'd made it four steps, then had fallen and caught himself on his hands and one knee. Michaela helped him to his feet and up the stairs.

Five doors stood along the second-floor hallway, but Philip led without hesitation to one down at the end. She opened it and peeked in, just in case he'd taken her to Nila or Nason. But no. In the dark room, she made out a king-sized bed and the mature furnishings of an adult's bedroom.

He stepped inside and stopped, as though he didn't know what to do next.

Neither did she.

Protect him from himself. Protect the kids.

She held out her palm. "Hand over the pills."

"Don't have them." He reached into his pockets, and when he withdrew his hands, he brought the lining with them, turning his pockets inside out. He'd had the bottle earlier, but he might've hidden it in his SUV.

"Fine. Sleep it off, then. And don't do this again."

He sat on the bed as if she'd pushed him. "I messed up."

"You did. The best thing now is to sober up." She motioned him to get up so she could turn down the covers. "You're not going to make any big life changes tonight. Tomorrow's a new day."

He ambled to a spot behind her as she tossed the extra pillows to the far side of the bed. His shirt plopped onto the comforter. She froze without turning. The soft brush of movement on carpeting told her he stood close. Shirtless, apparently.

Her heart broke out moves her backup dancers could only dream of.

Yet nothing could happen here. Nothing.

Even if he did make an advance, his disinterest while sober meant he'd regret anything that happened. And again, she wanted *him*, not alcohol or pills, to choose her.

She pivoted away and toward the door as he moved forward. Sheets rustled, but she didn't steal a glance.

"This wouldn't have happened if Clare were here."

Clare? He was thinking of his dead wife with Michaela in his bedroom? In the doorway, she turned. He lay on his back. Light from the hall cut across his chest and abs. She'd figured he worked out, but—

Do. Not. Go. There.

"Sleep on your side so you don't choke." The suggestion did double duty, both practical for him and an important reminder for her that, however nice the view, she couldn't excuse the state he'd put himself in.

He rolled away, revealing a giant tattoo spanning his back. Wings? The only way to confirm would entail turning on a light or getting closer.

She left without satisfying her curiosity.

11

*P*hilip woke to the sick stickiness of vomit. In his bed. Repulsion drew another heave, and he stumbled to the bathroom. When he finished, he pulled himself off the floor, locked his bedroom door to keep the kids from barging in, and cleaned. The process stretched on, interrupted often by more pressing needs—to vomit, to rest. He finished having remembered only portions of the night before.

His dealer had sold him what he'd said were the last painkillers he'd be able to get because a massive bust cut off the supply.

When Philip pressed him about when he'd be able to get more, he'd sidestepped the question. "Dope's cheaper and easier to get, and it's the same thing."

Philip had heard it all before, but he'd vowed he'd never cross the line to using dope—heroin. The medical grade, prescription painkillers left no mystery about what he was putting in his body. Meanwhile, heroin could be cut with any number of unexpected, deadly substances. "It's completely different."

"You'll run out long before anybody around here can get you what you want, and then, the differences won't matter."

Maybe another dealer could hook him up, but finding one carried risks. He could be recognized and exposed, and then what?

Besides, the lies and side-effects had been adding up. Discovery was one slip away, and what would that do to his job? His kids?

The supply issue could be a blessing in disguise if he used it as motivation to get clean. He'd paid and gotten out of there, planning to use the remaining pills to taper off.

After a stop at the liquor store, however, alcohol led to some other bright ideas that had eaten into his stash. Details after that got hazier. He'd seen Michaela, which meant he'd gone to the bonfire. Everyone would've noticed he was drunk, at least. Panic churned his fragile gut as he grabbed his phone.

A text from John, sent around eleven. *Get lost?*

He must not have reached the bonfire. Thank God. But where had he run into Michaela?

He might've dreamed of walking a dark road with her. Life since Clare's death had been one long, dark road, and it wasn't that much of a stretch to believe his subconscious would conjure one in a dream.

"Dad." Nila's voice pierced the door. "Nason ate all the marshmallow cereal, and I wanted some, and he's calling Helga names."

As if the unicorn could be called much worse than her given moniker.

Philip slid his phone into the pocket of his fresh blue jeans and picked up the wad of laundry that included the jeans he'd slept in, his sheets, and the mattress pad. If memory served, Nancy was coming to watch the kids today, and the evidence of last night needed to be gone before she arrived.

Nila tailed him to the washer, detailing Nason's offenses.

The boy ran up to defend himself as Philip stuffed the sheets and jeans into the machine. The mattress pad would have to wait for a separate load.

As he pressed the start button, another memory surfaced. He'd put all the remaining pills into the back pockets of his jeans to hide them from Michaela. He hit the controls to stop the drum from filling, yanked open the door, and pawed through the load.

"Dad, are you listening?" Nason tugged his pocket.

"I need you two to be patient." His voice was close to shaking with the effort of remaining calm. In the few seconds, the washer had gushed a flood of water. "Wait for me in the kitchen. I'll be right there."

"Why are you doing laundry?" Nila asked. "That's what you do when Nason has an accident."

"I don't have accidents!" A dull thud indicated Nason's stomp. "Only babies have accidents."

"No one had an accident. Go wait in the kitchen." His fingers found the tougher fabric of his jeans, and he pulled them out as the kids begrudgingly obeyed, bickering as they went. The pills were still in the back pockets. He'd spread them out, some in one pocket, some in the other.

He counted what he'd retrieved. No way had he taken enough last night to leave him with so few. He emptied the washer and collected strays from the folds of the sheets, but sudsy water had soaked several in the bottom of the drum.

On his way to the kitchen, he stopped by his private bathroom. He flushed the partially dissolved pills so he couldn't change his mind about them later. The good ones, he funneled into a bottle and stashed in his medicine cabinet.

When he reached the kids, he served Nila toaster pastries that quieted her complaints about cereal. Still filling in details of the night before, he left the kids munching at the counter and checked the garage.

His parking space sat empty.

He swore under his breath and paced to the kitchen. His head hurt. He couldn't think. The kids weren't helping. Nancy would arrive soon, and he had so much to hide. Except, he didn't know the extent of what he'd done and couldn't find out without questions that would bring even more trouble if he asked the wrong person.

He made coffee, but as he took the first sip, the doorbell rang. Nancy already. The kids ran to let her in.

Panic rose like bile. He was stuck without a car. Would she recognize the signs of his night? He'd showered, but the scent of alcohol could still be emanating from his pores. And the sheets were in the wash. He could blame the kids for that, saying one of them had slept in his bed and gotten sick, but if she mentioned it to them, they'd defend themselves.

And what kind of father used his kids that way?

Nancy set her purse on a stool beside Nila and glanced at him before greeting the kids.

He drew a breath. "I'm sick. Take the kids somewhere today, please."

"You're sick, Daddy?" Nila licked her fingers, her toaster pastries already inhaled.

He spared his daughter a regretful smile before focusing on Nancy again.

Showing no similar concern for him, the older woman laid her hands on the kids' shoulders. "Why don't you two go watch one of your shows?"

Nason lifted his bowl of milk and slurped down the cereal-reddened liquid, then dropped to his feet. They raced off, vying to reach the remote first.

Philip cleared his throat. "I don't want them getting sick too."

Nancy cocked an eyebrow like a school headmaster who'd

heard it all. "Based on what Audrey told me, this isn't a contagious illness."

As if his head and stomach weren't giving him enough trouble, his back muscles wound tight with dread. "What did Audrey tell you?"

"You came home around ten thirty, entirely drunk, with a woman."

Doubt and guilt stomped around his gut. Another memory surfaced, Michaela standing in his bedroom, asking for his pills. But Nancy only knew he'd been drinking, and she wasn't his judge, jury, and executioner. "And?"

"Audrey was concerned you wouldn't be able to care for the children, should something happen during the night."

Nila could've had another nightmare and crawled into his bed. That would've been a disaster. Still.

Nancy continued. "You set off the security system while attempting to enter the house. You also tripped on the stairs."

"I could've done that sober." It wasn't as if he'd gone on a rampage or caused an accident—except his car wasn't there, so he couldn't be certain about that second one.

"I told her she didn't need to stay over." She threaded her fingers together and met his anger with an even gaze. "But in the initial phone screening, Ruthann asked about the use of alcohol and drugs in the home. I assured her you provide a wholesome, stable environment for your children."

"I'm not allowed to have a drink because of the nanny?" He motioned with his coffee, sending a splash over his fingers. What a joke he was. He ripped a paper towel from the roll. "She's going to leave the first time I trip on the stairs?"

"No." Nancy gazed toward the living room, where voices of cartoon characters warbled, and pursed her lips. "I'm saying if it becomes habitual, she'll be uncomfortable, and that could lead her to look for other employment."

He wiped up his hand. "Then I'll find a new placement

agency who can bring in better candidates. I don't answer to my employees."

Nancy's mouth, still tightly drawn, took on a frown. "No one will find a better candidate than Ruthann. For the sake of the children, I sincerely hope this is a good match on both sides."

"I do too."

Her expression relaxed into regret as if she didn't know his stare disguised a massive headache and a sense of foreboding. He might have done something the night before that he'd pay for in more uncomfortable ways than this conversation. He dropped the paper towel to the floor. With his foot, he wiped up the spilled coffee. He didn't need to be branded a slob on top of everything else.

"I'll take the children to the lakeshore for some exploring and a picnic. That should keep us away until two."

"Thank you." He deposited the soiled paper towel in the trash and exited the kitchen, the victory too small to lift his mood.

Since Michaela had been involved, he'd approach her about the gaps, but gathering information without alarming her would require finesse. He finished his coffee, strategizing. After the last sip, he made the call.

Straight to voicemail.

Right. She was up in the air this morning.

Like everything else.

With no car and no way to locate it, he couldn't get to Gannon's, so he composed an excuse to cover last night and this morning.

Sorry, bad night. Nila got sick. Puke everywhere and still not feeling well. You'll be okay without me?

He hesitated. Throwing his daughter under the bus might be low, but Nila needed him to keep this job. He sent the text and poured another cup of coffee.

~

MICHAELA CAUGHT another stare from the soldier across the aisle, and the plane hadn't even taken off yet. She'd gone light on her makeup and worn her hair up to hide its length, but the flight attendant had recognized her. Perhaps if she hadn't used her frequent flyer miles to upgrade to first class, she'd have been less conspicuous.

She hunkered down in her seat and focused on her phone, which displayed a picture of Philip—one she'd spent the whole wait in the airport terminal seeking out on the Internet. His tattoo depicted feathered wings with damaged places where an underlying metal frame showed. The half-mechanical, half-angelic wings sprouted from a deep red heart—the real kind with chambers and arteries—that bore his late wife's name.

Given how he'd referenced her the night before, Clare still had his heart.

In a way Michaela never would.

She'd have to divorce the song she'd written from him, or her disappointment would keep her from polishing the lyrics and melody. As the flight cut south, she attempted to smooth out the rough spots, but she'd get further with a piano and the freedom to sing.

Thankfully, the flight to Illinois took under two hours.

After they landed, she stood to retrieve her bag from the overhead compartment.

The soldier's voice came from over her shoulder. "Let me get that."

She snagged the strap of the knapsack and tugged the bag into her hands. "It's light. Thanks."

"Can I ...? You're, um ..." His face and build were on the thin side, his complexion still spotted with acne. Eighteen? Nineteen?

"Let's get off the plane first, okay?" Her quiet question earned a conspiratorial grin.

"Yes, ma'am." He stood close to her elbow, quiet and blocking others from approaching.

Shielding the screen with her body, she checked her cell phone as she waited for the crew to open the cabin door. Philip had called. If yesterday hadn't happened, she'd have done a happy dance.

But yesterday had happened.

The soldier fell in step beside her in the jet bridge, stars in his eyes. In a quiet corner of the airport, she posed with him for a selfie. As he snapped the picture, she tipped up on her toes to kiss his cheek. The picture captured joyful surprise on his face and enough of her own to be recognizable.

"No girlfriend, right?" she asked as she stepped away. "Because if you have one, you might want to think twice before posting that."

"No, ma'am." He chuckled. "You don't have a boyfriend? I don't need some billionaire hunting me down and making my life miserable."

"No boyfriend." But hopefully a man who'd regret keeping her at bay when he saw her with someone else.

By the time she reached baggage claim, the soldier had uploaded the photo and tagged her, as promised. The conveyor belt jerked into motion with luggage from her flight. She replied to the post and reshared the image with a caption about supporting those in the armed forces.

Once in her rental car, she checked, but Philip hadn't reacted to the picture. Since her options were to go face her sister and father or to see what Philip wanted, she dialed voicemail.

"Michaela, when you land, can you call me back? I know how last night must've looked. I'm sorry. I'd like the chance to explain."

Interesting. If he could explain, maybe he had a prescription after all? Or, now sober, he might confess deep feelings for her. They could band together to get him clean.

She returned the call. "Okay, I'm listening."

Philip drew and released a long breath. "In high school, I took a hit during a game—football—that left me paralyzed. They did surgery, and mostly, I'm fine now. But last weekend, I wrestled with Nason, and the old injury flared up. The doctor prescribed painkillers to get me through until this stretching, yoga-type regimen they've got me on realigns everything, but in the meantime, I should've known not to drink. I'm sorry. I made a bad call."

She wanted to believe him. "But you said you're always on something."

"Honestly, I don't remember what I said, but I saw the doctor on Saturday. Since then, I've been on them. The prescription won't last much longer, and the pain's a lot better. I might not even finish out what they gave me."

"So why did it sound like you were talking about a drug dealer?"

"Oh, man." He laughed. "I'm really sorry. I was out of it. No. No drug dealer. Awestruck would fire me on the spot. My life is a lot tamer than all that."

Would he be able to laugh so easily if he were lying?

He had called himself a liar, but she couldn't believe he could do so this well.

"I should probably forget everything else you said too."

He hesitated. "What else did I say?"

"You open up to me more than to other people, and you care about me." Repeating his words made them more real. He'd been sincere about his feelings, if nothing else, and she'd proved herself last night.

This was happening.

Her and Philip.

"Look." He cleared his throat. "You *do not* want to get involved with me."

Why were the best things always in sight but never in reach? Or was this rejection not as firm as it sounded?

"Why?" Drugs would've been a problem, but what else could stand between them?

"I've got kids. They're always going to come first."

Now, she laughed. "Single parents date. Besides, I like your kids. Loosen up." She twirled a lock of hair that had slipped free by her temple. This would be far easier in person. "You care what I think enough to call and explain yourself, and when your defenses are down, you open up to me. Just admit you like me."

"Are you going to make me do this?"

His question left her feeling as though he'd thrown her to the ground and put his foot on her throat. She'd pushed him too far. Misread him.

She might as well hear him out. Whether he told her what he thought or not, he'd go on thinking it.

"I guess I am."

"I called because I inconvenienced you and owed you an apology. Now, I want to know where my car is, not how I can fall into a meaningless relationship."

Meaningless?

If looks could kill, the random guy looking for his rental car would've become collateral damage. "Is still having a job meaningless to you? Because without this relationship, you would've gotten yourself fired last night."

"I'm grateful, Michaela, but I was on a prescription. They wouldn't have fired me."

"If nothing else, you were drinking and driving." She pointed a finger, but only the steering wheel and windshield witnessed the shaming. "And mixing alcohol and a prescription. They wouldn't have been happy."

"Okay. True. Thank you for getting involved. I consider you a friend, but that's all I have to offer."

Enough. She pressed her open palm against the rim of the steering wheel. "Your car is about a mile from John's on a gravel trail because meaningless little me thought it best to not leave a clue in John's driveway—where the others might start asking questions."

"I meant a relationship would be—"

"I have to go be meaningless for my sister."

"Mic—"

She disconnected.

12

Philip winced as he got out of his SUV at Gannon's house on Monday morning. He twisted and stretched, trying to loosen his neck and back. Reducing how many pills he'd been taking left him with flu-like aches, and he'd compounded the pain by helping move the world's heaviest couch into Ruthann's apartment over the weekend. The discomfort had to be God's way of punishing him for the lies he'd strung together for Michaela on Friday morning.

Since he'd hurt himself after all, he'd considered going in for a legitimate prescription, but with his luck, all he'd get would be a lecture.

He hated this. The dependence. The lies. The cost. The fear. He couldn't lose his job over pills.

He had to see this tapering through, no matter how uncomfortable the process. He crossed an arm over himself and stretched some more as another vehicle parked by his in the drive. It'd be John, arriving for practice.

"I hired movers for the new nanny." He leaned to his other side. "Should've known to let them handle the thousand-ton couch."

A laugh rose. "Let me guess. She's hot, and you couldn't help showing off."

Philip dropped his arms and turned. A sedan—not the drummer's—had parked on the far side of his SUV. A middle-aged man wearing a button-down and dress pants stood between the vehicles. Tim, Awestruck's manager, pressed a key fob, and the locks clicked, followed by a few extra clunks that signaled his passenger had dallied too long in getting out.

When the door opened, a second man straightened, shaking his head at Tim. "Secured grounds. Who's going to jack it here?"

Smirking, Tim spun the key into his palm and pointed from the newcomer to Philip. "Have you two met?"

"A lot's changed since then." The man stepped closer, tattoo-covered arm extended for a handshake. He wore his brown hair short. His broad-set eyes were blue, his smile almost impish.

He looked vaguely familiar. Had they really met?

His T-shirt and jeans said his business here was more casual than Tim's. He could be a sound guy, a guitar tech, or even a fellow musician.

Oh. A musician.

A lot *had* changed. When Philip's former band toured with Awestruck, Matt had been their bassist. Even then, years before he'd gotten himself fired, the signs of Matt's addictions had been obvious. His face had been a collection of hollows and shadows, his body skinny and run down. He'd been fidgety and always drunk, high, or irritable about being sober—everything Philip worked so hard to avoid.

Matt's face had filled out to a healthy oval. He returned a firm handshake, his eyes clear.

Tim started for the door. Matt stayed focused on Philip. "I like what you did with 'Wreckage.'"

He scratched his cheek. Awestruck had debuted "Wreckage" at their first secret show. Philip had written the bass line, but not many people listened closely enough to isolate his contribution. A fellow bassist would pick out the sound automatically, like a former addict might recognize the signs of withdrawal.

"Thanks." Philip followed Tim toward the house to escape Matt's focus. "What brings you two here?"

"Making amends," Matt said.

Simultaneously, Tim replied, "Knocking sense into Gannon."

Matt scoffed at Tim's answer, and the manager stalked toward the studio.

Matt fell in beside Philip as they followed. "I'm an addict, working the steps. I would've come sooner, but with these guys, I needed significant amends to offer. 'Whirlwinds' is the best I could do."

They arrived at the studio's open door.

Gannon spotted Tim, and his face clouded with confusion. "What are you ...?" His voice trailed and his eyebrows pulled even lower as Matt made his entrance.

The former bassist lifted a hand in a wave. "Hey, guys. Long time no see."

Gannon looked back and forth between the visitors, as though to ask what was happening.

Apparently not as hung up on explanations, John moved in and greeted their old bassist with a handshake that morphed into a loose, back-slapping hug. "You look good. How've you been?"

"A lot better than the last time you saw me. Wanted to talk with you two."

Tim backtracked toward the hall and motioned for Philip to follow. "Introduce me to Michaela."

Apparently, Tim's way of knocking sense into Gannon meant letting the former bandmates work things out on their own. But what if Matt won them over? What if they decided Philip wasn't as much of an asset as Matt could be? As long as Awestruck produced an album, the manager wouldn't care whether Philip or Matt covered bass, so of course he had no qualms about leaving them alone.

Was it paranoia or sound concern that rioted to keep Philip in the studio? But refusing Tim would cause a scene, and the more attention he drew to himself, the more likely the others would notice he wasn't well. Philip would have to count on Gannon to protect his job.

In the hall, Philip fished his phone from his pocket. If Michaela resented being friend-zoned or suspected the truth about the pills, facing her with Tim as an audience could prove more dangerous than anything that might happen among the former bandmates in the studio. Then again, facing her in front of everyone when she showed up to work on the collaboration later would be equally risky.

"I hear you two are chummy." Tim put his hands in his pockets and let his expression ask for details.

"Friends." Philip's dry mouth made choking out the word nearly impossible.

"Call and see about breakfast," Tim said. "There's a restaurant by the marina in Lakeshore."

Philip knew which one he meant, but not the name, so he sank a couple of minutes in searching it out before dialing her.

"Yes?" Her curt greeting kept him on edge.

"Tim is in town, wants to know if you'll have breakfast with us."

"Tim who?"

"Bergeron. Awestruck's manager."

"Oh." Her tone brightened. "Sure. Where should I meet you?"

He didn't know how to interpret the change in attitude. Why would she want to meet Tim?

The manager hung close by, his expression asking for Michaela's response.

Philip nodded once, wondering which he'd regret more— leaving Matt with Awestruck or setting up breakfast with Michaela and Tim.

~

WHY WOULD tiny Lakeshore need both a Marina Café and a Marina View Bakery? In her hurry, she'd chosen the wrong location on GPS, so she'd first walked into the bakery. When the patrons didn't include any rock stars, she set off on foot toward the correct one, but she made the mistake of not letting GPS guide her there, so she'd snaked unnecessarily down one block and up another, passing Kim Piel's bookstore on the way.

The story hour this weekend would make that situation right, restoring her to Gannon's good graces. And now breakfast with Tim Bergeron.

The man had built as much of a reputation—within the industry, anyway—as the band he represented. If half the rumors about Tim's ability to work miracles proved true, he could get her a slot with Evie Decker.

Instead of having only a hit with Awestruck, she could have a song of her own climbing the charts. The song Philip had inspired. The song she'd finished over the weekend. Her anger had added a bit of spunk to the last verse of "Becoming Us," challenging the man she loved to love her the way she deserved.

Philip wouldn't. He hadn't even asked about her sister when he'd called that morning.

Even a casual friend would've, so Philip's line about considering her a friend had been empty.

But her fans would love her if she worked with the right

producer, one who'd ensure the perfect sound and emotion, capturing their loyalty. Evie Decker was that producer.

She stepped into the Marina Café and spotted Philip, who looked no better than he had Friday night. Haggard eyes, tired posture. A blond man sat across from him. Tim might be balding, or perhaps his hair had always been thin.

Philip drew his sluggish gaze in from the window and watched her approach without cluing in Tim. He gave no sign of a greeting. Didn't stand, offer a hug, or ask about her sister.

The biopsy went as well as possible, but my sister—and everyone else—is pretty depressed. Thanks for asking. It'll be a long week until we know the results.

A friend would want to know.

Thanks to Philip's lack of acknowledgment, Tim hadn't observed her yet, but no problem. She enjoyed the upper hand of surprise.

Creases around the manager's mouth and blue eyes put him in his forties, and he carried a little extra weight. He looked like a football coach. A man tough enough to keep his players in line and observant enough to read the game—all without getting off the sidelines.

"Hey, boys. Got room for one more?"

Tim rose instantly, shook her hand, and introduced himself. Philip moved down a seat, presumably so she could sit next to him, but she slid onto the bench on Tim's side of the table.

"After a couple of weeks here, you ready to head back to civilization?" Tim laid his arm across the back of the seat as she leaned forward, glancing over the menu.

She gave him a laugh. "I've enjoyed the peace and quiet while I've been here. I visited family near Chicago over the weekend, though."

Across the table, Philip slid his own menu to the edge of the table and watched her. "How'd it go?"

Now he wanted to know? If he hadn't thought to ask before she'd brought it up, he didn't deserve details.

"I made it into the city for some fun one night, so I wasn't too lonely." Her coy smile ought to cue their imaginations to invent non-existent love interests.

Sure enough, Philip's jaw pulsed, and he turned toward the window.

He had no way of knowing her trip into the city had been for an architectural boat cruise with her dad. He also couldn't know Dad had been so worried about Riley the whole time, he'd made for awful company. It wasn't that Michaela wasn't worried for her sister. She was. But Riley had come through the biopsy and had been resting at home with her husband and daughter to dote on her by then, and still, Dad couldn't be bothered to say much to Michaela, aside from harrumphing when she offered tidbits about her work with Awestruck or her hopes for her next album.

If Michaela's vague suggestion about seeing other guys pained Philip as much as it appeared, she might be able to push him far enough that he'd admit to wanting more than friendship.

"Anyway." She offered Tim another smile. "I'm writing new music, so this place has been good for me."

"Gannon first came here to write songs too. Well, that was the reason he gave, but we all know it was for a girl. Either way, he came through for the album, so who am I to complain?" Tim paused when the waitress came, and they all gave their orders —Tim, an omelet, her a fruit bowl and hot water with lemon, Philip coffee. Then, Tim refocused on her. "The new song any good?"

She couldn't have kept from grinning if she'd tried. She leaned back in the seat, bumping the arm Tim had rested there. To his credit, the manager moved his arm, but his interest stayed riveted on her.

"I think so. You know how much depends on having the right producer. I'm hoping Reese can convince Evie Decker to open up her schedule."

"I know Evie. You're not going to talk her into coming up here."

"Oh, I'd go to her. After the soundtrack collaboration is finished, of course, and provided Evie will fit me in. It'd be an honor to work with her. I love Reese, but the two haven't worked together before, so ..." She crossed her fingers.

"Tell you what. Send me what you've got. I'll forward it along."

"You'd do that?"

He resituated in his seat, his knee bumping hers. "Sure. Connecting talent to the right people is my job."

"Thank you so much. That means so much." In her excitement, she didn't even realize she'd laid her fingers on Tim's arm as she gushed until Philip jerked up from the table, excused himself, and strode off in the direction of the restrooms.

She folded her hands on her lap. Did he think she was too flirtatious? This was just how she dealt with men in the industry. They treated her better when she wasn't uptight.

Anyway, Philip had called her meaningless and told her he wanted to be friends. A friend shouldn't care about a casual moment between her and an industry professional. She had nothing to be ashamed of.

And yet, Philip's departure left her feeling just as guilty as when he'd left her in the parking lot of the pizza restaurant.

PHILIP HAD to get more pills. Somehow.

His reduced dose left him too sick to cope. Especially with Michaela and her games.

Sure, her initial interest in him had been as shallow as what she lavished on Tim now. But he'd believed what she'd said about how she actually liked Philip. He felt the connection too. He may have shut it down so he could focus on keeping his job, but that didn't mean he enjoyed watching her work her charm on someone else. She might develop real feelings for Tim, and then what? Or, Tim might allow things to go further than Philip had.

His stomach churned. Was he going to throw up?

Quitting had been easier in the past. He'd dropped the habit cold turkey the day Nila had been born and hadn't touched pills again until after Clare died.

But his use before the kids entered the picture had been sporadic. These last few months, he'd leaned on them constantly. He should've known he couldn't taper off this fast.

He measured out another pill. Which option for obtaining more carried the least risk? Perhaps his usual dealer had found a new source? The fact that there'd been a big bust worried him, though. What if authorities were working their way down the supply chain? If he got caught, they might make an example of a celebrity.

He didn't want to consider the horror that would put his kids through.

The worries eased as the pill kicked in.

Feeling more like himself, he returned to the table to find the coffees and water had been delivered.

Michaela sat closer to Tim than the bench required. Philip's bet? Tim saw through her and didn't mind the attention. And because Philip had been shut out of the meeting with Matt, now he got a front row seat as the first woman he'd connected with since Clare threw herself at someone else. Because his life wasn't awful enough.

13

Matt met Philip and Tim just inside Gannon's front door, and Tim left with the former bassist. Since Michaela's session with the band wasn't for a few more hours, she'd gone back to her condo. Probably trying to perfect her song so she could send it to Tim.

Meanwhile, Philip continued to the studio alone. Gannon and John were seated there, the remnants of a heavy conversation hanging in the air.

Philip dropped into an armchair and interlaced his fingers in an attempt to look relaxed. "What's the verdict?"

"I don't know." Gannon ran a hand over his face.

John seemed unruffled, as always. "He's come a long way."

"I'd like to believe that, but addicts are manipulative."

Gannon's statement underlined each of the lies Philip had told recently. Telling the guys he'd missed work Friday because of Nila. Telling Michaela about back pain and a prescription. Letting Nancy believe he'd only been drinking, not using drugs.

But Philip wasn't an addict. Addicts were helpless. He could quit, he just didn't want to. The pills made his life manageable, a tool he used, not an addiction.

"That wasn't Matt the addict we just talked to," John said.

"Even he said he can't guarantee he'll make good choices in the future."

"Taking recovery one day at a time is part of the program."

The program, presumably some sort of twelve-step deal, sounded miserable. One dark day after another with nothing to look forward to. Philip wiped a palm on his jeans. "What Matt does someday doesn't matter if we're buying one song off him. That's all we're doing, right?"

"He won't accept payment." Gannon rubbed his forehead. "I don't like breaking from writing our own music, and associating with him again ... I'm not sure I trust him that much."

"Forgiveness isn't optional," John said.

Gannon's mouth twisted. "I can forgive him without working with him."

The drummer pushed up from his seat. "I say we vote." He disappeared into the control room.

When the song rose through the speakers, the sound resonated, fuller and more polished than Philip had expected. Within three notes, he recognized why. They'd performed this song, "Yours," many times on tour last year. In one of the band's more subdued melodies, Gannon sang, "The mistakes I've made stretch two thousand miles into a past I can't take back."

Philip didn't know the full story, but he had heard that Gannon wrote the remorseful lyrics based on personal experience. The song halted.

"Oops," John called. "Wrong one."

Gannon drew a breath that looked like a precursor to a cutting reply, but he stayed quiet. Convicted by John's tactic?

A rough-sounding recording streamed into the room. The singer's voice couldn't hold a candle to Gannon's, and the drummer didn't have John's skill. The guitar was passable, but again, not Gannon. The song walked a fine line, edgy enough to be called rock while pulling up short of intensity that would keep it off mainstream radio stations. The lyrics described a whirlwind of consequences created by bad choices. The songwriter had good working knowledge of Awestruck's sound. The result aligned with their style while remaining different enough to stand out as a new fan favorite.

Resignation settled over Gannon.

John returned. "All in favor?" He lifted a hand to signal his vote.

Gannon silently raised his hand but kept his head down as if he didn't want to watch.

They had the majority already, but John waited.

Philip nodded his consent. For Nila and Nason, he'd ensure Awestruck's success, even if that meant playing a song by a guy who might be out for his job.

MICHAELA HAD to respect a fellow climber. Despite all she'd learned about Matt's falling-out with Gannon and John, by Thursday when she showed up to work, Awestruck was knee-deep in his song, "Whirlwinds." The man himself must not have earned a welcome in the studio, though, because Tim sat in the control room alone.

She sank into the chair next to him at the soundboard. She'd sent the manager "Becoming Us" that morning and wanted to put in one last good word with him before he had a chance to listen.

She ought to focus, yet satisfaction buoyed her when Philip seemed to track her movements. They'd chatted once or twice that week. Nothing groundbreaking. He had asked after Riley but accepted the simplest answer without question—they continued to wait on results. She'd asked after his kids, and she also hadn't pressed for details, though he hadn't said enough to satisfy her curiosity. Those children had certainly made quick work of infiltrating her heart.

Tomorrow, Gannon and John were leaving for their mysterious bachelor weekend, so today was the last she'd see Philip until the bookstore event on Saturday.

Tim made a show of tapping his laptop's touch pad before shutting the device. "Sent."

Her pulse spiked. "My song? Already?" She gulped, chiding herself for the pathetic eagerness, but she had to make sure she understood. "To Evie?"

"Yes, ma'am." He pointed toward the band. "Today's the day I hear the soundtrack collaboration, too, right?"

"I'm not going to kick you out." She pointed her toe against the floor and rocked her chair. "I'm surprised you weren't here earlier in the week."

"Miss me?"

Michaela edged a smile onto her lips, careful to maintain physical distance, lest she push Philip too far again. Hopefully, if he was still watching, he understood this was purely professional.

Tim's expression turned pleased before he waved his hand toward the window again. "These guys act like everything relies on their work in the studio, but there's a lot more to success. Besides, Gannon and his fiancée—you've met Adeline?"

She nodded. Despite her best efforts, she liked the woman.

"They're starting a business and have no idea what they're doing. To get Key of Hope running before the school year starts, they need all the help they can get, so I've been over there."

She leaned forward to ask him to explain, but before the words rose, her phone interrupted with a call from her sister.

The results must've come back.

Panic flashed over her. "Sorry. Excuse me."

She hit the icon to answer but didn't speak until she'd reached the privacy of the hall.

"Hey, Riley." She'd meant to say something cheerful. Maybe some kind of vote of confidence. Instead, her concern had stolen most of her vocabulary.

"It's cancer. I'm scheduled for surgery next week."

Michaela's muscles slackened. She leaned back to steady herself, but the wall stood farther behind her than she'd realized. She free fell the last couple of inches before her shoulder blades thudded into the drywall. "I'm sorry. I didn't think ... I can't believe it."

"Yeah. Me neither."

"Um. Well ..." Tears pressed into her eyes—did Michaela have any right to feel so upset when she'd spent years resenting Riley? But whatever Michaela felt, Riley had to be feeling worse. Michaela needed to do better than she'd done in the past. "When is the surgery?"

"Thursday."

"Okay. I'll come Wednesday night. I'll be there. I'll stay through the weekend, help out."

Riley sniffled. "You don't have to do that. I've got Darren. I'll be in the hospital for a couple of days this time. I won't be up for much company."

She was family, not company. "I can entertain Bailey, at least."

"We have Dad and Darren's parents."

"I'm coming. We're sisters." She stared at the opposite wall through a lake of tears. "I want to be there."

"Okay." Riley's shaky voice softened. "Then I guess I'll see you."

"Take care."

Silence replied. She put the phone away with shaking fingers. The band expected her, but she couldn't go back. She hurried to the closest bathroom and shut herself in.

THE DETERMINATION WAS UNANIMOUS: half an hour was way too long for a woman to spend in the bathroom in the middle of a workday. Philip had been relieved when Michaela hadn't lingered with Tim in the control room, but what, besides hurt feelings, might cause her to take off like that?

"You talked to her last." Gannon's suspicious gaze fell on Tim. "What'd you do?"

Tim held up his hands. "She sent me her song this morning, and I forwarded it to Evie. If anything, she's happy. I'm guessing she went to talk to her people about it."

He'd done more than connect her with Evie. For one thing, the manager had let her flirt her heart out at their breakfast on Monday. Philip had been glad not to have seen the two together since. He hated watching Michaela play those games. He hated how her behavior left him wondering if any of his own interactions with her had been genuine, or if she'd never stopped playing him. At least, not until a new mark—Tim—came along.

Okay. Realistically, Michaela's focus hadn't shifted that easily. Philip had insulted her a few times.

He hadn't meant to call her meaningless. He'd meant the kind of relationship she'd wanted would be meaningless. A meaningless romance. He could clarify, but he doubted she'd be moved, and if she wanted a meaningless romance, Tim seemed willing.

Philip had no right to hate the way she'd lavished the manager with attention.

But hadn't she said she didn't like who she became when she got ahead that way?

Five minutes later, she breezed into the studio with flushed cheeks and bright eyes, seeming to prove Tim's theory that she'd been celebrating the progress toward working with Evie.

Minutes later, they were playing through the collaboration.

The lyrics were comprised of a conversation between two people. Gannon's persona wanted Michaela's to choose him over fame.

In the last verse, Gannon sang, "I know you think you found true love, a crowd to worship at your feet, but love like that comes fast and cheap. With you, I'm playing for keeps."

Did Michaela see how fast and cheap her kind of success was?

She might, because a couple of lines later, a tear slipped down her cheek as she sang her part of the bridge. "I can't continue on my own. If you'll be mine, I'll be yours alone."

The emotion played into the line, the part where her persona admitted her way wasn't working, but she'd never teared up before.

As the song wound down, Michaela wiped her face.

After he'd played the final chords, Gannon pulled her into a side hug, and she cuddled against him for a second as if she needed comfort. But then, as they broke apart, her eyes lit as her gaze fixed on Tim.

"What'd you think?" Her question bounded out through a grin. "Good, right?"

The whole thing had been an act.

Again.

Tim gave a gently approving smile Philip had never seen from him before. Usually, to praise an Awestruck song, he'd clap, pump his fist, or shout, "That's what I'm talking about." This time, his response was ... tender.

Gross.

Michaela beamed. "The song's kind of possessive. Jealous and possessive. I like it."

"God wants us to love Him more than anything else." Gannon turned away to focus on his notes as he spoke, as if he knew the statement would fall on deaf ears.

"That was the inspiration?" Michaela laughed as if she expected someone else to join in. "I didn't get that at all."

Philip hadn't either, but John smirked and added, "We won't hold it against you."

Michaela looked to Tim for an ally, but apparently their manager wasn't entirely helpless around her because he shrugged, unsurprised.

She turned to Philip, making eye contact for the first time since she'd reentered the studio. A look he could've sworn was despair crossed her features, and she pivoted away again.

Concern for her welled, and then he remembered. She'd mastered getting men to respond to her—Philip right along with everyone else in the room.

Gannon's claim that addicts were manipulative came back to him. Addicts had nothing on Michaela. Or maybe, she had her own addictions.

14

Michaela navigated her rental down the alley and found only one empty spot remaining in the tiny lot behind the bookstore. Wedging into the narrow slot without taking out Philip's taillight or bashing in the door of Tim's car would take some serious skill. As she wiggled her car back and forth to line up, Philip and his kids got out of his SUV.

Tim and two others—maybe a father and a daughter there for the reading?—stood nearby, and through her open window, she heard the greetings.

"Lil' Mill." Tim held up a hand for Nila.

With a nudge from Philip, she high-fived him, and Nason rushed up for his turn.

"Mini Mill!" Tim lowered his hand and held it palm up. "Down low."

Nason slapped his hand, laughing.

The kids were friendly with Tim, and he with them. Here, she'd thought she'd made special progress with Nila.

I will not be jealous over an eight-year-old.

But she was. Philip might be no comfort to her, but she'd

counted on enjoying the kids' company today. A bright spot in an awful week.

At least, focused on greeting each other, no one watched the car gymnastics she completed to get situated in the spot. She opened her door the twelve inches the space allowed and slipped out.

"The guest of honor," Tim announced.

She straightened her shoulders and faked cheerfulness. "I didn't know you were joining us."

"Keeping busy. Plus, my daughter likes to read." Tim extended an arm toward the girl Michaela had assumed was with the other guy. "I thought she could read a story for us."

Michaela hadn't pegged him as a family guy. His daughter moved forward, and Tim settled his arm around her shoulders. The top of the girl's blond head didn't quite come to her father's shoulder.

Her grin was big and shiny—pink lip gloss appeared to be the only makeup her father allowed. "I'm Isabella Dubois, and I know who you are. I love your music."

"Aw, sweetie. I'm glad you could come."

"Where he goes, I go. Sometimes, anyway." Isabella eyed her father. "But this will be fun. Much better than the day camp he's been sending me to while he works every day. I'm the oldest kid there, but at least that means they're going to make me the star of their play." She ended on a note of pride.

Michaela understood the rollercoaster and congratulated her even as pity rose. She knew what it was like to feel like an afterthought to her father, and she knew what it was like to find solace on the stage.

Before Isabella could share more about her role, Nila advanced and slipped a hand into Michaela's.

Michaela squeezed the girl's hand in silent greeting.

"Have you met Matt?" Tim's question yanked her attention to the last man in their group.

Matt? This man was Matt?

The hodgepodge of tattoos on his arms and hands should've given it away, but when she'd met him on the set of *Audition Room*, he'd been kind of ... greasy. Now, his hair was short and clean. His wide-set eyes looked intelligent paired with his angular features. His five-o'clock shadow was a calculated fashion choice. Or the outcome of not having shaved for a day or two. Whatever. It worked.

"We did meet," she managed. "Once, a long time ago."

Not that he'd remember. The night of the taping, he must've greeted dozens of others.

Matt stepped forward and shook her hand. "*Audition Room*."

"You remember."

"Gannon knew you'd win from the first time he heard you sing. We heard a lot about you that year." He flashed a smile. "And he was right. An annoying habit of his when it comes to talent."

When they'd first met, she hadn't understood why Gannon had chosen Matt for a spot in his band, but this guy, with his self-assurance and—

"We should get in there."

At Philip's voice, she felt as though she'd been caught red-handed, staring at one man while the one she cared about stood directly behind her. The make-Philip-jealous plot had lost its luster. Especially since Riley's call, she didn't have the energy for schemes. She wanted comfort, and attention from anyone else was a cold one. She'd much prefer warmth like she'd seen in Philip's family.

Coming from him, reassurances would mean something.

She blinked. If she rode this train of thought too far, she'd find herself in tears.

～

PHILIP TEXTED his dealer as Michaela read the first story. The pills would run out the following day. He'd tried other contacts, but none had panned out. Kory had been supplying him for months. He couldn't have lost access as completely as he claimed. Philip must need to offer more incentive. More money.

"'But why can't I fly?' asked the little foal." Michaela had turned reading the book into a full-on voice performance.

Nila leaned forward and squirmed, hooked.

Michaela adopted a lower voice for the foal's mother. "'Ah, but you *can* fly.'" She glanced at the kids, stretching the moment before sharing the revelation at the end of the story. "'Do you remember how you felt after you shared your oats with Lily?'"

She made a dubious face for the foal's part. "'I felt happy, but I didn't *fly*.'"

Her gaze passed over the children, then lifted to him. Unbidden, an imagining of her curled up against Nila's headboard, reading to his sleepy kids, played in his mind. In her glance, she would convey both contentedness and a promise that after the kids were asleep, she'd be all his.

He dropped his focus and rubbed his forehead. He couldn't afford to entertain such impossibilities. Her expression just now hadn't held contentedness or promises.

Quite the opposite. At first, he'd seen only the bright actress, then a flash of uncertainty, like she knew she'd been made.

Still, the entire crowd of kids sat with rapt attention as she turned the last page. "'Why do you want to fly?'" The actress in her was back, voices and everything. "'Isn't it because you think it will make you happy? Any bird or airplane can fly, but love is a special gift. Your heart can soar any time you choose.'"

How was Philip supposed to follow such an animated act?

But since Michaela had worked out the order with Kim, he rose to take his turn as Michaela finished. He stepped carefully between cross-legged children, watching for fingers. Eager for Michaela to join them as she moved into the audience, his kids patted the floor between them. If she had any compassion, she would sit elsewhere. They already asked about her often enough.

But as the group applauded him for taking the hot seat, Michaela lowered herself to the place between his kids. In two-point-five seconds, Nason leaned on her and tucked under her arm while Nila took her other hand.

Now they'd get even more attached.

He swallowed his frustration. What choice did he have in front of the crowd when it was his turn to read Nila's favorite book? Nason fidgeted all through his sister's pick, but once Philip cracked the cover on the spaceship adventure Nason had chosen, the boy sat up, away from Michaela, attention riveted on the tale as if he hadn't heard this story fifty times before.

To be six again and adore such simple pleasures.

Nason led the applause when the story ended, and Tim took the spotlight. Just in time, too, because the bell jingled, and beyond the parents lining the children's area, the bookstore owner welcomed a new customer.

Kory.

Philip's dealer disappeared into the maze of ceiling-high bookshelves. Philip waited for Tim to start his story, watching as Nason leaned into Michaela again. At least the kids would be supervised while he slipped away.

He headed toward the bathroom until he'd crossed out of sight from the reading. No one but Kory browsed the shelves. That made things easier.

Philip found him at the back wall, by the marker for psychological thrillers. "How much is it going to take?"

Kory pulled a novel from the shelf and skimmed the cover. "We've been over this."

Philip plucked a book from the collection too. "There are very few problems money can't solve."

"This is one of them. I only came because I thought you had come around." Kory shifted his grip on the book, and Philip realized he held a small baggy with white powder.

"No." Philip jammed his book back in its place and returned to the reading, mind and heart racing.

A woman with a fancy camera had arrived. From the local paper? She didn't seem to notice Philip. Still, what if she'd inadvertently snapped an incriminating picture?

The sooner Kory left, the better. Tim finished his book and introduced Issy to the kids. As she read about a lost dog finding its way home, Kory appeared at the register with a book.

He was buying a book? Really? Philip swiped his hand over his face.

The store owner rang up the sale, using a stage whisper that drew glances from a couple of the adults.

Did people here know Kory? The guy was cleaner-cut than most TV or movie drug dealers. He even held down a respectable job. But in a small town, his side hustle might not be a complete secret. Would his appearance here tip someone off to Philip's habit?

Then again, only someone buying from him would know. There was safety in that—to protect their secrets, they'd protect Philip's. Hopefully.

The group clapped for the puppy who'd been found, and the noise overshadowed the jingle of the bell as Kory left. All that risk, for nothing.

"Are you kids ready for one last story?"

Tim's question resulted in a chorus of cheers.

He motioned toward Matt. "You might know Matt because he used to be in Awestruck. He has a new job, but he's still a friend, and he picked a book for you."

Matt waved with both hands in a show of child-like excitement. Philip hadn't realized the former bassist would be reading. Wasn't this an Awestruck event? Tim and Michaela made enough sense, but Matt?

Nila and Nason sought Philip out as soon as the last page had been turned. He wanted to take them and escape, but the families expected a meet and greet.

When a mother asked Philip to pose with her son, he sent Nila and Nason to Issy to keep them out of pictures. Twenty minutes later, he'd taken photos with all the kids who'd gathered near him, and Michaela motioned him to where she spoke with the photographer.

Attraction banded in his chest as he stepped closer, but as with Kory, he wanted what he couldn't have—affection, honesty, and a future Michaela didn't have to give.

She tipped an oblivious smile. "She wants a picture of all the readers for the Lakeshore paper." She waved in Tim and Isabella as she spoke.

The reporter called Matt over.

"I'm not here in any official capacity." Matt pointed toward Nila and Nason, who had taken a book off the shelf in the five seconds since Issy had left them. They grappled for control, on the verge of a fight. "I'll take care of this. You guys do your thing."

Philip took a step toward the kids, not about to let Matt fill in, but the photographer cringed an apology. "This'll just take a second. I promise."

Philip fell back in line. Matt hardly had time to kneel and ask the kids what book they'd picked before the photographer finished and Philip made it over to collect them.

Matt rose as he approached. "Are you feeling at home here? In Lakeshore?"

At the odd question, Philip glanced around the bookstore. Tim, Issy, and Michaela spoke with the reporter. The store owner helped a customer. Most of the parents and children had left.

"It's a small town," Matt prompted. "A different way of life."

"Sure. We're doing all right." More or less. He'd be better if he weren't getting cornered into chatting with the guy who seemed intent on replacing him within Awestruck. "Come on, kids, let's get packed up. You have your books?"

Nila clutched hers, but Nason scampered off in search of his.

Matt shoved his hands in his pockets and rocked on his feet. "It's funny being back."

Back? Only then did Philip remember Awestruck had been in Lakeshore when Gannon fired Matt. Afterward, Gannon and John had returned to California so Philip could audition before he left on a trip of his own.

"I wasn't here very long," Matt continued, "but I've spotted a couple of familiar faces. Kim, for one, not that I talked to her. Kory. Asher's still running the food truck."

The name passed so quickly, with so little weight, that Philip doubted he'd heard correctly. Had his anxiety about getting caught slipped the name in?

Matt watched him, unsmiling. He had said the name, and it had been no accident.

When Philip had concluded he'd be safe if someone realized why Kory had come to the bookstore, he hadn't considered that a *former* customer with less motivation to stay silent might've been present.

Across the alcove, Michaela joined Nason looking for the lost book. Philip's only option was to act as if the name—the whole conversation—meant nothing to him. "I live in Mariner, so I haven't gotten to know many people in Lakeshore, but I hope you're enjoying the reunion."

"Nah. Wasn't the greatest time of my life." Matt appeared to want to say more, but a glance at Nila seemed to change his approach. "At the time, I was convinced I was doing what I had to do, but I've found a much better way."

"Ah-ha!" Nason lifted the book he'd been searching for over his head.

Philip nodded absently for Matt. A better way? The phrase implied choices, and Philip didn't have that luxury.

Matt watched Nason trot back over. "Seeing this place where I was so lost … Looks a lot different now. That's all."

"Then enjoy your stay. I've got to get these two lunch before there's a meltdown." He herded them out the back and away from scrutiny.

BINGO. Michaela located Philip's SUV in front of a burger place on Lakeshore's Main Street, and the success lifted her low mood. She'd had Thursday afternoon and Friday to herself to acclimate to the news of Riley's diagnosis, but she still felt tremulous enough to burst into tears at the slightest provocation.

In this state, approaching Philip uninvited carried risk. They had hurt each other, but they'd also connected a few times. Since the call on Thursday, she longed to leave those petty disputes behind. She wanted real comfort. Perhaps Philip would pick up on the change, realize she'd gotten bad news about Riley, and rise to the occasion as she knew he could. If anyone could help her navigate this tangle of emotions, Philip could. He'd been down this path himself.

Inside, the little family stood at the counter. Nila struggled to decide between chicken tenders and a burger.

Deep in negotiations with her, Philip rested his hand between her shoulder blades. "How about you get chicken tenders? You can share one with your brother and try some of his burger."

"I don't want to share." Nason had both hands on the counter.

"Fine." Philip's tone said his patience wouldn't last much longer. "Then you and I can share, Nila. Order the tenders, and you can have as much of my burger as you want."

"But you like the burger with all the stuff on it."

"I'll take it off your part."

"But it'll still smell."

Michaela bit her lips together, restraining a grin.

"Fine." The word was even less true now. Philip worked his fist behind Nila, where neither child could see. His head angled toward the cashier. "Add a three-piece chicken tenders, a plain cheeseburger, and a barbecue cheeseburger."

Nason's head swiveled. "She gets *two*?"

Michaela couldn't keep silent any longer. "Bet you're wishing you'd gone with Gannon and John."

Philip turned, weariness heavy on his features.

"Michaela!" Nila clasped her hands as if she were about to recite a poem. "You're going to eat with us?"

"Sure, honey, as long as your dad doesn't mind."

Philip turned back to pay. "What I'm wishing is I hadn't given the nanny the morning off."

Michaela ordered a wrap, then took her water and number to the booth. Philip sat next to Nason, and Nila squirmed into the corner on her side, leaving Michaela plenty of room. The children spent the wait for the food telling her about their new live-in nanny, Ruthann, who wore dresses and took them to a museum and with whom Nason had "discovered" a shipwreck.

"A shipwreck?" She looked to Philip.

"There are a couple old beams washed up on shore." He leaned out of the way as the cashier delivered the food.

Philip divided Nila's two meals, leaving half of each on the tray. Nason eyed the leftovers hungrily as he started on his burger and fries, but for the moment, the kids were quiet.

"So why didn't you go with Gannon and John?"

"I've never been all that interested in hiking sixteen miles down a river canyon prone to flash flooding."

"Why on earth are they doing that?"

"John's wanted to go for ages. The hike is famous. The Narrows?"

Michaela had to shrug.

"While they're in Utah, they're going off-roading in Moab. That sounded better, but the kids already spend a lot of time with nannies."

"Well, at least this way, someone from Awestruck got to be at the story time."

He stuffed a bite of burger in his mouth instead of replying. So he wasn't thrilled about how the morning had gone. About hanging out near her? Or because of the unwelcome guest Tim had brought? A plop of barbecue sauce fell to his fries. Nila scrunched her nose, but it was Philip's annoyance that worried Michaela.

"I'm sorry Matt came. I didn't realize Tim would bring him."

"Tim tells you everything now?" He popped some fries in his mouth as if he hadn't just lobbed an accusatory question at her. He must not have noticed how she'd backed off.

"I've hardly talked to him, except at breakfast Monday." She willed him to take heed of her tone, realize how she was struggling.

"He sent your song to Evie."

"I haven't heard anything since. Maybe she didn't like it."

"It's been two days." Dismissive. Again.

She risked being more forthcoming about her mood. "Unbelievably long and discouraging ones."

"Tell me about it." Philip turned his attention to Nason, whose straw had stopped working.

Had something happened to him too?

That could help excuse his failure to guess she wasn't just

talking about a song. She could code the news about Riley to avoid upsetting the kids. Could she say "biopsy" or would children whose mother had been taken from them by cancer know the word?

"The straw's broken, bud. You can't bend the ones that aren't made for it." Philip removed the lid and set it on a napkin. "Be careful, okay?"

Nason nodded at the open-topped cup with the kind of eagerness she'd felt when she'd first been handed the keys to a car. Nila quietly picked the breading off her chicken tenders.

"If you don't like them, Nila, just eat the burger."

"I like them. Just not the outside."

Philip blinked slowly as though what he really wanted to do was roll his eyes, then returned to his own meal.

He treated her as he did the children. Offering a little guidance—be careful with the milk, don't eat what you don't like, don't be dramatic about Evie—and then leaving them each to carry on alone.

I can't continue on my own. When she sang that line in the collaboration on Thursday, the truth of the words had brought her to tears. People weren't supposed to be alone. People needed love. If only true connection and dedication weren't so rare.

And then Riley's situation ... Her sister might die, and then what? Were people right about heaven being a big reunion with lost friends and family? She'd loved her grandparents, but she'd go nuts if she had only their company for decades until her friends died. And goodness, what an awful thing to wait for.

Plus, that theory about the afterlife might not even be true. What if Michaela found herself on the other side just as alone —or maybe more—than she was here?

Something cold and wet touched her finger, and she snapped back to lunch with Philip and his kids.

Nason retracted his hand from the tray at the center of the

table, a chicken tender in his grasp, his eyes wide. The milk he must've tipped soaked into the paper beneath Michaela's wrap.

She plucked up the wrap and plopped a napkin on the liquid.

Though the puddle spread nowhere close to Nila, the girl lifted the paper beneath her food. Everything tumbled off, fries and tenders scattering over the table, the half burger bouncing to the seat. The meat patty separated from the bun and landed cheese- and ketchup-side down on the thigh of Michaela's jeans. Milk dripped next to the puck of beef.

"Nason! What did I tell you?" Philip rose to have better command of the table and began mopping up.

"Sorry." The kid set the tender next to what remained of his own burger, then eyed his prize as though he might not be sorry enough to resist eating it.

"Nila, put your paper down and pick up your food."

"But it's dirty now."

Philip's mouth went so tight, his eyes so hard, that he couldn't have been more than one protest away from completely losing his temper. "Good thing you had to have two meals so we have a spare."

The recrimination in his voice hit Nila hard. Her little fingers closed around the locket she wore every day as her chin pinched up and her eyes welled.

Michaela wiped her own eyes of the tears that had collected as she'd considered eternity. Hopefully, in the commotion no one would notice. She squeezed Nila's shoulder. "It's spilled milk. You know what they say about that." She collected the fallen food from her lap, the bench, and the table.

Nila shook her head.

Michaela folded all the spilled food into Nila's wrapper to discard later. She collected the other half of the burger from the tray and set it in front of the girl. "You're not supposed to cry when milk spills. It's a rule."

Instead of taking comfort as Michaela had intended, Nila pointed at her. "But you're crying."

"No, I'm not. See?" She flashed the pearly whites she paid so much to maintain and kept her focus on the girl, pretending she didn't care whether Philip had seen her tears.

Nila turned miserably to her food, and Michaela busied herself in trying to get the ketchup off her jeans.

"They got you, huh? Sorry about that." Philip's apology rang with far more sincerity than his son's, and far calmer than he'd sounded a few moments before. Maybe he *had* seen the tears.

He would ask about her sister.

He'd wrap her up in a hug and tell her she wasn't alone. He'd impart the secret of how to be at peace when death came close.

However, when she finished getting what she could of the red stain off her jeans, she found Philip working on his burger. The kids, as much as she enjoyed them, were a big distraction. Between their bargaining for the meals they wanted, the broken straw, and the spilled milk, perhaps she couldn't blame Philip for not guessing the biopsy results.

But for not *asking* about them?

That she could blame him for.

If he knew the secret to finding peace, she'd have to pry it from him, and she was no longer sure whatever comfort he could offer would be worth the effort.

15

---

*P*hilip stood in his bathroom and stared at his two remaining pills.

He'd held out as long as he could, even though withdrawal had kept him up half the night. Now, Sunday morning, if he didn't take something, he couldn't cope with the kids. Already, they thundered around the house. The nannies didn't work Sundays, so caring for the children fell to him.

He took one from his shaking hand, enough—he hoped—to get through church. Despite his failings, at least he could keep his promise to take the kids to learn about God.

If he had to quit entirely—and it appeared he did—he'd miss days of work. Maybe a week. He should've started the process on Thursday, so Gannon and John would've missed part of it.

Especially since Matt was suspicious.

What if everyone found out?

He couldn't be fired. Not just before the contract.

He forced himself into motion.

He fed and packed up the kids, trucked them to church, sang the songs, and delivered them to the children's teacher.

When he returned to the sanctuary, the prayer had ended, and the sermon was getting started.

Michaela's presence beside him had made this easier to sit through. Despite all that was wrong between them—his lies, her games, that misunderstanding about calling the relationship meaningless—he missed her. He should've been kinder when he'd shut her down on the romance front, should've tried apologizing again later instead of pretending the whole thing had never happened.

The pastor pulled him from his reverie with a verse about temptation. Everyone faced it, and God always gave a way to resist.

Supposedly.

If Philip's pathetic attempts at quitting lately were any indication, the next few days would be worse than anything he'd endured since losing Clare and, before that, his spine surgery.

Would God really give him a way to get through this without losing everything?

No. The God who hadn't saved Clare wouldn't save him. Philip would have to find his own way through this one.

But by two o'clock that afternoon, shaky, nauseous, and irritable, he recognized the only way forward was backward. Back to the pills, and if he waited any longer, he'd be too sick to do what needed to be done. He had to take care of this. Now.

MICHAELA ATTENDED GANNON'S CHURCH, though he wasn't there, to try to comfort herself over her concerns about death. Instead of feeling better, though, her doubts gnawed harder than ever.

Back at the condo she'd rented for the summer, she spent the afternoon on social media and songwriting, then planted herself on the couch and put in a movie starring her favorite actor. Thirty seconds in, she realized his strong jaw and warm eyes reminded her of Philip.

She switched the movie out for one based on a classic novel set in England. The hero's jaw was on the weak side, his forehead a mite too tall. She pulled a blanket over her jeans and sweatshirt and snuggled in.

Then, her phone rang.

Philip. Had he picked up on more than she'd thought the day before? And perhaps with the kids, he hadn't been able to reach out sooner?

"Hello?"

"Hey. Are you free?"

A bubble of hope formed in her chest. "Sure. What's up?"

"I need someone to watch the kids for about two hours."

"Oh." The hope burst, but the urgency in his voice softened the disappointment. Something had happened, and he'd called her for help. That was something. And hanging out with the kids might help her stop wallowing. "What's wrong?"

"I was working in the yard and cut my arm pretty good. I'm about to drive through Lakeshore on my way for stitches. Can I drop the kids with you?"

"Are you okay? Can you drive?"

"Yes. I'm almost to Lakeshore. How do I get to your place?"

She gave him the address. "Are you sure about this?" She might enjoy Nila and Nason, but she had no babysitting experience. "I could drive you and sit with the kids in the waiting room."

"I can drive, and the kids don't like errands like these since … everything." He had to mean everything with Clare. He must've chosen vague wording because of the little ears nearby. "They'll be much happier at a house."

"I don't have much around to entertain them."

"They packed some toys and games. See you in a couple of minutes."

He disconnected, and less than five minutes later, the kids waited on her step, each wearing a backpack. Philip watched from the SUV. As soon as she looked his way, he waved and backed out.

She pushed open the glass storm door. "Come on in."

SUCCESS HAD NEVER FELT SO hollow. Philip had driven an hour and a half to score. The kid he'd bought from had recognized him. The attendant of the gas station where they'd met had stared through the window while speaking into the phone.

Calling in a suspicious meeting?

Would such a run-down business have cameras to capture his license plate? Or would law enforcement get his name from the dealer?

And all for a supply that would last a couple of days.

Philip checked his mirrors for the millionth time, then turned into Michaela's driveway.

He smoothed the bandage covering his fictional injury, then rang Michaela's doorbell. By the time he got the kids home for supper, it'd be closing in on seven.

The door swung open, and Michaela's hair mirrored the movement, swinging over her shoulder. "All stitched up?" Her green eyes swept over his arms, lingering on his right shoulder, where the bandage raised the fabric of his T-shirt sleeve.

"Remind me to hire a landscaper next time."

"You do seem a little too accident prone for your own good. First getting hurt wrestling with Nason, now this."

She kept better track of his lies than he did.

He scratched his cheek. "You survived unscathed?"

"Yep. They drew me a couple of pictures, we went for a walk, did some more art"—Michaela motioned to the sidewalk, marked with pastel shapes that meant Nila had packed her chalk—"and now they're watching shows."

He followed her inside. Neutrals washed every surface with so much less personality than the woman who stayed here. He spotted Nason's cowlick and Nila's curls over the back of the couch as he approached. Nason wore headphones, while quiet music played from Michaela's laptop on Nila's lap.

"You guys hungry?"

"We ate." Nason leaned closer to his screen.

Philip lifted his eyebrows at Michaela, wondering what she'd fed them.

Nila supplied the information. "Eggs and carrots and apples. And orange chips."

Humor lit Michaela's eyes. "I had ingredients for a fantastic salad, but there were no takers, so we improvised. They polished off the bag of sweet potato chips. You do feed these two at home, don't you?"

"Most days." He asked the kids to pack up, then turned his attention back to Michaela. "Thank you for helping. I'd say I owe you lunch."

"Maybe two. After all ..." She pointed first to one child, then the other, looking pleased. This place may not be her home, but she seemed relaxed here. Even her clothes followed suit, flattering her shape without flaunting skin.

"Maybe two," he conceded. "Thank you."

He checked and found Nason slipping his tablet into his backpack. Nila remained curled up on the couch, engrossed in a show.

"Time to turn it off."

Nila promised to, and Michaela spoke again. "I thought you had that new nanny. Doesn't she live at the house?"

"Sunday and Monday are her days off. I didn't want to encroach on her personal time so soon." Especially not after

Nancy had warned him that drug use was a deal breaker. He needed to keep Ruthann as far from his habit as possible.

Nila hadn't turned off the laptop, and he caught a glimpse of the screen, but he couldn't have seen correctly. None of her shows featured that much nudity. "What are you watching?"

He stepped over to verify for himself. At another flash of skin, he plucked the laptop from her by the top of the screen.

"She wanted to hear some of my music, so I played her my *Audition Room* finale." Michaela's eyes shifted from Philip to Nila and back again. "I hope that was okay."

Philip would have no problem with the primetime television show, but that's not what danced on the screen. Still gripping the top of the display, he turned the device so Michaela could see her own music video. This must've been the one to earn a vulgar response. And no wonder. No eight-year-old should ever see this.

She went still and so pale her green eyes seemed to glow. "That isn't ... I played her *Audition Room*. She must've clicked another video when I answered the door."

"She's eight."

"I know. I didn't ... I—"

"Are you this desperate for attention?" He pushed the screen forward again, the hinge opening so the keyboard hung straight down from the display.

She grasped the laptop, folded it shut. "I didn't play it for her. I'm sorry. I never meant—"

He held up a silencing hand. They wouldn't do this in front of the kids.

Already, they stared at him, Nason clutching his bag, Nila with tears as thick as Michaela's. "I'm sorry, Daddy."

"It isn't your fault. You have your things?"

Nila peered over her shoulder to her backpack, which leaned against the coffee table. Philip circled the couch, swiped up the bag, zipped it, and motioned the kids to precede him to the car. He saw them in and shut the door.

Michaela stood on the front walk, shoulders hunched, elbows tight to her sides as she fidgeted. She knew she'd upset him, but he couldn't let her write this off as one troublesome video. The issue was so much more pervasive.

He stepped away from the vehicle and fought to keep his voice low enough to prevent the kids from hearing. "The sick thing is, you did mean for this to happen. You didn't make the video by accident. You didn't come on to me by accident. You didn't flirt with Tim by accident. You mean to live like this, while a million little girls are looking up to you. I hope you're proud, because who you are is no secret to any of us."

Michaela's top lip trembled, and her eyes collected enough tears to fill a birdbath.

He got behind the wheel before they fell.

As he navigated down the road, regret tapped his shoulder.

He'd been too hard on her. He was no role model either. But then, he went to great lengths to keep anyone from learning that, while Michaela published evidence on the Internet.

Now he had to debrief Nila. He couldn't let her turn into a Michaela, willing to leverage her body to get ahead, but what could he say about what she'd seen?

Even the pills wouldn't solve this problem.

MICHAELA HADN'T BROUGHT MUCH to Wisconsin, so packing didn't take long. One trip saw her carry-on, purse, and small duffle to the car, and then she wheeled her large suitcase to the door. There, she paused.

She'd go to Dad's first and stay there until after Riley's surgery.

After that, she didn't know.

Gannon and John would be home tomorrow, expecting her in the studio in the afternoon. Except, they'd said they didn't care if the collaboration happened. She'd alert them to her change in plans, and they'd all go on with their lives.

The car waited to take her away. Away from Tim and Tim's connection with Evie. Away from Gannon and the collaboration. Away from all her plans to resurrect her career.

She couldn't stay, though, no matter the cost. She couldn't face Philip or those poor kids. She couldn't face Tim or Gannon or John. Not knowing they all thought her a desperate attention-seeker who would corrupt an eight-year-old.

She'd never meant for Nila to see her music video. Never. Never in a million years.

How many kids had seen it? No wonder the parents of her youngest fans had thrown a fit. With Nila's teary face haunting her, she longed to undo it all. All the way back to before she'd won her first talent show, because every step had led her here.

She hated herself.

Hated how badly she wanted to be loved. Hated how little she deserved it. Hated how she looked, how she dressed, how she acted.

She had no excuses and no do-overs.

But she could step away from Awestruck and all the ways she'd humiliated herself here.

She tugged her suitcase from the house and put her phone to her ear to leave Gannon another voicemail.

"Are you mad at me?" Nila saved eye contact until after she'd launched her question from where she lay in bed, snuggly tucked in to sleep.

Seated on the edge of the mattress, Philip smoothed his hand over his beard, wishing he believed in a God who answered prayers for help. "No, sweetheart. But Michaela wasn't acting right in that video. She should've worn more clothes. I'm sorry you saw that."

Nila's fingers traced a ruffle in her bedspread. "If it's bad, why did she do it?"

"People do bad things sometimes."

"Will she go to jail?"

"No, but I shouldn't have left you with her. I'm sorry."

Nila shrugged and ran her hand up his arm, gently touching the edge of his bandage. His stupid, fake bandage. "Does it hurt?"

"Yes." Figuratively. He'd failed his kids today, and if he continued as a slave to these pills, he'd fail again and again. That hurt more than he could say.

When his daughter asked him to sing "Amazing Grace," he complied. He finished, stood, then noticed her big brown eyes peering up at him.

"Michaela has a pretty voice. I like her singing."

She did have a good voice—smooth, soaring, and strong—a perfect complement to Gannon. But beyond the collaboration, Philip would cut ties with her. He was too likely to mess up his kids himself. He didn't need to worry about someone else chipping in with additional damage.

"Is she a wretch?"

"What?"

"Mrs. Brennan says a wretch is a person who does bad things."

Mrs. Brennan had to be Nila's teacher at church. Despite his anger, he didn't want to call Michaela a bad person, but could he call her good? As if he had a right to make judgment calls about anyone. "I don't know, sweetheart."

"It's okay if she is, because God has grace, and He gives it to people who do stuff they shouldn't. That's what the song means."

"He doesn't give grace to everyone."

"Anyone who asks. That's what Mrs. Brennan says. Actually, Michaela *must* be a wretch, because Mrs. Brennan says we all are. Because we disobey God, we're supposed to go to hell when we die, but God has a-*maz*-ing grace." She accented with jazz hands. "He saves us if we ask Him to. That means, we go to heaven. He can save Michaela too."

All these years of singing the song to her, he'd never realized how closely she'd been paying attention. Had never predicted she would've sought out an explanation for the lyrics. "Did you ask God to save you?"

"Yes. Mom's in heaven, so I want to be too." She sat halfway up, eyes suddenly round. "You'll be there, right?"

Once upon a time, he'd thought so, but he'd seen too many unanswered prayers since to believe God bothered to change anyone's fate just because they asked Him to.

"Right, Dad?"

He couldn't steal her peace by sharing his disbelief. He'd taken her to church because Clare had thought faith important, and she'd be thrilled with Nila's half of this conversation. He had to answer, and this once, a lie wouldn't do. "I asked Him a long time ago."

It wasn't his fault God hadn't answered.

"Good." She laid her head back down, delicate locks curling against her pillow. "I love you."

"I love you too." That was the whole truth. He loved her and he loved Nason. If only the truth were enough to heal all the pain and secure a better future.

16

Michaela watched her father eat the eggs she'd poached for him. He'd undone the health benefits of cooking the eggs in water instead of fat by slathering half a stick of butter on his white bread toast. Good thing her main concern hadn't been to serve a healthy meal, but rather to initiate a healthy relationship.

Healthier, anyway.

As a child, she had hoped to make him proud early on with art or the feats of her day, but he'd never hung one of her pictures on the refrigerator or reacted to her tall tales—except when he told her to stop being so dramatic.

By the time she'd been old enough to do something nice like prepare his breakfast before he went into work, she'd given up.

But for as long as she was in town, she might as well make an effort. Too many people thought too little of her as it was.

His surprised thanks when he'd come down this morning to find a steaming breakfast ready had seemed a promising start, but then he'd fallen into silence as he ate.

Dad never had been much of a talker. Especially not with Michaela.

She took a bite of the whole wheat English muffin she'd gotten from the gas station two blocks down to accompany her own egg. "So, for dinner, I was thinking I'd make enchiladas."

Dad's eyebrows lifted, and he washed down a bite with milk. "Enchiladas?"

"Yeah. Sound good?"

He wiped his mouth with a napkin, eyeing her like he wondered what she'd done with his younger daughter.

She continued eating, waiting for him to process.

"Invite your sister," he said finally. "It'd be good to see she's looking after herself. Eating and all that. Run the menu by her, though, since there's no point in feeding her something she won't eat."

His immediate instinct to involve Riley didn't sit right, and the egg and muffin in her mouth turned tasteless. Riley had apologized for saying Michaela was like their mother, but that comment had come from somewhere. Some long-held resentment. Maybe a small part of Michaela had hoped that if Dad harbored a similar belief, this visit and her offers to cook and connect would counteract it.

Focusing on Riley *did* make sense. Riley was the one experiencing the hardship.

But Dad going straight to Riley without so much as a word of appreciation for Michaela seemed to suggest that whether Michaela was like Mom or not, whether Michaela was trying or not, Riley remained his priority and nothing between him and Michaela would ever change.

She chided herself for jumping so quickly to that conclusion. If she wanted to be unlike Mom, cooking for the whole group was the best way to differentiate herself.

She forced the food down her throat and lifted a smile. "A family dinner is a nice idea. I'll see if it works for her."

As he left for work, Michaela texted her sister. Waiting for a response, she cleaned the old vinyl kitchen floor and vacuumed the faded carpet in the dining room.

Still no response from her sister.

The speckled counters appeared to need a quick wipe-down, but the task grew more involved when she found an accumulation of grease and dust ringing the utensil jar, spice rack, and countertop appliances, which apparently hadn't been moved in years.

She took her rag to the painted faces of the cabinets, spending extra time on the grime that had built up in the cracks between the metal and the ceramic in the door pulls.

Hopefully Dad would appreciate all this.

Compared to her tiny LA apartment, the house was huge. And grimier than she'd remembered, even after all the tasks she checked off.

She ran out of steam, but still no word from Riley. Why had she thought she could pull her family together?

But then, miraculously, her sister messaged, asking if the next evening would work instead.

Michaela agreed and hopped online to find a recipe. If she wanted her family to appreciate her efforts, it'd have to be a good one.

"HEY, GUYS."

Philip turned a little too quickly toward the female voice. Michaela ought to arrive at the studio any time now, but instead, Adeline stepped in, followed by a curly-haired blonde.

Adeline motioned to her guest. "I'm giving Lina the grand tour. It's her first official day with Key of Hope."

Good thing she'd said her name. The last time Philip had seen

Lina, who also served as Awestruck's social media manager, she'd worn her hair straight. The different style transformed her to the degree that he might not have placed her without the prompt.

Gannon lifted a hand in greeting. "How're you liking Lakeshore?"

"It's peaceful." Lina's smile faded quickly. "Just what I was looking for at just the right time."

Sounded to Philip as if there was a story there, but rather than give space for her to tell it, Adeline asked Gannon where she could find some paperwork. Then, the women left again.

Still, no sign of Michaela.

Philip decided against asking where she was. They hadn't gotten much done in the morning as Gannon recounted how John had earned the gash on his knee, their drive through Moab's famous bathtubs, and the impromptu show they'd put on at some bar and grill in some dusty town when the band on stage had recognized them.

Now, John asked how the weekend had gone for Philip.

"The reading was a hit."

"It looked like it in the pictures the paper ran."

Before Philip had to expound, Tim appeared in the doorway and glanced around. He wouldn't seek out any of them so eagerly, but Michaela had him wrapped around her little finger.

Gannon crossed his arms and turned to Tim. "I noticed Matt in some of the shots."

"Oh, yeah. About that." Tim's focus settled on Philip like a punch to the gut. Had Matt told Tim his suspicions? "House's hand got crushed this weekend. He can't help with the show next month."

Philip drew air, recovering. At least this wasn't about Kory. Not that he wished harm to Eric Rittenhouse—House—who was Philip's righthand man on stage. Philip's gear wasn't as complicated as Gannon's, but if something went wrong mid-show, he depended on having a knowledgeable tech to fix it.

"Is he going to be all right?" Gannon asked.

If Philip had it together, he would've been the one to ask that.

"In a couple of months. In the meantime ..." Tim frowned at Philip.

He realized Tim's plan. "You want Matt to be my tech for this next show."

"There are worse choices with just a couple of weeks' notice. He knows Awestruck's old stuff, has familiarized himself with the new, is already nearby, and"—Tim flipped his line of sight to the other two—"tell me you wouldn't enjoy knocking him down a few notches."

Gannon answered with a smug smile. "I did that when I fired him."

"Not a priority for me," John said.

Tim pivoted from the Gannon-and-John tag team. "Miller? You're the one he'd be working for."

"Who's that kid who shadowed Charlie all last year?"

Charlie, Gannon's guitar tech, had been showing a younger guy the ropes, and apparently Gannon had met him because he supplied the name. "Riff. I agree. Move him up. He's trained for it."

"Why do you want us to work with Matt?" John's quiet question turned everyone's focus to Tim.

Tim's eyes widened for a fraction of a second, as if he were caught off guard.

Odd.

"It's not about what I want." Tim gained confidence as he continued. "The label is coming up for the show, hopefully with contract in hand. This isn't the time to break in new talent like Riff. It's too important."

"Matt's not a seasoned tech either," Gannon said.

"He knows exactly what Philip will need and when. Leaving him to make a living off landscaping with his family is a waste. He's talented and sober enough to act like it. He moved home to Fox Valley to get away from the bad influences he knows in LA. The old Matt never would've read to kids or declined a chance to get his picture in the paper, and he's no stranger to the equipment, the songs, or the pressure."

"If he moved to get away from bad influences, putting him in the middle of all the influences that come up for the show won't do him favors." Gannon motioned to himself, John, and Philip. "The three of us are clean, but a lot of the people around us aren't."

Gannon trusted him.

Also, the guy made a good point. Scoring at the show would be much easier.

"Right. You're unicorns. We're all very impressed." Tim brushed his hands together. "Have it your way. We'll promote Riff. Where's Michaela? I've got news for her."

"She's in Illinois with her sister."

Philip's brain slammed the brakes. She'd left? The entire state? And her sister. Of course. She'd been waiting on news. How had he forgotten?

Tim hadn't heard about the cancer scare, so Gannon filled him in, ending on the punch line. "Riley called Michaela Thursday. It's official. Cancer."

He'd seen her tears on Thursday and had written them off as an act because she seemed so chipper the rest of the day, but he'd misjudged her. Misjudged her completely. If she had been hiding that big of a disappointment since Thursday, she must be a master at sweeping pain under the rug. He remembered the sadness that had briefly shadowed her expression all the way back in the pizza restaurant, as she'd talked about faith, family, and her career. And yet the thing he'd judged her by that night was the way she'd hit on him.

Maybe sadness didn't excuse her behavior, but it did explain it. Was he just as guilty of acting poorly as he grappled with his own issues?

He'd been distant with Michaela at the bookstore, distracted at lunch, and vicious on Sunday. His regret over his outburst multiplied. "She didn't say anything."

But he should've seen she wasn't herself.

Gannon shifted his shoulder. "She left a voicemail Sunday night. Said she'd kept it to herself because she didn't want to give bad news right before our trip."

News about Michaela's sister wouldn't have ruined anything for Gannon and John. She must've kept quiet for other reasons. If she'd left that voicemail Sunday night, she'd done so not long after he'd stormed out of there.

He should've seen she was hurting. He should've treated her differently.

"You all right, Miller?"

He wasn't, and he couldn't pull himself out of the tailspin. He'd been a wreck over Clare's diagnosis. If someone —especially someone as unworthy as himself—had faulted him so severely for an accident like a child clicking a video in an unattended moment, he would've dished it right back.

Michaela had endured his outburst and left.

"Michaela and I ..." He swallowed. How much could he say without inviting questions about his fictional ER visit? "I saw her yesterday. I didn't know. We argued. Around six."

Gannon cringed. "She called around seven. We were flying back. I got the message when we landed."

Tim whistled.

Philip rubbed the center of his chest, but his discomfort burrowed deeper than he could reach. He'd been so focused on feeding his habit, he'd gone blind and deaf. He'd hurt Michaela, he'd put Nila in the middle ... And he'd refused to give Matt a chance at a job he could excel at. He was lying to everyone, inconveniencing people.

And he'd been illegally buying pills for months.

I'm an addict, making amends.

Matt had said the words so easily, but he'd turned his life upside down to have the privilege. Philip couldn't afford to lose so much. He either needed to quit or to find a better way to get the pills before he lost something he couldn't recover.

He cleared his throat. "When's she coming back?"

"She talked like she might not, but I told her to take as long as she needed, that the song would keep until she sees how things go with her sister. We have time before it's due."

"What'd she say?" Philip asked.

"Nothing. I left a voicemail." Gannon's brow furrowed. "If I'd known I was up against more than a cancer diagnosis, I might've tried a different tack."

"If she fled the state over a fight between you two, then you were more than friends." This accusation came from Tim.

"She was interested." Philip rubbed his forehead, embarrassed by the half-truth. Surely the guys could see the rest of the story, that he'd been interested too. If not for that, he would've had a much easier time keeping his head around her.

"You turned down Michaela Vandehey?" Tim's incredulous question gave him the chance to explain.

"I'm a single dad with young kids. I have to make decisions with my brain."

"As opposed to how I make them?" Tim crossed his arms as though his shock a moment before hadn't been entirely based on Michaela's looks.

Philip ignored him. "If I'd known about the diagnosis, I would've been more careful. I can apologize, but I doubt that'll be good enough."

"I want her in the soundtrack song." Gannon also crossed his arms.

Tim scowled. "And I'm going to tell Evie to forget it unless Michaela follows through on this collaboration. I'm not sticking my neck out for someone who quits, even if the fault lies with one of my supposedly *evolved* rock stars."

"Evie agreed to produce the song?"

"I came here to tell Michaela."

Working with Evie meant so much to her. An idea clicked into place. He could give Michaela an apology she couldn't ignore and solve his pill problem in one bold move, but acting on this would mean letting the others make assumptions about the level of his relationship with her.

A small price to pay to fix his life and keep Michaela's on the track she'd so desperately pursued.

"If you can spare me for a day or two, I can convince her to come back." He hoped.

"We've got a show coming up." Tim splayed his hands as if Philip had lost it. "We have a lot of work to do. You're doing new songs, and since you insist, Riff needs to be broken in."

"The sooner I leave, the sooner I'll be back."

Gannon and John exchanged a look before Gannon nodded his blessing.

Ignoring Tim's latest round of objections, Philip waited for John to signal agreement. The drummer saluted him with his sticks.

17

$\mathcal{M}$ichaela's childhood waited in a stack of boxes in her dad's attic.

On better days, she liked to think that if her life had a theme, it was that with enough determination, she could beat any odds. By looking back at times when that had proved true, she hoped to remind herself how she'd gotten this far.

She needed the dose of positivity because these days, her life theme seemed to revolve instead around the unavoidability of loneliness and rejection. That was all fine and good if she was ready to curl up into a ball and do nothing with the rest of her life, but since she had to prepare for that evening's family meal and couldn't leave her career on hold indefinitely, she needed to find hope somewhere.

Her old journals might contain the inspiration she needed.

After Dad left for work on Tuesday morning, she lugged a ladder from the basement. Perched on that, she accessed the pull-down stairs to the attic. The air in the unfinished space was thick and untouched by the air conditioning that kept the rest of the house cool. By the time she reached the boxes, she was panting. Dust from the cardboard stuck to the sheen on her arms as she lifted the flaps of the first box.

Teenage Michaela had been an avid journaler. A leather-like cover with a white marble print stood out among the collection. The first entry inside documented the first day of summer break following her junior year. She'd scribbled the last entry five years before, after graduating and just before she sealed up the box and toted it to the attic.

Five years to make her life—and break it.

She flipped open the journal.

Bible camp with Heather had been between junior and senior years. One long passage from that week signaled something monumental had happened. She paged back to the start of the day's notes.

Oh. She'd forgotten.

At camp, after she'd prayed to become a Christian, she'd doubted her eligibility. Even at seventeen, she had a history. After chapel, she told Heather the story of losing her virginity to a nineteen-year-old. She hadn't liked the boy—not as more than a friend, but he'd taken her to a party in the country. She'd walked with him into the fields because he'd said he needed her advice on a girl he liked.

When she learned the girl was her, and especially when it turned out "liked" meant "wanted," she felt stupid for not realizing his intentions sooner.

As she reread the retelling of the night, indignation welled. He'd fanned the flames of her insecurities, accused her of leading him on, said everyone else questioned why he'd brought a high schooler to a college party. He claimed he'd told them she was special.

She'd been too embarrassed to slip away from him and admit to the others that they'd been right, that she didn't belong, and would someone please take her home? One embarrassment had guilted her into another and another.

That night, she'd had a choice: set her social life ablaze or comply. She'd complied. Years later, when the creative director had proposed the idea for the music video, she'd also had a choice: rock the hole-ridden boat of her career in the name of modesty, or comply.

In both cases, she'd prioritized acceptance over her conscience, her needs, and her self-respect.

She kept ending up alone, no matter how much she sacrificed.

When she spilled the story of her spoiled virginity to Heather, her friend had said something comforting, something more than simply pointing out that she'd been a minor and he hadn't been. Something more helpful than shaming Michaela for the choices she'd never stopped regretting.

Michaela ran her finger over the indents her pen had made in the paper as she recorded the words.

"Your mistakes don't define you. Jesus says you're forgiven and new, so you are."

Your mistakes don't define you.

Maybe that had been true when her mistakes had been small-scale, but now that they were available for all to see, scarring eight-year-olds, her faults were harder to minimize with a mantra.

She swiped forward in the journal. The pages opened to the program for the talent show she'd won senior year.

She'd been in choir class for years, but the contest had been her first chance to command an entire stage. She'd chosen her own song, her own outfit, her own choreography.

Everything that hadn't clicked—her math grades, her family, college applications and scholarships, the revolving door of boys and friends—all her problems fell away, and for those three minutes, life had been as it should be.

Applause and cheers rose just a few notes in. A local TV station had televised the event, and a news station all the way in

Chicago had replayed a clip of her. Afterwards, her classmates had asked for autographs. Her crush had invited her to hang out.

She'd thought some label would swoop in and save her from her going-nowhere life.

She'd been wrong.

Her first record deal came with her *Audition Room* win two years later, but if not for that talent show, she never would've auditioned and become the darling of Season Eight. She wouldn't have known she had the fire in her. She wouldn't have tasted that first, addicting high. She read what she'd written back then.

I was one hundred percent myself tonight, and everyone saw me, and they all loved what they saw. Miss Klein says I have what it takes. I finally know what I want to do with my life, and I don't even care Dad didn't see me because he was off dealing with another Riley disaster.

Combined, the entries retelling the story of her lost virginity and of the talent show reflected the high and low of her teenage years.

Instead of seeing a lesson to help her move forward, she saw that she'd faced the same problem this whole time. No one really loved her. Mom had left. Dad and Riley humored her—at best. Men had been using and discarding her since junior year of high school, and whatever power she thought she had now was an illusion. Her failing music career proved fans would dump her, too, even if she gave her all.

She was a passing fantasy.

She nestled the journal back in the box, closed the flaps, and climbed down from the attic. If curling up into a ball were a viable option, she'd do it. But she'd promised her family a dinner, and if she failed to follow through, the broken promise would only ostracize her further.

~

BY TONIGHT, Philip would have far less to worry about. No more trouble getting pills, no more guilt over how he'd treated Michaela. He actually looked forward to seeing her, despite the hole he knew he needed to dig himself out of. Given his experience with cancer, he could be useful to her, and after so many mistakes, useful would be an improvement.

The doorbell rang as he tossed one last pair of socks into his overnight bag. He planned to drive himself to the airport and didn't expect anyone that morning, but the sound prompted him to get going. He zipped the bag and carried it to the kitchen, where Nila and Nason clamped onto him. "I'll be back tomorrow."

"Do you promise?"

As he confirmed for Nila, Ruthann entered from the front. "There's a Matt here to see you."

As if the kids' unwillingness to let him go hadn't already dampened his mood, the name doused the rest of his optimism for a smooth departure. "Visser?"

Ruthann lifted helpless shoulders. "He said Matt as if you would know. Want me to ask?"

"No." Philip worked around Nason to slip his phone from his pocket and checked the security app. Sure enough, the camera showed Awestruck's former bassist on his doorstep.

This had to be related to Kory, but if he expected Philip to confess anything, he was in for a disappointment. Maybe Matt saw that coming. Maybe that was why he couldn't seem to stand still on the step.

Philip promised to say hello to Michaela for the kids, said goodbye to them, and checked for the tenth time that Ruthann didn't have any questions. As he picked up his bag again, she lured them away with a promise of chocolate chip pancakes.

EMILY CONRAD

His last glance back revealed Nila staring after him, face streaked with tears.

She'd have nightmares tonight, but he had to take this trip. For Michaela, but also because he had a contact in Chicago who could ensure he never ran out of pills again. The cost would be exponentially higher than he'd paid Kory, but he had to function somehow.

First, he just had to make it out of Wisconsin. He pulled open the door and faced Matt.

"Hey, man." Matt didn't step back until Philip crowded him by joining him on the step.

A breeze rippled Philip's T-shirt, and the shadows of fast-moving clouds shifted over the faded remains of the flowers Michaela had admired. "What'd you need?"

"Tim said you guys shot down using me as your tech."

Philip started for his SUV in the drive. "And you're surprised?"

"Not at all, but you should know why I offered in the first place."

"Why's that?"

"Because I know what you're up to, and I wanted a chance to tell you a story."

Away from the house, the wind pushed harder. A cloud blew across the face of the sun. "What I'm up to?"

Matt nodded. "Let's start with the story. It's about a guy who found his best friend dead. Overdose. Wasn't pretty. Scared me straight in a way nothing else could in all the years I used."

The sun returned, but the warmth got lost on the breeze. "Why is that important to me?"

"Because you might think you've got your habit under control, but if you mess around with what Kory sells, it's only a matter of time until you take it too far."

"What are you talking about?"

178

Matt's eyebrows lifted as if to ask if he really wanted to play dumb. "He supplied me the entire time I was in Lakeshore."

Dark panic hit the throttle of Philip's adrenaline. He'd thought facing Matt would diffuse suspicion, but Matt was a lot more certain about what he'd seen than Philip had realized.

Why had Matt come here instead of getting Philip fired?

With the payday from the contract so close, Matt might have realized he could blackmail Philip. But he must know he could get a lot more if he edged out Philip and took over as bassist before Awestruck signed the new deal. That would require more effort, though.

Either way would be a nightmare. Philip needed that money. He needed to know, despite all his failings, he'd provided Nila and Nason with the lifetime of all the security and opportunities money could buy. He couldn't forfeit their futures to Matt.

"I'm not you." He tossed his bag in the back seat and opened the driver's door. "Don't project your issues on me."

"Sure. If I'm wrong about you, then forget it." Matt caught the door before Philip could shut out the conversation. "But if I'm right, think about this. Who'll find you the day you go too far?"

An answer played in Philip's mind, but he shut it down before the thought crystallized. Matt looked almost sorry.

The sympathy didn't make sense.

Still holding the door open, Matt tipped his head. "I'm a grown man who's been through rehab and meetings and therapy, and I'm still not over finding Auggie. It changed my life, and the visual is burned in my brain. It's worth thinking about how your death would change the lives of your kids. Especially if one of them is the one to find—"

"Get off this property." Because if images burned into a mind were a problem, Matt had singed one into Philip. The idea of Nason or Nila finding him scorched so deeply, he'd never eradicate the scar, no matter how hard he tried. "If I or any of my staff see you again, we're calling the cops."

Matt lifted his hands and took a step back. "If you ever decide it's time to change, I'm a friend."

"Get out of here." Philip yanked the door shut and watched Matt retreat to his own car.

Philip wouldn't overdose. He was careful. That was why he wouldn't make the switch from painkillers to heroin, why he was going to all the trouble and expense of sourcing pills from so far away.

He watched in his mirror until Matt pulled away. Only when the man was out of sight did he put the car in gear and start for the airport.

The wind batted the SUV as it cut down the highway.

The night Kory broke the news about the pills, Philip hadn't been careful. Nila had been the first at his door in the morning, unable to enter because he'd woken and locked it. If he'd died in the night, nothing would've stopped her from finding him.

She'd cried so hard when he'd left the house that morning.

That would be nothing compared to what she'd do if she came to him and he wouldn't wake up.

She'd be so scared. So devastated.

One hand white-knuckled the steering wheel while he wiped the streams of tears off his face with the other.

He was being ridiculous. He wasn't Matt. He was careful. He wouldn't overdose.

It would never come to the kids finding him.

Never.

His vehemence didn't quell the little voice inside him that believed otherwise.

18

*W*hile Michaela was at the grocery store, picking up ingredients for enchiladas, her phone rang. Reese. She let it go to voicemail, as she had Gannon's call on Sunday night.

The people who'd been lifelines in the past couldn't help her. She'd have to go back to work eventually to occupy herself. But she was done scrambling to please people in the industry when it cost her self-respect and hadn't earned her the security she'd longed for. If Reese wanted to drop her, so be it. Everyone ditched her sooner or later anyway.

Or ... Okay, she wasn't ready to lose Reese.

She'd better listen to the message.

As she picked out a couple of more tomatoes, her manager's voice played in her ear. "You may be friends with Gannon, but you have your own manager. Tim Bergeron burned a major favor getting you a spot with Evie Decker. You and I had a plan —collaboration first, Evie after—and I don't appreciate you working around me."

Tim had succeeded?

Reese should be happy, not annoyed.

Reese could lecture all she wanted, but light cut through the haze she'd been operating in. Her life might be a mess, but her career would get a healthy boost. What more could she ask for?

Not a friendly evening with her family, that was for sure, because a couple of hours later, when Riley and her family arrived, Riley scowled when her husband greeted Michaela with a hug.

Surely it hadn't been out of line, though, right? Maybe Michaela wouldn't know. After all, she'd offended Philip by how she'd interacted with Tim too. She vowed not to touch Darren again, even if it meant awkward maneuvering.

Still, Riley sat stonily at the table as the meal began. If not for four-year-old Bailey's animated stories about her day, Michaela suspected they'd eat in silence.

Halfway through dinner, the doorbell rang.

Dad made a show of laying aside his napkin and rising to get it. "Who comes around at dinner time?"

Probably someone who knew family meals had never been a revered event in the Vandehey house. But instead of voicing the guess, Michaela shrugged and shook her head.

Dad ambled off.

The interruption distracted Bailey, allowing Darren to turn to Michaela. "What's new with you since last week?"

She debated sharing the developments from the last couple of days—deciding to walk away from the collaboration, landing the spot with Evie. The stories would probably strike Riley as being boastful. In fact, lines had appeared on either side of Riley's mouth, as though she were annoyed Darren had chosen to fill the break in conversation by inviting Michaela to take the floor.

So instead of giving an in-depth answer, Michaela lifted her fork, stretching and snapping a string of cheese. "I learned a new enchilada recipe."

Dad returned alone and harrumphed into his seat. "Michaela, there's a gentleman caller here for you."

"A what?" She set her utensil back down, the food uneaten.

Dad offered no more explanation, so she went to the door.

Philip waited on the stoop. He wore a T-shirt with the logo of another band on the chest. The sleeves didn't hug his shoulders like some of his others, but still, he looked broad and tall and strong standing there, on the doorstep of her childhood home. He had a beard. Had any of the guys she'd dated in high school been capable of growing one?

She tugged her plain white T-shirt and smoothed her hand over the waist of her cut-offs. She'd dressed down today, expecting to see only family, but at least the shorts showed off her legs.

"How did you know where ...?" Her question about how he'd obtained her dad's address petered out. Between the Internet and locals, he'd probably found this place as easily as she'd found his home. Instead, another question took precedence. His eyes had been wounded the first time she'd seen him, but she'd had no idea how much more regret, sadness, and pain they could hold. "Are you okay?"

He focused on her as if preparing to tell her someone had died. "I've got a lot to tell you. But I'm here to apologize."

"For what?" Their relationship had been frustrating, but he had no way to know their argument had broken something in her. Did he?

"I dropped the ball by not realizing what was going on with you. Not asking about your sister. Overreacting on Sunday, when I'm the one who should've been ..." He rubbed his face. "You didn't play the video on purpose, and I shouldn't have lost my temper. Don't quit over what I said."

Ah, Philip had landed himself in trouble with Awestruck. This wasn't genuine remorse, only a play to stay on their good side. "Gannon put you up to this."

"This was my idea. I know how it feels to find out a loved one has cancer."

"You came all this way to see me. Of your own volition." Her voice came out breathless. The man of her dreams—one who had built the secure family she'd witnessed, the kind of home she'd written off as impossible for herself—had hopped on an airplane to come after her. Could it be that he'd finally extended to her the loyalty she'd known him capable of?

"There's a reason this has never worked, even as a friendship, and the problem has nothing to do with faults on your side."

A quick breath slipped past her lips. Philip showing up here and uttering assurance that, at least in one instance, her broken relationships weren't all her fault did more to clear the darkness than rereading her journals or the opportunity to work with Evie.

He focused on her in a way that seemed pleading. "I'm ready to change, and I ... need a friend. Maybe you do too. I thought despite everything ..." He looked around. "This is not a conversation I want to have on a doorstep."

Her hands were almost always either moving or touching something. Like now, she had one on the doorknob, the other on the frame. Occupied hands acted as a defense, an anchoring that Philip usually employed too. Except, tonight, his hands hung at his sides, still and unengaged in a way that seemed vulnerable.

Whatever had brought him here, he was at her mercy. He needed her. Badly.

"My family and I are having dinner." The statement made the gathering sound more ideal than it was, but Philip's company would make the rest of the meal exponentially more enjoyable for her. "Join us."

Hesitation swirled through his movement as he scratched

his arm. Those hands would go in his pockets next, his guard back up.

"Come on. You haven't eaten, have you? And then after, we can talk."

Decision settled across his features, and he lowered his hands to his sides again. "All right."

He stepped into the house and glanced around as if he respected this as personal space, part of her history that only her oldest and closest friends saw. A part she wasn't exactly proud of. He eased the door shut, and she led the way to the dining room.

Michaela introduced him to her family. He shook hands with her dad and Darren, greeted Riley and Bailey, who were farther away, and repeated everyone's names. She used the same strategy to memorize the names of new acquaintances, but with the shape he'd seemed to be in on the step, she hadn't expected him to rally this kind of effort.

"I'm sorry to barge in on your family." Philip aimed the apology at her dad and Riley, but neither replied.

"Don't be." Darren passed him the casserole dish. "None of us knows what to talk about, so a little extra company is welcome."

Her brother-in-law peppered Philip with questions about Awestruck, touring, and the new album.

Riley ate quietly, as if only she and Bailey sat at the table, but Philip seemed very aware of them, sadness shimmering in his expression when he looked their way.

After dinner, Michaela offered to handle clean-up. Dad walked Riley's family to the door while Philip stacked plates and brought them to the kitchen. Michaela had never done dishes with a man she was interested in before. None of them had had the patience for chores. They'd come to her for something else.

Philip didn't speak as he worked. His dedication to duty

EMILY CONRAD

increased her respect for him and amped up her curiosity about what had brought him there.

Her patience ran out when she reached the casserole dish with baked-on cheese. She left it to soak and tipped her head toward the back porch. "Let's go sit."

In the small, screened porch, a metal, gliding loveseat waited for them. Temperatures had risen to over eighty earlier, but following sunset, the air had cooled to somewhere in the seventies. She sat and folded her hands between her knees. He dropped to the seat beside her, hunched forward like when he'd shared that Nila might have her mother's gene mutation.

"Riley's doing the genetic testing," Michaela said. "We'll know in a couple of weeks."

He pulled one arm back, twisting to focus on her with sad concern. "How are you feeling?"

"Worried. Lost."

"That's normal, if it helps." He settled again, elbows on his knees.

"I've never liked being normal."

A low chuckle sounded. "It is a drag."

She sighed. At the thought of sharing what she'd been going through these last few days, her fears about never finding acceptance, her pulse hit fast and hard.

She would have to work up to revealing something so personal, if she spoke of it at all.

But there were things she could talk to Philip about that she couldn't discuss with her family. He'd been in similar situations with cancer. Surely he'd thought about what came after death, the way she'd begun to wonder. Right? Or was she the only one without answers?

Better to face the embarrassment of showing her weaknesses than to feel so haunted about the afterlife, on top of everything else. She swallowed. "I suppose wondering about

186

what comes after life, what the point of it all could possibly be, is also normal."

"Yes." He spoke solemnly, but if he didn't come through with more than that, she'd cry.

"Any advice?"

Philip considered her question so long that a storm of emotion gathered, but at the sound of his voice, the clouds inched back. "I don't know what comes next, but while we're here, I think the point is helping each other. Being there."

"Love." The word escaped on a wistful breath.

"There are worse ways to spend a life."

So true, but how could she spend herself on love when all her relationships eventually crumbled? She'd invested hours in her family the last two days, but neither Dad nor Riley had voiced more than the minimum, begrudging appreciation. "I'm not sure how that's supposed to work for me, since I keep ending up alone."

His eyes seemed to narrow in the darkness. "In what way? I just met your family in there." He spoke the end of the sentence slowly, as though he were debating saying more before he fell silent.

"They're a warm bunch, right?"

He shrugged slightly. "This is a rough time for them. The visit hasn't gone well?"

"Nothing's gone well. I should've learned a long time ago that people don't keep me around for my personality. Not them, not my manager, not anyone. I've been giving what I thought people wanted, but that hasn't led to any relationships where anyone wants me around for more than a pan of enchiladas or my looks or the occasional song."

"I do." He shifted back in the seat and looked at her, the sadness she'd seen on the doorstep again marring his expression. "But when I tell you what's been going on, you may not be interested in keeping me around."

She'd been afraid to confess her fears, but he hadn't left her alone with them. He'd confirmed what she'd hoped all along: life was about love. She might only meet frustration as she tried to live that out in many arenas, but Philip, sober this time, had offered ... not love—not yet—but companionship and potential.

And that, as Reese might've said if this were a professional negotiation, was the best offer she was likely to get.

She turned her hand up, opening it to him. "I'm interested. Nothing you tell me will change that."

PHILIP'S EYES had adjusted to the blue-gray darkness of the unlit porch. The pale beacon of Michaela's hand waited for him. If he chose to be honest with her, he'd have accountability that would mean changing his mind later wouldn't be easy.

For the kids' sake, he had to stay the course.

He closed his hand around Michaela's. The slip of her fingers between his sent the same flash through his nerve endings that he'd felt the first time he'd taken a girl's hand in high school.

Avoiding physical relationships for a couple of years must've resensitized him. And Michaela was different. For the first time since Clare's death, he hadn't reached out because of what he'd lost but in hopes of somehow gaining a future he wanted.

Not that having a hand to hold would win the coming battle.

"When I only had to balance my kids and Awestruck, I got by, but you made things more difficult. Kids only know their parents so well, and I used them as an excuse to turn down a lot of invitations from Gannon and John—like I did with you. The difference is, you didn't listen."

"Really?" She laughed. "That's the only difference?" With her free hand, she pulled her hair over her shoulder.

He tightened his grip on her to keep himself from touching her hair, her neck. To keep himself from letting attraction stop him from telling her a truth that had been fighting for release for weeks. "You get by my defenses."

"No has to be my least favorite word."

"You're the first person since Clare to see a side of me I tried to keep hidden. And to keep you from seeing more, I've been angry and defensive, and I've told you a lot of lies."

A new shadow appeared beside her mouth, indicating a frown. "You did warn me the night you'd been drinking that you're a liar."

He had no memory of it, but he wasn't surprised. He could still back out of this, come up with some new lie to redirect the big explanation he'd started.

Michaela squeezed his hand. "Tell me something true."

He put his hand on his biceps, meaning to push his sleeve up and show her his perfectly healthy arm. No cut. No stitches. But could he do this? In the dark, he could hardly spot the shadows that outlined her fingers on his hand, but he'd feel the absence acutely if this made her pull away.

A vision of Nila shaking his unresponsive body forced him into motion.

He pulled the sleeve up, exposing his shoulder.

Michaela hesitated, confused for a few beats, and then her cool fingers brushed over his skin, first one way, then the other. If not for the verdict he awaited, the touch would no doubt stir more feelings that had been dead for years.

He hung his head, still holding tight.

"No stitches."

He shrugged the sleeve, shifting it back into its rightful place, and waited for the reprimand.

"Where did you go that day?" Sternness edged her voice, but not shock. Not offense.

Maybe he could do this. Follow through, tell her everything. And maybe, when they were done, she wouldn't leave him to face the fallout alone.

19

"What happened that day starts back in high school." Philip faced Michaela, wondering if she had the patience for this and if he had any right to dump all his problems on her when she faced her own family crisis. He hadn't treated her well, and she could justifiably demand he cut the story short.

Instead, she nodded.

"My dad is a pediatrician. He worked a lot, but Mom arranged her teaching schedule to be home whenever my brother and I were. I thought we were all happy until the day of my brother's graduation party, when Mom announced she'd been offered the opportunity to teach for a year in England."

"She took it." Inevitability filled Michaela's voice.

"She said my brother and I were launching into the world, and she needed to set the example. I'd just finished my junior year. I waited for her to say it was all a joke. When she didn't, I thought Dad would stand up for us, say what I was too full of myself to say at age seventeen."

"Which was?"

"That I was a child who needed his mother and the security

of home." His voice thickened. All these years later, and he still felt for that child. "But Dad literally turned his back. I can still picture him standing there, hands on his hips, facing the table of sheet cake and balloons while my world fell apart."

Michaela leaned her head on his shoulder, and her hair settled against his arm like a silk sheet.

"He's a good man. He's seen me through a lot since Clare died, and there are few people I trust more, but back then ... He's changed a lot. Anyway, a month after Mom moved, I took a bad hit in football. I was paralyzed briefly. She came home for my surgery, but the painkillers lasted longer than her visit. That was when I first ..." He swallowed. He'd never told Clare the extra benefit of the painkillers. He hadn't wanted her to suspect his weakness for them. "Learned to treat pain—physical and otherwise—with pills. Back then, doctors weren't as stingy with the good stuff. On painkillers, Mom's absence didn't touch me. That I was missing all kinds of senior year activities because of the long recovery ... nothing bothered me."

He stared past the screens. Michaela's dad lived in an old neighborhood laid out in a grid. Around the black shapes of trees standing still in the calm night, lights shone from the houses around them. His own home growing up had been in a subdivision with curvy streets, lots of mature oaks, and more space between one new build and the next. The added luxury had done him no good.

"Eventually, the prescriptions ran out, I healed up, finished high school, went on to college, and spent my free time in a band. Dad made more of an effort with me and my brother. I think the problem with Mom was that he'd been absent in their relationship too. He reached out to her to try to win her back and became a new man, really, but Mom never came home to see it. After a couple of years, Mom asked for a divorce, and Dad gave it to her."

"The least they could've done was fight a bunch like mine."

Her temple shifted against his shoulder as she spoke, and he could imagine her sitting out here, the sounds of a shouting match filtering to her through the house walls. "That way, you could've been relieved when they gave it up."

"Instead, I grew up believing in a certain type of family— the dad provides, the mom keeps the home—the whole traditional picture. It was all an illusion."

"That's not always the case. You and Clare had something real."

"Why do you think that?"

She shifted sideways, resting the small of her back against the armrest, and let their linked hands lay on the ankle she'd pulled onto the seat. "You speak of her fondly. You both stayed in it until the end. You have two beautiful children from her."

"I loved her." Admitting the obvious made him sick because the love remained, except now his devotion pointed not to a woman but to a grave. And Clare would hate the man he'd become. "But parts of what we had were an illusion. I should've done better for her. I first spotted her during a gig at a bar. She was drinking soda, rebuffing passes, and looking all-around miserable, way too straight-laced for the scene. Meanwhile, I was in the band, dabbling in all the stereotypes. Women, alcohol, drugs."

He looked to gauge her reaction, but she focused on tracing the tendons on the back of his hand. He could distinguish the gentle glide of her fingertip from the line drawn by her nail, both leaving a trail of sensation like a comet tail, glowing in the night.

"I'm not sure if I thought, with a woman like her, I'd have a chance at the kind of happily-ever-after that my parents lost, or if I liked the challenge of winning the girl others couldn't."

Her hands stilled around his. "No wonder you don't want me. I'm neither of those."

She was wrong. About herself, and about what he wanted.

"You may have been in relationships, but I doubt the men you've been with have *won* you."

Her fingers tensed. She glanced at him twice—even in the night, her dark eyelashes and irises contrasted with the whites of her eyes—before she turned her face away. "They must've, or they couldn't have hurt me."

"Using someone and winning her are different." He would know. He'd used women more than he'd done right by them. Even now, he was opening up to Michaela because he needed something from her. "People can end up hurt either way, but winning takes effort. Doing things the way the other person wants because it's worth the sacrifice to have her in your life."

"I've got the sacrifice part down, only I don't call it winning. I call it selling out."

"Then those men used you. They didn't win you. In a healthy relationship, both people change in ways they can be proud of." He'd been proud of the choices he'd made for Clare. Not that he'd been perfect. "I hope you have that with someone someday."

She nodded silently as if she understood what he wasn't saying—that he wasn't the one. He hadn't put the effort into winning her and didn't have that to offer. Not right now, with such a black horizon in front of him.

Getting into his past had been a mistake. He should've just told her about the pills and been done instead of pulling her so deep into his story.

"You and Clare. What part was an illusion?"

He pulled his hand from hers. "From the start, I hid my partying from Clare because I knew she didn't approve. As we got serious, I cut back on drinking and drugs, and since she believed in saving sex for marriage, being faithful to her meant I waited too. When the band got signed, I dropped out of college and married her. The day Nila was born, I quit drugs because I wanted my kids to have for real what I'd thought I had growing up. Church became more important to me, but it never meant as much to me as to Clare. Those were our best years. Nason was only a few months old when Clare called me on the road and choked out that the doctor had found something."

"Cancer."

That day, he'd assured Clare the lump wouldn't be that. Promised it would all work out. "After she died, I quit believing in God, sobriety, and abstinence. But sleeping around left me feeling worse." And here they were, at the punch line. Fear vied to mute him, but if he didn't say this, he couldn't beat his habit. "The only thing that's helped me cope is the painkillers. I cleaned up while we toured last year. Then we settled in Wisconsin, and I had no show to get to every night, just two kids who need both a mom and a dad. Nothing felt right. Pressure and failure, everywhere I turned. I needed to get through somehow."

He didn't look to see what she thought of that. He wasn't sure what reaction he hoped for. What reaction would help. "Away from everyone I know, in such a rural area, when everything any of us do stands out so glaringly, pills have been hard to get. I had a dealer. You saw him that day outside Bryant's Subs. That guy who ran into me?"

The seat bounced as she shifted. "You told me not to be paranoid."

Philip gulped at the pain in her voice. "He was disguising our handoff. I wasn't feeling well that day because I'd run out of pills. To function, I had to go ahead with it whether you were there or not."

She stayed still, hard to read.

He continued. "The night of the bonfire, he told me there'd been a bust and he couldn't sell me any more. Ever since, I've been scrambling to get enough to stay out of withdrawal. I ran out on Sunday, got desperate, made up a story for you, and drove to meet a dealer farther away."

"Why not go lie to a doctor?" The dull expectation that had been in her voice when she guessed his mom had left returned.

"Even if I tricked someone into prescribing them, they track prescriptions, and people might recognize my name. The other dealer wasn't a long-term solution either. Part of the reason I came to see you was to line up more while I was in Chicago." Another way he'd used her. Shame wrapped hot fingers around his heart as the truth settled between them.

"And did you?"

He shook his head, then wondered if she could see in the dark. "Matt caught on. He came to my house this morning and asked who'd find my body when I overdosed. I tried believing it would never come to that, but I've been increasing the number, the toll the pills are taking on my life has been increasing. If I stay on this road, someday ..."

"It'd be Nila." Michaela's tone warmed for his daughter. "Who found you. Nila or Nason."

His hands shook. He pressed them together and rested his forehead against his thumbs. "I want to quit. I am quitting. It just seems impossible."

"You quit for your kids once before."

"I wasn't using as much. I had one less wound back then, and a lot more hope."

"Well ..." She sighed but didn't touch him. "Well, if the purpose of life is love, you don't have a choice. Aside from the risk of an overdose, this addiction could cost you your job, or you could be arrested, and then what would happen to your kids?"

He'd hardly heard anything after that word. Addiction. He wanted to argue against its use, but could he? He'd taken a flight to secure more pills. He'd been lying to everyone. He'd been paying through the nose. He'd risked everything.

Addiction.

As the label soaked in, her question registered. "They'd go live with my dad and Joan—he got remarried. They'd do much better by them than I have."

"You don't know the first thing about being a good parent, do you?"

Cut to hear the accusation that had haunted him for years, he lifted his head.

Shadows marked a notch in Michaela's furrowed brow. "If love is the point of our lives, love is the most important thing you can offer your kids, and you love them fiercely. I've seen it. I've gotten on the wrong side of it."

"Then love isn't the answer after all, because loving them isn't enough to get me out of this."

"Paired with rehab, I bet it is."

He wet his lips. "I can't lose my job. And I can't leave the kids that long."

"You just said they could go live with your dad."

"If I were gone and there was no other choice. He made it clear that he and Joan don't want to be my long-term childcare solution for things like tours. Maybe he'd make an exception for rehab, but sending the kids to Iowa for a couple of months would upset their lives before they're even settled in Wisconsin. There's the nanny, but she's so uptight about drugs ... Besides, going would mean telling Gannon and John. Even if they wanted to go easy on me, I would miss important Awestruck commitments."

She lifted her shoulders with what sounded like a frustrated sigh. "I guess you're sunk, then."

He resisted the anger that vied to slip over his disappointment like brass knuckles. He'd come for help he didn't deserve, and her reluctance to dig deep with him meant one of them understood healthy boundaries.

He stood. "We've all put a lot of effort into the collaboration.

I was in no position to criticize you over what happened with the video, so I hope you'll come back. Once your family situation allows for it." He couldn't discern if one of the screen panels was a door to the yard. He turned to leave through the house.

"You're going to need more fight than this to quit."

"Good advice." He stalked through the kitchen and hallway, out the front door. As he crossed the grass toward the street, he drew the key to his rental from his pocket and hit the button to unlock it before noticing someone leaning against the SUV, arms crossed.

Michaela. So the porch did have an exit.

He stopped in the middle of the sidewalk and waited for her to organize her disappointment, anger, and judgment into words. He'd taken enough of his problems out on her. She could choose to walk or to stick around and condemn him, and he wouldn't reciprocate.

She'd accused him of lacking persistence, but the truth was, he'd only been trying to avoid an argument with the one person he'd trusted enough to come to for help.

MICHAELA SHOULDN'T HAVE LET him get this close to leaving before they'd finished their conversation, but Philip Miller was a hard man to keep up with. He'd sped through years of his history, his ideas about love, and his current problem. She'd seen his confession coming as soon as he'd told her about the prescriptions following surgery, but she'd had no time to research options for recovery from a painkiller addiction, so of course she'd run out of ideas after the obvious choice—rehab. An idea that seemed to have offended Philip into leaving.

At least if the pills could be obtained through a doctor, they couldn't be too bad.

She'd wanted Philip to choose her, and he had. Sort of. He might've implied he wasn't interested in "winning" her, but he'd trusted her, and that was the first step. The next step was for her to help him get healthy.

This addiction was eroding his own joy, not to mention threatening his ability to care for his kids. She would help for those reasons, even if she weren't also invested in Philip because she liked the man who'd opened up to her. Who'd heard her fears without judgment and had offered her hope, even as he faced his own crisis. So, she would see him through this.

She straightened away from his vehicle and approached.

Philip didn't move, hands at his sides again. She stopped inches from him. Thanks to her flat sandals, her eye level was near his mouth, but she pushed her focus higher. His expression remained serious.

"We'll figure it out," she said.

"Good. The guys will be glad to hear it."

At the first sign he intended to step around her, she stilled him with a hand on his arm. Since he'd let go of her hand on the porch when his story got hard, her fingers had grown cold, but his skin remained warm.

"Not the collaboration," she said. "We'll figure out your problem. Together."

His mouth tightened. "You have enough going on with your sister. I shouldn't have tried to dump my issues on you."

"We're both in crisis mode." She shook her head and shrugged on the offbeat. "That means we get to lean on each other. I can't do much for Riley, anyway. She doesn't even like me." She moved her thumb on Philip's shoulder, wishing their connection wasn't so limited and fragile.

The movement seemed to catch his attention because he focused that direction a moment. "How can you think of me the same way?"

Remembering how much trouble she'd gotten herself in with what she'd thought was innocent contact, she lowered her hand from his arm. "I told you nothing you said would change this."

He studied her, troubled. "What if I want it to change? Because *this*?" He motioned between them. "This is hardly even a friendship, the way I've treated you. You deserve so much more."

From him?

She swallowed but didn't ask. He hadn't reached out as he spoke, so even if he wanted to give her more than a friendship, something was stopping him. Feelings of unworthiness, perhaps? Or was he just more focused on quitting the pills?

If so, he had a point. His health needed to come first.

"You'll be all right, Philip. You'll beat this once and for all. I have faith in you." She waited for the encouragement to settle. As his forehead smoothed, she stepped back. "Now, I just need to find someone who has faith in me."

"I completely forgot." He took her hand, apparently unguarded in his moment of realization. "Evie agreed to work with you."

"Reese told me." She left her hand in his, enjoying the warm strength and wondering how long it would last. "She's not happy I went through Tim."

His expression clouded. "She's the jealous type?"

"You're not?"

The shadows around his eyes deepened. "Why?"

"I wasn't flirting with Tim, but I got a definite jealous vibe from you."

She couldn't tell if the sound he made was from suppressing a laugh or a groan.

When he moved forward, he put his hands on her arms and tipped his forehead against hers. He closed his eyes and didn't move.

So this wasn't a kiss.

Michaela shut her own eyes, memorizing details about this moment. Over the softly scented summer air, she registered the linen scent of his soap, the warmth of his hands spreading up her arms.

"You keep saying you need to find someone who wants you around or who has faith in you." His voice came low as his forehead lifted away from her. "I want to be that guy, but what if I'm too flawed?"

"You're not. I've seen the good in you." She rested her hands on his waist, palms registering the softness of his shirt, the firm warmth of his body. When she lifted her eyes, she found him looking back.

Glints from the streetlights floated on his irises like fireflies. "I have a way to get clean that I think will work, but for the next week or two, I'll be nothing but a burden. Are you sure you want to deal with that?"

"We're both in crisis mode, remember? We can help each other."

He grimaced. "I can tell the guys you want me to stay here for moral support until after the surgery. One last lie to buy me about a week away from them and the kids. Thing is, in withdrawal, I'll be no use to you. We might even have to tell them I'm sick when the time comes for me to go back, because I might need a few more days."

She understood the grimace now. Withdrawal sounded intense, and she'd have to lie for him. To Gannon. "It'll be that bad?"

"What I'm on isn't that different from heroin. I mean, it is, but ... it isn't."

Oh. She hadn't realized. Her mouth went dry. She'd seen movies where characters went through withdrawal, and though she didn't remember what drugs they'd taken, heroin had to be one of the worst. "Is it safe to quit on your own?"

"People do it. I don't expect your help. If you aren't comfortable with me telling the guys I'm here for your sake, I can tell them my dad needs me."

"No." He'd invited her into one of the most important missions of his life, one that also deeply impacted his children. If she wanted to be a part of his life—and she longed to—she'd be a fool to walk away. "I want it to be me. I want to help."

"Are you sure?"

"Love is the point, right? You need to do this. For your own sake, and for your kids' sake. The least I can do is help."

"Maybe I'm not doing this solely for them." He slid his hand under her hair, gently resting it against her neck. "I want to live my life again."

"Then definitely." She covered his hand with her own. "Whatever I can do."

This time, when he drew closer and closed his eyes, he bent his head to kiss her.

A melody rose inside her, a new song she'd never get down on paper. With a hand in Philip's hair and one on his shoulder, she drew him with her, mid-kiss, as she let herself fall back against the SUV. He braced his arm on the window without missing a beat of this intoxicating song, but he kept his body from pressing against hers. She slipped a hand around his waist to pull him closer, but he resisted.

A couple moments more, and he broke the kiss. His hand slid from where he'd threaded his fingers into her hair. "I need to call the kids, break the news that I won't be home tomorrow."

She nodded, though rejection burned in her gut at the way he'd held himself back.

He studied her as if he could guess her pain. "In a week or two, everything will be different." He tipped her chin up with a gentle touch and brushed his lips to hers one more time. "For the better."

She'd been living off similar promises for years. Things

would be better when she got out from under Riley's shadow, when she won *Audition Room*, when she got a contract, when she cooperated with a music video director. Not one had provided the fulfillment she'd longed for.

She swept her skepticism aside. If she could trust anyone, she could trust Philip.

20

_M_ichaela glanced sideways to Philip, who hunched against the push bar of the shopping cart. The last ten hours had changed him. He sniffed, and his forehead glistened in the florescent lights of the department store. He dipped his face to his shoulder to hide a yawn, then blinked and refocused on the aisles ahead of them.

She'd picked him up from his hotel that morning with questions swirling behind her like dust kicked up by her tires. How did he feel about her? What did the kiss mean? Were they an item now?

None of those questions seemed appropriate now that she'd been reminded of the serious nature of his mission to get clean.

"Did you sleep?" she asked.

"A little." His stuffiness affected his enunciation.

"Are you sure you shouldn't check in somewhere? There're outpatient options." Between when he'd left last night and called this morning, she'd researched possibilities. "Doctors can prescribe medications to help with withdrawal."

"I'd be as much a slave to that treatment as I am to the pills.

Check Out Receipt

North Point Branch
410-887-7255
www.bcpl.info

Thursday, June 29, 2023
3:38:58 PM
01066

Item: 31183196788829
Title: The runaway
Call no.: Fiction OVE
Due: 7/20/2023

Item: 31183212668799
Title: To begin again
Call no.: Romance CON
Due: 7/20/2023

Total items: 2

You just saved $31.98 by
using your library today.

Free to Be All In
Late fees no longer
asseessed for overdue items
Ask for details or visit
bcpl.info

It'd go on for months, and I'd have to hide the process from the guys. This way, in a week or two, I'll be free."

If he made it that long, and even then, "free" seemed like a strong word. From what she'd read online, addiction was a chronic disease, not as easily remedied as a simple lapse in judgment. "Relapse is more likely if you do this alone. And when people relapse, they're more likely to overd—"

"I won't." His eyes snapped toward her, dark.

If he wouldn't accept help from the medical community, she'd have to do what she could to make sure he survived withdrawal. After all, he'd come to her for help. First, to tell her his story last night, and now, to take him shopping for supplies to get him through the next week.

In her reading, she'd seen that addicts were often encouraged not to engage in new romances for their first year of recovery. But if Michaela was integral to his recovery, they wouldn't have to wait that long, would they?

She chose not to dwell on it. Helping him get healthy was the important thing right now. Everything after that would fall into place.

He'd stocked the cart with groceries and toiletries. He turned into the men's clothing section. He took a stack of three black T-shirts—all the same size and cut—then a similar stack of gray. When he turned back again, she intervened.

"Another color too? How about green?" Her favorite color on him.

He shrugged as though she'd asked him his favorite color of daisy. "Whatever's fine."

She presented him with three hunter-green T-shirts, a size smaller than he'd selected for himself. If he cared about that or their V-necks, he didn't show his disapproval as he moved on to athletic pants. When he grabbed the first couple of pairs without looking at anything but the size, she rushed ahead to choose for him.

He shifted and rubbed his shoulder as she rifled through the assortment. "No one's going to see me. The idea's to have enough clean clothes on hand that I don't have to do laundry."

"I'll see you." She laid her first two picks on top of the mound of supplies in the cart. "And hotel staff will too."

"I'm not staying in the hotel." A yawn stopped him. While he had his hand by his face, he also wiped his damp forehead. "I rented a place for privacy."

"Well, *I'll* see you."

He checked their surroundings. The man browsing the farthest racks of the section seemed oblivious, but Philip lowered his voice. "Beyond dropping me off and checking in once in a while, you're not going to want to be around me, Michaela. It won't be fun or romantic or whatever you're thinking."

"You're going to want more pills, and if you don't have support, those cravings will win. If you refuse to check yourself into a program—inpatient, outpatient, something—you'll need me. For more than just a ride or a quick visit."

He released a long sigh.

"For Nila's and Nason's sakes, don't try this alone."

At the kids' names, he massaged his neck. Pain and worry spread across his features. "They were upset when I told them."

"That you aren't coming home today?" She rubbed his arm, but he didn't seem to register the touch. "Someday, when you tell them the whole story of what you did for them, how you quit for them, they'll appreciate this. You'll miss this week so you can be there for the rest of their lives."

He leaned against the cart's handle and rolled it out to the main aisle. "I'm always gone. That's what they're going to remember about me."

So his low mood extended beyond his attempt to push away Michaela.

"They adore you. This week is important for their sake. This is hard, but it's good."

"They want a video call every night. I don't want to scare them or snap at them. And the nanny. She'll recognize something's off, even if I fool the kids."

"Call them, minus the video. Send them pictures throughout the day. I'll help you." She'd enjoy looking for entertaining moments to capture for them.

Gratitude flickered across his face. That must mean she was making progress toward convincing him she'd make good company this week. She counted that as a win, but if getting the right to hang around had been so difficult—in fact, he hadn't even confirmed he'd accepted the idea—what more serious challenges would the coming week bring?

PHILIP'S HANDS looked steady as he moved his supplies into the back of Michaela's car, but he could feel a growing shakiness that would be obvious soon. He'd thrown up that morning, but knowing he had to stay hydrated, he'd forced himself to drink water. Even that wasn't sitting well. The clock was ticking. He should call the kids soon, possibly on the ride back to the hotel to collect his things, because he wouldn't be using video later.

He slammed the door and turned to take the cart to the corral, but Michaela had already disappeared with it. He dropped to his seat, but getting his weight off his feet didn't send the signal to rest to his crawling muscles.

He envied Michaela's energy as she got behind the wheel. She started the car and glanced at him. "How can I help?"

She couldn't. He'd enjoyed the kiss last night, but even in the moment, he'd felt off. Tense and apprehensive. He'd been in the earliest stages of quitting, and he wouldn't feel better until this was behind him. He hiked his thumb to indicate she should back out of the stall. "Let's keep this moving."

She checked every direction about a thousand times as she straightened the car into the aisle. Once she'd turned onto the street, she looked over again. "You can do this. It's going to turn out okay. Better than okay."

As if she would know.

"Why don't you call the kids? Remind yourself what you're doing this for."

In preparation for last year's tour, he'd set Nila up with a phone. The settings limited her conversations to family only. When he was home, the device usually lay buried and off in the little bag she toted around with lip balm and a coin purse inside. Today, though, she must have had it with her because she answered on the third ring, eyes as round and shiny as a doll's.

Nason's head bopped between her and the camera. "Hi, Dad!"

"Hey, guys. What are you two up to?"

He let them spend most of the ride to the hotel talking, and for a few minutes, his discomfort eased. But when the kids signed off with a chorus of I love yous, the pain edged back in.

He didn't deserve their love. But maybe, if he could endure this, he would.

When Michaela parked at the hotel, she unbuckled.

He lifted a staying hand. "I'll be back out in a few minutes."

"I'll go in with you."

If she knew how his stomach felt, she wouldn't campaign to stand sentinel. But she obviously didn't trust him alone, and he wasn't going to tell her about his rioting body, or she'd trust him even less. "I'm going in alone. No one knows me here, but you're local. You'll be recognized."

"No one recognized me at the store."

"A fluke." He grabbed the door handle. His stomach

wouldn't put up with drawn-out negotiations. "And us at a hotel is a tempting headline."

He didn't wait around for her reaction, but when he approached the hotel doors, he could see in the glass that she hadn't trailed behind him.

She gave him twenty minutes before texting to check in and, when he failed to respond, another three before threatening to come in after him.

Stomach issues. Be out soon.

Unless his gut revolted again. He carried his bag to the door and looked back at the room. He hadn't checked for forgotten belongings, but he had his phone and hadn't brought anything else he cared enough about to double back for.

To think, this level of discomfort was just the beginning.

He dragged himself through the motions, back to the car, where he dropped into the passenger's seat.

Michaela frowned at him. "Eye contact, please."

"What?"

She pointed at her right eye, unblinking. "When you're withdrawing from opioids, your pupils will be dilated."

She must've been doing her homework. He complied because he didn't have the energy to fight. Anyway, studying her eyes wasn't a punishment. "What color are they?"

"Brown." She pursed her lips as though she thought the question stupid.

"Not mine. Yours. Beneath the green contacts." Looking closely, he'd bet the lenses made her irises appear bigger, in addition to more colorful.

"Don't change the subject." Her mouth twisted with uncertainty.

Another yawn forced him to look away.

"I can't tell if they're dilated, but you still look miserable and sweaty, so ..." She put the shifter in reverse. "Where to?"

He pulled up the address on his phone and propped the

device in a cupholder, allowing the British lady on GPS to give the directions. He closed his eyes and forced his thoughts to linger on Michaela rather than how he felt. Her irises could only be so many colors. Brown, blue, green, hazel. But the variation of shades and flecks were endless. Pale blue would be stunning with her dark hair, but Michaela wouldn't cover stunning features.

The color had to be something she considered unremarkable, and since the most common eye color in the world was brown, he settled on his guess. "Brown eyes."

"Huh?"

"That's my guess. Your eyes are brown." And he'd bet they were beautiful.

"You'll never know. I've been wearing colored contacts since high school."

He couldn't imagine looking into Nila's face a few years from now to see a stranger's eyes staring back. "Your dad didn't care?"

GPS talked over him, instructing Michaela to turn, but she must've been able to track both his voice and the mechanical one because he felt the pull of the car turn as she answered. "He allowed it to save my vision. Before that, I wore cheap ones that ended up sending me to the eye doctor. Besides, he paid for glasses *and* contacts for Riley. It wasn't my fault I had perfect vision." Following another GPS interruption, the blinker clicked. "And maybe I partied some, but unlike Riley, I obeyed curfews, didn't crash the car or get arrested. I'd say I deserved the contacts."

Dark foreboding slithered in. He didn't want to scar his kids with his habit, but getting clean wouldn't prepare him to parent them well. What if Nila became as much of a handful as Michaela had been? Or what if Nason acted out? What if they grew to hate him or did half the things he himself had done after Mom left? Not having a mom changed a kid, and not for the better.

"Your eyes." His voice sounded raw to his own ears, and his stomach started to cramp and churn again. "What color?"

"You're one to talk. You have a beard. That hides part of your face all the time."

"Not the same."

She shrugged. "Every girl's got her secrets. No one, including the guys I've dated, has seen me without them—and makeup—in years."

He'd been right. No man had ever won her. Not her trust, anyway. No wonder she would hardly let him out of her sight.

Maybe she was a little career-focused, but he admired how, despite the pain he and her family had inflicted, she kept caring. Kept trying. So, as they'd stood on the sidewalk outside her childhood home, he'd kissed her in the belief that he might be able to do it. Win her over. Earn her love—once he cleaned up.

Today, he could see he'd gotten carried away. He wasn't the man his kids deserved, let alone the man he'd have to be if he had one more person counting on him. Those were lifetime commitments. Right now, he wasn't sure he could stand suffering another week. Another hour.

"Huh. Cute."

He cracked open his eyes as gravel sounded beneath the tires. Michaela parked in the drive of the small cabin. The blue siding had accumulated a coat of dust, and the bushes had gotten out of control since the photos in the online listing, but it was all his for the next two weeks. No maids in and out, no neighbors in the room next door or down below to complain about his odd hours.

Michaela hopped out. "Did I glimpse a lake in back?"

His energy lagged, frustration swirling in its place because he knew from last night how his muscles would crawl if he tried to sleep.

Michaela snagged a couple of bags and flounced to the door. "What's the code?" She pointed at the keyless entry.

He set down his overnight bag to free up his hand and check for the number on his phone. Once they made it in, Michaela unpacked supplies as he brought them in. When he hefted the package of sports drinks onto the counter, she was stowing frozen meals in the freezer.

"Thanks for the ride." He looped his hand through the strap of his duffle. He hadn't scouted out the two bedrooms yet, but the place wasn't big. They had to be through the doorway off the living room, on the other side of the kitchen counter.

Michaela turned from her work, shutting the appliance. "I'm not leaving."

"You have your family."

"They don't need me. You shouldn't be alone."

"So what? You're going to live here for the next two weeks?"

"I'll sleep on the couch if I have to."

"No." He braced a hand on the counter.

"No?"

Her objections were exhausting. He tried an argument she couldn't dispute as easily—a stare.

She assessed him, lips turned down with determination. "Fine. But you made the mistake of giving me the code, so I can get in whenever I want. And this is a lake with a ton of cottages. I bet it's not the only rental."

"Meaning?"

"I'm staying close."

He couldn't argue for his independence, couldn't do the most basic things like sleep and keep food down. She could do whatever she wanted. He didn't care.

"Also, have you figured out what you're going to do with

your rental car? We left it at the hotel, but you can't leave it there if you checked out."

He rubbed his eyes. Useless. He was useless.

"Never mind. I'll figure it out."

In this state, he couldn't imagine how she'd do that, but the rental car was the least of his concerns. He left her to whatever schemes she wanted to dream up and fell into the first bed he found.

Sleep mocked him from a distance, the word *useless* echoing through his brain.

The world would be better off without him.

Not that he'd act on the thought. After the kids, the person who'd be scarred worst by finding his body was Michaela. For her sake, he could hang on.

Couldn't he?

21

Michaela had stopped chewing her nails ages ago, but as she steered back toward Philip's cabin early Friday afternoon, she bit her pinkie nail down to nothing.

She'd only left Philip a couple of times since their shopping trip Wednesday morning.

She'd packed up her things at Dad's house and moved them into a cabin she'd rented down the street from Philip's. Dad didn't seem impressed by her choice to distance herself from the family, but he hadn't been impressed by her cooking and cleaning either.

Besides, Philip needed her, and staying in a cottage fifteen minutes away wouldn't prevent her from being there for family when the time came.

Aside from that trip to pack and sleeping in her own cottage for a couple of hours Wednesday and Thursday nights, she'd stuck close to Philip, though her patient had grown increasingly cross.

This morning, he had said some pretty nasty things to her over breakfast, so when she'd had to leave for Riley's surgery, she'd told herself she didn't care what he did.

But as she'd sat in the waiting room with her dad and Darren, she'd had lots of time to worry what he might do to alleviate his discomfort.

Discomfort seemed too nice of a word. He was ill, through and through.

Philip hadn't threatened to relapse, but finding relief that way must have occurred to him. She'd had his rental car delivered to the cabin, but she kept the keys with her, so he couldn't have driven, but he did have his phone. He could've used an app to get a ride somewhere, or he might've reached out to whoever he'd planned to buy from while in Chicago.

Now that the surgery was over and Riley was resting, Michaela had sped back, though he'd told her in no uncertain terms he didn't want her there. She half-jogged to the cabin door. If she found him unresponsive on the floor ... The thought was too awful to complete.

As she stepped into the kitchen, she spotted one of the living room recliners rocking. So he was still alive and kicking and watching some gory war movie. She grabbed a sports drink from the counter. She lowered herself to the chair across the side table from him and extended the bottle.

"I don't want it." Despite the sweat trickling down his cheek and the blanket he had pulled around his shoulders, he shivered.

"You told me yourself it's important to stay hydrated." She unscrewed the lid and held the drink out again.

He didn't accept the offer or stop rocking. "Just leave."

"I did. I'm back now." She set the drink on the table and leaned back in her seat. She didn't recognize the movie, and a gruesome shooting made her cringe and look away.

The window framed a view of the lake. Through the gauzy curtains obscuring the glass, she followed the path of a speed boat pulling an inner tube. All those people out there, enjoying summer, while she and Philip sat in this tomb.

He wiped under his eye. Was he crying, or were the tears part of his body's physical reaction to withdrawal?

"You know you can talk to me about anything, right?" she asked.

He stared at the screen. Though he had circles under his eyes and likely hadn't slept well since Monday or Tuesday, he used his foot to keep rocking himself in a motion that was more abrupt than restful.

"I'm proud of you."

He shook his head as if she'd insulted his dead wife.

"Seriously, it takes guts to fight like this, wrestle your life back from a disease."

He kept rocking.

"Don't people usually have to hit rock bottom before they do this? So, you know, it's good you saw the danger coming and found a way out. That's respectable."

"Nothing about this is respectable, and you're making it worse. Just leave."

She couldn't. The thought of the kids finding his body had to seem like a distant threat compared to his current suffering. Did he have enough motivation to endure?

"I read online that if people don't deal with the things that led them to use in the first place, they're more likely to relapse."

"I'm not a good dad. I dealt with it by using, but that made me a worse dad, so I'm solving *that* by not relapsing. Now if you don't mind, doctor, I'm dealing with not relapsing by getting my mind off it." He pointed at the screen he still hadn't looked away from, then dropped his hand and kneaded his thigh as if to work out a cramp.

"I can't let you ignore what's going on."

Philip huffed and rubbed his forehead. "You can't save me, Michaela."

She could try. "You're still stuck with the original problem. You think you're not a good dad, but that's not true."

"I'm gone half the time and the other half, I can't be both a mom and a dad."

"They don't need that from you. They just need you. To know you love them."

He planted his foot, halting the rocking motion as he pivoted toward her. With both hands, he pointed to the center of his chest, where sweat had dampened his gray T-shirt to charcoal. "I'm not enough. And don't try to tell me kids do fine without their mothers because all you need for proof that they don't is the two of us."

The two of them? Coming to help Philip had given her purpose, but shortly before, she'd doubted the point of her life. Felt lost, hopeless, disconnected, and used. If her mom had stayed, would everything have been different? Maybe not for the better. Mom hadn't been happy.

And with that heritage, what kind of mom would Michaela make?

What if Riley was right and Michaela was like her mother?

"Leave the original problem alone." He settled back into his seat. "I might not even have it in me to fix this one, but if I die trying, at least the kids will be better off."

"Don't talk that way."

"You're welcome to leave."

"You don't want to die."

"We all go sometime." His eyes fixed back on the carnage of a battlefield on screen. "If I overdose, I'll go out doing something I love."

"Philip! You're scaring me."

"So stop watching. Leave." He stilled and breathed out, eyes closed, enduring something. More nausea, probably. "I'd be better off."

"Without me?"

"Dead." He exhaled, peeled his eyes open, and climbed out of his chair. A hobbling walk replaced his normally assured, smooth movements as he made his way to the hall. A moment later, the bathroom door closed, but that didn't stop the sound of him vomiting again.

Dread shivered down Michaela's spine. Watching him deal with illness was one thing. But hearing him discount the value of his life? He was right. She didn't know how to handle this. She needed help.

Her dad wouldn't know what to do and might not even care.

Reese could probably produce a detailed plan, but she wouldn't want to get mixed up in this mess. Besides, she'd hardly forgiven Michaela for going through Tim to get to Evie.

Gannon had been understanding when she'd called to say she would come back, but that they were hoping Awestruck wouldn't miss Philip if he stayed in Illinois a little longer. Her mentor had sounded surprised at that, but he hadn't asked questions. So, so far she hadn't had to lie.

If she told him the rest of the story, he, John, and Tim would have ideas and a willingness to get involved, but they might also fire Philip. Even if they didn't go that far, there'd been so much tension over Matt's song. What kind of disagreements would rise if the bandmates disagreed about how to handle Philip? The tension would last a lot longer than withdrawal.

Perhaps someone from Philip's family could help instead?

She glanced at his phone. He'd given her the passcode so she could help him stay in touch with the kids, as promised.

She accessed his contacts.

Those he'd marked as favorites waited at the top in alphabetical order. Dad, Evan, Grandma and Grandpa, Gannon, John, Nila, and Ruthann.

He'd mentioned having a brother. That could be Evan, but Michaela didn't know enough about their relationship to risk calling him.

Philip had said his dad was a doctor and had called him a good man. He seemed like the best option.

Her exhale came out shaky. If Philip resented her calling his dad, she could lose this relationship, but he'd been talking like he might take his own life. Preventing a disaster of that magnitude had to come first.

She stepped outside and made the call.

～

MICHAELA CARRIED "AMAZING GRACE" for Philip when they called the kids to say goodnight that evening. She'd offered to warm up some dinner for him, but he'd declined. Did the crackers he'd eaten instead have any nutritional value?

When they finished the song, she slipped into the kitchen to let him wrap up the call. The numbers on the oven glowed 8:10. Had she made the right choice to call his dad?

When she'd introduced herself, Dr. Miller told her to call him Ed. She'd stumbled into an explanation, but after one fumbling sentence, he'd guessed the call was related to painkillers.

"You know?"

"I know it's been a struggle for him, but he led me to believe he'd quit."

"He did for a while." Once when Nila was born, and again when he'd signed with Awestruck. Did his dad know how many times Philip had been through this? "He's trying to kick it for good, but he doesn't want to go to a doctor or a facility." She hesitated, but Ed seemed concerned and even-keeled. She could trust him. She *had* to trust him. "Some of the things he's saying scare me, and he can't keep anything down."

Ed vowed to be on the next flight. In about twenty minutes, he'd arrive.

Philip had been trying to convince her to leave. Once he

found out what she'd done, he might throw her out, but Michaela couldn't quite regret her choice. Whatever feelings had inspired him to kiss her the other night weren't strong enough to help when pitted against an enemy like drugs.

Even his love for his kids might not pull him through this.

That was part of the disease of addiction. Love couldn't cure it any more than Philip's devotion could've saved Clare from cancer. In her head, Michaela knew this.

But if love couldn't save a person, what good was it? Philip had offered it as the point of life, and that'd seemed wise in the moment.

Maybe the problem was that the kids were so far away and Michaela, though closer, couldn't claim to love him. She hoped to get there someday, but first he had to survive until then.

And still be talking to her.

Should she have tried longer before calling in reinforcements? Ed hadn't arrived yet. If she tested out how Philip was feeling and things seemed more manageable, she could try to call him off.

She sliced an apple. The poor little fruit had no idea the pivotal role it played in her relationship with Philip. "Misery loves company," she mumbled as she selected a ginger ale to accompany the slices into the war zone.

The call ended, and she carried her offerings to the living room. Philip had already returned to rocking and massaging his muscles.

"How about you try a little something?"

"You want me to puke again?" The eyes that had reminded her of peaceful childhood memories had gone dark.

He didn't want the care she offered. Confirmed. But what about what he'd said earlier? Was he really thinking about dying? "If you don't care if you live or die, why do you care if you puke or not?"

With a resigned sigh, he held out his hand.

Resignation had to be the worst possible response.

"Do you really not care?"

"What do you want from me?" He stood and grabbed the plate. "Eat? Don't eat? How can I make you happy? Because this is all about you, right?" He whipped the dish away from her, aiming at the wall. The ceramic shattered, and apple slices bounced to the couch. "I've never met someone more selfish, always out to get her own way and be the center of attention. All the time, Michaela. It's exhausting. Give it up already."

Tears threatened, but she wouldn't cry. She. Would. Not. Cry.

Her lungs fought for air as if she'd tried to power through a marathon instead of intervening on behalf of a friend. Her sinuses and eyes grew heavy, and her adrenaline surged. She was going to sob. And if she didn't leave now, she'd do it in front of him.

Ed would have to take over from here.

Michaela left.

22

One of these days, when Michaela walked into the studio, Philip would be back. She hadn't heard a peep from him since his outburst on Friday when she'd fled the cabin.

Ed, however, had texted when he arrived and assured her he'd handle Philip.

Ever since, she'd been wondering what that entailed. Tough love? A trip to the doctor? Wrestling him into some program? How had Philip responded to his father's presence? Would he come back clean? Or would he revert to using? And what did he think of her, both for calling his dad and for leaving?

Whatever the answers, she believed Philip would survive with his dad there. Since Philip kept texting Gannon daily apologies and updates as his "flu" stretched on, he seemed committed to coming back.

Each time she walked into the studio, she held her breath, wondering if she'd have to face him.

On Wednesday, again, the anxiety was for naught. Tim and John stood talking near Gannon, who sat on one of the couches, strumming on an acoustic guitar. Shadows filled the control room. Except for the guitar in Gannon's hands, Awestruck's impressive collection of instruments and equipment waited, idle.

Gannon glanced her way. "Philip's really down for the count."

"I've never seen someone so sick with the flu." And she still hadn't. "But he refused to go to the doctor, so he brought it on himself."

Tim folded his arms. "I'm going there to drag him to a clinic myself if he doesn't get back here in the next forty-eight hours." He hadn't been in the studio all week. Perhaps he'd only come today to complain about Philip.

Gannon gave up on the melody. "He said he saw a doctor after all. It's a bug that's got to run its course."

Since a doctor had shown up on Philip's doorstep Friday night, he hadn't had much choice about seeing one. She crossed to the keyboard and turned on the power.

"So. Other business." When Tim paused, she looked up to find him watching. "You heard about Evie?"

"I did. Thank you. So much. Reese wasn't happy I went through you, but I think in the end, she'll come around."

"She couldn't have been that upset. I talked to her Monday night to hammer out some details for the collaboration, and she seemed fine. Of course, at that point, I didn't know if there would *be* a collaboration." Tim eyed her. "You and Philip worked everything out?"

A flush burned across her cheeks. "I don't think our relationship is what you're thinking it is."

"Leave her alone." Gannon put his feet on the coffee table. "You're the one who's always saying we've got work to do. How about you let us?"

John tipped his head toward the exit. "Gonna be late."

Tim checked his watch. Gannon's mouth quirked with amusement as John and the manager left.

Since Gannon hadn't picked up another melody on the guitar, she began working through one of the tunes that had risen from her experiences with Philip the week before. "Where are they off to?"

"Meeting with some of the crew. Lighting and our pyro guy, prepping for the show."

"Why aren't you going?"

"Tim wants you and me to smooth out a couple of spots for the collaboration, and John's the one with ideas about timing pyrotechnics with the drums."

She nodded, focus trained on her fingers as she felt her way deeper into the melody. Gannon tried a couple of notes on the guitar, accompanying her. With his simple contribution, the song grew toward its potential, closer to expressing the emotion that had inspired it.

The longing to capture her experiences in music banded her chest with tension, but the melody wasn't yet hers to control. Like waking from a dream, she could lose the whole thing with one wrong turn of her fingers. In that way, creating was a risk.

Recording their sessions helped recapture momentary perfection, but with the control room dark, the equipment wouldn't catch this. Still, stopping the moment for the insurance of a recording would mar the process for sure.

She pushed into uncharted territory. As it had only a few other times in her life, inspiration sang, illuminating a bar or two ahead of her. This journey wasn't just about her career or a future album or even about a song that she might someday distill from it. The music expressed everything about her family and Philip and wanting to be loved and …

She stirred from the dream, started to lose her way. Gannon picked up the slack, building on the melody where she'd left off until, without words, he passed control back to her.

This was how creating music was meant to feel.

She played until the tension left her chest. Gannon seemed to sense the end had come and left her to finish the last few bars on her own. As the last note quieted, she stared at the keys.

Times when she could create music that so perfectly expressed her mood on the spot were rare. She'd never be able to remember it all to recreate it. Even if she could, she'd have to trim it down if she wanted to use it in a pop song. Maybe, if she could remember a snatch of the music here and there, that would be enough. She inhaled and blinked.

Finally, she looked to Gannon.

He leaned forward, tapped his cell phone screen, and focused on her again. "Want to tell me about it?"

Michaela licked her lips, but she couldn't spill the story. Not without talking about Philip and how she wished she'd been able to reach him. Wished she could've saved him.

"Did your sister get to go home today?" Gannon asked.

She nodded. "After some time to recover, they're starting chemo."

"How are you coping?"

Michaela shrugged. "They caught it relatively early. Most women survive the stage and type she has, so ..." The majority of women with her sister's diagnosis might survive, but a significant percentage didn't.

He set his guitar aside. "You didn't choose that key because you're doing all right."

F minor had as much baggage as she did. She checked his expression again. He'd been a solid mentor during the good but tumultuous experience of *Audition Room*. He'd seen her cry and had given her perspective that helped her to face her biggest fears and worries.

But it'd been a few years, and he had a girlfriend now. Fiancée. Besides, back on *Audition Room*, her fear had revolved around the possibility the judges and audience might not love her. Since then, the sharp point of her fears had dug deeper.

Now, she feared no one ever would. Could she tell him that?

"If love is the point of life, why doesn't it solve more? And why is it easy for some people and unobtainable for others?"

"Love is the point?" He rubbed his palms together, as if this conversation would involve grabbing a shovel and literally digging deep.

"It has to be. Love is the best thing we've got."

"Except no one's perfect at love besides God, so a lot of what people try to pass off as love is faulty." He studied her, and she hoped her raw heart was far enough below the surface he couldn't tell the shape it was in. "The good news is, God offers perfect love to everyone. Jesus died for all of us. All we have to do is believe."

Belief. She couldn't quite muster that. Hadn't that been the problem at Bible camp? She'd soon doubted God could love her despite her past. As she replayed a snatch of the new piece, the cool, smooth keys beneath her hands and the mourning melody lent her courage to speak. "I don't see why such an amazing Being would bother loving me."

"He made you for a purpose, and He loves you deeply."

"Then why do bad things keep happening while all I've got are people around me who couldn't care less?"

"I could care *a lot* less." Gannon gave a playful frown and waited for her to roll her eyes before he continued. "I believe the Bible is true, and it says He loves us. Bad things do happen because humans brought sin into the world, but we still glimpse God's love in the good. All good gifts are from Him."

When was the last time she'd received something good?

Answers flooded in.

The collaboration was good. The scent of flowers filled her memory before she could even recall the visual of the bouquet from Philip, the stems in her grip, the petals' soft touch on her hand. She'd witnessed goodness in the way Philip loved his kids, the way Nila had taken her hand. Maybe even the way Ed had dropped everything to come to help his son. Philip didn't believe, and she didn't know where Ed stood. Could their actions point to a God they didn't believe in?

"Speaking of something good …" Gannon lifted his phone. "You seemed to have a song in you, so I recorded that. It won't be the best quality, but it should help you piece back together anything you liked."

She grinned. "All of it?"

"A twenty-minute song might push some boundaries with your audience, but I'll let you decide." Smirking, he focused on the screen.

Another gift.

Was it possible God loved her the way Philip and Ed loved their family? Could those flowers and this recording ultimately have been gifts from a Being she'd been ignoring for years?

It seemed too simple. Too good to be true.

AFTER THE LAST WEEK, Philip ought to be used to his heart racing. If Michaela had known how fast his pulse beat at times during withdrawal, she'd have called 911 instead of his dad. Good thing she hadn't been armed with a stethoscope at the cabin and wouldn't have one when, now just over a week later, she answered her door.

If she answered her door.

At almost nine on a Saturday night, when he knew she wasn't with Gannon or John—the only people she knew in the area—she had to be there. He pressed the doorbell.

The morning after he'd been drinking, when he couldn't fill in the gaps, he'd thought the guilt might do him in. Turned out, remembering his mistakes could feel worse.

As soon as he'd broken the plate, he'd known he'd crossed a line, not because of the broken dish but because, despite everything Michaela's contact lenses hid, he saw terror and grief in her eyes. Emotions that surged as he ran his mouth, lobbing accusations that had no basis in reality.

She'd left long before his ego and the fog of withdrawal lifted enough to allow him to admit his error. Then, half an hour later, as he got his head together, the door opened.

"Michaela." He wrestled himself from the chair. "I'm ..."

Dad stood in the kitchen, a suitcase in hand.

Instead of completing the apology, Philip swore. Not because Dad had come, but because Michaela had considered it necessary to call him in.

"She got scared, son."

He never should've let her near while he endured withdrawal. He'd known the symptoms would be emotional as well as physical. If he'd kept her away, he wouldn't have said those awful things. He would be able to hold his head up as he stood here, clean and sober, on her doorstep. She'd be proud of him for the end result, not hurt over what he'd done getting here.

He rang the bell again, but if she hadn't answered yet, she wasn't going to.

Maybe Dad had warned her off, the same as he had warned Philip not to focus on a woman when he had an addiction to beat. Dad had been helpful in other ways, but Philip had been through this before. He knew how helpful his relationship with Clare had been when he'd gotten clean in the past.

Michaela wasn't Clare, yet she'd proven herself kind and trustworthy, and his life was better for her involvement. Now that he was clean, he could return the favor. The future might hold good things for them.

He propped the flowers against the narrow window beside the door. Hopefully, the water the florist had poured into the bottom of the bag would hold them until she discovered them.

When he'd turned a corner the day before and realized he could come home today, he called the local flower shop and described the blooms he'd given her from his yard. The lady said they sounded like peonies.

He'd envisioned one hundred dollars netting a bigger bouquet, but at least these looked fit for a museum-quality vase. Red swirls scrawled across the white blooms, and the outer-most layer of petals formed a cup that contained the tissue-like profusion at the center for a much cleaner look than the peonies at home.

In case she answered after all, he walked away backwards, watching.

He pulled open his SUV's door.

Still no movement.

With one last glance at the flowers, he drove away.

He hadn't written out a card because he'd expected to give them to her in person, but Michaela would know they'd come from him.

23

———

"*Y*ou were sick for *so* long." Nila stretched the word "so" from the moment he pushed her swing to the farthest reaches of the chain. She came flying back toward him, her hair parting in the wind created by the movement.

"I'm sorry. It won't happen again."

Nason, who'd been jumping on the trampoline until a moment before, grabbed the swing next to his sister and climbed to stand on the seat. "You can't help being sick."

"There are some things you can do." Philip motioned him to turn around and sit down. Once Nason settled, he gave the boy a push. "And I missed you guys, so I'm going to do everything I can to be healthy from now on."

Nila gripped the plastic-covered chains of her swing and tipped her head back, giggling. "Are you going to eat lots of salad?"

Lettuce had to be Nila's least favorite food in the world, and she knew Philip wasn't a big fan either.

"I'm sure I can find another way. Unless *you* want to eat a lot of salad." He pushed her swing and sent her squealing with delight, legs extended, feet pointed awkwardly toward each other.

These two.

During detox, Michaela's and Dad's company had acted as a failsafe against using, but with Michaela at her own place and Dad back home in Iowa, he had to stay strong on his own. He'd longed to use that very morning when he woke to face the day. Pills had been part of his routine for a long time. The best part of his routine. Or so it had felt.

But for these two, he hadn't used. He wouldn't.

The door at the back of the house opened, and Ruthann stepped out, her multicolored purse resting against her hip. She waved and headed into the garage, off to enjoy her Sunday somewhere else.

"Did you have fun with Ruthann while I was gone?"

As the kids launched into answers, his phone pinged. He took it out, still giving the kids pushes with his free hand.

Michaela had texted. *Thank you.*

No. Thank you. Relief had his thumb twitching to respond as quickly as possible, but he weighed his options, then deleted what he'd typed and wrote instead, *Can we talk?*

Done praising Ruthann and all the fun they'd had, Nason vaulted off his swing and sprinted to the trampoline. Nila followed.

All this before Michaela replied.

We probably should.

Not promising. But she could've tossed the flowers and not messaged at all. He took her text as a good sign.

Seven? You can see the kids before I put them down. They've been asking for you to sing to them again.

They'd gotten attached.

He'd gotten attached.

He hadn't meant to allow that. Michaela's home was in LA, and she'd leave them all to go back. Her life there was too important to her—and he couldn't judge her for that when he left his kids often for his own career.

She replied that she'd see him then, but his mind wandered much further down the line.

Could they make a long-distance relationship work?

Memories of how she'd behaved with him early on stirred uneasiness. She'd be back in LA, two thousand miles away, with him oblivious, the next time she faced the temptation to compromise for the sake of her career. He didn't need her to stay near him, but he did need to know she'd be faithful.

He took a deep breath and scrubbed his palms against his eyes. He wasn't being fair to the woman he'd put through so much in the last few weeks. If she could forgive him, he owed it to her to believe the best.

BETWEEN WHEN MICHAELA parked in the drive and got out of her car, the door to Philip's house opened.

Nason hung back on the threshold.

Nila ran out and threw her arms around her waist. "I thought you'd *never* come back."

"I missed you too." Michaela returned the hug and let the girl lead her toward the house. "My sister is sick. I had to go spend some time with her."

"Sick like my dad was?"

"It's a little different. She's still sick." Michaela spotted Philip behind Nason.

He looked well. When he'd been withdrawing, he skipped shaving and only touched his hair to ruffle it. Today, his beard had been trimmed up, and his hair lay dry and combed. Instead of sweats, he wore jeans and a clean shirt. A hunter-green V-neck, to be exact.

Michaela squeezed Nila's hand. The girl expressed affection

so easily. Why did adulthood have to be so complicated? "Is your dad better?"

Nason peered up at the man behind him as if Michaela's question had inspired fresh doubts. "Are you better, Dad?"

"I don't know." Philip swung his son onto one of his broad shoulders like a sack of potatoes. "You tell me."

"You're still sick!" Laughter echoed in the front hall and through Michaela's heart as Nason kicked his feet. "I can tell. You're still sick! You should go to bed!"

"All right. If you say so." Philip started toward the living room, which would lead to the stairs to the second floor.

"No. Don't take me with you!" Nason pounded his back, fake horror brightening his voice.

"Oh, okay." Philip set his son back on his feet. "I'm not tired anyway, and we have company. We'd better stay with her."

Nason shrugged and jogged onward to the living room, but Philip turned back to give her a regretful smile. He might be carefree with the kids, but when it came to her, his expression said care was the name of the game.

In the ugliness of the previous week, she'd forgotten how good being with him and the kids felt. For the next hour, she basked in the easy company. She loved the kids' enthusiasm and the way they kept asking her to watch as they played in front of the couch where she and Philip sat. As they all interacted, she could tell Philip wasn't angry that she'd left him in his dad's care, and she struggled to hold his behavior against him when he seemed so different now.

Could she trust this? What if he seemed normal again because he'd relapsed?

No. Not so soon. After everything he'd endured to get clean, he wouldn't have.

He told the kids to get ready for bed and overcame their complaints by promising they'd sing for them when they came back down.

Once the kids thundered up the stairs, he turned to her. "Thanks for that."

She folded her hands. "It's easy to see why you love them so much."

He gave her a thoughtful look, but he didn't broach any of the topics they needed to discuss.

"This is for real?"

His forehead creased. "What?"

"You're clean now? For them?"

"Yes, but not solely for them." His hand shifted as if to reach out, but he curled his fingers and fell still. "How's Riley?"

"Time will tell. She feels okay and has a decent prognosis." Michaela had called her a couple of times. The conversations had been short, but friendly. "We got the results on the genetic test."

"And?"

The children made so much noise on the stairs, she thought for a moment one of them had fallen. But then they appeared before herself and Philip grinning, Nila in princess pajamas, Nason in a set with both trucks and dinosaurs on them. Wait. Make that dinosaurs *eating* trucks.

She laughed, imagining Philip and Nason in the kids' clothing section of some store, picking them out.

"That had to be record time," she said.

Philip lifted his hand, silently asking the kids to wait as he focused on her. "And?"

"She doesn't have it."

Philip waved the kids to join them on the couch. They bounced into the one-person-sized space between her and their father, blocking Michaela's view of how Philip took the news. Nonetheless, he'd touched her by making questions about Riley and the genetic test a priority. Until that moment, Riley had seemed like an afterthought to him. Maybe, when he'd said everything would be different once he was off the pills, he'd been right.

She hadn't memorized all the verses of "Amazing Grace," so she pulled up the lyrics on her phone as Nila snuggled close.

The first verse focused on being lost—exactly how she'd felt back home, before Philip showed up. To be honest, she'd felt lost for a long time. She'd called Gannon weeks ago because of that lost feeling.

Had grace found her? Because for the first time in ages, she felt hope for something bigger than a collaboration with Awestruck or Evie Decker. The second verse and its mention of belief ushered her into the third, both so closely mirroring what Gannon had said about goodness that tears flooded her eyes.

The Lord has promised good to me.

Good, despite the problems. Good like another bouquet of flowers, this one delivered to her door.

They finished the song, and she managed to hide her tears. Or so she thought, until Philip returned from tucking the kids in.

"Powerful song." He sat beside her in the same place, with just enough room for both kids to fit between them if they squished.

"Yeah. And a kind of weird choice for a six- and an eight-year-old."

"Their mom used to sing it to them."

"Ah." She hadn't realized she'd been invited into a sacred family tradition. Should she be honored? She opted to play it off lightly. "So you're not secretly religious or something."

"I believe in family, not faith."

She'd known this about him. He'd lost his wife. Nila and Nason might have gene mutations that could set them on a similar path. He valued his family and couldn't trust a God who wasn't equally protective of those Philip loved. Michaela had her own set of disappointments, and maybe she shouldn't be so quick to forget about them because of flowers and loving fathers.

Especially not fathers as flawed as Philip and Ed. Did they show great love in some circumstances? Absolutely. And they'd each failed miserably in others.

Maybe God was inconsistent too. Maybe that was why Clare had died, why Michaela's family had only the slightest idea how to love.

Philip brushed her hand with his knuckles and drew back. "I am sorry for how I behaved last week. Sorry doesn't begin to express it." He frowned and seemed to hold his breath, vulnerability replacing the steel that had been in his eyes the last time she'd studied them this closely.

"You were sick." But she couldn't bring herself to shrug. Not when she could still hear the crash of the breaking plate, the vitriol in his voice when he'd called her selfish.

"That's no excuse. I hurt you, and I scared you. Looking back at last week—and the way I've treated you since you arrived in Lakeshore ... I hate that guy. I lied to everyone. My good moods depended on pills, which is no way to live, and in my bad moods, I was cruel to you. I know I can never go back, but I understand if an apology isn't enough for you."

Was it? She picked at her nails, considering. "You're not the first to point out that I like to be the center of attention. I mean, you're the first I thought might kill himself." She stilled her hands to look at him and hammer home how real her concern had been. "But the rest of it wasn't that original."

He slid off the couch to kneel in front of her. If he'd reached for her hand, she'd have given it. Instead, he rested one palm on the cushion beside her and let the other hang at his side in that way of his. "I lashed out because I was angry with myself and how I felt. You were being a saint, and the kind of man you deserve would've been there for you, helping you instead of tearing you down. You shouldn't have had to be strong with everything you're going through."

The acknowledgment of her needs wrapped her in the kind of security she'd have felt if he'd embraced her. "I didn't think of it that way. You were in trouble. You needed to get clean."

"You acted selflessly. I never should've used you and your situation as my cover to get clean. I shouldn't have even suggested it. Yet, you let me, and I turned around and treated you horribly." He turned his hand and let his fingers rest against her knee. "I've had trouble thinking of myself as an addict, but when I look back at how selfishly I acted, it's hard to deny. I was out of control."

"And now?"

"I'm clean because my family needs me to be. It's like what we were talking about at your dad's house. Love's the best way to spend a life, so I'm trying."

She slid her hand into his. "I thought you'd be angry that I called your dad."

His hand closed around hers, warm and gentle. "You made a call I should've made myself. It wasn't fair of me to let you try to carry me through."

"I wanted to." She rubbed his forearm with her free hand.

"I know, but you didn't know what you were getting yourself into. I did, at least to an extent. It was unfair." He captured her hands in his and ran his thumbs over her fingers. "You don't have a medical background, and even if you did, I don't want to be that man around you."

"But you don't mind being that guy with your dad?"

"Dad's got thicker skin. He knew what he was walking into, and he knows how to handle me."

She smiled at the idea of Philip as a boy of Nason's age, getting into trouble and being assigned chores as a consequence. "How's that?"

"He'd credit prayer."

Philip's dad was a Christian? Or something else? Philip's idea about living for love appealed, but what if there *was* a good God to pray to?

The allusion to religion didn't seem to bother Philip, though. "He issued a lot of ultimatums and kept me constantly supervised."

"Did you have pills there that I didn't find?"

"No, but he couldn't know that, and a relapse wasn't the only danger. I've never been so depressed, and I never want to experience that again. I can't go back. I can't risk what that could do to my family."

She ran her fingertips up his arm and across his shoulder, then rested her palm against his chest. "You don't believe all those things you said about yourself, do you? About your original problem being that you're a bad dad?"

His ribcage fell with a sigh. "I'm not enough. The problem pills were becoming proves it again. But the kids already lost their mom. I'm not going to put them through losing me, too, whether by overdose or arrest. Our situation may not be ideal, but we're okay. Ruthann will be a stable figure in their lives, for a while, anyway. They've got a home here. They can make friends at school. We're not the traditional family I'd choose, but we've got other things going for us. Love will get us through."

She smoothed the pad of her index finger over the hem at the neck of his shirt. "You talk as if you expect to be single forever."

"Until recently, I did."

"And now?"

"I'm afraid I blew my chance with the woman I'm interested in."

She laughed but sobered when she remembered the warnings she'd read about addicts needing to remain single at the start of their recovery. But Philip wasn't an addict anymore, right? Her fingers curled at the neck of his shirt, her index finger slipping between the T-shirt and his skin. "Who's that?"

"Michaela, if you can forgive me, I'd like to date you."

"For everything before tonight, yes. I forgive you." She rested her hand along his neck. At the base of her thumb, his pulse beat with assurance. He'd come through. Alive. Clean. He'd promised everything would be different, and it was.

Maybe he wasn't a typical addict. Or maybe it was their relationship that was special, that would allow them to be the exception to that ban on dating.

They could be the exception, right?

She peered into his warm brown eyes, the ones that made her think of the home she'd always wanted. "But I hoped you'd say you wanted to *win* me."

He pulled her closer. When he touched her jaw, she bent her head and kissed him. After an intoxicating beat, he tilted his head, breaking the kiss. "What do you think I'm doing on my knees?"

For that, she kissed him again. The contact sent sparks through her veins and incinerated the last remaining pesky doubts. They were the exception. They had to be.

24

"*D*rumroll!" Charlie, Gannon's guitar tech, burst into the studio.

At the command, Wilson, the drum technician, slipped behind the drums and complied.

Michaela lowered her water bottle. She wasn't used to this many people in the studio at Gannon's place.

John and Gannon turned from their conversation with Tim, their expressions washed with mild amusement. With a flare that didn't match Charlie's heavier build and graying hair, the man motioned toward the door.

Riff, a wiry young guy, advanced with a silver box. Toward her.

Michaela glanced to Philip, who watched from a chair nearby. He'd been home almost a week, and they'd spent a couple of evenings together, but she didn't know where she stood with him much better than she knew her place with Awestruck's crew. Except for Sunday, when they'd sung to the kids together, he invited her to come after Nila and Nason were in bed. She'd questioned him on it, and he'd said he didn't want them getting overly attached.

Maybe she'd gotten overly attached herself because his precautions stung. Especially since he also kept turning the dial on their physical relationship back down whenever things seemed like they were about to get interesting.

None of her past boyfriends had acted so reserved in their physical relationship. Considering everything she and Philip had been through together, the limitations felt off.

Philip's tech carrying a box toward her and the goofy grins on the crew members' faces built on her base-level uneasiness. If they made fun of her and Philip teamed up with them against her ...

Riff extended the box. She took it, eyeing him for clues, but she didn't even know the kid's real name. Unless his parents had actually named him Riff. She doubted that. Riff scratched his arm, still grinning. He scratched his arm some more.

Philip had told her the tech was a stand-in for the normal guy, but the kid was an odd choice. He ought to see a doctor about the itchiness, because this wasn't the first she'd seen him scrubbing at his skin like a dog with fleas.

"Open it," Riff prompted.

She slipped off the lid. Nestled in a bed of pink tissue paper lay a microphone covered in black rhinestones. Relief and pleasure brought a laugh. Yesterday, she'd commented that she never used plain black mics at shows, but Gannon had vetoed the idea of painting one white or silver for next week's performance.

Gannon snorted. "You two stayed up all night making that?"

"No." Michaela focused on the roadies. "You wouldn't have gone to the trouble. Where did you find this?"

Riff gazed at the mic a couple of seconds. Admiring his handiwork, or about to fall asleep? "We made it."

"Bought the jewels last night." Charlie slugged Riff's shoulder. "Someone, who shall not be named, glued a couple to his fingers, but we're overcomers."

That brought another round of laughter before Tim suggested they put the microphone to use by running through the collaboration song. She complied, noticing again the possessiveness of the lyrics.

If you'll be mine, mine alone,

I'll help you through, I'll be your home.

Possessiveness her own relationship lacked.

So, when the group decided to caravan into Lakeshore for Gannon and John's Friday tradition of Superior Dogs, she looked for the opportunity to get a few minutes with Philip.

THE SUN SHONE as Philip got behind the wheel at Gannon's. Michaela hopped into the passenger seat. He hadn't expected her to ride with him into Lakeshore, but he welcomed the company. She'd been an important part of how he'd survived the week. Between time with her, extra workouts, activities with his kids, and calls from his dad, he'd managed without surrendering to his cravings for more pills.

To that end, he'd researched local activities to fill the weekend. "I found a list of local waterfalls. Want to come with me and the kids to find a few tomorrow?"

"I'd love to."

Anticipation, something he hadn't felt much in months—years, maybe—brightened his mood as much as the sunshine had. "Good, because I already told the kids I'd invite you, and they interpreted that as a guarantee you were coming. They're pretty pumped."

"It'll be fun. I haven't seen them in days." Her more reserved tone meant the excursion wouldn't be the lifeline for her that it was for him, but then she wasn't the one fighting for sobriety. "I'd like time alone with you too. After the waterfalls, we could go on a date."

"Would you consider a movie after the kids are in bed a date? I'm trying not to ask Ruthann for extra hours on the heels of last week, but company would be great."

"Sure, I guess."

"You're disappointed." He glanced over to confirm. He'd rather have the nanny upset with him than Michaela. "Okay, let's do it. Waterfalls, then we'll drop off the kids with Ruthann, and I'll take you on a real date. Someplace nice."

"I could cook for you at my place. I thought it'd be nice to get away from the house, so you don't always have to worry about the kids coming back down." Uncharacteristic shyness hooded Michaela's glance in his direction. "Maybe you could relax."

"Relax?" The very suggestion put him on guard. Hadn't he been relaxed around her?

She pressed her hands together between her knees. "That first time we kissed, you held back. I thought you wanted to work on yourself first, but we've spent three evenings together since you came home clean, and you're still ... reserved."

He kept his narrowed gaze on the road. "You want more of a physical relationship."

He was stalling. He'd known by the way she'd pulled him closer during their first kiss, and the way she'd tried to run her hand up inside his shirt two nights ago. Both times, he had thought of Clare and stopped her.

"Yes. I mean, not everything right away—it's only been a week. But I get the feeling you're not feeling the same chemistry I am."

She'd chosen an odd time to get into it. Gannon's SUV and a crew member's rental navigated toward Lakeshore ahead, and John's sports car hung in his rearview mirror. They only had the five-minute drive for privacy.

"Unless you're worried the kids will interrupt."

"No." Though that thought twisted his gut too.

"Then the problem is the morality agreement? Because not only do you seem uninterested in anything beyond a little kissing, but I also get nothing from you in front of the guys."

Lying and blaming the agreement would be easier, but he'd promised everything would be different. "You don't report to me, and I'm not bribing you with backstage passes or anything. We're not violating the agreement." The street swept down into Lakeshore, Superior and the marina to the left, the quaint downtown area ahead. "When we're in the studio, we're working. That's why I haven't reached out in front of the guys. But they know something's going on, or I wouldn't have gone after you to Illinois."

"So what am I supposed to think? You do like me, right?"

"Of course. Yes." He glanced over, but he couldn't look long as he followed Gannon down Main Street. Mid-summer, at the height of the tourist season, traffic flowed slowly and stopped often for pedestrians shopping the small businesses. "I'm not hiding our relationship. Really. Starting now, I'll make sure everyone knows, okay?"

"And when we're alone? Like, after the kids are asleep tomorrow?"

"I thought I gave you a heads up about this."

Her stomach fluttered. He'd never said he didn't want a physical relationship. Was that what he meant? "About what exactly?"

"I said after Clare died, I tried a lot of things to feel better, but nothing worked."

"Right. Drugs and one-night-stands. That's not what this is, right? I assumed that, the next time you had feelings for someone, you'd show it."

He did have feelings for her, and the other night, it hadn't been easy to resist peeling off his shirt and ... starting a chain of actions he'd better not imagine.

"If something's going on, I need to know. The longer you

wait to explain, the longer I'll be making up reasons on my own, and most of those have to do with you not liking me."

A block from the food truck, Gannon pulled into a spot. The vehicle a crew member drove pulled over a little later.

"I do like you. A hundred times over."

"Then what?"

A third spot waited, but Philip passed it. In his rearview, he saw John take advantage of the opening. Philip might get razzed about not parallel parking, but finding a space somewhere else would give them a few more minutes to finish up this conversation. "I've used women a lot the same as I used drugs, and I don't want to use you."

Michaela gave a bewildered frown. "It's not using me if you have feelings for me."

He turned a corner. Out of sight from the rest of the band and crew, he parked. "I do have feelings for you." Feelings bigger than any he'd felt for anyone since Clare. Michaela had seen his worst and hadn't run, except when he'd pushed her away. Even then, she'd known he'd be taken care of, having called his father.

But as his body ached to "relax" with Michaela, he couldn't deny his experience. He and Clare hadn't slept together until they'd gotten married, and their relationship had been different for it. Better.

He wanted better for him and Michaela too.

But that reasoning was so wrapped up with Clare, Michaela would never understand.

Her green eyes fixed on him like lasers out to blind a pilot.

He took a deep breath that was anything but cleansing. "Getting into bed with someone feels empty without ..." He cringed. She wasn't going to like this. "Getting into bed without a marriage commitment feels empty, and I've had enough emptiness to last a lifetime."

Disbelief and disapproval pulled at her forehead, her lips. "You want to wait until you're *married* again?"

Even to him, that sounded a long way off. Career-focused Michaela, still in her early twenties, had probably never seriously considered marriage. What had he been thinking of, mentioning it?

She swept up her purse and pushed open her door. "The others are waiting."

When he met her on the sidewalk, she gripped her purse with one hand and burrowed the other into her pocket. The signal was clear.

But he'd promised contact. He rested his hands on her shoulders and waited for those green eyes to fix on him. "You mean a lot to me. I'm not trying to upset you."

"Let's just go."

He kept pace with her. He'd said he wasn't hiding their relationship, and to prove it, he offered his hand. Her returning grip was loose, and sadness tipped the corners of her lips. They'd debut their relationship in the midst of their first fight.

MICHAELA DREW a breath into her belly, the way she'd been trained to breathe for singing.

She'd been telling herself the rejection she felt was all in her mind each time he maintained a boundary between them.

But no.

Philip had rejected her. Soundly. Again.

If he had genuine feelings for her, he wouldn't put this barrier in their relationship. They'd overcome a lot together, and their relationship ought to reflect their commitment to each other with a little more than handholding.

And who was he to mention marriage when he rarely allowed her near the kids? Clearly, he didn't plan for this to go that far. When Nila had seen that music video on Michaela's watch, she'd given him reason to think she wasn't fit to act as a mother to the kids.

Was he right?

How would she know when she hardly remembered her own mom?

She cared deeply for Philip, Nila, and Nason. For them, she'd change, if only Philip wanted her in their lives.

She slipped her hand away as they approached the group. The strangers at the front of the line got their orders and walked off, a couple eyeing Gannon but apparently not interested enough to try talking to him.

The man in the truck braced his hands on the windowsill and whistled. "The whole crew. A show of force like this can only mean one thing. Rehearsals."

Gannon nodded. "You've met everyone?"

"I see some regulars. Other than that, no. Let's start orders first. Two Superior Dogs, and ..." He pointed to Philip and Tim. "Same for you two?"

Both nodded. When the cook disappeared to put the hot dogs on, Tim raised an eyebrow at Philip. "Surprised he doesn't know your order. I thought you guys came here all the time."

"I didn't before, but I've seen the error of my ways."

The guys wouldn't think anything of his regretful smile, but she knew he'd skipped Friday lunches at Superior Dogs to buy pills near Bryant's Subs.

And now he'd changed.

Despite everything, she was proud of him for the victory.

The cook returned to the window.

"All right. Introductions." Gannon rested a hand on the shoulder of the man next to him, a sandy blond with a gauged earring and, in protest of Lakeshore's summer weather, a hooded sweatshirt. "Kyle performs with us, guitar and vocals. Kyle, Asher owns Superior Dogs. A Lakeshore legend."

Asher laughed. "If that's true, it's only because a certain band is addicted to loaded hot dogs."

After Asher shook with Kyle, Gannon listed off the names of the six crew members who'd tagged along and made up Awestruck's core onstage support: Charlie, Riff, Wilson, Kyle's tech, and the head sound and light specialists.

Asher turned his focus to Michaela. "And one lady in the whole group. I hope they're treating you well."

"Don't you worry about her," Tim scoffed.

The chorus of laughter had to have been a result of her new blingy microphone.

The gesture had been cute. If only Philip felt as strongly for her as the crew did.

But pouting wouldn't do, so Michaela rallied. "Like royalty. I've heard a lot about Superior Dogs."

Asher transitioned back into taking orders. When they had their food, they settled in the simple, white gazebo that overlooked the marina. Philip sat beside her, interacting with the group as if he didn't have a care in the world.

The pork and chili bowl she'd ordered took less time to eat than the massive, loaded hot dogs the guys favored, so she finished first. When her phone buzzed, she gladly took the excuse to get up.

Philip hardly seemed to notice when she excused herself, but for once, Reese greeted her enthusiastically. "Evie loves your song. She's off on a Caribbean vacation, but she called me because she's coming back early to get you in the studio."

"She is? Really?"

"I told her you'd be there tomorrow. You have three days to lay tracks before her next gig. I hope you're ready."

"That soon?" Michaela turned to scan the group she'd left behind. Leaving tomorrow and coming back three days later would mean she'd return in time for the show, but what would Gannon think of her spending time away so close to the event?

"If working with her is your dream, there's no time like the present."

"Right. Yes. I'm just surprised. The timing's kind of crazy with the Awestruck show coming up."

And with Philip. They had a lot to figure out, and he'd only been clean for a couple of short weeks. No others here knew about his problem, so they wouldn't know to keep an eye on him. Would he be okay without her?

Reese's low voice interrupted her thoughts. "You've really fallen for him, haven't you?"

"Huh?"

"I heard all about your little romance."

"From who?" Someone could've snapped a picture of them holding hands for that minute on the sidewalk, but the photo wouldn't have already traversed the country to Reese.

"Tim. Philip went to be with you for your sister's operation? It's my job to know these things, and when a client like you gets all quiet on me, I know something's up."

A client like her? That made her sound needy.

Maybe she was. She'd called Gannon for help this summer. She'd practically begged Philip for attention on the drive here only to be met with that humiliating refusal.

When she'd acted the opposite—independent—he'd come after her to Illinois. Maybe she ought to leave for a few days. He'd realize how much he missed her. How much he needed her. Maybe even how much he *loved* her.

Then, he'd prove his devotion with his actions.

"I'm not going to let some summer fling get between me and a golden opportunity." Michaela broadened her stance, both feet planted firmly on the path. A couple of days apart was just what they needed. And Evie was what her career needed. Two wins with one trip.

"Good to hear. I already booked your tickets. You fly out

tonight from Green Bay. Best I could do on short notice. I'm sending you the itinerary now."

Excitement and nerves stretched their wings in her stomach. Tomorrow. She'd be working with Evie Decker this time tomorrow. Was she ready? *Yes, yes. Yes, of course.* She'd gone into the studio with less in the past, and Evie would give input on the song's finishing touches. "Does Tim know? Awestruck?"

"I'm not the one who got the ball rolling while you had another project on your plate."

"Okay. I'll tell them." Her gaze collided with Philip's.

Oh, wait. How could she have forgotten waterfall hunting?

"I have plans tomorrow."

"This is Evie Decker." Reese's voice took on a decidedly serious tone. "You won't get this opportunity twice."

True. Philip hadn't had time to tell the kids she'd accepted yet, and in the end, their disappointment would turn into something good. She'd make it up to the kids, and Philip would make changes to keep her close.

Michaela Vandehey would not be needy.

25

Clean, Philip felt every discomfort he'd rather numb. Including regret about how his conversation with Michaela over lunch had gone. Now she and Gannon were both missing from the studio. Was she venting to him?

If so, she wouldn't find much sympathy from a man with Gannon's convictions, but he'd rather the lead singer didn't have a window into such a personal sphere.

He picked up a bass guitar and settled into his chair, hoping music would distract him from everything sobriety insisted he face.

Memories of Clare weren't the only consideration with Michaela. Abstaining from sex wasn't that different from resisting drugs. In both cases, the hard choice should strengthen his relationships, but his grip on willpower had never seemed so precarious. If he gave up self-control in one area, the other might not be far behind.

He pulled the electric bass closer. As soon as he played two notes, he could both hear and feel a problem. Earlier in the afternoon, Riff had cleaned the fret board and replaced the strings, but he'd done the work incorrectly. Hopefully his favored tech, House, would heal before everyone gathered to record the next album.

John, Wilson, and Charlie lingered nearby, but Riff must be in another room. Probably cleaning something else, for better or for worse.

In the hall, Gannon, Tim, and Michaela were standing in a cluster, the men facing Philip's direction, Michaela with her back to him, the ends of her long hair falling to the small of her back.

"You understand?" she asked.

"I'd be upset if you didn't go," Tim said.

Michaela wanted to go somewhere?

Gannon seemed less enthusiastic. "You came to get away and regroup. Are you sure you want this in the middle of that?"

Philip's grip on the neck of the bass tightened. She hadn't explained the call she'd taken at lunch, but he'd bet that was what she was discussing with Tim and Gannon. He'd forgotten about the ups and downs of dating. Maybe she'd decided to tell him her news tomorrow on the trails or at dinner. He'd give her the benefit of the doubt and focus on his job.

He turned away and found Riff in the office down the hall, a clipboard pinched under his arm. Coiled cords and other equipment fanned the floor in front of him, but the tech was on his phone instead of working.

"You switched the A and the E strings on this."

Riff whirled, shoving the device away. "Oh. Hey. Really?" He gave an apologetic cringe. "I wouldn't have done that."

He had, though.

Philip hesitated to hand the instrument over. Something was off, or Riff wouldn't have made such a basic mistake with this bass. Moving quickly to hide the phone didn't make sense, either, since no one on the team would begrudge a quick text.

"Everything all right?"

Riff scratched his cheek, then extended his hands for the

instrument. "This is a big opportunity, and then I go and do this. Can't believe it."

Philip passed him the guitar. If Riff couldn't pull his weight, they needed to know sooner than later, either by Riff coming clean or by his work doing so for him.

The roadie scratched his face again and knelt to riffle through a box. "I'm really sorry about this. It won't happen again. I'll be careful."

Philip waited until the tech straightened, a fresh package of strings in his grip. "Don't beat yourself up. Just double-check your work, and get this to me when it's ready."

"Yes. Coming right up. Sorry." He hunched over the instrument.

Philip let himself out of the office and closed the door again. In the hall, he hesitated as realization slammed into him. Riff was on something. Philip would guarantee it. And not just a small part of him wanted to reopen that door, find out what that something was, who he'd bought from, and whether his dealer could get his hands on painkillers.

"Hey." Tim waved to him from the entrance to the studio. "Let's go. Work to do."

Philip abandoned the door to the office. He wouldn't go back. To cement his resolve, he tried to pull up the awful image he'd pictured of the kids finding him. But he found the edges were softening on what had once been a crisp horror.

WHEN AWESTRUCK WRAPPED UP, everyone left so quickly that Michaela didn't realize she'd missed Philip until she saw only she, Tim, and Gannon remained in the studio.

She tossed a goodbye over her shoulder and jogged out. She found Philip behind the wheel of his SUV, engine idling as he checked his phone.

She leaned her forearms on the sill of his open window. "You weren't going to say goodbye?"

"I had to call my dad." The phone, which he'd rested on his leg at her approach, darkened on its own.

Her suspicion ebbed. If he'd been hiding something related to pills, he would've powered off the screen when she approached. "Everything okay?"

"Sure. He didn't answer, but I'll try him later." He squinted at her in the evening sunlight. "I can delay getting home. Ruthann's feeding the kids."

"Okay." As long as he made the suggestion, accepting didn't make her needy. Besides, she would leave in an hour. That had to be the definition of *not* needy. "Want to swing by my place?"

"I'll follow you over."

The whole drive, she rehearsed how their conversation would go. Ideally, he'd be apologetic about the limits he'd put on their relationship. He'd admit that few people would humor his ancient approach to dating. To make sure she didn't want to leave him, he might engage in more of a conversation about it.

If she'd set this boundary, her past boyfriends would've disappeared on the spot. Sex was the way couples showed they loved each other ... Well, maybe not entirely, but that made up a special part of a couple's bond.

Gannon's voice rang over her thoughts. *The things the world tries to pass off as love tend to be something else.*

Well, if Philip's abstinence plan was love, she couldn't see it.

She parked in the drive of her condo, and he pulled in alongside her. Michaela focused on breathing until he appeared beside her car and opened the door for her.

She peered up at him, willing herself not to be needy. "You really want to wait?"

Instead of softening and delivering the apology she'd hoped for, he stepped back. "I do."

She inhaled one more time, then unbuckled and rose.

He followed her to the door and caught up as she fit the key in the lock. She turned the knob and pushed her way inside.

He closed them into the quiet privacy of the condo. "I've been on your side of this conversation. I know how it feels. But this is something I need to do, and I know it can work out."

Wait. How could she have forgotten? "Clare asked you to wait."

He watched her, on guard.

No wonder his mention of marriage had seemed more like a barrier than an opportunity. "I'm not her. I never will be."

"I know."

Panic squealed through her brain like microphone feedback in an auditorium. She turned deeper into the condo, leaving him to follow or not.

The hallway to her bedroom had a tall ceiling and a skylight. Yellow evening light diffused downward. The carpet muffled her steps and silenced Philip's—if he even followed. She flipped on the light in the bedroom because the lake-facing windows didn't allow in direct sunlight.

Despite her hopes that her departure would wake him to the true depth of his feelings for her, leaving for California now seemed risky. It might not work. He might realize the opposite —that she didn't measure up. Or he might interpret her trip to mean she didn't care.

But the decision had already been made.

Courage to tell him her plan came easier when she wasn't even certain he stood in hearing distance. "I got a call at lunch. Evie's ready for me."

"Going right after the show?" His voice came clear and low.

She checked over her shoulder. He'd crossed his arms and leaned against the doorframe. Talk about playing it cool, independent, and unneedy.

"I'm leaving now. I'll be back in three days."

He stayed quiet, but oh, so focused.

She rolled open the closet door and stretched to pull down her carry-on.

"The kids were counting on you."

"I'm sorry. I wanted to come. I promise I'll do something with them another time. But you'll have fun without me."

"I'm sure we will." He spoke evenly, untouched by the regret she was feeling.

They were hanging on by a thread here. She grabbed a couple of tops and pairs of pants from the closet and dropped them in the case.

"The truth is ..." He spoke loudly, quickly.

At the sudden change, she looked up.

His expression turned pained. "I'm struggling."

The hallway skylight warmed the color of his hair and shoulders. He'd uncrossed his arms.

"With what?"

"You know."

Her focus zinged from one point to another on his face, his body, looking for clues about his state. He displayed no symptoms of withdrawal, but she might not recognize symptoms of him using again. "Struggling, or giving in?"

"Struggling." He returned her gaze with gentle focus, as if he knew what she was doing and felt her concern was fair. "But getting by. That's why I called my dad."

"Will you be okay?"

PHILIP HATED how he deserved her question and, even more, the uncertainty of the answer. He'd rather be strong, but Michaela seemed more drawn to his weakness than the façade of control he'd tried to maintain. "I'm here, then I'll be with the kids, then I'll call Dad again. I'll let the kids sleep in my room if I have to, so my reasons are right in front of me. Tomorrow is waterfalls, then I cleared our date with Ruthann." The corner of his mouth edged up ruefully. "Since that's off, I'll keep the kids close."

"I'm sorry." She crossed one of her arms over her body, shoulders drooping.

"I don't want a babysitter, and you don't want to be one."

She smoothed her hands over the clothes she'd piled in her suitcase as though she wanted to return them to the closet and call off the trip. "I've been working toward this for ages."

He nodded.

"It's Evie Decker. She's ready, so I'm going."

"Makes sense."

"I'll be back soon." Her green eyes reviewed him again. "You'll be okay."

"Are you convincing me or yourself?"

"I'm just saying, this didn't come out of nowhere." She pushed a hand into her hair and massaged her fingers against her scalp before dropping her arm again. "It's a legit way to grow my career."

Yet she stood there, posture slumped as if he'd asked her to choose him or her career. Today ought to be a fantastic day for her, and his old habits had added worry she didn't deserve.

He'd quit pills so they'd stop negatively impacting the people he cared about. Time to put an end to their power. He stepped into the room. "Don't worry on my account."

"I know. Because you don't need me." Her lips shimmered, dusty rose and perfect. Her hair fell in smooth, long waves, and her clothes skimmed curves that had the power to draw him, power she'd never understand. She had every reason to be confident, but the sheen in her eyes and the way she tipped her right ankle told a story of insecurity.

"You've helped me become a better person." He caught her hand, pulled her closer, held her to his chest. "I'm clean in no small part thanks to you. I'm here to support you too."

"I wish ..." She stepped back and peered at him, squeezing his fingers. "I wish you'd want me to stay. But ..."

"But what? I do." He'd promised to win her, to change for the better for her sake, and to help her do the same. That meant he wouldn't prioritize his preferences over her dreams.

"Not really, though, right?" She pressed her lips together. "You're still too hung up on Clare to even kiss me right."

He hadn't meant for her to realize the role Clare played in how he'd conducted himself, but exposed, the secret lost some of its power. Like his urge to use lost the sharpest edge when he told someone else about a craving. Openness turned his secrets from burdens he could hardly carry into obstacles he believed he could conquer.

She wanted an unreserved kiss? Done.

He lifted her hand and kissed the back, her skin smooth and cool against his lips. Mouth still tense, Michaela looked away. He turned her hand and kissed the base of her thumb, then the musical notes tattooed on the thin skin on the inside of her wrist.

Her attention fixed on him, and the signal that he'd ignited her interest quickened his breath. He released her wrist, and she gripped his shoulder, hunger evident in the way her finger-tips pressed into his muscle. He slid one arm around her waist, pulled her snuggly to him, and drew her hair away from her neck. She tilted her chin, and he kissed his way up until she gasped when he'd reached her jaw.

"Come here." She guided his mouth to hers in a kiss that sent his pulse roaring and rendered his lungs useless, the same as a free fall off a cliff would. He held her tighter, the exhilaration blocking all thoughts of what they might be tumbling toward.

She curved her back, tipping her head out of reach and returning him to solid ground. "I have a flight." Her hands rested on his neck, one thumb on each of his cheeks, her face a breath from his, her eyes alight. "But I stand corrected."

He ached to lean forward, kiss her again, jump off another cliff, but he knew how that game would end. He needed to stand by the choices he'd made before this high pounded through his veins.

He stepped back. "I'll see you in a few days."

"Take care while I'm gone."

"You too." He let himself out, climbed into the driver's seat, and ran his hands over his face. She'd only requested—and he'd only meant to give—a kiss. Seconds later, he'd been ready to fall into so much more.

If that was all the willpower he had, he might not survive the weekend.

26

$\mathcal{T}$he parking lot off the two-lane road in the middle of the woods wasn't where the directions indicated, but Philip turned in. This had to be the hiking trail to the first waterfall of the day. A sign at the far end of the gravel lot confirmed his choice.

"Let the fun begin." Gannon unbuckled.

Philip helped the kids out and called for them to stay in sight when they ran for the trail. They stopped to look over the edge of a small bridge spanning a brook.

Gannon joined him on the well-worn sand and gravel path. "I bet John would rather be here with us than finalizing seating plans or whatever he's doing."

Because of Michaela's absence, Philip had invited both of his bandmates along. John had bowed out to tackle wedding responsibilities. Two weeks and counting until the small lakeside ceremony.

"I don't know. He seems pretty stoked about getting married."

"True. Adeline and I want all of our friends and family at

our wedding, and I don't mind all the chores. But the waiting? That's the part, I mind."

They reached the kids, paused to look at the stream washing over a rocky riverbed, then moved on, the kids running ahead again.

"How long were you and Clare engaged before you got married?"

"A week." The band had decided to leave town suddenly, and he and Clare had known what they wanted.

Gannon laughed. "And I call John impatient."

"Aren't we all?"

Gannon chuckled as they came up on the kids again. Nason picked up a long, thin stick and poked a mushroom.

Nila plucked a purple flower from a clump of clover growing along the path. "This is for you, Dad."

"It's very nice, but just this one. Leave the rest for other people to look at." He held out his palm, and she placed the puffy bloom in his hand before marching ahead again. "Nason, let's leave the mushrooms alone."

His son ran after Nila, the stick dragging on the ground behind him, the trees towering above. Sunlight filtered down, illuminating layer after layer of green around them.

"Speaking of relationships ..." Gannon shot him a look.

He used to have to watch everything he said in personal conversations. With so much less to hide now, the invitation to talk actually brought relief. "It's a lot messier the second time around."

"Why's that?"

"History. Kids. I'm more set in my ways, I guess. Where I want to live. What I want to do."

Gannon nodded, too quiet. A trio of hikers proceeded toward them, equipped with gear the broad, flat trail didn't require. They said hello on the way by but didn't slow their stride.

Philip waited until their voices had receded. "You think Michaela's a bad idea."

"You're the one who said it's messy. Maybe the difficulty is less about the fact that you've loved and lost and more about ... Michaela's seeking, but she's not a believer."

"I know."

A few more steps.

"Are you? A believer?"

Neither of the guys had asked him directly before. He'd never argued when they talked about their faith and had sat in on most of the Bible studies they did on tour. He knew where they stood and knew he'd get lectures if he revealed what he believed. So, he'd kept his experiences to himself thinking, all this time, they assumed he was one of them.

The kids dawdled, looking up. As they came upon the pair, Nason was trying to convince Nila there were monkeys in the trees. At the threat of being passed by the adults, they abandoned the debate and scampered ahead.

"You do know faith isn't a requirement. Awestruck's not a Christian band, and we never asked you to pretend you believe something you don't."

Philip had enough secrets, enough problems. And didn't letting go of secrets lessen burdens? "I believed for a while, up until He killed off Clare. She believed and didn't deserve to die."

"I figured it was something like that."

"And you never said anything?" What else had Gannon noticed and not commented on?

"I'm saying something now." Gannon sighed. "I can't answer for God and everything He does. But if Clare believed, she's happy now. He didn't kill her off. He collected her to Himself. There's a difference."

"Telling me she's in Heaven isn't much comfort when we

need her so much here." No talent could turn Ruthann into Nila's and Nason's mother.

"I can't imagine the hole she left in your life."

"I wish I could do better for the kids, but without her, I keep failing them." Most recently, his extended stay in Illinois had restarted Nila's nightmares.

Gannon kicked a rock, and it skipped ahead. "Failure is the human condition. That's why we need Christ. Where we're weak, He's strong. I wouldn't want to try walking a valley like losing a spouse without Him."

"I guess I got through the valley on my own. Now, there's Michaela."

Holding hands, the kids stepped off the trail, picking their way a couple of feet into the thin undergrowth of the forest. He took out his phone and pulled up the camera.

"You're pretty serious about her."

"I could see getting that way." He'd much rather hike with her. Although, being off in the woods with Gannon meant no access to any of the temptations that had seemed unavoidable yesterday.

"She's the first you've been serious about since Clare?"

"That's why it's messy. Not because we have different beliefs. I've seen how selfless she can be. She's perceptive and caring. And the kids love her."

"A lot of people have treated her badly, and that's left a mark."

Philip glanced over. Was the warning for Philip's sake or Michaela's?

Gannon clapped his shoulder. "I hope it works out."

They reached the children, and he squatted to take the picture, Nason pointing at another "monkey," Nila looking up as if she believed him, and the forest encircling them.

He straightened, got the kids going again, then sent the shot to Michaela. *Miss you.*

~

MICHAELA CHECKED her reflection in the full-length mirror. Her one-bedroom apartment was tiny, but new. Between how much she'd spent on rent and how little time she passed there, splurging on décor hadn't seemed practical. She'd added just a few pieces to make the place homey. Now, she'd only stopped in to dress for a nice dinner out.

If she'd worn this little red number in Lakeshore, Philip wouldn't have taken as long to kiss her as he had on Friday. A delicious shiver shot through her at the thought of that good-bye. If only she hadn't had to leave for her flight, she would've explored the new territory more thoroughly.

She snapped a selfie and sent it with a text to Philip.

Wish you were here.

A reply arrived almost immediately.

Ditto.

He didn't have long to wait. She had wrapped up with Evie earlier. In celebration, Reese snagged reservations at an exclusive restaurant. Michaela would eat—and enjoy every bite, every moment of Reese's undivided attention—and then catch some sleep, get herself to the airport, and pick up where she'd left off with Philip.

He'd taken the kids hiking without her, but the area had dozens of waterfalls, so maybe they could try again next weekend.

She straightened the dress, checked her lipstick, then slid into her heels.

Reese's vintage, cherry-red coupe idled out front. A doorman stepped forward and opened the passenger side for Michaela, and she slipped in.

Reese zipped out into traffic. "I don't suppose you've caught any of the entertainment shows tonight."

"Is there buzz about the song already?" She pulled out her phone.

Sure enough, her name appeared in the title of a clip that had aired that night.

Michaela Vandehey to Complete Trifecta for Awestruck?

"Oh, about the collaboration? That's cool too." The palm trees lining the street passed quickly, the sky glowing with remnants of the sunset, but even with flowing traffic, it'd take a good half an hour to get to the restaurant. She clicked to play the video.

Behind the blond reporter, one Michaela had spoken with twice on red carpets, a screen displayed the words "The Awestruck Trifecta" and a professional photo of the guys.

"Following the close of last year's Letting Go World Tour, rock band Awestruck, responsible for hits such as 'Yours' and 'If I Let Her Go,' packed up and relocated to a small community in northern Wisconsin. Why would one of the country's most famous bands make such a move? It all comes down to love."

A slideshow featuring Gannon and Adeline played as the anchor narrated.

"Lead singer Gannon Vaughn reconnected with an old flame, Adeline Green. Though most of us were disappointed their relationship resulted in Vaughn pulling back from the spotlight, love seems to have given Awestruck's front man a fresh burst of creative energy that pushed the band's next offering, *Letting Go*, to the top of charts. The couple is launching a non-profit to teach music to youth in their community, but their focus is divided between that and wedding planning now that Vaughn proposed to Green this spring. The date is set for September."

Michaela glanced to Reese. "Is this the right clip?"

She nodded and motioned for her to pay attention.

The screen changed to feature a photo of John in the hospital. "A matter of days after his own serious wreck, drummer

John Kennedy was spotted out with a love interest of his own. Information about the reclusive couple trickled out slowly, so we'd only just learned Erin Hirsh is an automotive mechanic"—the reporter lifted her eyebrows as if to say there was no accounting for love—"when we learned they'd also set plans to tie the knot. Though information about the ceremony is scarce, rumor is, the pair will say, 'I do' before summer's end. Which brings us to Awestruck's third and final member, Philip Miller."

To a melancholy piano tune, the screen displayed a young, clean-shaven Philip sporting a tux and bowtie. Next to him, a blonde with bangs that would've been in style a decade ago grinned at the camera. She was wearing a white dress.

An ache settled in Michaela's chest.

This was his wedding day. This was Clare.

They looked so young. He was older than Michaela, but in this picture, both he and his wife must've been younger than Michaela was now. Nila was eight, so this must've been nine or ten years ago. Before grief haunted Philip's eyes.

She'd never seen him so genuinely joyful.

Meanwhile, the reporter summed up what Michaela already knew—the happy couple wasn't to last. More than she wanted his attention for herself, she wished she could restore the joy he'd lost—even if that meant he'd still have Clare.

"Following the loss of his wife, Miller stepped off the stage in preference for studio work until joining Awestruck in the middle of recording *Letting Go*. When asked if he was looking for love, the single dad had this to say." The anchor motioned to the monitor.

Philip, dressed to the nines, dipped his head to hear a reporter ask a question on the red carpet. Despite what the rest of his face said, Michaela noted his frustrated flinch. "I have my son and daughter. That's all the love I need."

"Of course," the reporter said, "the doting dad's devotion only bumped him further up the list of eligible bachelors. But, sorry ladies, this summer it seems Cupid's arrow has finally flown on the bassist's behalf."

Photos chronicling Michaela's career paraded across the screen.

"*Audition Room* Season Eight winner Michaela Vandehey is rumored to be collaborating with Awestruck. Whether or not anything is happening behind the closed doors of the studio, a source in Michaela's hometown caught this moment between the newly minted couple."

Oh no.

Philip had gone through withdrawal in her hometown. He could get in so much trouble with Awestruck if someone had captured the wrong moment.

Darkness shrouded the photo. A vehicle. A person leaning against it. No, two people.

Their first kiss.

She'd thought he'd maintained too much distance, but the way he'd braced himself around her looked protective. Romantic. Not the worst first kiss after all. She wouldn't mind having a better picture to remember it by. If the show hadn't led with that big intro, no one would know who appeared in the frame.

"Love is in the air," the reporter said. "Or it *was*. However, Michaela is rumored to have left Wisconsin for California to work on her next album. Will the distance do them in, or will the third and final member of Awestruck complete the trifecta of engagements by proposing by the end of the year? Only time will tell."

The clip ended, and Michaela pulled up Philip's contact information. But what should she send him?

If he lived in California, where she wouldn't have to give up her career to be close to him, she might not be opposed to the idea of getting engaged.

Then again, he toured for huge chunks of time, as did she. Why get hitched if they'd never be together?

To bring back that smile.

But even if she could make him happy for a moment, could she be everything the kids needed? Everything Clare had been to them and to Philip?

"I wonder who talked to them about me being here to work on an album." She tapped a fingernail against her phone, then slid the device back into her clutch. "It's just one song."

"About that." Reese's lips curled devilishly. "Evie has a proposal for you."

27

"Tim. What're you doing here?" In his surprise to find his manager on his doorstep at nine o'clock in the morning, Philip forgot common courtesy until Tim motioned to be allowed inside. Philip moved.

"Got some coffee?" Tim lifted a travel mug as he stepped into the house.

Philip waved him toward the kitchen, where he'd left half the pot for Ruthann.

Tim paused to look around when he entered the living room, then continued toward the kitchen. "Nice place. Kids like it here?"

"So far." This morning, Ruthann had coaxed them away from the TV with a promise of a new game involving the swing set.

"You know they don't bother to plow all the roads over winter? Just some of them, and even that's a process. People snowmobile to get around." Tim splayed his fingers next to his head, miming his mind blowing, then snagged the coffee carafe.

The whole band had spent Christmas in the area, so he'd

glimpsed the process of digging out after a storm. Surely Tim hadn't come to discuss the weather.

Tim tightened the lid on his mug, then pulled out a stool at the island and indicated for Philip to do the same. "Let's talk about this monster we created."

"What monster?"

"You don't know?" Tim sighed loudly. "Michaela should've called you, though Reese probably stopped her." He pulled out his phone and went quiet.

"Tim?"

"Evie wants to do an entire album with her." He didn't look away from the device in his hands. "She's coming back for a few hours to do the show, then she'll be gone."

Gone? She'd said her sessions with the producer had gone well, but she'd failed to mention they'd gone *this* well. Surprise and disappointment replaced the anticipation he'd felt at seeing her later.

Yet this didn't explain the visit.

"What do you mean, 'monster we created'?"

"I set her up with Evie. You didn't do anything, I guess, except this." Tim tipped the phone toward him.

Someone had photographed their first kiss?

"They're saying if you propose, it'll be a trifecta, all three members of Awestruck getting engaged in the same year."

Rumors came with the territory, but Tim must've come for a reason. Maybe Philip had been too quick to dismiss his contract's stipulations.

"If this is about the morality agreement—"

Tim put the phone away. "One could argue she's working with Awestruck, which is a conflict of interest, but Adeline recorded a song with us too. If we decide to can Michaela, we'll have to keep you out of the vote. Assuming she knows you can't pull strings for her, and this is as consensual as it looks, you're clear."

"Is that a possibility? Firing her?"

"No. Well, actually, not unless you start gunning for it."

Philip angled to see out the kitchen window onto the yard. Ruthann had set up a beanbag toss, and the kids were trying to sink shots while soaring on the swings. "Why would I want her fired?"

"Because she's using you."

Philip snorted. *Using* him? He was the addict in the relationship, not her. And even he was putting that behind him.

"Think about the picture. I'm sure you had other things on your mind, but you would've noticed a camera in your face, which means it was taken from a distance in the dark. Which means paparazzi were hanging around, not a neighbor with a cell phone. Someone tipped someone off, and it wasn't me."

He turned from the window to find Tim's expression as serious as the accusation.

"Michaela didn't know I was coming."

"But Reese knew because I mentioned your trip when we spoke Monday night about the collaboration. Michaela became a household name on *Audition Room*, so maybe if she hooked up with the right guy, some outlets would've run a story or two. But add in the trifecta angle and the single dad sob story, and yours is a match made in marketing heaven."

Heat pulsed in Philip's temples. Michaela wouldn't have done this.

Tim crossed his arms. "The last two albums Evie produced didn't perform as well as expected. That's how I talked her into taking on Michaela in the first place. My bet is, this publicity showed Evie that Michaela's star is rising, so Evie offered to do the full album to get in on the action. That photo is already benefiting Michaela. Don't get me wrong. Awestruck will get a bump out of this too, but for a struggling artist like Michaela, a relationship with you could be a game changer."

"Reese could've decided to leverage the situation without Michaela knowing."

Skepticism lined Tim's face. "I've seen Michaela in action."

Philip broke eye contact. She'd flirted with Philip the day she'd arrived so he'd help make the soundtrack collaboration a reality. She'd also gotten close with Tim when she wanted a favor from him. But those situations had played out over a couple of days while her relationship with Philip had spanned weeks. If she'd manipulated their relationship to further her career, she'd been incredibly deceitful.

Tim sipped his coffee. "We didn't actually create the monster, but we played into her hand."

"She wouldn't have done all that." If she'd wanted only a headline, she could've spilled one about helping him get clean. Instead, she'd called his dad and maintained his privacy. She'd sung to his kids when he couldn't. She'd forgiven him despite his many failings.

And he'd deserved none of it.

He'd interpreted her actions as selfless, but what if she'd simply been focusing on a bigger picture? A career she loved? He stared out the window again, on the blue sky and the sun hitting the trees. "I'll talk to her."

"Okay. We're getting questions about the nature of your relationship with her."

"No comment."

Tim nodded. "The show on Friday is the last time you have to see her. We can have her and Gannon work in the studio different days than you. We were going to have her join us for some tour stops next year, but we'll call that off."

"You're assuming she and I won't work out."

Tim lifted a hand helplessly. "Even if she were oblivious to Reese's maneuvering, she's staying in California. Everything else aside, long distance? We know how that works out."

"Are you sure she's committed to staying there? In LA?"

"Reese is talking like she is."

"And you trust her?"

"Okay. Talk to Michaela." Tim rose from the counter. "You want to ride with me?"

The band would meet at the concert venue today, an hour from both Mariner and Lakeshore, to finalize some plans. Philip could use the time alone to process. "I'll meet you there."

"Okay." Tim frowned at him. "For what it's worth, the single dad sob story ... You deserve to be happy. I hope I'm wrong about her."

The sense of heaviness this conversation had instilled compounded. He knew what he deserved, and happiness wasn't it.

~

MICHAELA PADDED over to her desk, her fuzzy slippers engulfing her feet. The cozy footwear suited the first day off she'd been granted all week. Eight a.m. here meant ten in Wisconsin. Philip would be at work, just one of a couple of reasons he couldn't help her decide about Evie's offer.

She pulled out the upholstered desk chair, plopped down in front of her laptop, and typed her query into a search engine. *How to make a big decision.*

Results populated, but simultaneously, her phone lit with a picture of just the man she wanted to talk to.

He'd used video call, but she answered with her camera off. She'd just woken up. A messy bun strained to subdue her hair, she wore not a stitch of makeup, and contacts had seemed like too much trouble. Plus, she didn't own a goofier T-shirt.

The overseas find featured nonsensical English—*Cats don't say moo every day*—paired with a very surprised-looking horse. She'd bought the top because the design made her laugh, and the fabric was soft and comfy, but she didn't want to answer for its oddness.

The sight of Philip warmed her like a hug. This man, with his warm brown eyes and his tragic past and his dogged determination to make a better man of himself ... This man had gone from claiming his kids' love was enough for him to kissing her for the whole world to see.

She took the phone with her to the bathroom. She'd get herself together, then switch to video. "Hey. Shouldn't you be working?"

"Shouldn't you be catching a flight?"

"How do you know I'm not?"

He frowned and studied the phone, probably wondering why she hadn't allowed him to see her.

And thank goodness he couldn't. She'd counted on him disbelieving what the entertainment show had suggested about her staying in California to make an album. His low tone and the knots on his forehead revealed he knew the show hadn't been all wrong.

"Okay. Evie made this incredible offer, so I delayed my flight to take time to consider. On the one hand, I'd love to spend more of my summer with you. And I want to find a waterfall with the kids." She grabbed her makeup bag. "On the other, it's quite an opportunity. I've wanted to work with Evie forever."

"Why not come back here while you make up your mind?"

Because around him and the kids, her priorities shifted away from the drive that had gotten her this far. "I'll be back on Friday."

"For a few hours."

Reese must've talked to Tim, who must've passed along at least part of the story. "My time there will only be that short if I decide on California right away." She skipped contouring to speed along her routine. Foundation and powder would do for today. "The other option is to write more material in Wisconsin before locking myself away in the studio. I don't want to write with Evie breathing down my neck. I mean, we'll buy some songs, but I have to contribute originals to keep the album authentic. And if I write in Lakeshore, I'll get more time with you."

Returning to Philip for a few weeks would be a no-brainer, except that, if she delayed the opportunity, Evie might change her mind as quickly as she'd extended this offer. Plus, leaving Philip and the kids behind wouldn't get easier after spending more time with them.

"But, whatever I choose, Awestruck's coming to California to record too, right?" Two weeks after John's wedding, the band would buckle down and lay tracks for their next album. Since they had the material ready to go, they'd make quick work of it. Then, they'd return to Wisconsin for Gannon's wedding, and their album would drop. After the holidays, they'd embark on another tour.

The band's time in California floated before her like an oasis. She longed to stay close to Philip—as long as being together didn't mean risking the best thing to happen to her career since *Audition Room*. "Are you going to bring the kids with you?"

"I don't know." His stormy tone played on her sympathy.

He was upset at the distance.

"I wish I didn't have to go, but this was kind of inevitable." She brushed bronzer over her cheeks and moved on to her eyes.

"Maybe."

"Are you ..." She paused with the eyeshadow brush mid-air. "Are you coping all right? How's staying clean going?"

"I've managed."

"I know we have something special. Our relationship means a lot to me too." She zipped along, adding a darker shade to the crease of her lids. "No matter what, we would face distance eventually. We've both got thriving careers. But this is the twenty-first century. We can talk on the phone and hop on a plane whenever that doesn't cut it."

"How do you think someone happened to take that picture of us?"

She lowered her makeup brush. How had he jumped to that? She pawed through her case for eyeliner. "There are cameras everywhere these days."

The knots on Philip's forehead grew deeper. A distinct line formed between his brows. "What have you told Reese about us?"

"Reese? I don't know. Not much."

"Did she say anything about a story on us?"

"If you're angry about the entertainment show and the whole trifecta thing, I was as surprised as you were." Eyeliner done, she filled in her eyebrows with deft strokes. She needed to get her contacts in so she could show him her face, reassure him of how she felt. "I'm just glad they didn't have pictures from our shopping trip or the cabin."

"Was Reese equally surprised?"

"I don't know." A few swipes of mascara completed her makeup. No false lashes today—she didn't have time. "I wasn't with her when she found out. Why?"

"Because I want to know who's behind it."

"Why does it matter? This is the nature of the beast. The industry." She grabbed her contact case. "Some photographer got a good shot and sold it to the show, who decided to help their ratings by making up an angle."

"Paparazzi don't spend much time in a suburb of Chicago. Reese tipped them off."

Distracted, she stabbed her eye getting her first contact in. "What?"

"Has she taken an interest in our relationship?"

"Maybe a little bit." Michaela blinked her watering eye and

swiped away the tears before they could undo the little makeup she'd applied. "Early on, she made a point of telling me you're single, but so what? Would you have done something differently?"

She ducked her head, slapped the other contact in, and straightened. Makeup and contacts a go, she nabbed the phone and hit the button to add visual to her side of the call. On his end, Philip rubbed his forehead as if to ease the knots and all the worries behind them. A second after she'd turned on her video, he seemed to notice because he straightened and fixated on the screen again.

She tilted the phone, ensuring the frame excluded her ridiculous shirt. "You said you weren't hiding us. If you're bashful, you shouldn't have kissed me on the sidewalk." She arched a brow, hoping the reminder of a part of their relationship that brought her so much joy would do the same for him.

"I don't like to be used, Michaela."

"I'm not using you. Reese may have seen the potential for a story, but I clearly told her I'm not with you for that."

"So you did talk about it."

"Um … yeah, I guess."

"If you're not in this for the story, why are you with me?" He leaned forward, and his face went off-screen, leaving her with a view of his shoulder. "Because I haven't exactly given you a long list of reasons to hang around."

"You're angry I haven't held a grudge? Seriously?"

"I would rather you have a grudge than an agenda."

Her own anger flared. "That isn't fair. Reese may have had an agenda, but I didn't know she would act on it. In fact, we don't know she did. This could all be coincidence."

"A pretty happy one, considering the story helped you snag Evie's interest." Philip sat back and crossed his arms. "She sees your popularity on the rise, and she wants a piece of the action."

"How dare you assume she's using me. Did it ever occur to you that, after three days in the studio with me, she might've decided I have talent? And it couldn't be that I have real feelings for you or that Reese took an honest interest in my life when she asked about you. Everyone has to be scheming."

His chin lifted. "Ask Reese."

She didn't have to. His suspicions about Reese and the story made too much sense, and perhaps Michaela should've seen the play for publicity coming. "If she did what you say, she was looking out for my career." Frustration infused her muscles, and she splayed her hand, but the effort to release tension failed. "So what if our relationship happens to be good for my career? Didn't you say I don't have to choose one or the other? I want both. Us—family—and my career."

"You can have both, but one has to take priority. Putting up with a manager who uses your personal life for professional gain is one step from doing it yourself."

"I wouldn't do that." She clenched her fist so tightly that her nails bit into her palm. She straightened her fingers again. "The story didn't do any harm."

"This time. What about next time, when your manager sees the perfect opportunity to get ahead by burning me? I've got secrets I can't have in the tabloids." He shifted, lifting his arm to reach for the phone.

"And I've kept them."

"But would Reese?"

"I wouldn't let her do that to you. She knows none of your secrets."

"But you already told me she didn't ask your permission for this story. Why would she ask for the next one? I need to know the kids and I are your priority."

"Which I can only show you by firing the manager who's been with me for years? Since she's the reason I've made it this far, you *are* asking me to pick between my career and you."

"Pick a priority. Yes." He watched the screen stonily.

"Then I guess it's singing. I had that long before I met you, and I'm not giving up everything I've worked for just because it offends you that people know we're together."

"Then I'm out." The video went black.

She stared at the phone, too shocked and angry to cry. While using, he'd lied to her and been aloof or mean, depending on the day. She'd forgiven it all.

After all the rejections she'd suffered, how could she have missed such obvious warning signs that this, like every other relationship, had been doomed to fail from the start?

28

$\mathcal{J}$im had reached a final number with the label, and the offer met the sky-high expectations their manager had been promising since before Philip joined Awestruck. Until tonight's meeting, that kind of windfall had sounded impossible, but tomorrow, the label would be at the show. Afterward, Philip's signature would secure the finances to fund any dream Nila and Nason could ever bring to him.

At least something was going his way.

More than something. The main thing. Providing for his kids.

As he stepped in from the garage, the scent of roasting chicken met him. He slipped his keys over a hook in the entry and made his way to the living room.

Nason sat on the couch with a book. On spotting Philip, he scrambled to his feet, but instead of running up for a hug, he shot toward the kitchen. "Dad's here!"

Nila sat at the counter, on the same stool where Philip had called Michaela two days before. His daughter looked as upset as he'd felt during that conversation.

"What's going on?" Philip laid his hand on Nila's back, but

her spine stiffened against the touch, the tear-stained dejection on her face taking on a hint of anger.

Ruthann poured gravy into a boat and sent Nason off with it, warning him to not spill on the way to the dining table. She cast Nila a glance, then took a covered bowl from the oven and pulled the aluminum foil off, revealing mashed potatoes. "Nila, do you think you can carry this? You'll need to use hot mitts and be sure to set it on one of the trivets we put on the table."

She slumped off the chair and accepted the task as Nason returned for salt, pepper, and butter.

Once Ruthann had dispatched them both to the table, she took a plate of already-carved chicken from the oven. "We saw Kensey at the library, and they had a nice time together."

Kensey. Did the name ring a bell? The kids had attended school here for half the year and had told him plenty of stories about their classmates. They'd made friends, but summer play-dates had gotten lost in the shuffle of nannies.

"Then why's she upset?"

Ruthann's makeup-free face remained smooth, not a worry line in sight. "Kensey invited her for dinner, but I said no because we had other plans."

"Oh." Philip reviewed the kitchen. When he'd said he would be home for tonight's meal, he hadn't expected the nanny to prepare a feast. Since Nila had spent so little time with friends this summer, he wouldn't have kept her home.

"She was excited to have dinner with you, and she helped me cook." Ruthann handed him the plate of chicken, padded with hot mitts, to carry to the table. "She was upset when you didn't come home at five thirty."

When he'd cited the time in a text, he hadn't known Tim would keep them. He also wouldn't have guessed Nila would care if he came home an hour late. But his tardiness hadn't only inconvenienced his kids, judging by the way Ruthann had the meal ready and warming in the oven. "It was an important meeting."

Ruthann lifted a bowl of green beans and a pitcher of water. "Just not to an eight-year-old. She dove headfirst into drama." She tipped her head and changed the pitch of her voice, indicating she was paraphrasing Nila. "She doesn't have any friends. No one loves her."

She eyed the milk, but Philip shifted the chicken to one hand so she didn't have to overload herself. "I wouldn't have minded if she'd gone with her friend, as long as you've met the parents."

"I thought family time would be more of a priority. And at the time she didn't mind. She was excited to see you." She glanced at him as if she'd realized too late her words could be construed as a guilt trip.

He wasn't taking the ticket. "It's important to me too, but I also want her to have friends."

"Okay. I'll check with you next time." Ruthann stepped into the dining area and set her load on the table, which had been decorated with a cloth and a vase of flowers. They really had gone to a lot of trouble.

"I'd like to enroll them in some classes too." Philip placed the meat on the remaining trivet and took his seat at the head of the table, facing his daughter. "Would you like to do ballet again?"

Nila didn't turn her tear-stained face his direction.

"If she gets to, I get to swim, right?" Nason grabbed for the mashed potatoes.

Ruthann held up a hand to stop him and focused on Philip. "Do you mind if we pray?"

A valid question. She knew they went to church some weeks. She couldn't know the kids were believers and he wasn't, and he wouldn't get into his reservations in front of them. But he also didn't feel comfortable leading a prayer to thank God for food provided by Philip and the job Nila resented so much.

"Nila, would you like to do the honors?" he asked.

She shook her head, still refusing to look at him.

Across from her, Nason licked his lips, far too focused on the meal to offer an acceptable prayer.

"I can." Ruthann spoke the offer kindly, so he nodded, though once again, she probably judged him. She rested folded hands on the edge of the table, and the kids followed suit. "Father, thank You for this beautiful day and all the fun we had and all the work we accomplished. You've provided everything we need and more. Thank You for this food. I pray You would bless it and help us to remember that all good things come from You. Amen."

Seemed to Philip more good things came from hard work and sacrifice than from God. He pushed down his resentment and focused on passing dishes. "Nila? Ballet?"

"You want to get rid of me more."

"What are you talking about? You love ballet. You make friends there. You get to dance and wear the costumes."

"They probably don't have ballet here. They don't have anything here. I wish we were back in Iowa."

As if Iowa were some land of opportunity. "What did you like so much about Iowa?"

"My friends are there. And Grandma and Grandpa's house is my favorite place to be. Grandma makes good food like this every night, and they always hug me and tell me they love me."

"I love you, too, sweetheart. I'm sorry I was late tonight, but I was working."

"You're always working."

"That's why we have this nice house. And my job is why Ruthann is here. And why we can afford ballet lessons. If they don't have any here, we'll find somewhere that does, and I'll make sure you can go, even if I have to fly you on an airplane every week to get there. That's what this job can do."

"An airplane?" Her eyes welled again.

"Don't worry, Nila." Ruthann's voice smoothed into a calming balm, though she shot Philip a recriminating glance. "You won't have to fly anywhere. There are ballet classes here. We'll find one and get you all signed up. And we'll find a swimming class for Nason too."

The boy cheered, but Nila continued to stew.

Philip couldn't claim his mood was much better than his daughter's. Since when was Ruthann the expert on how to interact with his children?

"Who's excited to hear Dad tomorrow?" Ruthann asked.

Dad? She spoke the way Clare would've, and it irked him.

Nason, mouth full, pumped his fist.

Nila scraped her knife on her plate in a failed attempt to cut her chicken. Philip moved to help her, but she leaned away.

Ruthann persisted. "How many times have you heard him?"

"Lots." Nason gulped a mouthful so large, Philip could swear he saw the lump moving down his throat. "And he sings to us at bedtime. But he's better at bass."

"I've heard him sing to you. I think he does a pretty good job, and 'Amazing Grace' is one of my favorites." She approved of something, at least.

"It's the only song he knows."

His one victory tonight tanked. "Really, Nason?"

Ruthann laughed. "I think he knows a lot of other ones, but he sings them for other people. I bet he saves 'Amazing Grace' just for you because it's special, and so are the two of you."

Finally, something had scored him some points with Nila, because his daughter's round eyes cast him a long look. From there, her attitude improved until she clapped her hands as Ruthann brought out the cake.

After the meal and dishes, the kids settled down with their

tablets, not having so much as chipped a plate, despite the jobs Ruthann had entrusted to them. How many times must she prove she knew them better?

He ought to drop the resentment and simply be grateful he could afford her help. He swallowed ground up bits of his pride. "Thank you for making dinner. Everything was great."

"Sure. Of course. Sorry it was rocky for a minute. Nila thinks airplanes mean saying goodbye. They're a symbol of separation for her."

And now she was apologizing for his daughter. And explaining her psyche. And pointing out another way Philip had scarred her. "Airplanes are also what bring us home again."

"She minds the goodbyes more than she loves the hellos."

He fought the urge to cross his arms and, in doing so, show his guilt. He knew his limitations. That was why he'd hired a good nanny. "When we go to California in a few weeks, is it best to leave her here or bring her with?"

"I'd say keep her here. If she goes, she'll miss the start of school and probably a few ballet classes. She would be behind everyone else, and she's already different enough. The other kids might ostracize her."

Ostracize Nila? Sweet, cute, and happy, she had everything going for her. "The kids should all be clamoring to be her friend."

"Not if they feel threatened or jealous."

The only reason they'd feel that was if they knew about Nila's famous father. If they knew about him. "Okay. Great. They'll stay." He took a breath, stretching his ribcage, but not releasing nearly enough disappointment and tension.

He and Ruthann settled details for the next day's show, then she left for her apartment. The kids played for a while and then completed their bedtime routines. They didn't ask him for the hymn, and he didn't offer. Lullabies seemed like a promise of an idyllic home life he couldn't keep.

After he tucked them in, he wandered downstairs and stood in the kitchen, staring at nothing. He didn't know his kids or what was best for them. He'd hurt Nila, and as Nason got older, the boy might grow to resent him too.

He should've sung to them. But the tradition equated to sticking a bandage on a much deeper wound.

He ought to be happy. Happy about the contract and the resulting security. Happy he'd hired a great nanny and made the right choice about Michaela.

Family was his priority. If she couldn't say the same, he wouldn't subject the kids or himself to the choices she'd make.

But he missed her.

And he missed pills.

How would he fill the hours between now and bed?

He'd imagined pills as his biggest problem. He'd forgotten the depth of the wounds that had driven him to self-medicate in the first place.

Michaela had said he needed to work on his root problem. His belief that he wasn't good enough. But how could he work on it when it was the truth? He wasn't even good enough for Michaela to choose unless she could get publicity out of their relationship.

This pain had to stop.

A deep breath in. A deep breath out.

He'd failed his kids enough. He wouldn't fail them by using.

Another breath.

Find something to do.

Another breath.

He couldn't go back. Couldn't get hooked again. He'd quit because feeding his habit had monopolized too much time and money, and it required too many lies. He'd quit because he didn't want his kids finding him dead.

He changed into workout clothes and hit the in-home gym as though his life depended on it.

~

MICHAELA PUT her earbuds in and sank to the velvety pink chair in the corner of her bedroom. She would spend most of the week here, throwing together song ideas in anticipation of working with Evie next week. She'd hoped at least five of the songs on the album could be her own. Reese had said she didn't have to contribute so many, but the songs Reese had procured from songwriters weren't powerful or memorable. If she wanted an album she could be proud of, she needed to contribute substantially.

As far as originals went, she'd have "Becoming Us," which she and Evie had already recorded. She'd also developed a song from the melancholy tune she'd captured with Gannon's help while Philip was withdrawing. And she'd written an angry song based on the way Philip had broken up with her over nothing on Tuesday.

So, basically, she had nothing but Philip to go on. She and her career were inseparable. Even in breaking things off to prevent her from "using" him, he'd given her career one final gift, one more song.

When he saw her at tomorrow's show, perhaps he'd come to his senses. He had to see that her accidentally benefitting from a harmless segment varied wildly from her maliciously using him.

She was ambitious, not evil. She wouldn't hurt someone she loved to get ahead.

And Reese wouldn't either.

But enough with that maddening situation. Reese had just forwarded Evie's work with "Becoming Us." Listening to her dream-come-true ought to lend a little inspiration for other songs.

She settled deeper into the chair, tweaked her earbuds, and let the music play.

Twenty minutes later, she paced. She'd lost track of how many times she'd listened, but this version of the song wasn't growing on her. Reese had flooded her phone with praise for how it'd turned out, but this didn't sound like a Michaela song. This sounded like ... like a Kira K song.

The song had been drowned in a crowd of effects, and the melody she'd hummed to herself continuously after it'd first come to her played at a tempo twice as fast. She'd tried singing it that way in the studio at Evie's request, but they'd agreed it didn't work. And yet, here it was.

Another melody interrupted the song. Reese calling.

Disappointment crushed her windpipe, but Reese spared her the pain of speaking by dominating the conversation, speculating how well the song would do.

Was she right?

Finally, Reese seemed to wait for Michaela to reply.

"It's great. She really did something with it." Did that pass as a compliment? After all she'd done to work with Evie, she couldn't very well bash the result. Besides, she could sacrifice for a song that accomplished all Reese predicted. "Is this the final version?"

"I sent it on to Jamie, and she loves it. I don't think we'll need any changes. Are you ready with something else for Monday?"

Suddenly, her songs lined up like dominos. If she allowed Evie to edit her heart out of the first one, Evie would do the same to all the others. Reese expected the album to win awards, but at what cost?

"Don't you think 'Becoming Us' sounds a little rushed?"

"No." Reese stretched the word to accommodate a boatload of skepticism. "You're the one who wanted to work with Evie. You need to let her do her job."

Michaela swallowed again, but her throat wouldn't loosen up to allow her to speak without belying her emotion.

Reese seemed to catch on regardless. "You need to get serious about what you want. No more games. This is exactly what you campaigned for. Don't show everyone just how unprepared you are for this level by being impossible to work with."

Michaela dropped back to the chair and clenched her fist until her nails dug into her palm. The physical pain pushed back the emotional storm long enough for her to get a couple of syllables out. "Of course not."

"Good. Now. Send me what else you have so we can decide what we're going to go ahead with on Monday."

Michaela understood she'd been cut from the "we" who would make the decision.

She called Gannon for advice, but he didn't answer, and she couldn't bring herself to leave him yet another panicked voicemail.

She hung up, debating pros and cons of continuing to work with Evie. No dream came free or easy. Working with talent meant compromise. At least this time, no one had asked her to remove layers of clothing, as they had for the music video.

They were more concerned with removing her heart.

29

*A*fter a knock, the door to Philip's dressing room swung open.

Gannon stepped in and shut the door behind himself. "What's going on?"

The pending show and contract combined to amplify John, Tim, and Gannon's energy. Knowing his low mood would stand out like a wrong note at a pivotal moment, Philip had left Awestruck chatting it up with the support bands and escaped here to avoid questions.

Unsuccessfully.

Concern and pre-show restlessness battling it out, Gannon snapped his fingers and bumped his fists together as he dropped onto the couch. "Okay, truth is, Tim told me."

Philip had been scrolling on his phone, but knowing Gannon wouldn't give this up, he slid the device onto the coffee table. "Were you trying to warn me or protect her?"

"When?"

"When you said she'd been hurt a lot."

Gannon shrugged. "Are you sure Tim's right about her?"

"She didn't know about the story, but she wouldn't have

changed anything if she had. She said her career is her priority."

Gannon grunted, his struggle to sit still evident in his bouncing foot. This was a good day for him. It ought to be for Philip too. The contract would put millions at his disposal. How many people realized their dreams of making so much for doing what they loved?

But what good would millions do in the hands of a failure?

"She was a good kid on *Audition Room*, but she worshiped the spotlight." Funny, coming from the guy who got more energy off performances than anyone else in the band. "I tried explaining how Awestruck has become who we are. I thought I could set her up to stay true to herself. When I saw her video, I knew it hadn't worked. I'd already been approached about contributing to the movie soundtrack, but I wasn't sure I'd want in until she inspired the song."

Suddenly, all the lyrics about the dark edge of fame made a lot more sense.

"She wants the whole world to love her. She thinks adoration will make her feel better, but only God's big enough to fill that void." Gannon's focus fixed on Philip. "I know you don't want to hear this, but the same is true for you. We've all got voids we can't fill except with the divine."

The God who had failed Clare wouldn't give Philip what he needed. "You're right. I don't want to hear it."

"Noted." Gannon rapped his knuckle on the coffee table. "All right. The kids are coming soon?"

"Any minute."

"Focus on them. You've got something good there." Gannon made his way to the door.

It said a lot about the singer that he hadn't told him to focus on the show or all the contract would bring. Despite how shows amped up Gannon, he understood as well as Philip that the career would never satisfy.

Michaela didn't get that yet. How much damage would she do before she figured it out?

Philip rose to follow. Interacting with the others might help cheer him up. But as he stepped out of the dressing room, his vision settled on Michaela.

He hadn't realized she'd arrived, but there she stood, made up like a rock'n'roll princess. She'd teased her locks and pulled the top half back. At the ends of her hair, the waist of her dress cinched in before blooming into a choppy-layered skirt that came to mid-thigh. She'd completed the look with short, black boots. Heeled, of course.

A gaggle of musicians and crew surrounded her.

Gannon stepped forward and touched her arm. She turned toward the greeting and, in a flash of smokey eye makeup and green irises, seemed to spot Philip.

"Ready for this?" Gannon asked her.

She refocused without more than a glance in Philip's direction. "Yes, but if you get a minute, I have an Evie thing to run by you."

As Gannon answered, Philip turned away.

If she wanted love, as Gannon claimed, she hid it well. But maybe that was the trick. She wanted love, realized it was hopeless, and had settled for fame. Philip couldn't reach what he wanted either, and he too knew how to settle.

Tonight, highs would be easy to come by for both of them.

NILA CLUNG to her nanny's skirt and peered Michaela's direction. The leather bodice and layered chiffon skirt, so different from Michaela's usual clothes, must intimidate the girl, but Nila clearly wanted to say hello. Michaela longed to go over, get on the girl's level, and coax her out of her shell. She'd love to tease Nason too.

But she couldn't.

The nanny and Nila stood next to Philip. Nason held his dad's hand.

She'd never seen Philip in the heavy black boots he wore or the black jeans, but the gray T-shirt matched his everyday look, as did the thinly veiled pain in his expression.

How could he look so wounded when *he'd* dumped *her*?

Everything was such a mess. This distance between her and a man she had such feelings for. The fact that Nila couldn't run up for a hug. The promise of being in the studio with Evie on Monday to produce an album she didn't believe in.

She'd sacrificed Philip and the kids for that opportunity.

Was love the point of life?

If so, she and Philip should've been able to find a compromise to stay together. If they could talk again, they might be able to work it out. With him in her corner, with his kids to count on for giggles and sweet moments, she could handle whatever working with Evie brought. She'd have it all, and she'd make sure Philip did too.

Besides, she might yet rectify the Evie situation. She'd asked Gannon to try to find a few minutes for her tonight. Of course, as soon as he'd promised a conversation, he'd been pulled away to meet fans. Now, a crew member with a phone in each hand and a headset over her hair hurried Michaela's direction. The multitasker pulled her into the hall to review some last-minute details before bustling off.

Michaela hesitated to rejoin the others. More than she wanted a one-on-one with Gannon, she longed to talk to Philip.

Florescent lights stretched at even intervals down the hall, away from where everyone else gathered. Doors lined one side. Her own dressing room was closest. Next, a label secured with masking tape indicated one of the support bands had been required to share space.

Chords rose from the stage, and the roar of the audience

gave its approval. The second band, Tickertape Tragedy, had taken the stage. Afterward, Awestruck would go on.

Her heels marked her steps against the worn linoleum flooring. The second support band had been assigned a room. The next door had no paper. *John Kennedy* was scrawled directly on the tape. Philip's room was next.

The security guard at the end of the hall stood with his back to her. She laid her fingers on the metal knob. Philip would've passed her to get here from where she'd left him with the group, so she wouldn't barge in on him if she entered. Would he stop back in, giving them the chance to talk?

If not, he'd never know she tried.

She let herself in.

The room held a dressing table and mirror, a small couch, a coffee table, and not much else. A black duffle lay in the corner, and two kids' backpacks leaned against one side of the couch. No sign of the nanny's belongings—she'd been wearing her purse when Michaela last saw her.

She saw only one option for concealment—the tiny, attached bathroom. If she waited there, Philip would be in the dressing room with the door closed before he saw her. She'd have at least a couple of seconds before he backed out of the room and away from the conversation.

She flipped the bathroom light on. Old, but clean. Good enough. She extinguished the light, stayed in the shadows of the bathroom, and waited.

Writing lyrics on her phone proved a poor way to pass the time. She kept getting lost in scenarios like what she'd say to Philip or what she'd do if the nanny and kids came instead of him. The small of her back ached from her heels, but she refused to stand barefoot in this dingy bathroom. She eyed the vanity. If she sat on the high end of the warped countertop, she might do building management a favor by pushing it back down again.

The quick rattle of the doorknob stopped her breath. She froze except to turn her head and see if she'd get Philip himself or would have to deal with the nanny.

The newcomer was neither. Riff, dressed in all black like the rest of the crew, eased the door shut again. Focused on Philip's duffle, he knelt and reached into the bag. As he rummaged in there, he glanced at the door.

He stood and made for the exit.

He was *stealing*.

She couldn't let that happen, and though it'd be hard to explain how she'd caught him, perhaps the fact that she had would score some points with Philip.

She stepped from the shadows. "What do you think you're doing?"

Riff's eyes and mouth opened farther than she'd imagined the sleepy guy capable of. He lifted a hand as if he could block her from recognizing his face. "You can't prove anything." He yanked open the door and ran, slamming it behind himself.

His reaction proved he hadn't come for above-board reasons, and if he'd stolen something, she *could* prove her case. He'd have the missing property on him. Except, his hands had appeared empty. Uneasiness turned her to the duffle bag.

Riff had seemed off since she'd met him. If forced to name one person on the crew as a potential drug user, he would be her pick. And if she was right, he was the perfect person to help Philip relapse.

Philip wouldn't. Not after all he'd done to get clean. Not with his kids here.

But she'd seen his face earlier. Despite being the one to end things, he was as heartbroken as she was. No doubt he still felt inadequate with his kids, and he was under a lot of pressure with the band too.

Crushing anxiety built in her chest, limiting her breath as if someone had yanked the strings on her laced-up top. She checked over her shoulder. If Philip had given up on sobriety, he might come any time for the pills Riff had left him. Would he dare perform high the night of such an important show for Awestruck?

Yes. She'd rarely noticed anything off about Philip while he'd been using, so of course he'd expect to be able to hide it. Even if he couldn't, one sign of addiction she'd read about was continued use, despite worsening consequences. But she'd also read about the likelihood of an overdose in a relapse. His tolerance would be lower. His old dose would hit in ways he didn't expect.

She couldn't let him do this. For so many reasons.

All she saw in the open bag were clothes. The black cotton of a T-shirt, the pale blue of jeans. She squatted, pushed her hair over her shoulder to clear her view, and peered down along the edge where Riff seemed to have reached.

She plucked out the small baggy.

But this wasn't filled with pills.

The bag contained powder.

Powder.

Heroin?

He'd said it wasn't that different from the pills, but was that true?

She should not have this in her hand. She'd made her share of mistakes, but she'd stayed away from hard drugs and didn't want to be caught with a substance that could land her in jail or on every tabloid cover. This stuff ruined lives. It killed people.

It could kill Philip.

How could he do this? To himself? To his kids? His poor father, who'd dropped everything to help him get clean.

Philip had sworn he'd never do this.

Addiction. It was a disease. She'd read that. A disease that pure willpower couldn't force into remission.

Her fist closed around the baggy. She flushed it in the bathroom and scrubbed her hands at the sink. Maybe when Philip came looking for the drug and found it gone, when Riff told him about seeing her, he'd rethink. He'd get scared of being discovered, and he'd choose to stay clean.

He'd given that whole speech about never escalating to heroin.

Surely, this had been an isolated moment of weakness.

If only she could believe that.

Feeling as helpless and hopeless as if she were watching a plane crash, she let herself out of the dressing room. She could tell Gannon, but Philip had predicted she would burn him, and getting him fired would fulfill that prophecy. Besides, if his association with Awestruck ended, what would stop addiction from taking over?

The kids, in theory, but in her research, she'd read about foster systems overloaded with kids displaced because of the opioid epidemic. Philip would vehemently deny he'd ever let his problem go that far, but wouldn't they all?

She could call Philip's dad again. As his father and a doctor, he'd know what to do, and he'd proven his willingness to go above and beyond for his son.

"Hey." A man's voice from behind froze her in her tracks. "You wanted to talk to me?"

Gannon.

She pivoted on her heel, pressing her hands to her hips to hide a tremor.

Gannon, her mentor, the best ally she'd had in her career, studied her, eyes narrowing. He glanced at Philip's door and back to her. "Everything okay?"

She rubbed her forehead, fingers quivering. The harder she fought to regain her composure, the worse the pain in her throat grew. "No."

30

"*L*et's talk." Gannon led her to his own dressing room, a mirror image of Philip's.

She lowered herself to the couch and toyed with the top layer of her skirt. He'd left the door open, so they didn't have a guarantee of privacy or much time before Awestruck would go on. Their conversation would only get so far. She'd asked for this to discuss Evie, and the best course of action regarding Philip remained calling his dad.

"I don't like what Evie did with my song." Speaking the truth aloud made her objections more real. Emotion, already running high over the situation with Philip, turned its force to her career, and the pressure of tears mounted as she explained the hurried version of the song.

"What does Reese think?"

"It'll be the next hit." She picked at her nails and blinked, willing her mood to rise. "That *is* what I wanted."

"Maybe a little too much."

"Huh?"

Gannon grimaced as if he regretted his words.

"You think I should turn down Evie's offer or make Reese

stand up for me." The bold approach matched his advice to not sell out. To not sacrifice her peace of mind. Only, she'd never have peace of mind if she blew up her career over artistic differences with success so close.

He sighed. "What's this whole thing with Philip?"

"It's ..." She could not discuss him when that trauma had left deeper wounds than the disappointment over her songs. Her songs weren't a matter of life and death. Philip was. "There is no 'whole thing' with Philip."

"What happened to your theory that love is the point of life?"

"Nothing happened with it. Philip and I aren't in love. We were a two-minute segment on an entertainment show."

"That's it?"

Of course not, but even before the piece aired, Philip had had reservations. She had other responsibilities besides talking him into loving her when his heart had never been available in the first place. He may or may not still harbor feelings for Clare, and he definitely needed to work out his relationships with the kids, but he could only do that if he avoided the black hole of heroin.

She'd been a fool to think they were the exception to that advice about not dating during the early stages of addiction recovery. She couldn't save him.

She needed to move on with her life, and she could end Gannon's inquiry into their relationship by playing off the same silly suspicion that set Philip against her—that she'd been with him to boost her career. "Yes. A segment. And I'm glad it helped get the ball rolling with Evie, but now I have that to deal with. What do I do?"

Gannon studied her, a coolness in his expression she didn't usually see. "Were you using him from the start?"

She'd been tempted to at first, but she'd quickly come to like him and to hope for a future together. A future they'd never have because he was the one who couldn't quit *using*.

An eruption from the crowd signaled Tickertape Tragedy wrapping up. Awestruck ought to be waiting in the wings, but Gannon didn't budge.

He'd understand so much more if she told Philip's secrets, but she'd given her word not to. She tried to sidestep the issue. "If love is the point, love of music and love of fans count for something. You're the one who told me that a career in this industry, done right, can change lives."

Though unintelligible, a two-beat chant picked up. The fans were demanding Awestruck. Gannon remained still. "It can change lives when done wrong too, and if all you're chasing is the spotlight, that's doing it wrong."

So he was holding the fallout with Philip against her, but perhaps the advice still pertained. "And I only want to work with Evie to advance my career, so I should listen to the part of me that's worried she'll edit the heart out of my songs."

"It sounds to me like you have good reason to be concerned."

She inhaled through her nose, exhaled through her mouth. The exercise didn't ease the tension in her chest. "What if this is my last chance, though? This is a huge opportunity. It's Evie Decker."

"Michaela Vandehey is more important to me—and she's just as lost as ever."

Lost. Like in "Amazing Grace." Except instead of only being "once" lost, the condition had proven an ongoing state for Michaela.

She'd last felt found when she'd won *Audition Room*.

And before that, at the school talent show.

And once, for the space of a couple of hours, at Bible camp.

"You're listening to people who're far too willing to take advantage," he said. "That's how your music video happened, and it's how your relationship ended. Now your music itself is at stake. You won't find peace like this."

He didn't understand her career or her relationship with Philip. Defensiveness broke through her anxious tension and spilled out in words. "I learned from the music video mistake, and the situation now with Evie is different. As for my relationship ..." She put air quotes around that last word. The more she thought about her and Philip, the more certain she became that he would have used any excuse to push her away. The entertainment show happened to be the most convenient. "Ever think maybe Philip's not all he's cracked up to be? That maybe he's another of those people who are taking advantage of others? Maybe the fact that it's over means I've actually grown a backbone to recognize what's best for me."

"And what's that?" He crossed his arms, clearly not expecting to be impressed by the answer.

"In that case? My career."

"You're addicted to the spotlight, Michaela. This won't end well."

Addicted? He thought *she* was addicted?

That was rich.

She rose, considering storming out, but she'd let Gannon think too little of her for too long. "Sure, let's talk about addicts. I just flushed Philip's heroin stash."

Gannon stood as she blew the secret—and any chance she'd had of retaining Philip's trust. The lead singer studied her. He must've seen her sincerity, because one of his fists clenched.

"There you are." Tim stepped into the doorway, glanced back and forth between them, then motioned for Gannon to head for the stage.

Gannon's vision raked her face. "How long has that been going on?"

She gulped, guilt on the rise. She'd spoken in anger and

self-defense. Not her most noble motivations, but perhaps this would turn out best. Gannon might fire Philip, but he would also try to help.

If anyone could.

"I think it was a first, but he was using other things before." She left out the word pills because they had an audience in Tim. Telling Gannon was questionable enough. She wouldn't let another person in on the secret.

Gannon rubbed his face, grief on his features.

Tim advanced into the room. "Who's using what?"

His star didn't spare him a glance. Instead, Gannon focused on Michaela. "Thank you for telling me. As for you and Evie ..." He sighed and shook his head, appearing to struggle to redirect his focus. "Artists often have different ideas than the people they work with. We've disagreed on songs within Awestruck, with Tim, with labels. It's not a moral issue this time, so you have to decide what you can live with for your music and pick who you trust."

"I trust Evie to make the album a hit."

"If that's what's most important to you, take the opportunity."

As he gave his blessing, she realized it was what she'd wanted to hear. Working with Evie meant not rocking the boat of her career. And perhaps by compromising on this album, she'd gain a bigger platform that would lend her the clout to call the shots for herself in the future.

Yet why had Gannon made the recommendation with such a heavy voice?

Tim ushered him from the room before she could press, but she could imagine the bomb she'd dropped on her mentor would lead to the low mood. Perhaps the situation with Philip was the reason even she didn't feel relief, though her decision was now made.

She would work with Evie.

Tonight, she'd stay just long enough to perform the duet, and then she'd leave, putting Philip behind her as soon as possible.

~

IF RIFF THOUGHT the favor Philip had requested gave him freedom to skip out on his job, he had another think coming. Charlie had noticed Riff's absence and fixed the loose cable that had prevented Philip's bass from playing, but not until the others had performed half of the encore without his contribution. Still no sign of Riff when the show ended. Charlie accepted the bass as Philip left the stage.

Wherever the roadie was, he'd pay for this. Riff's absence would send questions flying, and Philip could far too easily be pulled into the crossfire.

"Philip." Gannon's voice cut after him, hardly audible above the crowd. The singer bumped his arm. "We need to talk."

"I know." They cleared the area visible to the audience, and Philip scanned the hurrying crew, already beginning tear down. "I'm going to go find him, wherever he is."

He rounded a corner and leaned to see between crates that would soon contain their equipment. An uneven shape back there could be a person's feet.

A hand closed on his arm, the grip rough. Philip whirled.

Gannon's focus blazed, steady and hard. "I don't think you understand."

Did he think the label noticed the debacle? An equipment malfunction wouldn't cost them the contract. They'd shown their ability to roll with the punches tonight. Any band that couldn't was doomed. "The label will appreciate our flexibility. Don't worry about it."

He shrugged out of Gannon's grip and started down the narrow aisle toward the legs he'd spotted. Riff must have found a nook to shoot up in back here. Had the kid forgotten all about the encore? Philip had been counting down the minutes until he'd be alone himself, but he never would've let his need to escape seduce him into using here. This narrow walkway made the shortest path from the stage to the dressing rooms. Discovery was inevitable.

He kicked Riff's shoe as he reached him. But Riff wasn't sitting, as Philip had thought.

He lay flat on his back, unmoving.

Philip and Gannon dove to their knees on either side of the tech.

Gannon pressed a finger to the roadie's neck and slapped his cheek. "Hey, Riff! You with us?"

He wasn't—at least, he wasn't conscious—and the reason why protruded from his arm.

Bile rising, Philip pressed the back of his hand to his mouth.

Gannon spotted the syringe. "We need some help back here!" The singer had lungs, but could he compete with the crowd to get the message out? When would they give up asking for a second encore? "Is it heroin?"

Philip opened his mouth to answer. Earlier, he'd cornered Riff into telling him what he was on and had paid him to score some for himself. Had the heroin been laced with something? He shook Riff's shoulder. "Come on. Wake up!"

"Philip!" Gannon reached for his phone. "What is it?"

His pulse hit so hard, his vision blurred. Why did Gannon believe Philip knew?

"Hi, Dad!" Nila's cheery greeting hit like a kick while he was down.

How was this happening? How was this nightmare real? He rose to block his daughter's view. Even as he turned her away, she craned her neck to see. Thankfully, Nason stared up at him, half-asleep.

"Sorry." Ruthann motioned toward the dressing rooms,

then pointed ahead, indicating toward the spot where she and the kids had watched almost the entirety of the show. "Nason needed an emergency bathroom break right at the end, so we ..." Her gaze dropped to Riff. She already held Nason's hand, and she grabbed Nila's shoulder to pull both kids away so quickly that Nason stumbled into her.

Philip returned to the guitar tech. Gannon had his phone pinched to his ear with his shoulder while he worked his knuckles against the center of Riff's chest, trying to wake him.

Everything about this—the syringe, the color of Riff's lips, the kids, Gannon's desperate effort to save him—wrung Philip's gut. Matt Visser had said he couldn't rid himself of the vision of finding his friend dead from an overdose. Not only would this image stick with Philip, but also the physical, helpless panic.

The feeling of the world ending.

When he'd approached Riff, the tech had looked so terrified, Philip had hurried to reassure him. "It's okay. I'm not going to get you in trouble."

What lies.

God, I'm sorry.

The prayer tore from his soul. He'd known all along he wasn't enough, and his near relapse tonight proved it again, but now he also saw his guilt. He didn't understand God or why Clare had died, but as he'd sung a thousand times to his children, he'd come through many toils and snares, and most of them, he'd brought on himself. And on his children. And his friends. And Michaela. And his family, his dad. For all he'd done, he deserved to have the natural result—to be unconscious on the floor like Riff.

The only reason it hadn't yet come to that was grace.

God's grace.

A wretch like him, who'd played a part in this, who'd gambled with the life of his children's father, had no right to tell God how to do His job. Not regarding Clare or anything else.

As Gannon spoke to whoever he'd called, Philip shot a look over his shoulder. Ruthann had gotten the kids fifteen feet away already. The distance continued to grow, though Nila peered back as she tripped along.

They needed to save Riff. For Riff's own sake, for the kids' sake, for Philip's sake—because this could've been him.

God, please.

Philip bent over him, watching, listening, and feeling for breath. Before he could discern any signs of life, pounding footsteps rushed their direction, and someone pressed Philip away. "We've got him."

Gannon retreated to allow access for the two members of the crew who'd come. The woman, one of their assistants, had a fat, plastic pen. She pried off the cap as the second crew member took Philip's place on Riff's side, crowding him out.

He climbed to his feet, dizzy, and wiped his face. Wet. With tears. Because he'd made this happen. Maybe Riff wouldn't have bought tonight, wouldn't have used, if he hadn't been emboldened by the fact that Philip had a habit too. This was his fault, and his kids had seen it, and it could've just as easily been him.

Only, he would've waited until he was alone. No one would've found him until his body had grown cold. There would've been no rescue effort. Just crying, confused, terrified children.

Philip may be standing, but he needed help as desperately as the man on the floor.

Riff's foot moved. He stirred, opened his eyes, moved to sit up. The drug they'd administered to counteract the overdose had worked.

The part of Philip that was relieved cowered, dwarfed by his horror.

That could've been me.

Over and over, the thought played.

Gannon turned and laid a hand on Philip's shoulder. "We need to talk."

Philip heard the anger but nodded, unable to peel his gaze away, though crew blocked his view of Riff. Soon, paramedics and perhaps police would join the group. In other circumstances, Philip would've been at the center of the gathering.

Or worse, he might've needed the group but distanced himself from the help, the way he had with God as Clare died, the way he'd done repeatedly with Michaela. The way he was tempted to try to do now with Gannon.

He'd enclosed himself in distance and self-help, and he was dying. He couldn't hide any longer.

It was time to be found.

31

*P*hilip's bedroom door opened, and footsteps tiptoed to his bedside. Another couple of rustles, and he felt the dip of the bed. A small finger tapped his shoulder.

"Dad? Are you awake?" Nila's whisper implied that she cared about not disturbing his sleep, but he knew what would come next.

Sure enough, another tap. Three fingers this time. "Dad, are you awake?"

Her volume had increased, and she'd only get louder from there.

He opened his eyes just far enough to see the clock. Five a.m.? But he'd gotten clean specifically so the kids could always wake him, and each morning since last week's show, waking had seemed like an undeserved gift from God.

He grabbed a long, slow inhale and rolled to face her. Vision still blurry with sleep, he had to blink a few times before he determined that instead of her pajamas, she wore a white dress. Nila displayed her biggest grin as he shifted to sit up.

One day, when she resembled Clare even more, she'd get married. She'd know by then—if she chose to have the test—

the mystery of her genes. Whatever the test revealed, he didn't doubt two things. First, his little girl would still believe in amazing grace. Second, and because of that, she'd still be grinning.

"What's this?" he asked, though he should've guessed this would happen when she'd asked him to hang her new dress for John's wedding on the back of her bedroom door the night before.

"I want to see it as I fall asleep," she'd said.

As long as Nason wasn't off, trying to eat cereal while wearing his fresh white button-down, they'd be all right.

"I waited all night, and it's morning now." She lifted a headband braided with little artificial flowers. "Can you help?"

"Go change out of the dress, then come back, and I'll help you put the headband on. You can wear that this morning, but you can't wear the dress until Ruthann does your hair."

She chewed her lip, debating, then nodded once, left the headband, and disappeared. He wouldn't have long before she returned, so he forced himself out of bed and pulled on a T-shirt. That and his sweatpants would do until he changed for the ceremony.

When Nila returned, he slipped the headband over her soft curls. She disappeared with another grin into his bathroom, and he waited to hear her reaction to her reflection.

"Will Michaela be at the wedding?"

"No. She's working." He'd had no contact with Michaela since the show—if the little they'd seen each other that night counted as contact. She'd gone after her song, before the show had ended, long before the encore and Riff's overdose.

Between Gannon and Riff, Philip had learned why she'd made such a quick exit, but he hadn't worked up the nerve to call her and apologize. He'd done that so many times already. Before he tried again, he needed to take care of business within himself, his family, and the band.

To that end, every day since, he'd either seen a therapist, attended a recovery meeting, or taken the kids to church. He had a long road ahead of him, yet he also had more hope than he'd felt in years.

Nila emerged from the bathroom, the headband crowning a distraught face. "How come people like you always work so far away?"

She meant people in the music industry, and he wasn't sure how much longer he'd number among those.

He sat on the edge of the bed.

Instead of firing him, Gannon and John had required him to take steps to deal with his addiction. Awestruck needed a bassist and wanted it to be him.

Philip would complete all the steps they'd required, but he was no longer as certain about staying with the band. Awestruck might be a light in the darkness, but that meant darkness pressed close. Drugs were easier to come by. Plus, the highs that came with performing meant steep lows on returning home. And tours meant months away.

After a long meeting with Tim, discussing his options, he let Gannon and John sign the contract without him. They'd found a way to leave the door open to whatever he decided without him entering a commitment he couldn't keep.

Then, he'd spent the last week considering the best next step. He might be able to face the darkness with the accountability and support of his new system. Openness with Awestruck, therapy, support group meetings might carry him through.

And God.

Each time Philip had come up empty this week, God had provided. Provided a phone call at just the right time. Provided a verse once when he'd flipped open his Bible. Provided a reminder of grace through Nila humming her favorite song.

God may have chosen to take Clare, and Philip still didn't

understand the purpose in the heartbreak, but only a good God would've spared him. Only a good God would bother with the little details that had kept him afloat.

Philip didn't have to understand God to trust Him.

So, He could lead him down the straight and narrow, no matter where his career took him.

On the home front, the kids would be in good hands with Ruthann. She'd been shaken by the overdose, but she'd helped him with the kids as they processed what they'd seen. And though she'd frowned her way through Philip's confession about abusing painkillers, determination had settled over her features when he'd promised to take his recovery more seriously. She'd stay on but wouldn't take any nonsense if she suspected a relapse.

Fair enough.

He was free to continue with the band.

A lifestyle of constant coming and going, the kids raised by one parent or a nanny or boarding school, was common enough in the industry. They made sacrifices to live the dream.

Exactly the example Mom set.

The realization hit hard.

Philip had first known abandonment when Mom left to pursue her dream. His family's financial stability hadn't mattered to him and wouldn't matter to Nila or Nason. He had longed for someone to stand up for what he needed when he was a kid. How could he fail to stand up for what Nila and Nason needed?

As he'd been lost in thought, Nila had attempted to braid her hair. She bumped the headband, displacing it, but when she tried to pull the accessory free, her locks tangled around the flowers.

He motioned her closer and threaded a couple of strands free at a time. "Would you rather I didn't go away so much?"

She nodded, winced, touched her hair where the movement had pulled, then lowered her hand again. "And Michaela too."

"Michaela gets to do her own thing." He loosened the headband enough to slip it off and work more easily a couple of inches from her scalp. Her hair smelled softly of shampoo, and her chin bunched with what he guessed was concentration to stand still. "But you know what I'm going to do?"

Her forehead wrinkled with the effort of looking at him without turning her head. "What?"

He untangled the last few strands and lay the headband on the bed. "I'm not going to go away next year. I'm going to stay home with you and your brother."

He'd told Michaela that family was his priority. However that might look for anyone else, for Philip, it meant learning to take care of his kids—himself.

MICHAELA PARKED in one of the last spots of the tiny lot. Pine needles and leaves had been pressed into the old asphalt by tires and the boots of many, many hikers. She didn't know John well, but judging by the trees tattooed on his arm, getting married at the edge of the forest on the shore of Lake Superior suited him.

The secluded beach was two miles from the lot by trail. The couple had arranged for guests to reach the site by shuttles that looked like stretched golf carts. One waited now, complete with a spray of flowers on the back and a tuxedoed chauffeur.

Michaela held the skirt of her emerald maxi dress so the fabric wouldn't tangle around her ankles as she walked. Tripping and falling? Not on the agenda tonight.

She'd done far too much falling this summer as it was.

"Michaela Vandehey?"

A fan? She'd assumed anyone close enough to John to be

among the thirty or forty people attending the tiny ceremony would be immune to starstruck interest.

The petite woman who'd apparently spoken grasped the forearm of her companion. "John said you were invited but wouldn't tell us if you were coming."

She'd RSVPed before spilling Philip's secret at the show. Since the concert, she'd spent long days holed up in the studio with Evie. She'd wanted to reach out to Gannon for an update about Philip, but she was trying to break the habit of caring so much about him. Philip had broken her heart, and even if, by some miracle, he'd responded well when Gannon undoubtedly confronted him, he was a long way from being capable of a solid relationship.

So, instead, when she'd had a few minutes to spare, she'd checked in with her sister and Dad. Riley had started chemo and was battling fatigue, but emotionally she seemed to be staying positive.

But Michaela's choice to focus on her family didn't mean she'd completely doused her curiosity about what had become of Philip. Was he okay? Getting help? Who was looking after the kids? How were they coping? The tabloids had been eerily quiet on the subject, so she hoped to find out tonight. Knowing might help her move on. And while she was here, she could also seek out Gannon's advice once more.

This week, she and Evie had worked on recording a song they'd bought. The process didn't bother her as much when Evie's taste didn't override Michaela's own songwriting. However, their next task would be one of Michaela's originals. Gannon ought to have ideas for how to steer Evie's vision the right direction from the start. Perhaps that would help prevent a repeat of what had happened with "Becoming Us."

The approaching couple reached her. Still with her arm threaded through her date's, the woman extended her hand. "I'm Kate, one of John's sisters. This is my husband, Tanner."

After they'd exchanged pleasantries, the chauffeur handed her into the cart, and Tanner joined Kate in the seat behind Michaela.

"I still think they should've used horse-drawn carriages for this," Kate said. "Would've been magical, but when I asked Erin, she said she trusts engines more."

Michaela agreed with Kate on the subject of horse-drawn carriages, but for the sake of feeling like she belonged here, she offered one of the few bits of information she knew about Erin. "Makes sense. She is a mechanic."

"She's a *technician*," Kate giggled.

That sounded like an inside joke.

Michaela decided to steer toward a subject she knew better. "It's crazy how they're fitting this in despite everything Awestruck has going on."

"Their schedule is always packed. Besides, I haven't ever seen John this happy. They're good together. She draws him out of his shell, and he grounds her." Kate shot Tanner a gooey-eyed look that suggested she considered their relationship similar. "He wouldn't have put this off for anything."

Tanner settled his arm around his wife. "With the new contract in the bag, I'm sure they all feel like celebrating."

She puzzled over Tanner's statement. Who was "all"? Did the wording mean they hadn't fired Philip? Or had John not told his family about dismissing him to keep the drama away from today's ceremony? Unsure how to pry into band politics, she focused on the passing scenery.

Paper lanterns had been scattered along the trail and into the forest. The ceremony would end at sunset, and now, about an hour beforehand, the glow from what Michaela had to assume were electric candles cast the palest yellow against the white lanterns. Even without horse-drawn carriages, the effect after dark would be magical.

As they neared the beach, the sound of waves washed over

the noise of the cart, and soon the chauffeur pulled to a stop. They climbed out and walked the last, short portion of trail between two lines of lanterns. Wooden boards had been laid on the beach, first in a path, and then broadening into a giant oval more than large enough for the forty-something chairs, a string quartet, and a platform for the ceremony. Lanterns, airy fabric, and flowers were everywhere, especially on and around the pergola up front.

Beyond that, teal waves washed toward shore. Short sandstone cliffs jutted out into the water on both sides of the beach. A few boats had been anchored in a loose semi-circle. Security to maintain the perimeter? Or had some guests come by water?

Michaela chose a seat toward the outside, halfway back.

She listened to the conversations around her, but no one talked about Awestruck. Gannon and Adeline must both be in the wedding party, because neither mingled among the guests. As the time for the ceremony approached, Tim arrived with his daughter. He didn't seem to notice Michaela as they took seats farther up.

The time listed in the invitation arrived, and guests filled most of the seats. She peered over her shoulder, toward the trail. A small group stood at the mouth of the path. She made out John in a light gray suit. Four people, all old enough to be his or Erin's parents, lingered, as did Gannon in gray pants and a white button-down. Another man cut through the group.

Could John have a relative who looked that similar to Philip?

The man passed through the group, holding hands with a girl in a whimsical white dress. It was him. Philip and Nila, an adorable pair all dressed up. Adorable most days, actually.

How she ached to be part of that.

But it was all a façade, a façade she'd expected Gannon to handle.

Instead of the gray John and Gannon wore, Philip's pants

were navy, his shirt white, no bowtie or boutonniere like the other two had. He clapped John on the shoulder, then strode toward reserved seats on the center aisle in the second row.

So, he wasn't in the wedding party, but Philip ranked as a guest of honor.

Despite everything.

She'd been afraid Awestruck might go too far with the information she'd shared, but what if they'd done the opposite? What if they'd turned a blind eye?

The music changed, and she realized she'd stared at Philip and Nila through the entire time the parents had been seated. John, Gannon, and the pastor had taken their places up front. If the ceremony was starting, where was Nason?

A girl younger than Nila acted as flower girl, and Michaela saw envy in the way Nila leaned to watch. Philip whispered something to his daughter, looking entirely too handsome and happy.

How could he have been the same person whose drugs she'd intercepted a week ago?

Delighted murmurs rose from the back of the seating area, and Michaela twisted again but couldn't see until the child reached her row. Nason carried a book-sized box, which must contain the rings, tied with a ribbon. As ring bearer, he wore the same style outfit as Gannon—gray pants, a white shirt, a little boutonniere, and a bowtie. John's two huge pit bulls, each with a collar made to resemble a white shirt collar and bowtie, followed at his elbows.

When the brindle one stepped toward the seats, sniffing, Nason said, "Stay with me. Stay with me."

Chuckles went up, but the indignant commands worked. Then, two rows later, the dog strayed again. She heard the murmur of Nason trying to call him back. That failed.

"Camo."

The dog lifted his head toward his master's call and broke

formation to join John up front. There, the dog promptly sat on —or very close to—John's foot and panted out at the crowd, earning more laughter. Nason reached the platform a moment later, and John had both dogs sit off to the side while Gannon accepted the box. He said something to Nason, pointed toward Philip, and sent the boy to join his dad.

Erin, in a simple but elegant white gown, lingered at the mouth of the trail. Adeline squeezed her hand, then advanced without her. Her blue knee-length dress flattered her, and her side-swept braid made even Michaela wish she'd done more with her own locks. Up front, Gannon's smile morphed into a goofy grin. Someone was dreaming more about his own wedding than the one playing out before him.

Philip nodded a silent greeting to Adeline the moment before she stepped into the invisible line stretching from him to Michaela. When the maid of honor proceeded onward, Philip's focus remained stationary. He'd noticed Michaela, and he seemed as surprised to see her as she'd been to see him.

Everyone stood, blocking her view of Philip. Erin had started down the aisle. She wore a headband of flowers and walked with a woman, her mother probably. John and Erin focused on each other, grinning. Though they seemed to see only each other, their joy was contagious, because all around Michaela, the other guests smiled too.

When they all sat back down again and she caught a new glimpse of Philip, even he looked happy. But then he cast a more sober glance over his shoulder, to Michaela. They both had a lot of explaining to do.

32

"That's what you want?" Tim grimaced at Philip in the diminishing light of sunset.

The ceremony had ended, and staff hurried to rearrange the seating area into a dance floor with a buffet and tables off to the side. A waiter nearby whipped out a tablecloth with a flourish. He set a lantern in the center of the smooth surface and added a couple of sprigs of flowers.

As he moved on, Philip made himself nod. He would miss Awestruck. The music, and, now that he'd finally let himself benefit from it, the brotherhood. He'd been in the band for the money, though, and he no longer believed the kids needed financial support from him more than they needed him, present and involved. "It is. I'll record this album with them, then I'm out."

"Well, don't tell them tonight." Tim motioned to where John and Erin posed on the beach for the photographer. Near them, Gannon and Adeline held hands and whispered, waiting in the wings for shots that would require them. "Wait until tomorrow for Gannon, after the honeymoon for John."

"I mentioned it to Gannon already. He wasn't that surprised."

"Disappointed, though."

Philip shrugged.

"Man." Tim winced. "You sure you can't make it work?"

"If the others had kids their ages, bringing them on tour might work, but without that, they'd have no friends. I leave them here, and I miss out on their lives."

"So if I talk Gannon and John into adopting elementary-aged children, you'll stay?"

Laughter burst from Philip. "Yeah, that's a realistic option."

Tim tipped his head, only begrudgingly acknowledging the humor. "Getting them to adopt kids would be easier than finding a bassist who fits what these two want."

"Matt's got himself together."

"Several steps ahead of you on that one, but I hardly convinced them to take a single song from him."

"I bet he'd be willing to meet the same criteria they set for me. In fact, I don't get why they considered me different."

"Matt crossed lines you didn't, and when it blew up, he wasn't about to change." Tim studied Philip before turning his gaze back toward the photoshoot, more to avoid eye contact, Philip suspected, than to watch the proceedings. "I didn't know you were hiding a problem to begin with, so maybe you've got us all fooled, but you seem sincere. Like you'll actually stick with sobriety."

"I hope so." He gulped, feeling compelled to go deeper, though talking about faith still felt unnatural. "I pray I will."

Tim assessed him again. "You too, huh?"

"You ought to give it a try."

"Prayer?" Strings of lights over the dance floor came on, and music started. Tim stepped backward, as if to rejoin the party. "I've let problems stack up so long, I don't even know where I'd start."

Beyond Tim, Michaela bent to talk to Nila and Nason.

Philip watched her animation as she spoke with them. He'd rather go join that conversation, but they all looked happy, and he needed to finish this talk with Tim. He refocused. "Probably couldn't start in a worse place than I did."

"With heroin?" Tim smirked. "True."

He'd never taken the heroin, but why split hairs? He'd turned to drugs because he'd rejected God. The whole thing had been as foolish as Nason or Nila moving out tomorrow and trying to provide for themselves.

He glanced back to them in time to see Michaela pull them into a group hug.

If his children ran away from him, everything they did to get by would break Philip's heart, but the pride behind the initial rift would hurt him worst. So between him and God, he had to believe his own pride, and not his drug of choice, had been the problem.

Michaela waved goodbye to the kids. They scampered toward the dance floor, and she angled Philip's direction.

Tim used her advance as an excuse to wander off.

Per usual, she'd dressed beautifully, but not practically. Earlier, they'd enjoyed temperatures in the mid-seventies, but with the sun setting, the air hovered in the sixties already, far too cold for a California girl to be comfortable in a halter top. He'd offer her his jacket, but he hadn't worn one.

"Now that you've checked me out, care to explain yourself?"

"I wasn't—" He had to stop there because his gaze caught on the way the dress draped over her curves. He tightened a fist, willed his focus back. "I owe you. Thank you."

She shifted, leery, and put a hand on her hip.

"Riff almost died that night, and if things had gone differently, I would've. No doubt about it."

"Oh." She turned as if to scan the crowd for the tech, but

Riff was off in rehab. Michaela pulled her hair to one side, and the soft light of the lanterns accentuated the delicate contours of her shoulders. "You owe me more than a thank-you."

He owed her more than gawking too. "I've apologized to you so many times for so many things. I'm waiting until I can do it right next time."

The start of a smile gathered at the corners of her eyes. "What does that involve?"

Probably nothing she was thinking of. He had been too quick to push her away over the entertainment show, but now more than ever, they wanted different things. "I'm not sure, but for starters, a little more distance, therapy, and church between me and my last near relapse."

Her eyebrows rose. "Therapy?"

He nodded.

More lines appeared on her forehead. "Church?"

"Everything changed that night."

"It must've." Her voice hardened, as if she understood his belief and her disbelief amounted to irreconcilable differences. Of course she did. Way back on the first day they'd met, she'd sat in a pizza restaurant and told him she couldn't both believe in God and do what she had to do for her career.

He tried to soften the disappointment with a smile. "So, like I said, thank you."

"Because I told Gannon, and Gannon forced you into therapy and church."

He knew what she wanted. If outside forces were to blame for his new convictions, they didn't go deep enough to keep him from her.

"Gannon and John did require therapy if I wanted to stay with Awestruck, but by that point, I knew I needed help. Professional and divine."

"Wow." The word sounded neither happy nor skeptical.

"Amazing grace, right?" He ought to continue and drop the bomb that he'd chosen not to stay with Awestruck beyond recording the next album with them. She wouldn't understand the decision, but maybe that was why he ought to tell her.

They both spoke simultaneously and stopped to motion the other to continue.

Michaela took the offer. "I'm glad you're getting help. That's half the reason I came. To make sure you did."

"And the other half?"

She pointed toward the buffet tables. Gannon and Adeline were filling hors d'oeuvre plates. Out on the sand, John and Erin were posing with family members. Meanwhile, as the sky darkened, the glow of the lanterns seemed to strengthen, casting yellow pools across the tables and dancers.

"Same thing as always. I need advice. For all the good it does me." She avoided eye contact, but her green irises focused on points nearer and nearer to him until, finally, it seemed she couldn't help herself.

Her wounded expression cut him. He wished he could heal her, but he wasn't enough. Had never been, in any sense. God would have to rescue her, as He'd rescued him. Still, he prayed that God would let him help.

"Gannon is probably wiser, but if you want to talk to me ..." He shrugged. He'd been learning a lot lately, and he felt good about his decision regarding Awestruck, but he probably wasn't a good source for advice. Still, for Michaela, who'd stuck with him through so much, he would try.

IT WAS hard getting used to, this concerned way Philip focused on her as if he'd defend her or fight for her good. It shook her conviction that she'd done the right thing when she'd walked away.

"It's about Evie." She sighed, embarrassed she'd been stuck on the same problem for weeks. "We recorded a song we bought, and that went okay, but next up, we're working on one of my originals. I'm trying to figure out how to stand up for what I think is best for the song. I don't like what she did with the first original song of mine, and I want to make sure it doesn't keep happening."

Philip looked out toward the lake, where the lights of the boats she'd spotted earlier bobbed in the deepening evening. After a sigh, he pulled his focus back. "If she ruined your song, why are you still working with her?"

Could she blame the glow of all these candles for how soft his eyes looked? Warm instead of wounded. "It's frustrating, but it'll help my career, and since it's not a big scandal like the music video, it seemed like my best option."

He studied her, and she did all she could to keep from shivering.

"What's your main goal for your career?" he asked.

Her hair shifted as she tilted her head, allowing cold air new access to her skin.

"It's a valid question," he said. "Reese hasn't asked you that? For career planning?"

Reese hadn't, but Michaela couldn't let him turn this into another attack on her manager, so she threw some ideas together. "To get to the point where I get to do an all-stadium tour. Where I never have to think about money again. Where people come to me to make the kind of music I want to make, and those albums go platinum."

"Okay. And to get there from here, is there any line ..." He stopped and seemed to regroup. "Don't take this the wrong way, but what's the line you won't cross to get there? At what point do you refuse to do something because, once you do, you're not living your dream anymore?"

She glared. "What's the *right* way to take that?"

"Pretend you believe I'm asking because I care. What's the line when the dream isn't worth it anymore?"

"I wouldn't hurt someone."

"What about yourself?"

An ache grew in her stomach, and she pressed her hands over it. "The dream is my whole life, the only worthwhile thing I have. I can't hurt myself with it."

"But you're not happy. That's the problem. Mine, anyway."

"Not everyone can live a fairytale." She smoothed her hands over her dress and away from the pain that was more emotional than physical, anyway. "My career hasn't worked out the way Gannon's did. Or yours. So here I am, doing my best. Once this album does its thing, everything will change. Reese thinks it'll be the one to go platinum."

"The next high's always the most important one." He spoke softly, almost to himself.

She considered letting the comment slide, not taking on the hopeless task of exacting an apology from him, but the slur hurt too much. "This is not the same."

"You're chasing highs, Michaela, and they're never going to do it for you. As long as career highs are what your life is all about, you'll never be happy."

As if the man who'd never wanted her knew anything about making her happy. "Look who's become a sage."

"No. But I have changed the highs I'm chasing."

"Because you found religion." Faith amounted to nothing more than another excuse to push her away. "You're all about Jesus now, right?"

"Not that I'm good at it, but yes. God and being there for my family are the two things I'll cross any line for. No boundaries. For them, I'll quit drugs, the band, whatever it takes. But for the fame-and-money fairytale?" His expression soured. "You said it. Not everyone can live that life. Some of us are better off without."

"You're one to talk."

He acknowledged the point with a regretful laugh and broke eye contact again. "Remember the difference between the men who use you and the ones who try to win you?"

"If you're going to claim you did everything you could to win me—"

"I wouldn't. I did horribly by you." He glanced toward the dance floor, where Nila and Nason were jamming out. He took a step in their direction, and candlelight flickered in his eyes as he looked to her one more time. "But as bad as I did, fame's doing worse, and you're allowing the mistreatment because you think you'll finally find love. But God's been offering you love this whole time. Jesus died to win you."

She gaped at him. He really believed all of that? She couldn't even think up a joke to make light of his sudden change. Even he seemed awkward about it, backing away a few steps with a sad smile, then turning toward the dance floor.

She watched him join his children. He took their hands, twirled Nila, then mimicked Nason's goofy moves, setting his own kids and several of the adults to laughter.

When she'd had a moment with the kids just now, she'd explained that she had to go away for work. They hadn't seemed upset—surely, if they'd felt pain like what she'd endured as she'd said goodbye, they couldn't have buried it the way she'd buried hers.

So, Philip's plan to protect them had worked. Unfortunately, as always, no one had looked out for Michaela.

She scanned for Gannon.

John, Erin, and several older adults had joined him and Adeline.

Talking to him now would mean pulling him away, and his advice would likely be similar to Philip's. Similarly impractical.

She shouldn't have come.

She wove around the tables and followed the perimeter to the card box. After slipping hers inside, she left.

Alone.

Like always.

33

Seven months later

Michaela's heel clicked on the black tile as she stepped into the dressing room. She eased the door shut and leaned against its solid promise of a moment's peace. More tile covered the entry and swept along the mirrored wall on the right side of the room. The narrow counter and vanity lighting there provided enough space for a whole kick-line of women to prepare for a show, all for her tonight.

The mirror doubled the massive bouquet of roses Reese had sent. Next to them, stylists had fussed over Michaela before tonight's show. Only Reese had used the left side of the room, a lounge with plush white carpet and black leather furniture. No one had touched a key of the baby grand.

Michaela considered sitting on the bench, but she'd spent everything on stage.

On stage over the last few months. She had nothing left with which to soothe herself, no music bubbling up to numb the pain.

Since her album's release, she'd spent more time in hotels, passing through dressing rooms, and on stages than in her own home. She'd also spent the entire time at the top of the charts, resulting in tonight's honor.

She should've mentioned performing at this theater that night in August at John's wedding, when Philip had asked for her career goals. Artists dreamed of performing here, and she'd packed the house. Fans had screamed and sung along with every song.

"Becoming Us" had exploded. The whole album had. To capitalize on the interest, she'd been touring aggressively, winning fans and fame and fortune by giving it her all.

Jesus Christ died to win you.

Philip's voice came back to her often in tired moments like these, but how could the love of God be so simple? How could it be a gift, just waiting for her? No one loved that way.

Fatigue could get her to fantasize about anything, including perfect, free love.

Singing songs she didn't like about a man she wanted to forget every day—sometimes at two different shows—took a toll. But she was getting closer to her biggest goals, and eventually, her emotions would catch up with her. She'd be as happy as she ought to be.

She rubbed the bridge of her nose and pushed away from the door, the hem of her black slip of a dress swinging against her upper thighs. She ought to dig out her coat. Even after the exertion of the show, this room felt like a walk-in freezer.

A knock chased her.

Silence and solitude. Luxuries even this place couldn't stock for her.

"It's open." Though with any luck, Reese wouldn't hear her say so.

The woman would have some itinerary change. Some event to squeeze in to capitalize on their time in New York City.

"Nice digs."

Her steps halted. She'd spent enough time thinking about Philip to know his voice, and maybe the heating system worked better in the hall, because he brought with him a comforting warmth.

Although, this could simply be where she broke with reality.

She might be imagining him.

A mental breakdown would net her a nice, quiet vacation.

She perched on the stool at the vanity, but she refused to take her makeup off in front of any version of Philip, real or imagined. Instead of facing the mirror, she swiveled toward the voice.

He held a much smaller bouquet of flowers than the one from Reese. Peonies, though. He wore a T-shirt and jeans like always. Oh, wait. A hunter-green V-neck. She laughed despite herself. His shoulders looked broader, stronger than she remembered. His expression was far less guarded than it used to be. Easier to read.

She rose as the difference dawned on her. He'd shaved.

The beard had accented his jawline, but his facial structure hadn't needed the help.

When he smiled—just a gentle lift of the lips, really—she could see every nuance of the movement.

How her fingers burned to touch that skin.

"You look good," she managed.

"You look beat."

She dropped back to her seat and pulled the zipper on one of her heels to slip her foot free. "You're as charming as ever."

He smiled again. He really needed to stop doing that.

But at least she wasn't cold anymore. She focused on her foot, curling and straightening her toes to work out the aches. "How'd you get in?"

"I still have some connections."

"Mostly with pig farmers, from what I hear."

He stepped closer and set the vase of flowers on the counter in front of her. In her peripheral vision, she saw him tip the card in the roses from Reese to read the inscription, then stepped away again.

Finally, satisfaction sailed through her. Philip Miller was checking out the competition.

"Is that all you know about Iowa?" he asked. "Pig farmers?"

"Pig farmers and your dad and now you." She unzipped her other shoe.

He'd mentioned quitting Awestruck the last time they'd spoken, but she'd assumed he wouldn't follow through.

He had.

He'd recorded the album with them, taken a much smaller chunk of the massive contract than he could've, and moved to Iowa. Awestruck was off touring without him.

"How's your sister?"

"Her oncologist says they've now found no evidence of disease." It'd been a long road, and chemo had taken a toll. Riley lost her hair, and Michaela had paid her own hair stylist to work her magic on a wig. The favor had seemed insignificant in comparison to the hardship, but Riley seemed to have appreciated it. Still appreciated it, actually, since her hair hadn't grown back in yet.

The news of her sister's remission brought another genuine smile to Philip's face. Michaela remembered how hard she'd had to work, once upon a time, to brighten his expression like that, and now it seemed to come so easily.

The change prompted her to wonder about his life now. "If Iowa's not all pig farmers, you'd better tell me about it."

"We live in a rural neighborhood. The land can be flat, but we're in rolling hills that leave you thinking there's a dramatic view over the rise." He shrugged. "Mostly, it's more of the same, but Nason seems to like it."

The idea of Nason with boundless hills to explore sent a whisper of contentedness through her. "And Nila?"

"Nila's all about dance. She tells me she's going to be one of your backup dancers in a few years."

As if Philip would ever allow his precious daughter into Michaela's world.

Michaela couldn't blame him. She wanted good things for Nila. Not this world of rejection and loneliness.

She touched a finger to one of the graceful peony blooms. "How's the degree coming?"

She heard, rather than saw, Philip's smile this time. "You've been keeping tabs on me."

"It's not every day someone walks away from an opportunity like Awestruck." She pivoted toward him. "I had to know what you considered a better offer."

He chuckled. "You think I'm crazy."

"You turned down millions to move to Iowa and go back to school, and you want to argue that's the better deal?"

"We've argued enough, haven't we?" No one else looked at her with his steady kindness.

Others were too busy keeping an eye on what they could gain from her.

Had she ever understood Philip? To an extent, but he'd changed since then. For the better.

And he'd left her behind.

Or he should've left her behind.

Yet, here he was, gentle and grounded and kind.

"We have." The delicate scent of the flowers wafted to her, fragile instead of the overpowering aroma of the first bouquet he'd given her. Or maybe all her senses were dulled these days. Maybe success in this industry required a certain amount of numbness.

Okay, not *all* her senses. Now that she'd gotten past the

initial rush of Philip's appearance, gooseflesh crept across her arms and legs from the cold room.

Philip shifted. "I came to deliver the apology I promised."

She adjusted a fern in Reese's bouquet, as if she preferred the roses over the peonies. "And you thought intruding on one of the biggest shows of my career would be the best timing?"

"I figured you'd be in a good mood here. I don't know if you've heard, but this place is kind of a big deal."

She didn't have the energy to defend herself against the unspoken concern she heard in his voice. "So you flew up from Iowa."

"It's not the first time I've flown somewhere just to see you."

Nope. Not buying it. "Last time, you were also hoping to score some drugs, if I recall correctly."

"But I didn't."

Her eyes flitted to the mirror. Just for a glance, for a moment of the fantasy that he cared, that this time was different, that the man she kept singing about deserved the songs after all.

A notch between his eyebrows marked determination and sincerity. "That was the last day I used anything."

Her mutinous feet moved against the cool tile, turning her.

"You helped me get clean, starting with listening to my story that night and ending a few weeks later by flushing some tainted heroin down the toilet."

"You haven't used anything since that day."

"I haven't." His mouth tightened. "I can't say I haven't been tempted, but God is good. My life is good. The kids. I don't want to jeopardize any of that for a high that'll come and go and leave me to find my way out of that maze again. I'm managing my life differently now."

Maybe for an addict, God really was the answer.

"Anyway." He swallowed as if nervous. "I promised an apology." He tipped his head toward the couch.

The invitation drew her onto the lush pile of the carpet. The couch's supple leather chilled her legs when she curled into the bend of the sectional. Either Philip noticed or couldn't keep his focus with her wearing her short skirt because he tossed her a throw from off the back of the couch before dropping to the spot next to her.

She covered her legs, unsure if she should be offended or grateful. "Let's hear it."

He narrowed his eyes toward the coffee table, as though trying to recall a memorized speech. She inhaled to temper her disappointment as she realized that this would be nothing more than a robotic recital of a script he'd written up at a recovery meeting sometime in the last seven months.

Thoughts apparently gathered, he turned toward her, eyes so rich with promise that she lost her breath.

"Michaela, I lied to you. Repeatedly. And I pushed you away because I had a habit to hide, but also because I knew deep down I didn't deserve the blessings in my life, and certainly not another chance at love. Though I tried blaming God for the bad things like my mom leaving and Clare's death and cancer genes, I was convinced the heartbreaks were what I deserved."

This man, this pulled-together, thoughtful, handsome man, believed all that?

"It's not, Philip. No one deserves that."

"True, in one sense. God didn't design the world to have heartbreak, but humans didn't stick to His plan, and I'm not innocent. I was so angry that God would take my kids' mom that I turned around and almost killed their dad too."

He lowered his gaze and scraped at his thumbnail. "Seeing Riff overdose, I was forced to admit my way wasn't working. I needed God if I wanted any hope for this life or the next. I needed to trust that, despite the pain, He's good." Philip focused on her, one side of his mouth pulling with a hint of hope. "And He is, because He met me there, despite everything

I'd done to myself and all the people I cared about. I'm not enough, but God is, and from now on, He gets to show how strong He is through my weaknesses."

How could this mentality encourage him? Even after proving his strength by staying clean all these months, he didn't consider himself enough. "I don't get it."

He shifted forward, as if being a couple of inches nearer would help him explain. "God's giving me a fresh start. Because of Him, I can sit here, after all the times I've failed, and apologize with the hope that I'm not doomed to repeat my mistakes. I'm still flawed, but I'm changing. Whatever the future brings, I won't handle the challenges the way I handled the past because of God."

A fresh start. Flawed but changing. That made more sense. Couldn't she claim those same things were true of her? She'd gotten a fresh start with the new album. It had its flaws, sure, but her actions hadn't elicited a moral outcry this time. *That* was a change.

She studied Philip's features. She couldn't claim her fresh start had brought her the peace she saw settled in his face. "And shaving is an outward sign of that?"

"You once accused me of hiding. Maybe I was. If not behind a beard, then behind lies and other defenses. I wanted to show you how serious I am about being open."

He'd gone to the trouble of coming here clean-shaven, in a shirt she'd picked for him, with flowers she loved, but what did he want? He lived in Iowa. Did she ever perform there? "We don't even talk anymore."

Regret shifted the skin near his mouth and eyes. "I'd like to change that if you would. The kids would love hearing from you too. They begged to come along tonight."

He'd mentioned her to his kids? He was okay with her talking not only to him, but also to them? She knew how seriously he took such things, and joy welled, but reality promptly flushed it away.

"You don't approve of my life, of my choices." He hadn't mentioned her contacts, but she remembered the conversation where she'd complained about his beard. He'd accused her of hiding herself behind makeup and contacts.

And he was right.

Everything authentic about her got utterly squashed whenever she showed it to the world. Why risk exposing the few parts of herself she'd managed to shield?

He seemed to focus near her hands, then interlaced his own fingers and lifted his gaze to meet hers. "I just want you to be happy and to know you're loved. By God. By the kids. By me."

Loved? The word rushed through her with a sense of freedom she'd always imagined happy families felt in each other's company. But again, reality haunted her.

She and Philip had tried this and failed. They'd lost touch. If love equated to months of silence, she didn't want it.

He touched the blanket where it lay over her shin but withdrew his hand before speaking. "I'm not here to criticize your choices, but if this"—he motioned to the dressing room around them —"doesn't work out ..." He laughed and gave a nervous smile. "You could always move to Iowa. Try a new beginning of your own."

So impractical. This whole thing. "Right. Because I'd be happy there."

"You might surprise yourself."

Maybe she would, because she found herself leaning closer to him.

He'd certainly surprised her. His easygoing warmth made her wonder if Iowa wouldn't be so bad. As long as Philip was there with Nila and Nason.

But how could she walk away from everything she'd sacrificed so much to build?

He rested his hand on her shoulder and brushed his thumb over her cheek. "Forgive me?" The nervous playfulness had vanished, and his voice deepened with emotion.

"I forgive you." Her own voice had turned husky, but so be it. She might not drop everything to move to Iowa, but he deserved to know she cared as much as he did. "You really ... You flew here only to see me?"

He nodded. His hand sent warmth clear across her shoulders and down her arm. "More than enough reason. You should know I've always appreciated how much of yourself you're willing to give to causes you believe in."

She lowered her eyes. Her donations to cancer research should've been anonymous, but word had gotten out. Reese, probably.

Philip shifted his hand, drawing her attention back. "I've been one of your causes. But I don't want to be a cause for you, and I don't want to see you that way either. I'd like us to be the kind of friends who uplift each other." He chuckled. "For more than the sake of inspiring a few songs."

Embarrassment flamed her cheeks, incongruent with her unstoppable grin. "You recognized yourself."

His hand slid to the side of her neck and touched her cheek again. "I recognized the woman I fell for."

He was going to kiss her, wasn't he? She slid her feet to the floor so she could edge closer.

The door burst open, and Reese stepped in. "Okay, I've got you booked for Late—"

Reese stopped in her tracks, looked from her to her guest.

Philip gave Michaela one last smile, then withdrew his hand and stood.

Reese didn't apologize or offer to come back later. She'd considered Philip a help to Michaela's career when he'd been part of a famous band. These days, she probably saw him as a threat. Someone who might convince Michaela to move to Iowa.

Would she do that? Ever?

She'd envied how Awestruck had moved to Wisconsin to be near Adeline, like she was some kind of Helen of Troy. That was Michaela's dream—to have that kind of pull over someone. Not being the one who got pulled.

Still, for Philip ...

He moved toward the exit.

"Wait." The warmth he'd brought would follow him right back out the door, and she was freezing in this stupid excuse for a dress.

He moved closer, opened his arms to her, and wrapped her in a hug.

She melted into the embrace. She hadn't felt in ages as steady as she did with his arms around her. But this couldn't last. He'd leave her here to live her life. How would she cope? She shivered, and he lay a hand on the back of her head, cradling her with tenderness no one showed her. No one else.

"Call me." He studied her face as if Reese weren't right there, as if Michaela had gone ahead and let all her emotion spill out in tears. He stepped back, slow to withdraw his hands from her shoulders.

She nodded. If she opened her mouth, she'd sob, and she couldn't do that. Not in front of Reese. Not when she'd been granted the life she'd fought to obtain for years.

He turned and stalked past Reese. "Take better care of your artists. It's freezing in here."

Reese met the burly command with a level stare, and Philip continued to the door. There, he stepped toward a small box on the wall. A thermostat. He hit a button about six times and let himself out.

34

Nine months later

So, this was how it would end.

Michaela pressed her heels against the base of the paper-covered bench in the doctor's office. Large posters of the inner workings of the human ear, nose, and throat decorated the otherwise plain walls. Not a speck of Christmas cheer in here, though the holiday loomed at the end of the month.

To think, it'd been well over half a year since she'd done that show in New York. Had that conversation with Philip in that swanky dressing room, and turned down his invitation to Iowa because she was so sure happiness would catch up with her.

It had. A couple of times.

But it had also fled, as skittish as a stray cat.

The specialist rolled his wheeled stool away from her. "We can do surgery, if other options don't work, but vocal cord nodules can come back. I recommend beginning voice therapy for the long run. Short term, ten days of complete voice rest."

Michaela opened her mouth but hesitated to disobey his

order so soon. But obviously, this had to be discussed. "I have shows booked solid for months."

The doctor clasped his hands loosely. "Technique will help, but the schedule is the leading reason you landed in my office."

The muscles in her legs tensed. Her voice, which she'd built her entire life around, was failing her in the heart of her dream. But then, could she call this the dream? Because each time Philip invited her to Iowa, something he'd been doing more and more often, her desire to accept grew.

"Ten days. Non-optional. Start immediately."

The problem had begun mildly. She'd lost some of her range and had to resort to lip-syncing two songs in her lineup that went too high. Saving her voice for performances and conversations with Philip hadn't prevented the problem from worsening. Her throat hurt and her voice was hoarse when she spoke. When she sang, even the notes she could hit caused pain to shoot like a bullet from ear to ear. She'd lip-synced an embarrassing number of times, but the laryngitis wouldn't go away.

Because she didn't have laryngitis. She touched her neck. The lump tightening her throat as the news soaked in had nothing to do with her new diagnosis.

"Do you have any other questions?"

She gave a jerky shake of her head.

The doctor offered a look of practiced sympathy. "Rest and voice therapy will work wonders, but it'll take time. You still have a long singing career ahead of you, as long as you manage this correctly."

She bit her lips together and nodded. *Manage* this?

He left her to show herself out.

Alone, she blinked at the full-color illustration of vocal cords on the wall.

How would she tell Reese she needed time off? A vacation would impact not only Michaela's income, but the livelihoods and investments of a long string of people. And fans' backlash in response to canceled shows could be brutal.

She wanted to call Philip, as she did whenever something happened. Big or small. They were in contact daily, but lately, she'd restricted most of their interactions to text so he wouldn't hear the rasp in her voice. Whether she texted or called today, she knew what he'd say to the news the doctor had delivered.

He'd tell her to draw the line he'd been talking about at John's wedding.

She needed to take this break.

But how could she?

Her pulse fluttered as she pulled on her jacket and collected her purse.

Maybe she couldn't call Philip, but reaching out to two of her other contacts would brighten her mood.

Before leaving the exam room, she made a goofy face and sent a snapshot of it to Nila and Nason. As soon as they got it, she was sure to receive two funny images in response.

The prospect gave her the courage to leave the privacy of the exam room, but as she stepped into the lobby, the weight of having to break the news to Reese grew too heavy to carry all the way to the car.

At least she had an excuse to text instead of call. That should spare her the brunt of Reese's disapproval. Besides, Reese ought to recognize that no one could make money off a nonexistent voice.

The diagnosis is vocal cord nodules. Ten days complete voice rest, starting immediately. Doctor's orders.

She frowned at the words on her screen, but she had no choice. The text sent, she slipped the device in her purse.

Outside, the California sun shone. Green strings of Christmas lights twined around the trunks of the palm trees surrounding the parking lot.

Her phone chimed. She checked Reese's response as she continued toward her car.

You don't have time for that. I'll schedule a second opinion.

The sun had warmed the interior of her coupe. Still, Michaela felt a chill as she peered at the reflective glass of the medical offices. Reese had already gotten her in with a highly recommended specialist, the one who'd just given her the diagnosis.

I don't want to risk my voice. I want to heal this right.

There. Philip would be proud she'd advocated for herself, as he so often urged her to do. She'd send him a screenshot of this conversation.

Reese's response came fast. *Hence the second opinion.*

I trust this doctor. She refused to run around to a million doctors until Reese found one who said she could keep going until she entirely lost the ability to sing. Besides, she still wanted to forward this to Philip. She wanted him to know he'd been wrong to worry about her so much. She'd stand up for herself on truly important matters.

Reese launched a series of replies, outlining reasons why she couldn't obey the prescription for rest. Each one made her throat throb.

She couldn't send this chain to Philip.

Refusing Reese could result in Michaela getting dumped. With no manager, her career might end, and if Reese wasn't exaggerating, she might face hefty financial losses for not performing.

But her voice simply wouldn't comply. She'd have to lip-sync, and fans would grow suspicious, since her normal speaking voice had even deteriorated.

She fiddled with her phone, Philip's name tempting her among her favorite contacts.

They'd seen each other a couple of times since he'd come to her show in New York. As part of her ongoing mission to grow closer with her sister, she'd brought Riley to the premiere of the movie that included the collaboration. Philip had met them there. He'd also driven to meet up in the Twin Cities and, on a separate occasion, brought the kids to Chicago when she'd been in those areas for concerts. They texted or talked most days, and now that both kids had cell phones, he'd allowed her as one of their limited contacts—hence the goofy pictures they constantly traded.

She'd never had a best friend she understood as poorly as she understood him. Why did he care about her? What did he get out of it?

Fans, she understood. They were in love with the fantasy. Philip knew her better than that.

Reese loved her for the money—and would run her into the ground to get it. Philip didn't make a dime off her.

Men had their reasons for wanting Michaela around, but even when she and Philip had dated, he'd never taken advantage.

He—and the kids—simply accepted her for her. Who else ever had?

Heather. And Heather had claimed God not only liked her but loved her. Philip and Gannon had said the same.

Jesus died to win you.

What did He get out of the deal?

Even less than Philip.

She'd suspected love to be life's purpose, but the idea that love could be freely given stood in opposition to how she'd lived her whole life. That God might offer love and wait to be accepted sounded too good to be true, except for one thing: Philip had been loving her that way for a year.

Once he heard about the nodules, his voice would thicken with sincerity as he admonished her to stop letting Reese call the shots, find a way to pursue singing without surrendering her health or her peace of mind.

She could so clearly imagine his steadfast belief in her and his desire to protect her from Reese that her heart rate slowed its panicked race.

Until Reese's name appeared on her display, and her pulse kicked up again like a stadium of booing fans.

Michaela didn't answer. She couldn't let Reese talk her into yet another poor decision. She'd made far too many of those already.

This is the line, Philip.

Doubt poked her as soon as she'd thought the words. She'd crossed the line long ago, hadn't she?

Well, no more.

All the effort was killing her.

God, I'm sorry I turned away from Your love. Show me the way.

Her heart settled into a peace she hadn't felt since long, long before—if ever.

Yet, her career troubles remained. She needed a way out.

Would that mean giving up singing entirely?

She swallowed and pulled up Gannon's contact information with trembling hands. Philip had suggested finding a new manager, and that might be a viable solution.

How proud would Philip be if, the next time they talked, she told him she'd finally taken his advice?

Gannon might have an industry connection that would pave the way. Besides, she owed him a thank-you for all the other help he'd given. He would happily talk to her about God, help her better understand the love she'd rejected for so long, give her directions for what to do next on that front.

Then, with his advice or on her own, she'd part ways with Reese. Even if the move meant leaving singing behind for good.

She'd tasted the dream, and she was ready to let it go.

35

$\mathcal{M}$ichaela peered through the windshield at the houses tucked against the hillside by blankets of snow. She passed *119* on the left, which meant *124* would be...

There.

The blue house was the last structure before the road climbed over the rise. Beyond the house, fields of snow, punctured by broken cornstalks, stretched to a valley of gray-brown trees, bare limbs reaching for the winter-mint sky.

She parked in the drive, pulled on gloves, and zipped the thick coat she'd ordered online two days ago. She hadn't owned boots like these since her childhood, and the rubber soles left her ready for adventure like she hadn't been in years.

She was so late getting here.

God worked much quicker than she did. In the two days since she'd turned to Him, He'd changed her. Changed her so much, she could see the opportunity to be here, though it'd come through a setback, as another good gift.

She was through explaining those away.

She rang the doorbell and listened for the thunder of children running and, perhaps, the yips of the puppy Nila and Nason had earned with a summer of begging.

At the crackle of tires on the gravel road, she turned. The vehicle slowed half a block away, at another home.

In the quiet neighborhood, noise was the noticeable rarity, movement almost jarring.

Since no one had come to the door, she sat on the step to text Philip.

What're you up to today?

A feather of clouds overhead moved slowly, measurable only when compared to the stoic branches of the tree in Philip's front yard.

Her phone's vibration would've startled her if not for the cushioning of her gloves.

Finished my paper this morning. Took kids exploring. Hoping to wear out The Terror.

He'd included a picture, him holding up the adolescent Labrador whose boundless energy had resulted in the nickname. Nila and Nason peeked in from the edges of the frame. The very upper corners showed they were off in the woods somewhere. Philip wore a hat, but still no beard. His smiling cheeks were pink, right along with those of the kids—about the only part of them visible around their hoods, hats, and fully zipped jackets.

How long do you think it'll take until you're home? I just got a delivery confirmation on something I sent you. She added a cringing face and sent it.

No one steals around here.

She checked the quiet street. Yeah, she didn't doubt the crime rate was low.

Chuckling, she typed another reply. *But it might freeze.* Another cringing emoticon for good measure.

What'd you do? Send me flowers?

She sent an emoticon with zipped lips.

No other response came, but she imagined him surveying the woods, debating, and finally choosing to turn his party of explorers back toward the house. At least she hoped he would.

Fifteen minutes later, a dog barked. She focused on the rise. A boy raced a dog along the gravel shoulder. Nason and Fern "The Terror" Miller.

Philip and Nila wouldn't be long.

Michaela's muscles itched to run to meet them, but she held herself still. Enough was broken in her. She didn't need to add a twisted ankle to the list of things God needed to heal. Besides, she'd failed to tell Philip a few key things she couldn't exactly blurt out now.

She should've thought this through a little better.

Please, God, let me say the right words.

Even when she couldn't speak.

But surely the Lord had known all along that He had His work cut out with her.

Trailing behind Nason, Philip and Nila appeared together. She wore a pink-and-purple jacket, and her hands moved as if she was telling a story. Philip had his head down listening, hands in his pockets, his silhouette crisp against the shining landscape.

Michaela stood.

Nason must've spied the movement, because he slowed, leery, while the dog veered left to right, tromping through the snow at the edge of the ditch.

Philip lifted his face, and her breath caught.

Nason had gotten close enough to recognize her, because he shouted her name and burst into another run, tugging the confused dog along with him. Fern caught on fast and reached her first. The dog planted two paws on her thighs, and Michaela knelt to pet her and hug Nason.

Seconds later, Nila stopped a foot from her, panting, and Michaela hugged her, too, before straightening. As she did, she watched Philip jog after Fern and step on the leash to stop the dog from running into the street.

Oops. Nason must've let go.

"Dad said you sent us a present," Nason said.

She opened her arms to indicate herself, but before Nason could decode the movement, Philip laid a hand on his shoulder. "How about you take Fern in and help your sister make some hot chocolate? We'll be in in a bit."

Grinning, the kids trooped up the front steps.

"Make sure the dog has some water," Philip called.

"Okay." Then the door slammed, and there she stood, in the quiet of an Iowa winter with Philip.

He didn't know she'd had any voice problems. Didn't know she'd finally chosen to believe God. Didn't know she'd reconnected with Gannon, and he'd helped her find a new manager. Didn't know how badly she longed to be more than friends.

He'd gone so far out of his way to see her so many times that he must want more, too, but he hadn't made a move, and she knew why.

He wanted to mean more to her than her career.

And finally, he did. He and the kids.

But she didn't have a voice to tell him so.

He tugged the string that would cinch her hood. "You finally learned to dress for the weather."

She nodded. She'd dressed for the cold but had been growing uncomfortable, anyway. The sight of him helped, though. Always did.

He stepped closer, eyes narrowing. "You seem quiet. Did I leave you out here too long? You're frozen solid?" A grin broke free. "I could warm you up."

She nodded again, hoping he'd make good on the offer.

He chuckled and brushed a finger along her jaw. The cold air, hard at work on her face and his bare hands, couldn't numb her to the sensation.

The humor in his expression turned careful. He tipped his head slightly, brown irises alight with the sun as he searched her face. "Is something wrong? You're supposed to be down south somewhere."

Time was up. She had to reveal her secret. Her gloves allowed her to text, but she'd go faster without, so she pulled her right hand free, opened a memo app on her phone, and started typing.

I've been ordered to ten days of complete voice rest. I'm on day three.

He studied her as if able to read her face better than the words he'd skimmed. "Why?"

Vocal cord nodules.

He sighed, clenched his jaw, and proved he was angry at someone else by pulling her into a protective hug. "I'm glad you came."

PHILIP LOVED his kids and the changes he'd made for their sake, but tonight, their bedtime couldn't come quick enough. If only he could send them to sleep without dinner. He took the chicken from the fridge and grabbed one of the easy recipes his stepmother, Joan, had given him in the early days of their time in Iowa.

"What's a n ..." Nason stumbled to sound out the word.

"Nodule," said a computerized voice.

Philip looked away from the chicken to see Michaela smiling proudly, both kids crowded close to her at the table. She'd found a text-to-speech app, apparently. Her answer to Nason's question must've been made up of small words, because the kids read the answer.

Philip didn't need the explanation. Any solution Michaela tried would only help so much with how many shows Reese and her label expected of her. If something didn't change, the nodules would keep coming back until they ended her career.

He shouldn't hope for that, but he'd grown sick of how they pushed her around, sick of how she always did what they told her. She loved the large audiences their advice brought, but he'd much rather she perform for smaller crowds who liked her for her.

Her choices could ruin her voice, her ability to sing for anyone, even the kids.

Anger shoved ideas at him. *Go, confront Reese. Sue the manager and the label.*

Funnily enough, Michaela wouldn't stand for him taking over her life like that.

Since he couldn't make her decisions for her, he prayed God would lead her to better choices.

She didn't look worried as she typed her half of the conversation with the kids. And honestly, Michaela didn't need to sing for them. They'd stopped asking for "Amazing Grace" around the time Nila's nightmares had subsided—when they'd moved here. Nason considered anything resembling a lullaby "for babies."

But Philip would miss her singing.

No wonder she'd been avoiding conversations with him lately. He'd chalked the disconnect up to conflicting schedules. Instead, she'd been hiding from him.

Didn't she see Reese was bleeding her dry?

"Does it hurt?" Nila asked.

Silence.

"What's that word?" Nason asked.

"It says, 'Not when I'm quiet.'" Nila's older-sister voice came through loud and clear, but this once, Nason seemed not to mind.

As the question-and-answer session continued, Philip dumped the meal ingredients together and slid the chicken in the oven. As much as he wanted to send the kids to complete homework in their rooms while dinner cooked, the tactic would be useless. They'd find excuses to come down and be close to Michaela.

They'd missed her as much as he had. Almost, anyway.

At least it was a school night, so he could send them to bed around eight thirty.

The kids did their assignments at the table while he and Michaela carried on a half-written conversation about his progress toward finishing the business management degree he'd abandoned when his first band got signed.

Awestruck had paid him generously for his work on the last album, and he would continue earning royalties on his contributions to the albums he'd been a part of. So he didn't need to work while he studied. Afterward, he planned to invest in a concert venue. Nothing crazy, just a place for local and regional bands to get some exposure, for people to make and listen to good music.

After dinner, they played a board game until he could finally tell the kids to get ready for bed. Nason headed for his room while Nila put the game away. On her way back through, she paused at the table where Philip had been struggling to figure out where to start with Michaela.

"Will you be here in the morning?" Nila asked.

He wanted her here. Badly. Simply the sight of her had raised his hopes. He'd almost kissed her in the driveway.

But she didn't want his life.

Michaela pecked away at her phone and turned it toward him. *I got a hotel, but I'll be here with you and the kids as much as you'll let me for the next week.*

A week. His heart soared as though she'd promised much more. What would it do when she left again?

And how would the kids feel?

Her staying at a hotel instead of in the guest room would

help, but, wow, did he long to keep her under his roof. Yet another warning that Fern might be the only member of the house to bounce back after Michaela left again.

Both Nila and Michaela peered at him, hope welling as they waited for his verdict.

Regardless of how this might end, he couldn't refuse the time she'd offered. "We're going to see her every day for a week. How does that sound?"

Nila jumped and threw her arms around Michaela. Philip opened his mouth to reprimand her for being so rough—and to warn her that they'd have to say goodbye again soon—but the joy on Michaela's face as she returned the embrace stopped him.

They were all goners.

He got up from the table and let the dog outside. Afterward, he checked on the kids, then came down to find Michaela had collected her purse.

"Leaving already?"

She held her phone, so it only took her a second to type a reply and turn it toward him. *Freshening up.*

She looked perfect, as always. Didn't she know she didn't need to worry about things like that with him? Still, he held his peace and made his way to the living room.

Fern had curled up in an armchair next to the Christmas tree. She wagged a guilty tail as if she expected him to kick her out, but he chose a spot on the couch instead. There, he spent the next fifteen minutes coaching himself on not falling any further for Michaela. They had no future together.

Where was she, anyway?

If she thought she had to paint on another layer of makeup for him to love her, wasn't that just another sign that the time still hadn't come for him and her? That it might never?

All of his practical reasoning was for naught when she appeared in the doorway of the living room. No wonder she'd been gone so long. She'd pulled her hair into a loose braid. He'd rarely known her to style it all back, and the fact that she had accentuated the other changes she'd made.

He stood to meet her as she stepped closer. She'd washed off every trace of makeup. He brushed his thumb over the dusting of freckles on her cheek, but before he'd finished, his attention fixed elsewhere.

Her irises were blue with gray flecks, like wind-whipped water on a deep lake.

He cleared his suddenly thick throat. "What's all this?"

She bit her lips, then released them with a small smile and turned her phone toward him. She already had a message typed on the screen. *You're right. I need God's version of love, not Reese's. The schedule was too much, and she still wouldn't adjust it when I was diagnosed with nodules. Gannon helped replace her.*

He read it again. Michaela's mention of God, the fact that she'd replaced Reese ... She'd really taken these steps? If she had, the future he'd been trying to tell himself they couldn't have was theirs for the taking. He held his breath as he lifted his gaze to her face.

Her expression seemed to hold both relief and hope.

"You really believe in God now? And you fired Reese."

She nodded.

He longed to kiss her, but he pulled her into an embrace instead. This was the first time she'd brought up God, and he wouldn't follow it by diving straight into romance. "I'm proud of you."

She leaned back, keeping one arm around him as she typed one-handed. The words appeared on her phone. *Unconditional love like God's would be hard to imagine, except there's you.*

Amazed joy washed over him. She really thought that highly of him? If so, it was all God's doing.

Michaela resumed typing. *I hope I can perform again, but I can't belong to that dream anymore. I want to start working toward a new dream with God and with you.*

She waited until he'd read the message, then put the phone in her pocket.

How many times had he begged God for this? For another chance at love, for a chance with Michaela. And now, suddenly, all those prayers had been answered with a yes.

A glorious, undeserved yes.

He tightened his arms around her. "I'd love that." He dipped his head and brushed his cheek against those freckles. "I love *you*."

Her cheek rounded against his with a smile, and her arm moved, as though to get her phone back out.

In no mood to read, he stilled her. "Some things can be said without words."

Her lips pulled into a smile so unchecked he was certain she would've laughed, too, if she had a voice. Instead, she snuggled closer, and he watched her blue eyes close in anticipation of a kiss.

He remembered the details of how it'd felt to kiss Michaela during their short-lived attempt at romance. Back then, he'd tried to convince everyone, including himself, that he'd come through the valley of Clare's death and was ready to begin again. In truth, he'd been lost in that valley and incapable of finding his way out, let alone starting over with someone new.

Michaela had been lost in a valley of her own.

The desperation and pain that had haunted them had also poisoned their kisses.

Not so now that God had found them both.

Now, as their lips touched, Philip felt awe, joy, and hope. This was it. The other side of the valley, and the real new beginning. A dream that, as he kissed Michaela, became true.

≈

Bless the Lord, O my soul,
and forget not all his benefits,
who forgives all your iniquity,
who heals all your diseases,
who redeems your life from the pit,
who crowns you with steadfast love and mercy,
who satisfies you with good
so that your youth is renewed like the eagle's.
Psalm 103:2-5, ESV

Spend more time in Lakeshore with an email subscriber exclusive.

Food trailer owner Asher has seen too many tears he couldn't dry. Determined to be part of the solution, he avoids romance and all the heartbreaking drama that comes along with it.

At least, that's the plan until his heart decides it has a mind of its own. If he can't rein it in, he's destined to break not one but two women's hearts.

Subscribers to Emily's email newsletters will have the opportunity to download *Between the Two of Us*, which is a prequel novella to the Rhythms of Redemption Romances, as a welcome gift.

Sign up at emilyconradauthor.com.

AUTHOR'S NOTE

Philip and Michaela went through a lot, and if you're reading this, I imagine that means you stuck with them. I hope you found the ending worth it. Theirs is my favorite happily-ever-after of the series, perhaps because even I was a little surprised at how their story came together in the end.

But what a journey getting there.

As I write this note, I'm conscious that the subject matter may have hit close to home. It did for me too.

After I wrote this story but before its publication, a family member of mine faced an ovarian cancer scare, and I got just a small taste of what Riley's family experienced. If you or a loved one are newly diagnosed, one place you may find helpful information and support is ovarian.org, which is the website for the National Ovarian Cancer Coalition.

Likewise, though the circumstances differ, my family has been touched by addiction. I did my best to research and get things right, yet *To Begin Again* is a work of fiction. If you're facing addiction, whether in your own life or the life of a loved one, I strongly encourage you to reach out for help from an expert.

Alcoholics Anonymous offers resources and information on local support groups at AA.org. For Narcotics Anonymous, visit NA.org. Family members of addicts can begin to find support through Al-Anon (al-anon.org) or Nar-Anon (nar-anon.org).

If you're facing either of these situations, my prayer is that you would sense the Lord close by, and that you would see His healing, delivering hand at work. I pray that one day, you would look back on the story you're now living and marvel at how God worked it all for good.

DISCUSSION GUIDE

1. Which character did you relate to most? Why?
2. People and events from the accounts of King David were a source of inspiration for The Rhythms of Redemption Romances. What similarities can you find between Philip and Michaela's story and the biblical accounts of Michal and Palti mentioned in 1 Samuel (18:20-29 and 19:11-17) and 2 Samuel (3:13-16, 6:16, 6:20-23)?
3. Philip was angry with God for taking Clare. If you had a friend wrestling with similar pain, how might you support them?
4. What was your initial impression of Michaela? How did that idea change as the story progressed?
5. Michaela's dad and sister blamed her for her mom's choice to leave. How did Michaela try to resolve that tension? What else could she have tried?
6. How did Michaela's attempts to help Philip backfire? What did she do that was truly helpful?

7. In what ways did Philip undermine his own sobriety, even after he quit taking pills? How did he behave differently after finding Riff?

8. Philip turns his life over to Christ before Michaela does, and the dynamic of their relationship changes. How can we maintain friendships with people whose beliefs differ from our own?

9. Philip chooses to walk away from something he'd previously considered a dream-come-true, and Michaela ultimately risks her own aspirations by making changes she isn't sure will work out for her career. What factors are important to consider when making decisions about pursuing a dream or aspiration?

10. Describe a special lullaby or bedtime routine from your childhood or that you do with your children or grandchildren.

11. If you read *To Belong Together*, how was John and Erin's wedding similar to or different from what you expected?

12. The next book in the series, *To Believe in You*, follows Matt. What has he overcome so far in the series? What challenges do you think he might face in the book to come?

13. Share a line that stood out to you as particularly meaningful or helpful.

ACKNOWLEDGMENTS

This story was made possible by those who have faced addiction and bravely chose to tell their stories.

I also relied on my critique partner, Janet Ferguson, and my team of beta readers: Danielle, Elizabeth, Jane, Jessica, and Kendra. Thank you each for your contributions. Since I don't have kids, Jessica and Kendra provided the extra details that helped flesh out Nila and Nason. Elizabeth generously shared insights into a few aspects of the story, including what it's like to be a nanny. I appreciate the help bringing the story to life!

The story would not be what it is without the wise feedback of my editor, Robin Patchen. Judy DeVries and my volunteer proofreaders, Sarah, Teresa, and Maria, helped me look like a better grammarian and speller than I am. Any proofing mistakes or other errors are all my own.

Tickertape Tragedy is named after my friend Jake's band. I used them as Awestruck's opening act with his blessing and in appreciation for his years of friendship.

Thank you, reader, for coming along on this journey. You have so many options for entertainment. Thanks for choosing a book, and not just any book, but this one.

Lord, thank You that we are never, ever too lost for You to find and rescue.

ABOUT THE AUTHOR

Emily Conrad writes contemporary Christian romance that explores life's relevant questions. Though she likes to think some of her characters are pretty great, the ultimate hero of her stories (including the one she's living) is Jesus. She lives in Wisconsin with her husband and their energetic coonhound rescue. Learn more about her and her books at emily-conradauthor.com.

facebook.com/emilyconradauthor
twitter.com/emilyrconrad
instagram.com/emilyrconrad

ALSO BY EMILY CONRAD

The Rhythms of Redemption Romance Series

EmilyConradAuthor.com/RhythmsofRedemption

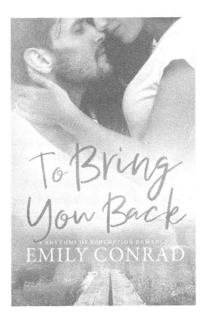

To Bring You Back - Book 1 - As if her biggest regret wasn't hard enough to forget, now the man she never should've loved is famous. And back on her doorstep.

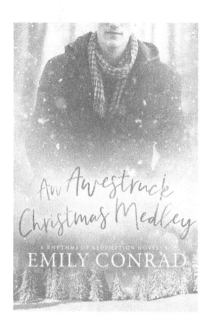

An Awestruck Christmas Medley - Book 1.5, a novella - Four hundred miles of snow-covered terrain, not to mention troubled relationships, stand between the men of Awestruck and a Christmas spent with loved ones. Gannon's made a promise he's determined to keep, and he's not about to let a blizzard stop him.

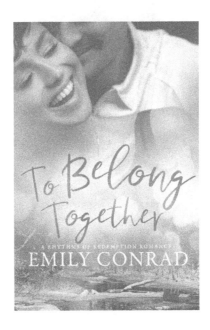

To Belong Together - Book 2 - Drummer John Kennedy can keep a beat, but he can't hold a conversation, so he relies on actions to show he cares. Unfortunately, when he's instantly intrigued by a spunky female mechanic, he can't seem to convey the sincerity of his intentions. Could God intend this pair of opposites to belong together?

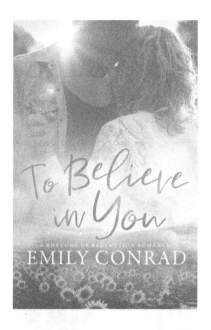

To Believe In You - Book 4 - Bassist and recovering addict Matt Visser has been transformed by faith and a year of sobriety. Just as he wins the trust of his beautiful but cautious coworker, Lina Abbey, a new truth about his past reveals a wrong he can never right. Both he and Lina need something more trustworthy than Matt to believe in. Otherwise, history will repeat itself in all the worst ways.

Subscribe to emails at https://www.EmilyConradAuthor.com for updates on new releases, or find all the latest on the series at https://www.EmilyConradAuthor.com/RhythmsofRedemption.

Stand-Alone Title

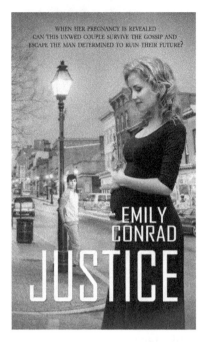

The love of a lifetime, a quest for justice, and redemption that can only be found by faith.

DID YOU ENJOY THIS BOOK?

Help others discover it by leaving a review on Goodreads and the site you purchased from!